Blood Hunted

Ariel Rae is R. A. Desilets's adult pen name.

Consider checking out her young adult work:

Carter Ortese is Trouble
Break Free
Start Small
Girl Nevermore
In a Blue Moon (Blue Moon #1)
Hipstopia (The Uprising #1)
The Collapse (The Uprising #2)
My Summer Vacation by Terrance Wade
The End Diary

Blood Hunted

ARIEL RAE

SPACE FOX
BOOKS LLC

To the little fox inside all of us.
Be adorable and vicious enough to survive.

This book may contain circumstances not suitable for younger readers and is recommended for adult audiences.

If you'd like to read about the content in this book, please visit the publisher's website spacefoxbooks.com for additional descriptions for any sensitive topics.

Preface

I was ten when I found the door to Faerie.

I had dreamed about it, tucked in the woods nestled in a small grove of pines. After that, I tromped through the forest behind my house, looking for the door. A few weeks later, I stumbled upon it. A bright golden brown door attached to nothing but the ferns in front of it. It felt like magic, and on a certain level, it was.

My tiny hands and legs were too weak to open the door more than a few inches. The ferns in front of it were too thick for me to pull it open wider than that. I tried to wiggle through the narrow gap, but my shoulders wouldn't fit. It was too stuck to close either, so the gap in the door remained wedged open.

When I got home to my family, I prattled on about what I had seen, excited by the prospect of magic in our very backyard.

I had glimpsed the realm beyond. It held a world with turquoise skies and chestnut brown lands. It held rich hues that were candy to my eyes. The clouds rolled with orange colors, and the sun shone a faded purple.

Of course, none of my family believed me. What family would believe a girl claiming to see a door that led to another world? Instead, my mom made me strip and check for ticks, worried about lyme disease.

Once the barrier had been broken, opened by the hands of a ten-year-old, it didn't take long for the Fae to find us. First, it was the Fae, who were monsters in their own right. Soon after, the other monsters of Faerie found their way over.

By the time I was nineteen, I had learned three solid rules to navigate the hellish earthen landscape:

1. Never negotiate. You will always lose.
2. Never trust a pretty face. You will always be led astray.
3. Never mention how I started the apocalypse. Because no one left alive knows, and my life depends on secrecy. For only the one who opened the door is immune to magic and only the one who opened the door can kill the Fae king.

When I turned twenty-one, I started my quest in earnest to kill the king. Even if it was the last thing I did, I would destroy every Fae on the planet. I would slaughter them until my blistered heart felt whole.

One

My mark sat at the end of the bar, leaning into a woman who appeared perfectly enthralled by his presence. I sipped the lukewarm beer the tavern served. This place was nowhere near as nice as some places I had seen in my travels. I watched the male Fae from across the room.

No matter how many times I had done a hunt, I still could not deny how physically attractive the Fae were. As much as I loathed them and enjoyed seeing their entrails spread in the aftermath of the bloody wreckage I left them in, they glowed with ethereal beauty.

This male was no different. His cheekbones were high lines perfectly carved and chiseled, as if cut from marble. Fae's eyes matched nothing on Earth, and his swirled with the glow of a pink lilac flower. Their irises churned whenever they used their magic, like he was doing to the unsuspecting woman who smiled pleasantly at him.

Saving her tonight wouldn't be an act of nobility. No, it was an act of revenge. I fiddled with the hilt of my sparrowbone dagger through my shirt, sheathed uncomfortably against my upper ribs. It was the one place the Fae overlooked whenever we got intimate. They never cared enough about my pleasure to bother removing my shirt.

I had tracked this target for two days, watching his comings and goings around the court. We hoped he had information on Lord Finian, as once I found a Lord, I would be closer to finding the king's court. Once I found the king, well…

Letting the dagger go, I took a long swig of beer and ditched the glass at my table with a few coins to pay for it. I weaved through the crowd as the woman grew closer and closer to the Fae's mouth. She licked her lips, eying him with desire.

I stepped in between them and pounded on the bar, causing the woman to jump and the Fae to scowl. "Can I have another beer? Cold this time?" I called out.

The woman shook her head. After compulsion was used on humans, it was as if they were coming out of a dream. "I should, uh, get going." She rolled her shoulders and got up, acting as if she hadn't been under the spell of a Fae, and walked out of the bar.

The Fae leaned over me. "You're going to pay for that." A wave of his magic washed over me, making the hair on my arms rise, but it had no effect on me. All it did was create a wave of pleasure across my skin.

This was foreplay. This was where I excelled. "Oh, yeah? And who is going to make me?"

The bartender slid a drink to me, but knew better than to get involved in whatever was going on between me and the male. He made himself scarce without waiting for payment.

The Fae's eyes swirled as he looked me up and down. "You should beg for mercy."

I smiled pleasantly. "Why would I go and do a thing like that, when I can tell you I don't want to?"

He bristled. A glint entered his eyes, one I had seen dozens of times before. The moment hung between us, and I worried this Fae would differ from the others. But they never did. All of them acted the same when presented with a challenge. They wanted to conquer it. Conquer me. Receiving a rejection from a human was like pouring gasoline on a Fae's already ignited libido. The word *no* never came out of a normal human's lips. They wanted a hunt. They wanted a game. Much like me, except my end goal was my pleasure and their death. Normal humans could not reject Fae.

I could. And that rejection made them want to crawl on top of me and tear the word from my lips. It was my secret weapon.

"You won't beg?"

"No." I shrugged and took a sip of the new beer. It was tepid. I sighed, wondering when I would get back to living with small luxuries. I missed cold beer. This court was by far in the worst condition of those I had visited, remaining a burned out husk instead of being rebuilt. There weren't many places for Lord Finian to hide, except I still had found no leads.

"No." His lips struggled to form the word. Frowning, he turned to his own drink and used magic to make the glass burst with condensation.

"Neat trick. Care to help a girl out?" I shook my beer at him.

"No." He scoffed and took a sip of his drink, which looked like white wine, though I couldn't be sure. His pink eyes roamed over me as his lips pursed around the rim of the glass.

If I had my way, I would kiss those lips before I killed them. I would do a lot of things to this male before he died underneath me.

"What?" I asked, keeping my voice light and airy. "I might make it worth your while."

"And how is that, girl who says no?" He placed the glass back on the bar and leaned forward.

"I could tell you what you've been dying to hear for the last thirteen years."

"And how do you know me well enough to know what I want to hear?"

I reached up and traced my fingers along his jaw. "Because it's what every Fae hopes to hear." I allowed myself to get close enough for my lips to brush against his ear. "There's nothing you can do to seduce me. I will *always* tell you no."

He shuddered and pulled back, eying me with a hint of suspicion. The Fae told stories about me, of course, but the allure of someone's being able to tell them no was too good to pass up. "How can you do that? How can you resist?"

I pushed the beer toward him.

With a wave of his hand, he turned the beer cold with his magic.

Taking a long swig, I gave him a genuine smile. This court had little in the ways of comfort, so this was a small respite. "Thank you."

"Now answer me."

"I don't feel like it." I winked.

His lips parted in a frown as he took a few large gulps from his glass. "Upstairs. Now." His magic once again swept over my skin.

"We'll go upstairs when I am good and ready to."

"But we *will* go upstairs?" His voice dipped into a growl.

Closing the gap between us, I traced my tongue up the side of his neck. His skin tasted of melted caramel on a hot summer's day. I got to his ear and whispered the single word that would make him want to strip me bare right on this bar. "No." The beer tasted extra sour going down, unlike his skin. Every Fae had a distinct flavor and smell. This one was particularly delicious.

It made me almost feel sorry for what I needed to do next.

His eyes flashed, pulling back from me. "What is your name?"

"Why does it matter?"

He casually sipped his drink, but his irises were blazing pink. Magic darted around me, and I could feel the urgency of his compulsion against my skin. Like all the Fae before him, he wanted to change my mind. "Because I want to know what to call you when you are begging for mercy underneath my grip around your neck."

"Charming. Do you say that to all the ladies?"

"No," he spat. The rest of his drink disappeared in a flash. "Are you done?" He didn't wait for my response, but grabbed my hand and pulled me toward the exit. "You have a room here, right?"

"Yeah."

"Which one is it?"

"Why should I tell you?"

Even from being towed along behind him—Fae were *strong*—I could see his jaw clenching. We got to the staircase, and I practically tripped up them as he hauled me to the second floor. When we reached the landing, he whirled around on me and pressed me into the nearest wall. His body became flush with mine, and I could feel all of him.

"What is your name?"

"I won't tell you."

"What is your room number?"

I feigned disinterest, though I would tell him, eventually. I wasn't done toying with him yet. "Why would I tell someone when you aren't doing anything for me?"

He growled and nipped at my ear. My body reacted, pushing against him even as he caged me against the wall. "Your room."

The magic poured around my skin, trying to find a way into me. "Now."

I pulled on his shirt, bringing our lips together. He was ruthless, pushing against me until the weight of his chest against mine knocked the wind out of my lungs. His tongue parted my lips, and I gasped. A growl escaped him as his hands trailed down my hips.

"Let's try this a different way. My name is Torin." His teeth sank into my lower lip. He sucked it into his mouth before letting it go. I breathed. "I want you to know that so you can scream my name."

"You think pretty highly of yourself."

"Only because you will."

"No." I smiled. "I won't."

His fingernails dug into my skin as he played with the hem of my pants. "Your room."

I may hate the Fae, and I may have an agenda to get out of this, but I was still human. I had needs. I liked to feel wanted, and I enjoyed his being pressed against me, promising more to come. Fishing in my pocket, I presented him with a key with the number four etched into it. With a snarl that did nothing to detract from his attractive features, he snatched it from my hand and dragged me down the hallway.

"No, don't," I said, voice dripping in mockery as I kept pace with him. It didn't matter how half-hearted the words came out, they still had the same effect. The Fae heard *yes* their entire lives. From humans, they heard demands for more. Often, if the Fae got too bored with appeasing their human lover, they would kill them. For a human to sleep with a Fae was a death sentence.

For everyone except me.

He shoved the key into the lock, threw open the door with a bang, and pulled me into him once more. I barely had time to latch the door behind us before he was on me. His bruising kiss claimed me. We backed up toward the bed, and soon my knees buckled underneath me as he tossed me backward on top of the mattress.

"You say one thing, but your body tells a different story."

Despite being sore, I bit my lower lip. I was a sucker for my own hormones, and this… I craved. The air filled with the impatience I felt during every hunt, knowing how the night would end. Now that I was so close to it, my whole body thrummed with excitement.

"What does it matter what my body does if I am telling you something different?"

He scowled, as if the thought never occurred to him. It likely hadn't. The Fae were used to getting what they wanted because their compulsion was strong, and most humans fell for it every time. The woman at the bar would have given this male whatever he asked for, except I intervened.

"Tell me you honestly don't want this." He crawled on top of me, pressing his knees into my thighs. "Say it again."

"No."

His eyes narrowed as he tilted his head. With deft fingers, he roamed around the top of my pants. Every time he brushed my skin, I shivered. "Take off your clothes."

"No." I gave him my sweetest smile.

"Fine," he said with resignation. He grabbed the bottom of my shirt and pulled. My eyes widened as the fabric tore clean in half, revealing the belt I kept my sparrowbone dagger sheathed in. His eyes met mine, and he tried to pull away, but I wrapped my legs around his waist. I rolled us over while his magic tried desperately to compel me.

He slapped me, and I thanked the universe that Fae had spent so many years relying solely on their magic, which made them soft.

I yanked out my dagger and poised it next to his throat.

Such a waste. I had been looking forward to tonight, to have a brief moment where I'd forget everything in the universe and get off. But no. This male—Torin—had the audacity to give me his name and do something no other Fae had done before. The others had been overcome with a desire to get me to scream yes, and they had failed to notice the slight bulge underneath my shirt.

But he had actually tried to get me naked.

Fear crept into his pink irises as he realized who he had gone to bed with.

"Scarlet," he said, like a death whisper, and I supposed it was.

"Where is Finian?"

Torin sucked in a breath, shaking his head. He opened his mouth and a brief scream came out of his mouth. Too much noise and not enough soundproofing.

With a sigh, I thrust the knife into his neck. Bright red blood spurted out, because we bled the same. It splattered across my neck, my chin, my shirt. It flooded onto the bed, but he wasn't dead yet. His hand reached up and cupped my jaw, forcing me to look at him. His mouth gaped open and closed, as if he were going to say something, but only a gurgle of his blood spilled from his mouth.

His fingernails scraped against my chin, and my jaw ached from the power of his grip. Pink lilac eyes glared into mine, as if he could transfer his thoughts into my mind, but his magic was no good to him. Not even the most powerful Fae could take a sparrowbone dagger to the throat and recover. His grip tightened, and I sucked in a breath as his fingernails bit into my skin. He scraped away a small part of me during his last throes of life in attempted revenge, but his hand fell away from my face, dropping lifelessly to his side.

I jumped off him. My job was done, but my body wasn't happy.

Normally, I slept with the Fae I killed. Normally, I was satiated for at least a few days. I wanted more. I wanted to feel the magic everyone else claimed was so pure and vibrant.

I wondered, what did it feel like to be captured by something other than my own whirling thoughts and the need for revenge? What would it be like to lose myself in someone so completely? I wanted to lose my sense of self, my sense of duty.

What would it be like to trust someone I took to bed?

I breathed out and went to the bathroom, shedding my torn shirt and blood splattered pants. No mission was complete without a change of clothes, which I had stored after booking the room under a fake name. Showering quickly, I rushed to leave the scene as soon as possible. Just because we were alone now did not mean the manager wouldn't come to check on us. Places like this tried to be a middle ground, a place where Fae and humans met without the use of magic, but of course, the Fae never stopped using their magic. That was the problem. If they could have joined our society without magic, maybe the war wouldn't have happened and my family would still be alive.

Maybe I wouldn't be carrying the burden of hunting down the Fae king.

I towel dried my hair. The irony of my name was in the color. There was power in a name, and my nickname was chosen because of the amount of blood I left behind, not because of my hair or eyes or lips. I had light eyes and dark hair, a reflection of the dark side of the moon as it crested with the sun's reflection.

Scarlet was the perfect nickname, because Fae expected a wicked red haired beauty slaying them. But it was me. Black hair cut crudely in a chin-length bob with pale, unassuming features. The name had turned into the perfect disguise.

I leaned forward and gazed into the mirror. I swore. That

bastard had nicked my skin. *Ass.* I ran a tissue against the wound and dropped it into the toilet, flushing it into oblivion. With a sigh, I went back to the scene of the crime and grimaced as the pretty Fae's face seemed to gaze at me with wonderment. He was dead, I told myself as I took the sparrowbone from his neck. Deader than dead. The deadest.

A part of me hated this.

A part of me loved it.

Frowning at the bright blood on the end of the dagger, I washed that too, careful not to split my skin. Once I was clean and dressed, I dropped a heap of coins on the nightstand, a request to the inn's manager to not share this information readily. I could not stop a Fae's compulsion, because if a Fae questioned manager, she would tell them the truth about this night, but maybe the money would help her disappear. No one wanted to get caught up in a murder investigation, especially when Fae were involved.

As for murdered humans, we were a dime a dozen. We died all the time, and the Fae swore it was not their fault. It was, though. I had seen it when I was younger, and I had never let myself forget it.

I sheathed the dagger, laced up my boots, and walked out the door, leaving the bloody scene long behind me. The name of the male Fae became a whisper on the wind.

Two

My hair was still cold and damp when I stumbled into our underground compound later that evening. Out of the three people in the room, it was Marcy who glanced up first. She gasped at the sight of me and crossed the basement in moments. Her fingers gripped my cheeks.

"What happened to your face?" She tilted my face to the side to get a better angle on the cut.

Her squeezing fingers made my lips pucker together. "Nice to see you, too."

"Who did this to you?" Her green eyes blazed, but with the color of an angry human. Blond wisps of hair curled around her delicate features.

"The better question is: are they dead?" Anya asked in a bored tone from across the room. She fiddled with the end of a knife, always twirling something deadly in her hands, not that she could ever wield a weapon against the Fae. One tendril of magic would be enough to bring Anya to her knees, much to her dismay.

"Yes," I said, stepping back from Marcy's grip. Her scrutiny was too much sometimes.

"Oh no, you don't," Marcy insisted. She snatched my wrist and dragged me over to where she had stashed the first aid kit. "You know how dirty Fae fingernails are? We cannot risk your dying because of an infection."

"I'll be fine," I said, even as I let her guide me to sit on the stool as she checked my face.

"She'll be fine," Anya agreed, her light brown eyes flicking over us.

"It's better to be safe than sorry," Quinn added from his corner. He was poring over his computers again. I swore that guy never stopped thinking of ways to end the Fae from behind the screens.

Even after the Fae invasion and subsequent war, most of our technology still worked. The problem was making it work against the Fae. Once they had influence over us through compulsion, our military and police laid down their weapons. A single swipe of mind erasing wiped our top scientists out. They left our society in shambles, with no solutions and the nation's guns happily being burned by the hands that originally made them.

It took years for us to discover sparrowbone, and even that was by chance and not by our invention. A few teens had traveled into Faerie only to come back with scars and weapons. Sparrowbone was toxic to the Fae, slowing down their magical healing long enough to fight. As soon as I had the opportunity to, I stole my dagger and two knives. Sparrowbone was equally useless in the hands of a normal human. Whenever a Fae compelled someone, the human would submit instead of fighting.

To be honest, the war was over far sooner than most of us expected, but the hollowed shells of cities proved it all happened.

Courts arose out of the ashes, made to the ruling Fae's specifications. Every Court was different, depending on the Fae in charge. This one was a disaster.

As Marcy prodded my face, I looked around our headquarters. In the past month, it had become well lived in, which made me feel edgy and unsettled. This was not a home, nor was it supposed to be. The hairs on my neck stood on end as I thought about the implications of someone's finding us here.

My anxiety almost got the better of me when Marcy pressed alcohol against the cut.

I hissed. "Why?!"

"Because infection is still real! It's a really real thing. Now, stop moving."

"You'd think the Fae Slayer would be able to handle a minor scrape."

I scowled at Anya. "You want me to cut you and pour alcohol onto it?"

She shook her head. "I'd rather be out there hunting with you."

"We've been over this before, Anya. You're—"

"A liability, I know." Her light brown hair hung in sharp, awkward angles around her face. She didn't dare go to a hairstylist or anyone outside of the compound, as any outside contact could put our mission at risk. These three humans could ruin my life if the Fae caught them. Their relationship was to Scarlet the Fae Slayer, not the real me. They could never know my true name, but if they were captured, they could easily confess everything they knew about me to the Fae, including my appearance. That would make it a lot easier for the Fae to track me down.

"It's not that I don't want you to come," I added, trying to appease her.

She slammed her knife into the table. It stood on end; the tip balanced in the worn wood grain. "Obviously. But I wish it were me. I want to end every single one of them like you do. I want to watch them suffer, want to see them cry out in pain."

"The crying out part would ruin the stealth of our operation," Quinn muttered as he typed a few more commands. "Scarlet, you still hoping to find the Lord of this court before we move on?"

"Finian? Yes." I nodded as Marcy applied a small bandage over my face. I'd keep it on while I was at the compound, as I knew it would make her feel better. She was right, after all. Fingernails were horribly dirty, and unlike other humans, I could not go to a Fae healer and ask them to rid me of my ailments. Magic, even the good kind, had no effect on me. If I got an infection, without getting access to expensive and rare antibiotics, it could be a death sentence.

"There," Marcy said, staring at my face for a few more beats. "You know, I wish we could do more for you too." She murmured the words, meant only for me and not the other two in the dingy basement space. "There's more to life than death."

I shook my head. "As long as the Fae are around, that's all life will ever be."

Marcy's fingers left my face as a frown marred hers. "There are still other forces in the world. Your heart might be full of hate for them, but there's still love between us." She gestured to the other two in the basement.

"Of course there is," I said. My broken heart almost felt whole when I thought about the four of us against the world. After my family died and they lost theirs, we had found each other, and that was a prize worth keeping. It was worth fighting for and killing for, and nothing would stop me from keeping them safe. "But until the threat is gone…"

Marcy waved her hand. "Remember, you deserve more than

what you have, okay? You are worthy of love and trust, and you're worthy of our friendship." A forced smile parted her lips. "We're here for you, and we'll keep being here as long as we can be."

"Speaking of which—" I stood up, and my stool scraped against the floor. "—we should move locations."

Quinn groaned. "Do you know how long it took me to set up these computers again? It's almost impossible to get internet now."

"Then find us another place with access, because we're getting too settled. This place is too… lived in. They will sniff it out, eventually."

Anya rolled her eyes. "Always paranoid."

"Don't I have a right to be?" I cut a glance her way.

She hadn't been the same since Paul's death, and his demise happened because we didn't move. We got too comfortable. To aid our escape, Paul had confronted the Fae. He allowed them to use his body, however they disgustingly needed, as the rest of us slipped out the other exit. I remembered the timber of his voice as he bit down on the poison capsule. He gave into them, said he was theirs after the poison had already taken its hold. He was likely dead in ten minutes or less, which gave us enough time.

His voice, arched and needy, had chased me into the next court.

Our numbers had dwindled significantly, and we couldn't afford to lose anyone else, nor could I imagine it. I glanced at Marcy, who tossed me a weak smile. "I can prepare our kitchen supplies for the next move. We got a good number of dried goods stored away this time, so it should make the transition easier."

Anya stood and stretched her hands above her head, knife rotating languidly as she twirled her wrist around. "I can gather the weapons. Quinn?"

"Yeah, yeah. Fine. Let me do some research on hot spots and where we could head to. But, Scar?"

"Yeah?"

"Can this wait until tomorrow? I might have a final hit for us, and if I can pinpoint the Lord's location, we'll be one step closer to finding the throne."

Finding the throne. My blood became alive at those words. The Fae king was elusive, living somewhere in secrecy. He had heard the stories of the Fae Slayer and went into hiding after my third or fourth kill. It was only a few years ago, but felt like a lifetime. By the time I had realized my true powers and decided to kill the king, he had already made himself scarce.

Some powerful Fae he made. Just a male who hid the moment a woman gathered too much power. I would never kneel to someone as sniveling and feeble as that.

"I hate the idea of staying in this place one more night, but if you're sure you can find Finian's—"

"I'm sure." Quinn's face reflected determination and confidence. He had been so close in the past to weaseling out the higher Fae, but our need for secrecy always cut time short. We could never stay in one town for long, because once word got out about the Fae's deaths, they would try to find us. Any dead Fae was a neon sign pointing to our location, and I had already killed three here.

Though, finally killing a Lord would be an accomplishment.

"Okay," I nodded. "Forty-eight hours. That's all I am letting us afford. Anything beyond that is borrowed time." *Though we might be on borrowed time already.*

Quinn's eyes brightened. "Let's get it done then. Marcy, I need snacks!"

Marcy rolled her eyes. "Fuel for the computer nerd coming up." She tossed me a wink before turning to the hot plate and pot in the corner, dumping in water, spices, and some dried bits of meat and vegetables. The smell was incredible, even though there wasn't much to it. Whenever I was away from the compound hunting, I craved the simplicity of this life, this world, this unreality we lived in. Marcy was right, there was more to life than death, but until this was over, I could never have these small moments permanently. They were fleeting, over as quickly as a cursory glance.

"Anya? Can I have a word?"

She approached me slowly, as if she waited for my reprimand. Her well-defined shoulder muscles rolled as she considered me.

"Let's go up to the fifth floor. Get some fresh air." I wrinkled my nose and tried to give her a genuine smile. Most of those had died the moment the Fae invaded my house.

"Happily," she said with a wary smile.

As long as I was with her, going to the top floor was less of a risk. The Fae might be able to take over her mind, but I could easily knock her out and kill them if needed, so long as they thought I was in a stupor too. We had gotten out of more than one sticky situation because of their assumptions.

Anya got pissed with me once, as she assumed I had used her as bait. I would never do that to my friends, and she realized it was a mere coincidence the Fae had found us.

They always found us if we stayed stagnant.

As the old wheezing elevator opened onto the hollowed out fifth floor, Anya stepped into the light breeze. I watched goosebumps rise on her skin as she spun around in the open air. I wished I could give this to them every day. Most days passed in underground basements, hiding in seedy places people and Fae were less likely to look. My friends barely got to see the sun, let alone breathe fresh air. I felt guilty, but any exposure to the outside world put them at risk of capture and compulsion.

"While I hate the ruins, I do like how every single building now has a rooftop terrace."

I snorted.

The sun settled near the horizon, casting bright pinks and oranges into the sky. I remembered how the sky in Faerie had been lit up like this when I nudged the door open.

I wished I could go back and slam the thing closed, board it up, and set it on fire so no one would ever find it. But it had reached out to my mind with its tendrils of evil magic and planted those dreams in my head. The visions coiled so thick I had to chase the power into the woods; I had to find the hidden door, no matter what.

Two weeks was all it took for ten-year-old me to open the door, and two months later, the world had ended as we knew it. I remembered the look on my mother's face when the male had forced my father to—

"Scar?"

I shook off the memory and clenched my fists together.

"You know why I put up with all of your rules?"

"Because you know what's good for you?"

Anya shook her head, a devious smile on her lips. "Because you burn with as much anger as I do. I see it every time I look at you."

"You don't get to survive the Fae war without battle scars."

"Some people did." She wrapped her arms around herself. "That's why my sister trusted them, because nothing bad happened to us. That's why she's a servant now. I wonder how long it will take until they tire of her. She seemed stronger than other people, but everyone succumbs with need, eventually."

I knew my body did, and their magic did not affect me. Though, I had to wonder if I loved the sex or the *aftermath* of the sex. The moment their body was penetrated by my dagger, the moment of realization, the moment—*Yes, that was it.* Because already I wanted another mark, another Fae to carve out of the world. Humans would win this.

Unfortunately, after the Fae were dead, we would have to deal with the magical creatures which had crossed through the portal too. We could fight the beasts once we had our weapons back, when people could finally wield power at their fingertips.

"Is Marcy okay?" I asked, uncertain where the question had come from. I spent so much time away from them, I felt it prudent to use this time wisely and check in with my crew.

"In what way?" Anya glanced over her shoulder at me, her light brown hair catching the last rays of the sun. I shrugged in response, and she kicked a piece of ceiling tile that had fallen to the floor. "She loves you."

"I know."

"Do you love her?"

I licked my lips. I wasn't allowed to love. Not when I had to seduce and maim and kill. Not until this was over. It would be over some day, and maybe then. Maybe I could entertain a future with the soft-cheeked blond who had kind green eyes. Maybe I'd be able to spill the secrets of my family's last day on earth. Maybe life wouldn't be so hard.

That version of the future felt less possible than winning the lottery. Everything would have to align perfectly for something so miraculous to happen. It would hurt more to hope and lose that future than to never hope at all.

"I want the best for her. For all of you."

"A neutral response, and why would I expect anything less from you? But I know the truth behind your calloused heart, Scar. I know." Her eyes flashed before turning back into the breeze. Anya had more to offer the world than her thick exterior, and I wished she could fight by my side. I trusted her.

By the time we headed back, Quinn told me it'd likely be a few more hours before he discovered the Lord's safe house, but he had determined one of his hang outs was the local Fae club, Ceilidh.

With that information, I took my leave. I had to prepare for the next hunt, and ever since Paul's death, we had been wary of my spending too much time with them in hiding. If they were found, we wanted it to look like three innocent friends hiding out together, instead of having the Fae Slayer in the mix. I took one last glance before exiting the basement, and the three of them felt so amicable, so at peace. They might have needed me to save the world, but I did not know where I fit in once we succeeded.

A part of me wondered if I could get back my innocence. Violence and sex had become so intertwined for me, and I wasn't sure I wanted one without the other. But at least I didn't need to face this problem now, as there were plenty of Fae who needed to meet their untimely end at my hands.

Three

I weaved through the hollowed streets and burned out husks of buildings. The original city was still here, but covered in dirt, grime, and fallout from the endless use of magic. The Fae found it funny to make things collapse, and in the wake of many buildings falling down, they left the humans with whatever this was. Not quite a safe haven and not quite dangerous. It varied depending on the Court, but this one was bad.

This town was in a limbo. It wasn't quite the wilds, as there were enough Fae to keep the roaming monsters at bay, but it wasn't a safe haven for humans either. They carved cities and courts like this one all around the United States. Every Fae Lord and Lady made a place for themselves and provided a modicum of safety to their residents from the external monsters. Quinn had spoken with people across the globe, and it seemed as if it was much the same everywhere. Once the Fae had access to our planet, there were no safe corners. They destroyed and took everything, reshaping the landscape into what they thought it should be.

Except Australia. Apparently, there was something about the poisonous snakes that made the Fae stay away. At least, that was the rumor. For all we knew, the king could have been hiding in Australia, and maybe that's why no one spoke of anything bad happening there. Though, I hoped not. Getting across the planet would be incredibly exhausting without air travel.

I headed to an apartment complex someone turned into a temporary hostel. For the last few nights, I had used this location as my hiding spot. It was far away from the taverns and inns, as well as from the compound. Exhaustion weighed on my shoulders, and I wanted a long bath. I wanted to soak myself long enough to forget the feeling of Torin's lips pressed against mine, how his body had promised me more. Frustration weighed on me, because it hadn't gone the way I hoped.

I wanted to forget how much I enjoyed his skin resisting the dagger while I pierced it through his neck.

Sighing, I realized none of it would ever be enough. Sex would never be enough on its own. I wanted to be captivated, to feel passion and desire. I wanted something *more*. Taking a life felt dangerously powerful, but it still was not *enough*.

The receptionist behind the counter looked up as I walked in. "Lola, hi. I wasn't sure if you were coming back."

I had paid for four days up front, and a fifth one if she would keep my fake name out of the Fae's mouth. Of course, I would never give someone my real name, nor would I give them my alias. Scarlet the Fae Slayer attracted too much attention.

Lola suited me fine for now. I stole it from an old neighbor.

"Yeah, one more night, I think. After that, I will head out."

"May I ask you a question?"

I shrugged as I held out my hand. She placed the key in my palm. I gave it to her in the morning every day, in case I didn't come back. It made no sense for me to hold on to things that were not mine.

"What is the rest of the world like?"

"Much like this."

She blinked her pretty blue eyes at me. "I heard New York still has skyscrapers."

"I haven't gotten that far."

"Oh, but you seem so well traveled."

I frowned, wondering if she was trying to gather information. Sometimes inns and hotels would act as a superhighway for the Fae who were hunting specific people, usually those on the run. I was not on the run, but something quite the opposite. If she was asking questions about my life, there was probably a reward posted for a runaway. Obviously, I was not the runaway in question. Even so, I didn't need to give her a reason to be suspicious.

"You must be mistaken. I travel throughout the state to establish trade routes for my father. He's in the antique business." The lie and truth tasted horrible on my tongue. My father had been an antiques dealer with Lola's father—*been* being the operative word. The Fae had destroyed him, in a similar way to my mother. And they made my brother watch before killing him, too. A child.

Lola's family had survived and kept the business, so her name became one of the rotating identities I used to keep the Fae off my trail. Seeing her name on a hotel log wouldn't raise any suspicions, as she *did* travel for her father.

I swallowed the lump forming in my throat. "You see, he needs to establish new clients. A few of his recently went missing. We think due to being Fae Followers, but we can't be sure. Anyway, I am drumming up some new business for him." I blinked innocently, glancing around at the furniture in the sparse lobby. "Say, you wouldn't—"

She waved her hand, a blush creeping onto her cheeks. "No, no. We don't have the means to get anything as fancy as antiques, though I am glad to hear your father is alive and well. Mine did not fare so lucky, and I've been forced to run this place ever since."

The disdain in her voice was unmistakable. She was after the reward money. I wondered whose face was plastered over the boards this time. Likely someone who had enough resemblance to me to spark her interest.

"Well, I might be able to cut you a decent deal." I pulled out my fake business card for Lola Scott, Antiques Broker, and passed the paper on over to her. "We're down in Coventry. If you ever feel like coming by."

The address was wrong, enough so if the Fae caught wind of the Scotts it should keep them safe. Besides, the real Lola and I looked nothing alike, so most would realize I was using this as a facade, anyway. It had been years since I had seen the Scotts. The last I heard, Lola wasn't doing so well, and by now, they might be dead. The point was I borrowed stories, enough to make myself believable wherever I was staying, and I shed my identity like a snake at the next city.

If I ever saw Lola again, she wouldn't recognize me now.

"Oh, I rarely get out of this place." The girl behind the counter smiled at me. "It was nice to chat with you, Lola. Appreciate you staying here."

"Yeah, no problem." I padded off to find my room, key in hand. I made a note to ask Quinn who was being searched for now, because if I remotely looked like her, this could pose a problem for me. At least the receptionist seemed satisfied, or at least as satisfied as I could make her without having Fae magic at my disposal.

Back in my room, I had a single knapsack full of supplies,

continuously packed and ready to run. I kept one here and at the compound as a backup. Either would work in a pinch if I had to get away, though I hated leaving things behind. I had lost too much already.

Locking the door, which really had no power over the Fae, I filled the bathtub with water and salts for a soak. If I was going to hunt again tonight, I wanted to rid myself of this tension.

When I first slept with a Fae, I had hesitated before I sliced through the sinew and muscle into the jugular. It had been a weakness, a moment where losing my virginity truly hit me along with the intensity of the decision to make sex as much my weapon as it was theirs.

The Fae hadn't been suspecting it, as he was my first victim. That Fae had been almost kind. That Fae had an inkling of what could have been construed as feelings. He knew it was my first time, and he told me he'd be gentle. He had treated me with tenderness, which made me hesitate. It had made me weak.

After that moment of softness, I destroyed the last of my good nature by plunging the knife into the Fae's neck. I decided never again. If I was going to meet violent Fae head on, then I'd have to meet them with the same level of viciousness they had toward humans.

A few kills later, I craved devastation.

Though, out of all the Fae I slept with over the years, I remembered him, my first. His eyes were the color of robin's eggs, complete with flecks of red strewn throughout. I had never seen another with those eyes, and I wondered if it had been a rarity in the Fae world.

Maybe I had destroyed something beautiful.

But they had started it.

I eased my body into the hot salt water and breathed a sigh of relief. If Quinn's information was good, maybe I could sleep with the Lord tonight. Even if Quinn didn't find the Lord's manor, I could track him at the club. If I were going to get admittance into a Fae club and attract the attention of a Fae Lord, then I needed to look flawless at Ceilidh. It also meant scrubbing the dark splotches from under my fingernails and removing the trace of caramel from my lips.

Salt water always did the trick.

Sinking low, I wondered what the Lord looked like. I had heard rumors of his stunning long brown hair and forest moss green eyes. Rumors of his chiseled chest and tight shoulders made me want to conquer him all the more. Fae were attractive, but rarely were they built like the Lord was rumored to be. They had no need for extra bulk, since they were not soldiers. When one had the capability of disarming an army with nothing but a thought, why bother lifting weights? Of course, I heard rumors that their glamor could change them to be whatever they needed to do, but if they ever did, I didn't see it.

Besides, why would they bother changing themselves when they looked as good as they did? Plenty of people would throw themselves at the Fae as Followers.

I clenched and unclenched my hands several times, letting the tightness from earlier today relax into the warm water. A knock sounded on the door, and I nearly jumped out of my skin. My heart raced as I grabbed the dagger, never leaving it far out of my sight. I crept out of the bathroom, leaving a trail of salt water in my wake.

"Who's there?"

"Marcy."

My heart skipped a beat. Marcy knew better than to come here. She knew the consequences of us being caught together, of someone seeing her and using her against me later. I pulled the door open, glanced around, and yanked her inside.

"What are you doing?" I growled.

"You're naked."

Right, that. I swallowed, shaking my head. "Marcy, what are you doing?"

"Quinn got it," she said, voice timid.

My anger flooded out of me as quickly as it had come in. This was a message, an official direction of where to hunt for the Lord. "He'll be at the Ceilidh tonight. Scarlet, the club *is* his manor."

I held back a laugh. Of course it was. Why hadn't I checked there already? Because Fae liked their comforts, and most Lords and Ladies were unwilling to go without. The night club was in the court's heart, sure, but it still was a loud and unruly place. It was never where I would expect a Lord to hang out.

"Were you followed?" I asked Marcy.

She shook her head.

"Good. I need to get dressed and head to—"

She tugged on my arm. The action stopped me cold. "Scar, I might not see you again after this."

"You say that every time."

Her blond hair fell in front of her face as she shook her head. "This feels different. This feels… final."

"You and your feelings." I reached up, tucking the lock of hair behind her ear. The heat of her skin against mine was too much. "Nothing is going to happen to me."

She ran her tongue over her lips. "Scar, what if—"

"No," I said, tone final. "I'll be fine. All of us will get out of this town, and I am going to kill the Lord, but only after he tells me about the king's location. You'll see. We'll get the information we need, and we'll be out of here before anyone knows."

"You've already left three bodies in this city. It feels dangerous to stay."

"I told everyone to pack. Force Quinn to move to the next safe house. Now that I know where the Lord is staying, there's no reason to sleep at the compound for one more night. I know Quinn hates leaving his precious hot spots behind, but he's going to have to if we want to stay alive."

Marcy nodded, taking a step away from me. "I'll try. Do you need my help getting ready?"

I laughed, looking down at my utterly naked body. "Unless you can smell any of the last Fae on me, I think I'm good."

"What did he smell like?"

"Caramel."

"Oh, that's why you smelled like the circus I remember going to when I was little." Marcy barked out a laugh. "For a few moments, I thought you were hiding candy from me."

"Never."

We stared at each other for a few beats. "You should head back." My voice felt too soft in the space around us.

"Yeah, I should."

Marcy looked me over one more time, and I had to resist the urge to do a very Fae thing and rest my hands on my hips. The Fae would let anyone get a good, long look at their bodies. Clearly, I had been around the ego-maniacal beings for too long.

With an exhale, I stepped back toward the bathroom and the warm water I had left behind.

"Promise you'll be careful?" she asked as she unlatched the door. Her green eyes searched mine as her fingers brushed over the door handle.

"I promise I'll be as careful as I can be while in the nest of vipers."

Her eyes roamed over mine, as if searching for a better answer, one I could never give. "Okay. See you later, Scarlet." She slipped out into the darkening evening, and I went back to my bath. In another five minutes, I'd get out and prepare for tonight. I wasn't leaving anything to chance.

At the club, I would have my dagger concealed as normal, but also a knife stuck in my boot. If someone disarmed me, I wanted a backup. Calling Ceilidh a den of vipers was putting it mildly. Most humans who went in did not come out without a Fae latched onto their arm like a succubus. The Lord would have guards, because Marcy was right. I had been leaving bodies in my wake. By now, he must be on high alert, knowing full well how Scarlet was in his city. Heck, he might have spread this information in order to lure me into a trap, because it felt too convenient.

Quinn said it would take him a few more days, but suddenly the information was in his hands and ready for me? Yeah, this was definitely a trap. Unfortunately for them, I had worn different wigs during my first three killings in the city. Brilliant red hair for two, becoming the very name I gave myself, and blond for the last one.

Tonight, for the Lord, I would go as myself. No more dressing up, no more hiding. If the Lord was luring me out, he was going to get me as I was. Nothing special, nothing different. I would be ready; I'd be expecting this to go south. The knife in my boot assured me I would make it out of this.

After a few more preparations and applying a light amount of makeup, I traveled into the night. I headed straight for Ceilidh to uncover as much as I could about the king before the Lord died at my hands.

Four

Ceilidh was at the edge of town, but I could hear the music long before I reached the club. They had converted an old warehouse into a nightclub, and it amazed me that Fae wanted something so ordinarily human to rule over, but here they were. Complete with VIP sections, bottle service, flashing lights, and a DJ. Every night there was a Fae party, and all the humans were invited.

It likely was to bring future Fae Followers and servants in. The club presented the guise that servitude to Fae could be fun, luring younger men and women out only to enlist them into Fae enchantments. Compulsion was a hell of a drug.

Clubs like Ceilidh disgusted me, but they were often the best hunting grounds. Still, I had to put on a convincing show, as if I belonged there and wanted to be part of the crowd.

With a bat of my eyelashes, I got past the bouncer. They lazily felt my body for weapons, but he either didn't notice mine or didn't care. I wondered if it was the Fae's arrogance that allowed them to be so nonchalant about security or if they were expecting me. It would be a rather elaborate trap, but I had been eluding the Fae for years. Maybe my weapon was a dead giveaway, so they rolled out the red carpet.

If the Fae knew what the bogeyman looked like, would they be so frightened of me? The reason Scarlet the Fae Slayer's story spread like wildfire was because of the mystery. To them, I might as well have been darkness incarnate, a creature of the night, the monster under the bed that every child feared.

I had never seen a Fae child, but the adults had to come from somewhere. The question was: where? Even after thirteen years of our vague coexistence with the Fae, none of us knew their history. Why weren't there Fae children? And if there had been children, would I have felt differently about killing the Fae?

While I wanted to believe the humane part of me would feel guilt, my mouth watered at the idea of the Lord's blood seeping through my hands.

Weaving through the crowd, I made my way to the bar. Strangely, there were human bartenders, but perhaps that was to make people feel more comfortable buying spirits. Faerie wine was something humans rarely messed with, because it was like taking a dose of ketamine and ecstasy. Humans felt good afterward, but also ridiculously tired.

Though some still drank it and partied. To each their own.

I leaned over the bar, meeting the eyes of the men surrounding me. Most of them were humans, which wouldn't help me reach my target this evening. I needed to get into the VIP section. I needed to be noticed by the ones who mattered.

Twirling my fingers through the ends of my short black hair, I fluttered my lids until a bartender handed me my drink. One drink to nurse the entire night, so I wouldn't look suspicious, but I wouldn't get drunk. I trailed around the outside of the dance floor, glancing in at the bodies undulating like waves in the crowd. Fae and humans mixed, and seeing them like this, I could almost forget that *consent* was a word most of them knew nothing about. These people looked happy, but was it from the Fae magic or because they wanted to be here?

Judging by how many Fae's eyes were lit by magic, I would bet most would have no say in how this night ends. Despite my boiling blood, I had to keep my face neutral. People frequented this club after all, which made me wonder what humans saw in the Fae.

Other than how obnoxiously gorgeous they were.

Continuing my trek around the dance floor, I finally spotted three Fae worth paying attention to. Their jewelry was a bit more glamorous, their cheeks higher, their eyes sharper, and the colors of their irises unique and distinct.

I took my drink and danced through the crowd, taking a moment to lose myself in the bass's beat. The music rose and washed over me like a wave as I passed by person after person. Hot bodies were slick with the smell of sweat, and the pheromones Fae gave off before they had sex ignited me. The air tasted like Fae, and the people smelled enraptured. The grinding and closeness of their bodies was intoxicating on its own. Sweet smells invaded my senses, and I allowed myself to drink in my surroundings.

After all, I had to look the part, like a love-struck girl looking for someone to sleep with.

Once I was a foot away from the taller Fae in question, I forced myself to knock against a human male. He whirled around, pushing against me with an angry jealousy. Humans could be so predictable when they were caught up in Fae magic.

Bingo. I stumbled backward, right into the Fae in the middle of the dance floor. Half of my drink sloshed at his feet, barely missing his shoes with expert precision.

"Oh my gosh!" I looked up, aghast and glaring at the man who walked into me. "How dare you do this to the Fae!"

The man looked confused for a moment. "I didn't! You walked—"

"Your poor shoes!" I said, bending over wiping the single drop of liquid off the tip with the edge of my dress. "I know someone who is an excellent cleaner, and I—" I gazed up at him.

He stared down at me.

The man who had run into me was already being hauled away by guards. In a club like this, the guards barely needed a reason to escort a human out, but if someone accuses a human of acting against the Fae, they were gone. Nothing bad would happen to him, except maybe a sore butt from being thrown onto the streets. This was a means to an end, and while the man might be furious he couldn't get into Ceilidh again, I had met my mark.

I was sure of it.

"Hello," the Fae said, grabbing the underside of my chin and lifting me back to my feet. "And your name might be?" His green eyes swirled as a wave of compulsion wrapped around me, passing me by with no effect.

"Lola." I figured it would be easier to stick with the truth I told the receptionist, in case anyone came asking around. Lola was here. She had been in the city and had been obsessed with meeting one of the Fae at the club.

"Lola." The word rolled off his tongue with a sexual longing. The lightness of his voice made my body long to lay with him, only to cut him down moments later.

Not yet, I told myself.

"Yes, that's me." I made my voice timid and coy. "And you might be?"

"Raskos."

"Raskos." I ran through the database I knew about, the Lords and Ladies. As far as I knew, there was no Raskos, though things changed all the time with the courts. I tilted my head to the side, trying to make myself seem interested but innocent. "And your companions?" I nodded toward the other two Fae with him.

"This is Cumina and Morna."

I blinked a few times. From afar, I hadn't realized the two guards were female. Cumina and Morna had cropped black hair cuts with fierce angles. Their jaws and shoulders were sharper than most of the feminine Fae I had met. They looked identical, save for the style of clothes and the color of their eyes. Morna wore a vest and black trousers with golden eyes, and Cumina had silver eyes and wore a red blouse with flowing pants. Their skin was deep umber, as dark as a clouded night sky.

"A pleasure to meet all of you."

"The pleasure is ours, Lola." The way Raskos said the name was like a light breath across my skin and goose flesh appeared all over. It drew my attention back to him in an instant. I wondered how I would have reacted had it been my actual name on his lips. I also wondered if this male could lead me to where I needed to go. Unfortunately, there was only one way of figuring that out.

"Would you care to dance?" I blinked a few times. "It's the least I can offer, with my clumsy—"

"Lola," he rumbled, closing the distance between us if he glided on air. "Say no more." The spark in his eyes was from his magic. The tones of his iris were like staring into a moss covered forest. He was stunning.

I nodded in what I hoped appeared to be blissful compliance. He took my hands and guided me to the middle of the floor a few steps away. The crowd parted around him as if he were a tsunami, and with his grip on my hands, I knew his compulsion was just as powerful. I didn't have to feel it to understand the effect it had on everyone else. He parted the world around us, bending everything to his will.

I would have to be careful to play into his expectations.

My hands were drawn to his body, despite his guidance. Raskos was like wine and staring at him made something come alive inside of me. *Raskos*. I tried to wrap my brain around where I had heard that name before as he draped his arms around me, pulling me close. Our bodies connected in a way I hadn't felt for years, but that was the atmosphere in the club. I might be immune to Fae magic, but this many delicious scents in one place was enough to tease any person, even someone as jaded as myself.

Raskos.

"Raskos," I whispered his name on my lips, leaning in as if I was going for a kiss before burying my lips against his neck. The smell of him was familiar and foreign, something vaguely… like candy? My lips ached to taste him, figure out where I knew him from, because something about this Fae was different from the others.

I could feel Cumina and Morna's eyes on us, watching like everyone else in the club was. If this didn't get me into the VIP section tonight, I'm not sure what would. Surely, a Lord would want to come out and play with someone that a higher Fae took interest in.

Surely.

Except as I was dancing and trying to get close to this male, I felt a tap on my shoulder. A fully armed Fae soldier stood behind me, and my blood froze in my veins the moment I laid eyes on him. Fully armed soldiers did not show up at a club. Not when they had magic that worked on people—worked on everyone except me.

"Hello," I said, trying to be moon-eyed over the dance with Raskos. "How do you do?"

The male Fae tilted his head to the side and looked at Raskos. "I'm cutting in, Finian. You can find another human to partner with tonight."

Finian Raskos.

I was an idiot. He looked familiar and resembled a high Fae because he *was* a Fae Lord. And Cumina and Morna must have been his bodyguards. I gritted my teeth, fury rushing through me.

The Lord shrugged as he walked backward in the club, away from me. This newcomer—this fully dressed soldier who had no jurisdiction here—took over the dance. It was awkward with his layer of leathers and swords at the ready, but I tried to keep appearances. On the surface, I was a giddy girl named Lola who was in town to sell antiques for her father's market.

Since when did Lords listen to soldiers? My pulse spiked because this didn't feel right. The Lord was not in the VIP section, and soldiers were here and at the ready.

"How are you doing this evening, miss?" The Fae's voice was like liquid fire along my skin. Something about him fueled the burning hunger deep inside me. And his dark amber, almost black eyes hadn't flashed any color yet. No magic use, so I could answer freely.

At least, sort of freely.

"Well, sir. I can't believe I was dancing with the Lord himself. I never thought I'd be so lucky. And now his personal guard?" I tripped on the last part, forcing it out like a question.

The Fae chuckled. "He wishes." His grip on my arms shifted as he dipped me into a spin, arching me away before whipping me back into his arms. I could only hope he didn't suspect who I was, not with him so close and completely engulfing me. There would be no way out of this if he knew.

"Well, if you are not his guard, then why the armor?" I parted my lips in a pout.

"One can never be too careful these days. Don't you agree?"

"Of course. I didn't mean any offense." I blinked innocently up at him. He had height on me, about eight inches. Most Fae were taller than me, being five-six myself.

His eyes flashed, searching for something.

Sputtering over a few more lines, I hoped if he were using some kind of compulsion my words would act as a buffer between him and the truth. "I only mean that Fae seem so powerful. I couldn't imagine you needing armor to protect yourself against anyone. If I had a strong Fae like you by my side, I would feel so safe. May I ask your name?"

"Voss."

"Voss," I repeated, hitching my breath on the end of a sigh. "That's a beautiful name. But I shouldn't be surprised. Fae always have such beautiful names. Not like mine. Lola seems to roll off the tongue all right, but—"

"But—" he interrupted, pulling me close against him. His grip shifted to my waist, clamping on my dress and digging into my skin. "It's not your name. Is it, Scarlet?"

There was no time to think. I simply acted. My fingers went to my sheath, and the dagger came out right in the middle of the dance floor. I thrust it into the small space between his armor, where the shoulders met his chest plate. Cursing, he stumbled back from me with my dagger still wedged into his bloody shoulder.

I growled. As much as I would miss my dagger, I had my knife. There was no time to get the weapon back.

I whirled and ducked through the crowd on the dance floor,

flinging the emergency exit doors open and leaping over the stair railing. I launched myself down to the bottom floor as quickly as I could, pulling open the steel exit door with a heave and nearly falling into the street.

Maybe Marcy had been right. Maybe those had been my last moments with her, and I had ruined it by not saying goodbye properly.

Another male Fae appeared out of the shadows to my left so I darted right into a narrow alleyway. I realized my mistake as a stunning female Fae blocked my path from the other end. Both Fae prowled toward me, swords out.

Screw this.

I reached into my boot and drew the sparrowbone knife.

"Oh. Oh, gosh." The female laughed. Her voice came out ethereal, caressing my skin like the glow of the moon. "What on earth are you planning to do with that?"

"It's good for the eyes." I twirled it expertly in my hands. "Besides, I'm out of daggers."

"It's good for the eyes! Like a home remedy?" The female laughed again.

I was holding something in my hand that could kill her, and here she was, laughing in the face of danger. Damn it, I kind of liked her.

Something crunched behind me, and I pressed my back against the wall so I could watch the male Fae too.

"Listen, we don't want any trouble." His hands were up, turquoise eyes steady on me. While he held a sword, there was no expertise behind it, no practice. If I were to break through either of them, it would be him, but he was also closer to the club's exit.

The female seemed as if she had more wits about her, poised and certain.

"Yet you funneled me down an alley to corner me."

"Well, okay. That's fair. Isn't that fair, Elspeth?"

Elspeth growled. "Oh, we're giving out true names this time around? Very novice of you, Penn."

Penn's face reddened. "At least we're even."

"It's not like humans can use that against Fae."

"Can't you?" Elspeth looked at me, her eyes sharp. Clearly, the boogeyman rumors had spread far and wide.

I smirked despite my predicament. I was not getting out of this, so I might as well have a little fun.

"Maybe I can. Who knows? You'll have to wait and find out." I took the opportunity and lunged toward Penn. He dodged my attempt at getting the knife straight into his eye, but he didn't realize his face wasn't the true target. I kicked out, slamming my boot into his kneecap. He yelped and stumbled backward a few feet. I darted around him and got only two feet before I had to back up once more.

"She certainly cannot use our names against us." The deep rumble came from Voss at the end of the alley, appearing as if out of the shadows. He tore the sparrowbone from his shoulder and tossed it back toward me. It landed on the asphalt with a clang, spraying his blood in droplets against the pavement.

I arched an eyebrow. *Was this another trap?*

"You gave it back to her?!" Penn exclaimed as he rubbed his knee. "She just tried to—"

I shoved the knife back into my boot and scooped up my dagger, readying the weapon while narrowing my eyes at Voss. "What's the meaning of this?"

"You'll never trust me if I leave you unarmed." He shrugged.

"Trust? You talk of trust?"

"Yes, a thing two people with a mutual goal might come to find in one another if they so choose to work together." A dark amber sparked in his eyes. "I can't believe it's true. It doesn't work on you at all."

"Obviously. How else would I have been able to kill as many as I have?"

"How many was that, exactly?" Elspeth asked, hands on her hips. "Because I only started paying attention when she got to a baker's dozen."

"Would have been one more tonight." I scowled at Voss. "If you want me to trust you, you could walk away and let me finish my job."

"I need Lord Finian alive, unfortunately for your plans." Voss stepped around Penn and leaned casually against the wall. He was well within striking distance of my dagger again, but he seemed at ease with my being armed. No fear of the deadly slayer I had turned myself into. Most Fae trembled when they realized who I was; they begged for mercy. Voss merely stared at me as if I was a curiosity.

Maybe that's what made me lose my edge.

"Well, I need him dead for my plans, so I guess we're at an impasse."

Voss chuckled. "I think you need my help more than you need Raskos's body on top of yours." There was a challenge in his stare. He knew I slept with the enemy before I killed them. I was like the Fae Followers and everyone I hated, but my decisions were out of duty, a means to an end. I refused to be put in that same category as them.

"So what of it?" I spat.

"We've been looking for you for a long time, Scarlet. The girl who is immune to magic, the Fae Slayer. You're wanted by the king."

42

"I've heard." I matched his bored tone with my own.

He stepped close to me, shrinking the distance between us once again. I could slash his throat open, but for some reason, I waited.

"I don't think that's such a good idea."

"Shush, Penn. Your concerns are noted, but are unnecessary." Voss reached up and tugged on the end of a lock of my hair. "*Whereas she was the reflection of the full moon, he glowed like the midday sun.* The quote makes a little more sense, does it not, Elspeth?"

"You're the sun?" I rolled my eyes. "Not likely." His skin did seem to glow, despite the darkness of the surrounding night. His hair flowed around his ears, brilliant blond, while his eyes were swirling pools of dark liquid amber, almost like staring straight into a solar storm.

He was right, whatever that quote was. We were similar opposites.

"What is that from?" I asked.

"Nothing that concerns you at this moment. We need to talk about your deliverance to the king."

I slashed out at him, but he jumped back before I connected. "I will do no such thing."

"You can and you will, because if you don't discuss this with me, then I have orders I must follow."

"Orders from who?"

"The king himself. And if you don't come back into the club with me and put on a good show, then I will have to drag you off by your hair right here and now." He reached his hand out toward me. "Put the weapons away and dance with me."

I slashed out with the dagger. He hissed as I got a knick on his small finger. It was practically a paper cut, but it was enough to enrage him.

"Oh dear," Elspeth barely said before Voss had me pinned

against the wall with his hand covering my windpipe.

His other hand expertly disarmed me in a second. It was a blink before he precariously pressed me between him and the cold brick. My body reacted the same way to him like it did to every other Fae. Violence created a vacuum in me that nothing could ever fill.

A growl escaped his lips as he leaned next to my ear. "We're being watched. I can't talk freely here. You need to trust me. Come back into the club. I'll pretend I was wrong and you're another innocent girl who was temporarily under a spell. Otherwise you *will* die tonight."

"Why—" I choked on the word, and he eased his grip slightly. "—should I trust you?"

"Not here." The look in his eyes was final, shutting down any more questions on the tip of my tongue. I knew better than to ask again. If we were being watched, then I needed to get out of here, and if the only way to do that alive was with him, I had to trust him. At least I had to trust him for now. He could have killed me. He could have kept my dagger. If he wanted me dead, my body would be lifeless in the alley.

"What do you need me to do?"

Voss's wicked smile made my stomach curl into a fiery pit. "Drink this." He offered me a flask from inside his pocket.

I sniffed it, shaking my head.

"Faerie wine is the only way to explain how you were immune to compulsion this evening. You must drink it."

"But then I won't remember anything."

"A single sip. You will."

"But you'll have a hell of a hangover tomorrow," Penn added.

"And there's a cure for that," Elspeth added.

I looked between the three of them. There was no way out of this alley unless I wanted to die or work with them. "And I have to drink it now?"

"Yes, now. Before we go back into the club and give everyone the false alarm." His voice had dropped into a hushed whisper, but I could feel their magic pulsing around us. He was glamoring something, making other people see another scene in the alleyway, or perhaps making them hear something else. I wondered how it worked, what it would look like if I were an outsider staring in.

I stared at the flask. "There's no other way?"

"Afraid not."

Rolling my eyes, I brought the flask to my lips. I felt as if I would regret this decision, but the alternative was an untimely demise. "Bottoms up."

Five

From the moment the wine touched my lips, I knew this was a bad idea. But I also couldn't kill all three Fae, especially not one so heavily armed. The wine tasted like fresh out of the oven bread oozing with butter and a side of bright fruit. I wasn't sure how those tastes went together into one sip of liquid, but there they were.

The effect was instant, and *weird* did not begin to explain the way the world pulsed around me. I may avoid compulsion, but the Faerie wine hit *hard*. It rose inside my stomach, turning my body into a pool of mush. A happy pool of mush.

After a few seconds, I stumbled forward into Voss. It was a single sip, something he promised would get me out of this mess. But what if he was the mess I needed to avoid getting into? And what did it say about me that I wanted to get into that mess?

He reached out, steadying me with heavy hands on my shoulders.

I blinked furiously, trying to rid my eyes of the swirling colors in front of them. "Has my head always been this heavy?"

Elspeth chuckled. "That was fast. Here." She scooped up a dagger from the ground—my sparrowbone, I realized—and handed it to Penn. "She can have this back once Voss is satisfied."

"Sexually?" I slurred, falling farther into Voss's steady grip. I looked up, catching his eyes. Standing next to him felt like getting a tan. There was something deeply mesmerizing about looking at him.

"Not sexually. Not for you, no." Voss tightened his grip around my shoulders. "Though we are going dancing. One hour from now, you'll be sober. We'll talk then, after you put on a good show."

"Your words feel like liquid fire along my skin."

He frowned. "Does it feel like that with every Fae?" Wrapping his arm around me, we walked toward the exit I had burst out of earlier.

Well, he *walked*. I stumbled. My legs were gelatin, my vision labored, and everything about me felt light. I tried to dredge up old memories, anything to make me focus on why this was a bad idea, but every single horrible thing was gone. As if it never happened. As if the Fae war had never been.

What would peace have felt like? This? A peaceful world, *that* would have been something to see.

"No, most Fae feel like…" I tried to think of a good word to put behind the urgent desperation I felt before sex. There were a lot of emotions coiled up together around Fae and sex. For me, it wasn't about the sex. It was about the… "Death. Like kissing death."

"I suppose that's what you are, isn't it? The kiss of Scarlet is the kiss of death." He pulled me close. "Or should I say *Lola*."

"Why does that name feel so good on a Fae's lips? I am jealous of my friend."

"You should not use your friend's name for anything. What if—" Penn shut up as Voss tossed him a look over his shoulder.

"No, he's right." I let out a breath. "The last time I heard about her, someone said she had gotten insanpheria. Slow way to go," I muttered, leaning more heavily on Voss. The Fae brought over the disease, and it acted sort of like dementia, but spread like a toxin. There was no cure yet, but thankfully it was rare for someone to catch.

If Lola had contracted the toxin and died because of my cover story, I might be doing her family a favor.

My body sagged more. "Am I slurring?" I asked. I didn't feel like it, but my mouth was doing weird gymnastics every time I tried to speak.

"Yes," Penn said. I could hear the scorn in his voice, though I wasn't sure why he was so angry with me. Oh, wait. The kneecap thing.

"I'm sorry about your knee," I muttered.

Voss snorted. "Apologizing. How absolutely adorable."

"I'm sure it hurt," I stated.

"It *did* hurt. And apology not accepted. You're drunk." Penn's voice dripped with annoyance.

"Your loss. If it makes you feel better, I'd do it again."

"How is that supposed to make me feel better?" Penn exclaimed.

Voss laughed. I liked his laugh. It felt like caressing a fire.

The leathers of Voss's armor dug into my side, but I couldn't find the body control to move away from it. When we got to the second landing, the sound of the club surged over me. The pulse went straight into my head and made the ground ripple under my feet. I wanted to carry myself away into the music.

"Why couldn't we hear this from outside?"

"Because of the wine. Everyone else hears it just fine." Voss pushed open the door, pulling me with him as we entered the dark club.

While there were no strobe lights, the wine made the dancers look like they were hopping forward in time, slipping from this moment to the next. The world was a record skipping forward instead of playing the song straight. It was beautiful to watch, like a meteor shower on a cloudless night.

Voss led me through the crowd, weaving in between the bodies on the floor. The humans seemed to part around him as they had done for the Lord. Again, I felt a pang of jealousy, wishing I had such abilities. My job would be so much easier if I had magical powers too, but no. I had to be human, a human fighting against barely beatable creatures with nothing but my secrecy and sex.

And now the secret was out.

Stupid.

As soon as I felt the negative thought pop up, the wine dragged me back down, washing me with a feeling of greatness. Voss was warm, and he was leading me exactly where I needed to be.

But I couldn't remember why I needed to be here.

Lord Raskos eyed us as we walked up, me still a stumbling mess by Voss's side. "The girl is still alive, I see."

"The girl isn't who we thought."

"But compulsion—"

"Doesn't work on people who are drunk on Faerie wine." Voss tilted my head up, as if this proved the point. "How much did you steal tonight, little fox?"

I held out my fingers to indicate a bit, and let my fingers slowly drift apart. I still wasn't sure why Voss was lying for me, and my head swam with the need to figure him out.

"And she's really sorry about it," he added.

"I'm not," I giggled.

Did I just *giggle*? What was this wine doing to me?

He tightened his grip on my shoulder in a warning.

Lord Raskos's eyes dropped the length of my body. "I thought I saw her stab you."

"I was worried I was going to jail." I blinked wildly, staring between the two of them. "Am I going to jail?"

Raskos waved a hand. "I have plenty of wine, though I'd prefer you ask next time. A pretty thing like you should have whatever you want." A smirk spread up his face. "Including as much wine as you need." His mossy eyes flicked to Voss. "You can leave her here if you want. There is something about her that intrigues—"

"I'm afraid I'm taking her for the night," Voss said. "You're right. There is something about her, and I'm claiming it for myself."

I opened my mouth to protest, because he was *not* going to claim me for himself. I had to get to Raskos, and I wanted to stay here.

But his hand went around my jaw, covering my chin. His fingers brushed along my lips in a move that could have been seductive, but I knew he didn't trust my words. The wine made everything hazy around the edges, but a few moments would fill in with clarity. I hated it, because every time I felt as if I had a grip on the real world, I got lost in something.

Like how warm his fingers were. The calpuses brushing along my lips.

I bit him.

"Yikes," Lord Raskos said as Voss shook off his hand. "You can have her then."

I smiled sleepily at Voss, licking a small bead of blood from my tongue. "You taste like the sun."

"Hmm." Voss gazed at me.

"I think she's going to keep you mighty busy tonight. You sure you don't want to dump her on my lap?" Raskos settled back, gesturing to his trousers. His slithering smile twisted his features into something vile.

I would kill him.

"Yes, I think she will. Let's go." Voss didn't give me a chance to say anything else as he dragged me along with him onto the dance floor. The crowd moved around us again, but soon settled as the music swelled. He pulled me into him, dancing along with everyone else, which was awkward against his armor. "I can't believe you bit me," he whispered into my ear.

"I'll do it again." I licked the skin on his neck.

"This is the wine talking. You want nothing to do with me."

"True. But I can make it worth your while."

"How so?"

"I'm the only one who can say no to a Fae."

He leaned back, giving us enough space so he could see my face. "Is that how you do it? I've always wondered, but you never left any survivors."

"That would have been stupid of me, to not kill the person I was trying to kill."

"Oh, so you *do* call us people?"

"Fae," I spat, annoyed by the wine on my tongue.

"So that's it?"

"What's it?"

"You say no, and they let you flay them alive?"

"Let's try it." I leaned close to his ear. "I will never sleep with you. You will never seduce me. And I certainly won't enjoy sex with you."

His body went rigid against mine for a second before he found the rhythm of the song again. "It's not that easy with me."

"Sure, it's not. That's why you hesitated." I patted his chest plate, losing myself in the music and the feeling of him against me. The room swam around us, but it felt less blurry around the edges. Still, the wine loosened my tongue. "I'm sorry about stabbing you." I caressed the blood on his shirt.

"You made quite a scene."

"Why does no one seem to care about it?"

"Because most of them didn't see it."

"You put up glamor to protect me?"

He sighed. "Why don't we dance until you hate me again? It will be much easier to discuss everything I need from you once you can focus."

"Fine by me. I enjoy dancing." As if to prove the point, I spun away from him and did a few moves on the dance floor that were not dancing at all, but rotating through a bunch of fighting stances. Voss eyed me curiously, and I laughed at the stupidity of this night. I should have been getting this attention from Raskos. I should have been splitting his neck open. He needed to…

Suddenly, reality snapped back together, and Voss's eyes widened.

He gripped me once more and hauled me against him. I struggled to push away, but he whispered, "Trust me. If you suddenly seem sober, this won't work. You're still drunk."

"Why should I trust you when you *forced* me to drink Faerie wine?!" I hissed.

"Because Raskos would have had you killed. Those two Fae you saw earlier? They were assassins, assigned to be his temporary guard by the king himself to find you and kill you."

Morna and Cumina, the tall almost-identical Fae with gloriously handsome features and flawless skin from earlier.

"What is it to you?"

"We want the same thing, little fox."

"And what's that?"

"To kill the king."

My tongue dried out. I hadn't heard him correctly. For a Fae to want to kill the king was treason, something they could be tortured for. I had heard the stories while working in clubs to find my marks to kill. Captured traitors found themselves locked away with little food or water, kept on the brink of insanity, a fate worse than death where they would be made to bleed blood and magic daily.

I wanted to kill the king more than anything. But how could I possibly trust Voss? This could be a trick from a pretty face. The hair on my arms rose as his fingers trailed down to my waist, moving me into him. While there were layers of clothing and armor between us, I might as well have been stripped naked. Everything he said made me feel as if I knew nothing about the Fae I had been hunting for years.

"I don't believe you."

"Why not?"

"Because no Fae goes against their king... it would be..."

"Stupid?" he finished for me.

"Asinine might be the better word. A death sentence?"

"Ah, but none of them have had you on their side."

"I might be the Fae Slayer, but what makes you think I need your help to get close to the king?"

He chuckled, running his fingers up my sides. He reached around my shoulder and dragged me closer still, so my head rested on his chest. His heart beat was strong enough to hear through the armor. "Because the king sent me to assassinate you."

My body screamed at me to run, but I could feel the cold, calculating eyes of other Fae watching us. Any move I made to get away from him would ruin the ruse of the Faerie wine.

He had me trapped in more ways than one. I'd have been impressed if I wasn't so pissed off.

A human should never make a deal with a Fae. There was so much at stake, and so little information I had to make this decision clearly. I had been drunk on Faerie wine not moments before, and what was to say that it still wasn't in my system? How could I trust myself?

"How many people are looking for me?"

"All the king's horses and all the king's men."

"That isn't funny."

"Isn't it?"

"How many?"

"Including Morna, Cumina, and myself, there are nine."

My throat closed. *Nine.* Nine assassins ordered directly from the king himself, if this Fae were to be believed. But I had a hard look at Morna and Cumina. They were not the normal Fae on guard. They had the look of warriors, Fae who would tear out entrails and ask questions while the blood was still warm. If the other six assassins were anything like them, then I had to take my chances with Voss.

"I'm not making any deals."

"Nor would I expect you to."

"What's in it for you?"

Voss dipped me backwards, and I was forced to look into his eyes. They were molten swirls of rich amber lava. "Killing the king means more freedom for me than you could ever know."

I narrowed my eyes. "You look pretty free to me."

A smirk quirked the side of his lips. "You'd think that, but *look* around you. What do you see?" He brought me back into his arms, and we were dancing to the music again in a flawless move. He had fluidity and grace, even with the armor packed tightly around him.

"People who are at the beck and call of Fae."

"And many Fae who take advantage of that. This isn't freedom for your people or mine. This is letting those obsessed with power continue to win. Greed rules all. It ruled in your old world and mine."

"So why not kill the king yourself? Why recruit me to help?"

"Because, little fox, you know the saying. *Only the one who opened the door can kill the king.* He's immune to everything else. Everything."

"And you've tried?"

"Only a fool would do that."

I scowled, because that's what I had said.

"I wouldn't *try* unless I knew I could succeed. And before now, I have seen plenty of other Fae try and fail at the task. I've seen the king stabbed, his heart cut out, his eyes ripped from his skull. I've watched crows feast on his guts, and despite that, the king comes back whole. You, however, can kill the king. The only human not influenced by our magic and curses. The only human capable of committing the most vicious act this planet has seen. The only one capable of saving us all."

"What do you need saving from?" I asked.

"You think I care to be an assassin? Watching blood spill over my hands day in and day out? You think I don't crave a world where my brethren can live beside humans instead of using them as mindless slaves for the taking? We destroyed our world. That's why we left the moment the door opened. And we'll do it again if things don't change. Greed took everything from us in Faerie. I won't let the mistakes of the past repeat."

His eyes blazed bright under the flashing lights of the club, and damn it, I believed him. I hated how I believed him, but something about his words was too compelling to ignore.

"And if I say no to working with you?"

"Well, we may have a contingency plan for that."

"Of course you do." I scowled. "Do I want to know what the contingency is?"

"The one called Anya. She went up to the fifth floor without you."

My heart went cold. If they knew Anya, they knew where Quinn and Marcy were too. My friends were in danger, but it seemed Voss was the holder of this information alone. If Morna and Cumina had known, they would have easily slipped inside and slit everyone's throats to get to me. At least, that was my assumption based on their serious expressions.

"I need time to think about it," I said as my heart kicked up in my chest. In reality, I needed no time. I would do what I had to for my friends, but I had to get Quinn and Marcy out. They had to run as soon as possible. Trusting Voss with my life was one thing, but trusting him with my friends' lives was another. If he had Anya, the other two needed to know, and they needed to escape.

"I figured as much. We can talk tomorrow night at the Sparrow Hawk."

"If any harm comes to Anya, it will be a no. You hear me?"

Voss hand cupped my chin, and our eyes met. His lips were inches from mine. "I wouldn't have it any other way. I'll walk you out. Raskos is watching, and it'd be better if we're seen leaving together like two lovers would."

"As if I would ever sleep with you."

Despite his earlier words, his muscles tightened, as if wanting to rise to the baited challenge, but just as fast, his eyes settled to a mundane nonchalance. He might have instincts, but maybe he was different from other Fae. My words tapped into something primal within him and still he stomped it down.

He grabbed my hand, and we walked casually out of the club. Humans and lower Fae alike watched us as we passed, several of them with looks of jealousy and contempt. I wanted to tell them they could have Voss for all I cared. There was nothing sexual about this.

Penn and Elspeth, who were waiting by the exit, peeled off after us as we walked out of the club, down the stairs, and back outside. Once there, I pulled my hand out of his scalding touch.

"Until tomorrow, then." I approached Penn and narrowed my eyes at him, holding out my hand.

Penn glanced at Voss. "Do I really want to give her the stabby object back?"

"Again, she'll never trust us if we don't."

"Fat chance of me trusting you either way, especially until I see Anya alive and well."

Elspeth frowned, and I tried to not read too much into it. There wasn't much I could do for Anya at this moment. I either put a small amount of faith into these dangerous strangers, or I tried killing them. Even if I brought them down, I had no idea where they were keeping her. She might die before I found and freed her. It wasn't worth the risk.

Penn sighed, passing over my dagger. He took a long step back to open up the space between us, and I smiled when I noticed the slight hobble in his step. Maybe I was a stupid, weak human, but I could pack a good kick to the knee.

"See you at the Sparrow Hawk, Voss." I twirled around and marched down the street, refusing to look back even as tears sprang into my eyes.

Tonight had been a massive failure. Raskos still breathed, assassins were after me, and worse, a Fae was attempting to make a deal with me. Blood rushed to every part of my body. I had no way of knowing if Voss was telling the truth about wanting to kill the king. Trust was a fickle and elusive thing, and I wasn't sure I could ever trust the Fae.

Except now it seemed like I had no choice.

I got back to the compound in less than ten minutes. My feet pounded into the pavement, driving me forward at a breakneck pace. I had to check on the rest of my friends, because they had found me, found *us*.

I was stupid. Killing as many Fae as I had, even if they had been higher Fae, was a rookie mistake. It brought the king's troops straight to our doorstep, and we hadn't planned to move for another day. I cursed myself, but there was nothing I could do about it now, save for trying to make up for my mistakes.

When I reached the exterior steel door of the compound, a note with a scrawling script was tacked on the outside. I tore it down and stared at the words, taking several moments for my eyes to adjust under the weak moonlight.

Scarlet,

Anya is safe. Inside. Call this a show of faith. You can trust us, at least with some of your secrets. Morna and Cumina will not be so forgiving. We are allowing you the choice to join us without consequence to your friends. However, I am not the most patient male. If you run and I have to follow you, I cannot promise the same thing twice. I would need leverage next time. So consider the warning leverage this time, as I know you humans always expect there to be a catch.

See you tomorrow.

V.

I burst through the door. The steel clanged against the other side and made ceiling dust fall into the stairwell. I leaped down into the basement and raced through the hallway until I was safely inside the dark space.

Quinn had fallen asleep at his keyboard, and Anya and Marcy had been sleeping, until I startled them awake.

"What is it?" Marcy asked, eyes wide with worry.

They were here. They were fine. That's why Elspeth frowned, because Voss had… Well, he hadn't *lied*. I had assumed. He said my friend left the compound, not that he had her in his possession. *Fae and their tricks.* I clenched my fists at my sides; the note crinkled in my fist. As angry as I was with Voss, I knew I had no other option. I had to either trust him with my life or trust him with theirs.

And I didn't trust him, so I would carry this burden.

At least with everyone awake, I could update my friends on the night's affairs.

I pressed my eyes shut and fought back tears. "We need some tea or something. I have a lot to tell you."

When I finished the story and the tea had settled the last of my nerves, the three of them exchanged stricken glances. A somber mood took over the basement, because we knew there was no way out of this.

"I'm sorry," Anya said, shaking her head. Her brown hair danced around her chin as tears pricked her eyes.

"I'm fairly certain they know everything. I'm not sure how long Voss and his group have been watching us, but if I were to place bets, I'd say they've been here for a week at least. He said that to frighten me, so I would know the consequences if I tried to act against him. But he has done nothing to compromise us, so I think he's telling the truth when he says he wants a truce."

"Or he wants to give you a false sense of security," Quinn said, running his hands over his shaved head.

"It's the same means to an end, isn't it? He wants me to go with him, and now I have to. It's no longer a decision or a deal. He's played his hand, and I have to play right into his."

Marcy frowned, her green eyes igniting. "There has to be another way. We could run. We've slipped into the shadows before."

"There are three of them, Marcy. This isn't like the last time where there were two bumbling Fae. One is outfitted to the teeth in Fae armor and weapons. Penn and Elsbeth looked like they could handle themselves in a battle too." At least Elspeth did. My lips turned down, because I had thought about this from every angle. One of them was watching the compound right now, I was sure of it.

"I wish we had unburied that secret passage." Anya crossed her arms over his chest.

"With what? A backhoe?" I shook my head. "There was no way of getting the tunnel unearthed without the proper equipment, and what an advertisement that would have been. 'Secret lair going into place over here. Please, no one pay attention.'"

Marcy giggled, and her airy laugh was music to my ears.

"I can't believe you are joking at a time like this." Quinn scowled, his hazel eyes sweeping across the room. "I guess we will have to move."

"I don't want you to tell me where you are going, in case everything goes south."

"How will you find us again?" Anya asked.

"Maybe I won't." I let out a breath.

This might be my last night with them—my companions for the last two years. Ever since I started hunting Fae, our ragtag group had become my family. I depended on them and looked forward to seeing them once a mission was complete. They made me feel more human than I did when I was out there in the wild. When I was among the Fae, I felt more like an animal, hunting and prowling like a predator in the night. These three kept me connected to the part of myself that ran on feelings, not instincts.

"I don't like this." Anya got up and paced the room again. She had been crossing the basement on and off, ignoring her tea until it grew cold.

"Do you see another way out of this?" I asked, leaning back in my chair. I gazed at each one of them in turn, because the answer was written on the walls.

For the second time in my life, I was helpless.

The first time, the only reason I survived was because the Fae didn't know I was there. My brother—*he* had sacrificed himself to save me. We were in the pantry closet. His hand was over my mouth as we stared at the intruders, as they...

"There's no way out." My voice was slick with finality. "Voss and his crew have me cornered, and they know it. They wouldn't have let me go if they thought I had any chance of getting out of this offer."

"And if it's a trap?"

"Then you'll have to find someone else with the magical gift to kill the Fae." I worked my jaw for a moment as I looked at Anya. "Besides, if Voss wanted me dead, he would have let Raskos take me home. Morna and Cumina were not normal Fae; I know that now. I was blinded by my ambition and ignored the warning signs leading us to the club. We should have moved days ago." I let out a breath. Moving would have meant letting another Lord live, as we had in many unfortunate courts.

"You should make him prove his loyalty to you."

"What?" I looked across the room at Marcy.

She nodded, as if she could see the solution as clear as day. "He's asking loyalty of you, right? Trust? Well, you ask the same for him in return."

"Careful, Marcy. This sounds a lot like a deal," Quinn cautioned.

"We want to kill the king anyway, right? So you tell him you'll work with him to kill the king, as long as he kills a Lord with you."

I sucked in a breath. "You think he'd agree to those terms?"

"It's two Fae for one deal, right? And it forces him to show you if he's telling the truth. He kills a corrupted Lord with you, the worst of the worst, and then you kill the king with him. If he's willing to kill a vile Lord, I think it's safe to believe he'd also want to kill the king."

Quinn glanced mournfully at his equipment. "If you got him to agree to kill a Lord in another court, it'd show everyone Scarlet has left town. We could stay here. This was the best hot spot I've found."

I pondered his thought process. It would be easier for my friends if they could stay put. If we made Scarlet the Fae Slayer appear elsewhere, they might stay safe. The assassins wouldn't bother looking at Raskos's territory any longer if I slaughtered a Fae in a different court.

"If I make a deal with him, I'm bound to it regardless of whether he ends up being treacherous." I tapped my foot on the ground, not liking the idea. "I could tell him it will be the only way for me to trust him. If I'm careful with my wording, it shouldn't be a deal."

"You'd have to be *very* careful." Anya's eyes flashed. "One wrong word, and you are bound."

"Yes, but she's only bound to kill the Fae king, which is what we want, regardless." Marcy pointed out the obvious. "If she accidentally gets into an agreement with the Fae, the worst that happens is we still get what we want. It's a win."

My heart thrummed. Making a deal with a Fae was like digging my own grave. This night had been a step into uncharted territory. I hated it. I wanted my routine back, the prowling in the dark, the choosing of a mark, the making the mark bleed and die at my hands. It was a simple life. Violent, but simple.

I chewed on one of my fingers, breaking off a callous near my nail bed. "This isn't what we planned, but I think Marcy is right. I think this is the only choice we have, and I'm sorry to say our journey is ending here and now." I let out a long wavering breath, not trusting myself to say more.

"It was great working with you, Scarlet." Anya crossed the room first and held out her hand.

I stood and clasped it in my own.

She smiled. "When you're done killing the king, turn around and put a dagger into the Fae blackmailing us, okay?"

Choking on a laugh, I nodded. "I'll see what I can do."

Anya dropped my hand. "We'll kill them all someday. For everything they've put us through."

I swallowed, thinking about what Voss said. Not all of them were like that, at least according to him. But he *was* Fae, and he was forcing me to work with him. Everything told me not to trust him, and yet his mention of greed resonated in me. Isn't that what the Fae at my house looked like back in the day? Greedy hands roaming over my parents. Lips flaring with the taste of their fear.

Anya pulled me into a hug, and our chests thumped together. She went back to her bed, pulling the knife out of the table as she went. A quick and quiet send off, despite the years of knowing each other. I appreciated that about her.

"I'll find out where the king is. We'll come to you if we can." Quinn pointed to his equipment. "If you get him to agree, leave a note at the Sparrow Hawk. I'll pack up if we need to, but if we can stay—"

My lips set in a grim line of understanding. "I'll see what I can do, Quinn." I echoed my earlier words to Anya.

He clapped me on the shoulder. "Godspeed, Scar." He turned to his computers, continuing onward as if he hadn't been dead asleep when I came in an hour ago. That guy would burn himself out someday, and I was glad I wouldn't be here to see him waste away in front of that machine.

When I turned around, Marcy was only one foot from me. Her cheeks were pink. "Can we go up to the fifth floor?"

Letting out a breath, I said, "I don't see why not. Voss is probably out there, but hopefully the ruse tonight kept the others at bay. We should stick to the shadows, just in case."

🙠 ✄ 🙢

We nestled in a corner of the rubble, which had an overhang of wire mesh holding together a layer of concrete overhead. The rubble covered enough to obscure us from prying eyes on the compound, but I was positive I felt a Fae's gaze Fae lingering in our direction.

Marcy kept her distance. I didn't blame her. Saying goodbye was hard enough without something starting between us. I never had time to think about how I felt toward this girl with delicate features and light hair to match her eyes and skin. I wished I could pinpoint what it hung between us.

Admiration, maybe? Understanding? A bit of love?

We had suffered at the hands of the Fae. Marcy and I were the only ones with mutual stories of witnessing our family's deaths. Quinn and Anya lost as many people as we had, but they lost them on the battlefield, out of eyesight.

Not in their house.

Not coiled with fear and rage.

Not seeing the tears in their own mother's eyes as...

"Hey." Marcy reached over the gap between us to squeeze my fingers. "Stop going back there."

I swallowed. "I don't try to."

"But you can't help it."

"No."

"It's okay if it fuels you, you know? But don't let it... burden you. Your parents would have hated that."

I thought of what my brother's arm looked like when they separated it from his body. I thought of his scream, the echo it made in my brain. It was impossible to block it out. Those moments in time looped on repeat, over and over. I feared they wouldn't stop even after the King was dead.

I forced myself to focus on Marcy's hand on mine. "We've never said what this was, did we?"

"Seems pointless now," she said, dropping her hand from mine. "Life takes us in different directions, but perhaps someday it will take us again in the same one."

"And if it doesn't, it's probably best not to dwell on what could have been." I followed her train of thought exactly. It was a grim outlook, but that's the world we lived in. Once someone exited my life, there was very little chance of seeing them again.

We gazed out of the broken side of the building, watching the clouds roll over the stars and the moon trek across the sky. Having fewer people meant peace surrounding the world. In the wilds, the howling creatures juxtaposed the quiet of the empty streets. Hoswisps, venomous beasts that came over from Faerie, surrounded the courts, adding an eerie background of bleating chaos. They were distant, almost like hearing a police siren from my youth, but the sound served as a warning. The threat of the wilds made any town without Fae just as dangerous as the Fae courts.

I wondered if Voss was telling the truth about wanting to create a new world. I wondered if there was such a thing as hope, trust, and love in a place of empty tomorrows.

"And if we're being honest," Marcy added in as a whisper in the dark, "you never really wanted me."

I looked at her in earnest.

"You wanted the idea of me. This girl who understands you on more levels than you let other people, but I've seen you Scarlet. Sex with Fae changed you."

Frowning, I distanced myself from her by another few inches. "Explain?" It was as much of a demand as a question.

"You feel the most alive after you've killed, and that's something I could never give you." She gazed at me with gigantic eyes. "You like it. It empowers you, and that's okay. We need some badass women to free us from this disaster we've found ourselves in. But at the end of the day, what is a big old softy like me supposed to give you?"

"Love, kindness, a connection to the part of me I long for?"

Marcy shook her head, a sad smile playing at the corner of her lips. "You haven't been connected to that side of yourself since your family was tortured and murdered in front of your eyes. Things like that change us. I guess I was hoping... I was hoping when this was over, I could be that anchor for you."

"You still could be."

She snorted. "No, you like it too much. You'll be with a Fae. I can feel it."

"I will *never* be with a Fae." I stood, dusting off the back of my pants. Anger pulsed through my veins. After everything they had done to us, how could she say that? "Never."

"Don't be so dramatic. There are more of them now than us, and who else would survive being brutally stabbed during sex and survive?"

"The Fae die."

"But they wouldn't if you didn't go for the parts that count."

"You make it sound like—"

"You like violence."

I stared at her, waiting for shame or guilt or anything to well up in me that would prove her wrong. Any kind of emotion to show how it wasn't true. I didn't love the violence; I had a job to do, and that was it. But her words struck me, sticking to the coldness of my heart with their echoes of truth. I did like violence. Raskos being taken away from me this evening was the biggest blow to my ego. I wanted to hurt him, I wanted to feel the power coursing through me as I did, and I wanted to get off on it.

"I wished I didn't." I breathed out.

Marcy stood finally, stepping up to me and kissing my cheek. "We all wish things could be different, but you're Scarlet the Fae

Slayer. You will succeed, and when it's over, I hope you have a very long and happy life."

"I will see you again." Marcy was my hope, the tether to the human side of me. I needed to see her again if I had any chance of keeping the quiet, patient side of myself alive.

"Maybe. Hopefully. But if we don't, I promise to continue watching over Quinn."

I shrank back. "I'm sorry, Quinn?"

"He needs someone to remind him to eat before he dies of exhaustion."

Rubbing the bridge of my nose, I laughed. "Fair point."

"Let's sleep before you have to pack and leave us behind."

I begrudgingly followed Marcy inside, but before we slipped the elevator doors shut, I gazed out at the hollow building across the road. I swore I saw a flash of turquoise eyes. A part of me knew it, but the hairs on my neck rose anyway. Penn watched from the shadows. I'd kick his other kneecap tomorrow to even out the score.

Packing for the Sparrow Hawk was a somber affair. We worked together in uniformed silence. There was a lot on the line if things didn't go as planned, and it felt like we were preparing for a funeral instead of a journey into the unknown with the Fae.

That was if Voss accepted my counteroffer.

I couldn't believe I was going to negotiate with a Fae. Everything in my being told me not to, but I needed some assurance he was telling the truth about his vision of the future. What better way than taking one of the more corrupt Lords along the way? I had decided on three names, Lords and Ladies who were worse than Raskos. I hoped Voss would agree to one of them being the first target before we went to the king.

And if he didn't, I would still have to go with him, regardless. At least this way, I could try to carve out a bit of power for myself.

Besides, there was the matter of how to reach the king. At this point, killing Fae hadn't given me enough information to figure out the king's location, and if I had a bounty on my head, it wasn't like I could walk into his court by myself. If Voss wanted to kill the king, then he must have a plan. At the very least, I could hear him out, but trusting any words from a Fae's treacherous mouth was a dangerous game.

My skin crawled as I drew the drawstring closed on my pack and hoisted it onto my shoulder. I had both knives, one attached to my thigh and one in my boot, plus the sheathed dagger at my side. Quinn had given me his sparrowbone necklace in the shape of the tiniest sword ever. The chain felt heavy on my neck, like it was larger than a typical parting gift. I laughed at him once for having it, because what could something the size of a thick toothpick do against a Fae?

But I'd take any protection I could get, even something small enough to conceal and stab a Fae in the eye.

"Well," I said, "that's all, I guess."

"Remember, you have to trust someone. Even if that's not Voss, you need allies on your side." Marcy clasped my hands in hers, and I nodded.

"And don't trust the wrong one," Anya snorted.

"And don't drink any more Faerie wine," Quinn added.

"So helpful, Quinn." A thought flitted into my head indicating how Faerie wine could be useful, but my memory from last night was hazy at best and it dissolved before I could grasp what it meant.

"Anytime."

The room turned cold after that, because there was nothing more to say. With a final nod at my friends, I slipped into the street and headed toward the Sparrow Hawk Inn, which was on the outskirts of the court.

Just two weeks prior, I had slit a Fae's throat at the inn. It felt like a lifetime ago that I watched the blood cascade over my hands and soak into the mattress. Sometimes I felt bad, because what did the employees do with the remains I left behind? Typically, the Fae got involved in carrying on an investigation, but what of the bloodstained sheets and floorboards? How did the humans carry on in the wake of my destruction?

This was a world full of harsh realities, and I wasn't the only one who killed inside the inns. Typically, it was humans who got the brunt of the violence, but I couldn't help but wonder.

I was a few blocks away from the Sparrow Hawk when I felt the icy trail of eyes on me. I froze and turned in a slow circle, looking at the broken foundations around me. "Yes?" I announced, keeping my voice steady.

Elspeth stepped out of the ruins. "We're not meeting at the Sparrow Hawk."

Narrowing my eyes, I widened my stance to prepare for a fight. "Oh? Why is that? Is there someone else coming to take me away?"

She rolled her birchwood eyes toward the sky. "Mother, help me. No, I am here to escort you to the horses so we can get to the next destination faster. Besides, Sparrow Hawk was compromised by Cumina last night. Seemed she had a little too much fun with a human male, and they are wrapped up in sheets together. We cannot risk her seeing you with Voss again."

"Why should I trust you?"

Elspeth took a step forward, and I took a step back. "For Mother's sake, look!" She held out another missive in the same scrawl as last night.

Little Fox,

Ever the questioning one, aren't you? Have some faith in Elspeth. She's worth your trust. I'd trust her with my own life.

V.

I snatched it out of her hands, waving it. "And I'm supposed to believe this is from Voss?"

"Why are you so difficult?"

"Why is he not here?"

"Because he likes to prepare everything meticulously before travels, so he sent me here to fetch you."

"Why not wait outside the Sparrow Hawk?"

"Again, Cumina cannot catch us. Will you come with me and stop making me angry?" Her eyes swirled with light brown and yellow. Her magic reared up around us, causing the hair on my arms to rise. A few pebbles floated in the air, but other than the chill along my skin, nothing happened to me.

"Frustrating, isn't it? Not getting everything you want when you snap your fingers?"

"Infuriating!" Elspeth threw her hands out. "Fine, go to the Sparrow Hawk. Cumina will kill you, and then we will find someone else. Though, I don't want to spend the next two years on horseback searching for another person who could actually kill the king." The frown on her face made me smile. "Oh, you were joking. Very funny. Hilarious." She turned and stalked off through the ruins.

I ducked into the ruins after her and trailed behind as we weaved away from the Sparrow Hawk and toward one of the lesser known stables across town. I understood the need for secrecy, especially since I had almost outed myself last night to several assassins. As much as I didn't trust Fae, something about Elspeth felt honorable. Maybe that would be my downfall. Marcy had reminded me to find an ally.

Maybe she was it.

Elspeth's hair swirled behind her as if caught in a magical breeze as she walked through the ruins. Her locks coiled in perfect waves around her shoulders, glowing a bright auburn. Whenever we passed by a section where the morning sun cut through the hollowed out buildings, her tresses reflected bright red. The shine on Fae's hair was ridiculous. How were humans supposed to compete with that?

We weren't.

When we arrived at the stables, Elspeth made a coughing sound in her throat. "I refuse to deal with this one ever again."

Voss peeked his head out from the stables, a huge sack in his hands. A frown creased his lips. "What did you do?"

"I came willingly." I shrugged innocently.

Elspeth threw up her hands and marched into the stables, pushing Voss's shoulder as she passed him.

"That does not appear to be the case." He frowned.

"I have something I need to talk to you about before I decide to make this journey with you."

He cocked an eyebrow. "I thought I was clear. The journey is not optional."

"Sure, you can take me however you want, but my hand still has to be the one to perform the task, right?" I arched an eyebrow at him, but didn't wait for his response. "So if you want me to be compliant, I have—"

"Careful, little fox. Are you going to make a deal?"

"No, not a deal. You want me to trust you, yes?"

He licked his lips, a smirk playing on his mouth. "Penn, take over." Voss tossed the saddlebag back into the stables. Penn grunted inside as Voss leaned against the door frame. "I'm listening." He crossed his arms over his chest, sizing me up.

"You want me to trust you, and I have discovered a great way to establish trust." I placed my hands on my hips, standing up straighter.

He narrowed his eyes, sweeping his vision lower for a mere second. "A proposal for an establishment of trust. A mutually beneficial notion for both of us. I am listening."

"And this is not a *deal* to establish trust," I added, because the way he was phrasing it made it seem like a deal.

He chuckled.

"You want to trust me to kill the king, and I want to trust your word for a better tomorrow. What better way to establish trust than a practice run?"

"A practice run?"

"We need to kill the king, but how will we know how the other will react in battle or in times of crisis if we don't practice beforehand? So we should practice."

"We can practice on the road."

"No." I stepped forward. "We can practice by killing either Lord Treborne, Lord Alpin, or Lady Burke."

"Alpin's off the table."

I scowled. "You said you wanted a better tomorrow. By all of my accounts, he has killed as many—"

Voss's vicious stare made me shut my mouth. "Your information on Alpin is outdated. Some of your trust needs to go into me when I say he is not one of the bad ones."

My teeth mashed together. Everything I had seen suggested otherwise, but maybe it was a front. There were layers to the Fae, and I hated to admit that I didn't care to find out most of those layers. Nuances made things complicated. It was easier to kill someone and move on than it was to analyze everything they did.

"Fine. How about the other two?"

"Treborne. We can kill Treborne."

"And we kill him my way."

His eyebrows came down low on his brow. "You're asking me to sleep with this male?"

Penn laughed from inside the stables. "Sleep with Treborne. Elspeth, are you hearing this?!"

"I'm *asking* for us to get him alone, not make it some big, messy affair. And an easy way to do that is through my method of getting someone into bed."

Voss looked me over, chewing my words. A dark blond eyebrow quirked up into the hair swept across his forehead. He had stupidly gorgeous hair like Elspeth, with perfect shining blond locks. I wanted to scalp him for it.

"This is a deal."

"No!" I stepped forward, desperation clawing my throat. "It's not a deal, it's—" I stumbled over my words, wondering how to backtrack.

The colors swirled in Voss's eyes as he took another step closer to me, gesturing out with his hands. Eyes swirled like that when contracts were being sealed, deals being made between Fae and human.

"It's not a deal!" I screamed.

"Relax," Voss smirked, putting a hand on my shoulder. The colors died away in his irises, and his eyes went back to their dormant black. "I couldn't make a deal with you if I wanted to."

"What?" I stumbled backward a step, making his hand fall off my shoulder.

A smirk tugged on his lips. "I was playing with you. The same way you played with Elspeth. Doesn't feel good, does it?"

I scowled. "I don't understand."

"A deal requires Fae magic to bind two people to the contract. You, little fox, are not bound to our magic, so there is no way to make an official deal with you. But I can accept the offer, as the traditional terms of another living being. We will kill Treborne together, as he's a despicable male not worth feeding to stray hoswisps. And once we do that, you'll trust me for my words?"

"I trust that you want to kill the king for the same reason I do, but I'm not sure I should trust you for anything else."

"A wise choice of words. Clever of you trying to find a way around negotiation, but there is never any bargaining with Fae. It's best for you to remember that in case your powers ever stop working." Voss's eyes flash, but I couldn't discern the emotion behind them.

"Are you both done?" Penn's voice traveled from inside the stables. "If we have any hope of leaving before the others discover our plans, we should head out now."

"So, where are we headed?" I asked.

"Exactly where you think, to Treborne's land."

"And after that?"

Voss glanced at me and chuckled. "For you to find out when we get there. You'd think I would give you the location of the king's court without being by your side for the slaughter?"

I shrugged. "It was worth a shot."

"As most things are." Voss headed into the stables, and I followed him. The mares were outfitted with the same regalia as Voss, leathered armor that showed more than weathering along the edges.

"What are these from?" I pointed to the bite marks around the ankle coverings of each horse.

"Hoswisps and the charred marks are from fire pauldrins."

"Why are they called—"

"Less talking, more riding. Let's go." Penn threw a saddlebag at me. I grunted, barely able to catch the thing in time. "Put your bag in there and load it onto your horse."

I blinked, but did as he commanded. Penn had shorter hair than most Fae, closely cropped around his head with dark curls to it. His turquoise eyes were like something out of a tropical magazine, but still they held none of the inklings of someone with a royal history. None of these Fae had royal eyes. All the high Fae I had met had some distinct second color inside their eyes. Even Raskos had flecks of dark bark in between the moss green spires in his eyes. Assassins from the king wouldn't need to be high Fae, they just needed to be good at their jobs.

I knew Voss was good at his job. He had tracked down me while the others had failed. Regardless of what Voss told me, I knew Fae had been searching for me. They wanted me dead. I heard my name whispered with heated animosity in the darkest corners of the places I visited. Still, Voss had been the first one to find me, and the first to corner me.

I had to respect him for it, even if I hated him.

"How is your head, by the way?" Penn asked.

"Fine," I said. "Why?"

"Faerie wine usually leaves a hell of a hangover for humans." Elspeth led her horse out of its stall, gliding by me as if floating on a cloud.

"No hangover," I said.

Penn looked at me. "Huh."

"What does that mean?"

"Nothing. Leg up?"

"No." I tried to jump into the stirrup, but ended up falling short. Voss gripped my waist and tossed me onto the horse with no regard for how I landed slightly sprawled on top of the beast.

"Penn's right. We need to leave, and there is no more time for your pride."

I glared at him as he led both of our horses out of the stables and onto the road. He jumped onto his own in one fluid motion, and I wished I had more riding lessons in my life.

My group usually hired a carriage to bring us from one town to the next, because of the need for coverage and stealth. My friends rode together, and I took an aimless walk through the forests and trees. We made sure I could walk each journey during the daytime, because at night the world erupted with the chaos of Faerie wildlife. Plus, the wildlife from earth that had survived were mostly predators.

"How far is it to Treborne's place?"

"About two days' ride, and there isn't a good place to stay between here and there, so I'm afraid we'll be camping in whatever we can find."

"Isn't that a death sentence?"

The horses picked their way across the rubble, and my body tried to get used to the lurch and sway of the one I rode on. It was a dabbled color with a white mane and sleek coat. She was a stunning mare, full of power that I could feel underneath the saddle.

"Only if you fall asleep."

"You expect me not to sleep for two days?"

Voss glanced at me. "I expect the three of us to keep watch, because I don't trust you not to careen off into the distance the moment we're out of the city."

"The thought had crossed my mind."

"Do you want Treborne dead?"

"Yes."

"And the king?"

"Yes, definitely."

"Then stick with us. It's as simple as that."

Was it? I wondered what Voss got out of this. Sure, he had his vision for the world with his speech about greed and corruption. He had ideas about how Fae were taking advantage of humans, but that didn't mean our situation was simple. Everyone had something to gain, something more to take, and there would always be something more to give. The question was, *what*? It made no sense for one of the king's own to want him out of the picture.

"Does he not pay you well?" I guessed.

Penn snorted, and Voss gave him a glare. "What? She asks hilarious questions."

"The king pays me nothing."

"Then why work for him?"

"As I recall, we're on our way to kill him, so what makes you think I'm still working for him?"

"What *made* you work for him? Your literal use of language frustrates me."

Voss arched an eyebrow. His cool black gaze spread across my skin. "Obligations I'd rather leave behind. Isn't there something you'd like to leave behind?"

I swallowed, because I flew back to that place I never wanted to be again.

Tears streamed down my face as I had run out of the house, fleeing the scene of bloodied corpses and dead eyes. I had screamed myself hoarse the moment the Fae had left, screamed until I had no voice left. It had died in my throat and didn't come back for days. My father was missing an eye, while his muscles twitched in the aftermath of his death.

Not to mention my mother or brother.

Not to mention the way their entrails gleamed like tinsel.

I blinked back to the present. "I have a lot of things I would rather forget."

"How many of those include murdering Fae, I wonder?"

"None of them," I answered honestly. "I would go back and kill them again if I had the opportunity."

"Would you?"

"Yes."

"Penn and Elspeth, watch this one tonight. We can't afford her deciding to slit our throats if the other's back is turned."

I rolled my eyes. "You assured I wouldn't. I can't get to the king without you."

"True. And his location will be a guarded secret until the last possible moment. For the safety of my crew."

"I'm still not sure why we gave her the sparrowbone back," Penn sighed.

"If it makes you feel better, Penn, I am also fairly good at kicking things."

Penn grumbled under his breath, something that sounded like a Fae word for bitch.

"Yes, how is the knee, Penn?" Elspeth asked sweetly.

"You are all very cruel." Penn guided his horse forward a few more paces, lengthening the space between us.

Voss chuckled. "He's a sensitive thing, isn't he?"

"Only because she got him good. Did you see that thing? It was the size of a grapefruit."

"Good," I said.

"I was telling you we *didn't* want trouble!" Penn yelled from his position up ahead.

"Then you shouldn't have been in my way!"

Voss's chuckle turned into an all out laugh, and the way it filled the air was a deep caress across my skin, making every part of my body thrum. "I'm sure you'll be fine after another day's rest, Penn."

He humphed from the front of the line.

Elspeth kicked her horse to join him, and she dropped her voice into hushed tones, leaving Voss riding beside me. I wasn't exactly a prisoner, but there wasn't anywhere to go other than into the wilds, which was like signing a death warrant. Voss hadn't killed me yet, and if I was still alive in two days' time with Treborne's pulse fading under my blade, then I would accept Voss's words with sincerity.

"What happened to you?"

"What?"

"To make you hate us?"

"Where do I start?"

"At the beginning." His eyes flashed into liquid amber, like he was trying to use magic before quelling it. His irises faded back to black.

"My house was near the portal. That's why I found it when I was ten. My family, because of our proximity, was also the first to die."

"And yet, you survived."

I ran my tongue along the pointed part of my canine tooth, wishing it was sharp enough to cut into my skin. "Something like that."

"They must not have been very smart Fae to leave someone as powerful as you alive."

"They didn't have a choice."

"Why?"

"My brother covered for me." I let out a hollow laugh. "Why am I telling you this? It's not like you care. My family is dead. They died in the first wave of invaders, because that's what you are. That's what you did. You invaded. You destroyed our defenses, and you took and took and took, and now this is all we have left. Vague cities, a small semblance of what life used to be, harsh wilds, and dangerous battles every single day."

"How is that different from the world before?" Voss's horse was next to mine. I could reach out and slap him, but I'd risk falling off my ride.

"My world had actual cities, cars and buses that took people from one place to another, decently safe woods to walk in, and a police force."

"You had pollution, crashes, different predators, and the need for protection. And sometimes people needed protection from that protection."

I opened my mouth and snapped it shut. I pushed my horse forward, choosing to ride in the middle of the group. Voss might have a vision for the future which included humans and Fae, but accusing humans of... I shook my head. I was only ten when the world changed. I was ten. I remembered things being good before they came. I remembered dressing up for Halloween. I remembered being excited about Christmas.

I remembered my parents shutting off the news whenever I entered the room. They had strict rules about internet usage and social media. I remembered how vigilant they were.

The need for protection.

Didn't the need grow the moment the door opened? After I had broken the seal, hell broke loose. The world became chaos, dark, and night. Everything became a grisly ruin of what it once was. And here Voss was telling me it had been horrible, as tragic as this world now. I refused to accept it. The Fae had ruined everything. I opened the door, and I started the apocalypse. No one was supposed to know, but now these three did. I was trusting the hands of my enemies, and never in my life had I felt so hopeless.

    Except in the pantry.

    Except when my brother stepped outside to save me.

    Never again.

Eight

We rode until my ass fell asleep and my thighs ached from gripping the saddle. Elspeth tried to teach me how to ride with the flow of the horse so it wouldn't hurt as much, but it didn't work. I never had grace. My precision came from being sly, hence Voss's annoying nickname for me. I never had to learn other skills because I had something no Fae could get from anyone else.

It was my weapon and my curse.

By the time I slid off the back of my dappled mare, Switch, my legs almost collapsed underneath me. I stretched several times, feeling joints popping over my body from disuse.

"How is this better than walking?" I asked as my neck cracked.

"If you have to run away from hoswisps tonight, you'll be thankful you have the energy." Penn went about setting up camp like this was something he had done a million times before.

Elspeth watched him from a nearby log, seemingly unable or unwilling to help. She looked bored, as she did most of the time.

"Noted," I replied.

"I'll take the first watch," Voss said.

"Great. I feel so safe."

"You should. He's good with a bow and sword." Penn gestured toward the small pile of tinder he had created, and Voss waved his hand, coaxing a fire from nothing. "Plus, he has magic to back it up."

"I'll be sure to let the wilds know you're leading Voss's official fan club. I'm sure they'll be so impressed they will let us be." My back cracked as I twisted to the side. It hurt.

"You don't have to be so…" Penn's turquoise eyes swept over me, but he pressed his lips into a thin line and didn't add anything else.

Turning back to Voss, I said, "I bet you wish you had our guns at your disposal. Think of how many hoswisps you could kill with an assault rifle."

"And how many nearby predators would hear the shots and come running from miles away? It wouldn't be the hoswisps you'd have to worry about in that case." Voss shook his head. "For someone who has eluded capture for so long, some things you say make very little sense."

"Maybe if the Fae had taught us about the dangers they had brought in, people would be a little more prepared for the new reality."

"Here we go again…" Penn muttered.

Voss narrowed his eyes at me, and with another wave of his hands, the rest of the logs caught on fire. Stupid Fae magic. It made everything easy for them.

Elspeth sighed and picked underneath her long fingernails, getting all the loose dirt out. She still looked prim and proper, even after the day's ride.

During our rest breaks, Voss and I had spent the time bickering, because I couldn't stand the truth behind his words. Before the Fae came along, there had been a beautiful planet with wildlife and quiet nights. Quinn had cautioned me once of looking at the past through rose-colored lenses. He had been alive a decade longer than me, but there was still a distinct line between before and after Fae.

My scope of the world hadn't been fully formed before I opened the Fae door. I had been too young, but I wanted to deny it. I wanted to throw the revelations right back into Voss's pretty chiseled face, but the scathing comments wouldn't come.

So instead, I kept arguing my point, no matter how futile it was. "You could have at least given us a fair shot to figure it out. The Fae didn't have to take out our leaders or our guns or any of that."

"Is that what humans did throughout history? Warned places of war before it happened? No, they waged war, tons of battles where hundreds of thousands died. You act like humans are better than Fae, but humans would just as soon throw each other into the dangers of the dark."

"You have an answer for everything!" I was annoyed, and my arguments felt childish and forced on my tongue, and yet I couldn't stop myself.

"And you have a very black and white world view."

I huffed, sitting down on a fallen log near the fire. In truth, I was too tired to argue anymore, and I knew I wouldn't get anywhere with him. Something about Voss made me want to bicker. I needed to prove him wrong and show him that my world was worth saving—the one before the Fae came over. But reversing the damage done was impossible. My family would still be dead, no matter what happened at the end of our journey together.

Speaking of which, I needed to clarify something. "What happens once the king dies?"

"One of the princes will rise to power," Voss said. "Such is the way of the world, but we can hope the prince will be worthy of the power and wield it with honor and dignity. We can hope they will encourage the other Fae to do the same." He unpacked the horses, leading them farther away from camp to graze among the grasses. The Fae had chosen a large clearing to sleep in for the night, likely due to needing to see for a longer distance. It would be easier to run from a swarm if needed.

"You don't know which prince?"

Voss shrugged, clearly done with this conversation. "The king's power chooses when it leaves him, usually through proximity."

I considered his words as the three of them continued to get camp prepared.

The setting sun brought a sense of foreboding. Everything I had learned screamed at me to run into the comforts of a structure. Indoors. Being in a city surrounded by Fae was the only way to guarantee safety at night, which was ironic, given how unsafe Fae were for humans to be around. I understood the need for Fae, at least on a temporary level, but long term... We'd be better off without.

I watched as the orange orb crept toward the horizon, casting long shadows around the group of three. They looked at ease being out here with Voss standing at attention, gazing out into the distance to assess any incoming threats.

"You'll want to sleep," Penn said as he pushed a bedroll toward me. "It'll be a long day tomorrow, and when we arrive in Lord Treborne's lands, there will likely be a party to attend."

"A party?"

"Penn, we don't know if we'll get an invite." Elspeth sniffed.

"Elspeth, he's obsessed with you."

"Really?" I asked.

Elspeth rolled her eyes. "Unlike what you believe, Scarlet, I have never killed a human. Never. Treborne finds the prospect of corrupting me... very tempting."

"Huh." Then he'd love my little party trick too. "Have you ever killed a human, Penn?"

"Sadly, yes, but it was during the first war when they took up arms. I got shot." He lifted the hem of his shirt, showing a small white scar the size of a bullet. "I made the men turn their arms on each other." His shirt fell down around his waist again.

"It was brutal," Voss added, coming to settle on the opposite side of the fire. "Penn isn't much of a fighter, but he can glamor people to believe they are in an entirely different dimension."

"That's..."

"Horrible," Penn stated, looking distraught by the admission. "There was so much blood. I had never seen guns before in my life, and I had no idea... I thought they would be like arrows, leaving some survivors like me. But no. Bullets were much worse."

"And you?" I asked Voss, though I didn't trust him for a genuine answer.

"Me?" Voss smiled. "I kill anyone who wrongs me."

"Fae and human?"

"I've killed Fae before the portal opened, yes. And humans, well, many people have tried to kill those I care about, especially during the war. As one of the king's assassins, I can handle myself in battle, so I'm sure you can imagine how that turned out for the enemy."

"Not well."

"Not well indeed." Voss stretched out his legs. "I will never be ashamed of protecting the people I care about. That could include you, little fox."

"I don't need your protection."

"Maybe someday you will."

I crossed my arms over my chest.

As if sensing we were doomed for another battle, Penn told me to go get some water from the stream with Elspeth. I glared at him, but was parched enough to listen to the instructions.

"Besides, if you're gone, maybe I can convince him to stop inciting arguments with you." Penn nodded at Voss.

Voss shrugged, like we'd be hard pressed to find middle ground. I had a feeling he was right.

I took the heavy cast-iron pot, and Elspeth trailed after me. We picked our way through the short brush on a trampled path down to the riverbed. The river flowed steadily and clearly, but there were a lot of rocks to traverse before we reached the actual water.

As I hopped onto the first large stone, I asked, "If you stayed clean after this entire time, why come on the journey to kill the king now?"

"Is that a legitimate question?"

"Yes."

"There are some things worth sacrificing for. That includes my personal *cleanliness*, as you call it. The king had no love from me. He's a cruel male, and I refuse to accept him for what he wants to be."

"And what's that?"

"A false god. He's always believed himself to be the savior of our race, but the Mother will always have that position."

"Huh."

"There's no *huh* about this. Our land was lavish and beautiful, and it was driven to ruin by the hands of males who thought they deserved more."

It felt similar to what Voss said. Maybe there was some truth behind his words after all. If there were numerous Fae who felt this way, then maybe there was hope for us living side by side. But the moment I thought that, the flash of pain scarring my mother's brow seared back through my memories, and it was hard to shake.

How much pain the Fae had caused, not just to my family, but others, would it be possible to heal from that?

I dipped the cast-iron pot into the stream, letting the cold water wash over my hands and forcing myself to be present. Once water filled the pot to the brim, I dragged it back out.

"And what will you do once the king is dead?"

"What?"

"After," she clarified.

I glanced at her. To me, there was no *after*. This was it. My entire life had led to the death of the king. Marcy had said once this was over, maybe we could find each other. But I knew she was right. She craved safety, and I was anything but safe. Not with the way violence was carved into my heart.

I said, "There's no point in considering a future which hasn't occurred yet. Why talk hypothetically when a band of hoswisps could kill us tonight?"

"Smart words from a girl who sleeps with Fae."

"At least I'm smart enough to get off before they die."

Elspeth let out a laugh, and it felt like moonlight drifting along my skin. "You know, if I had killed humans, I would have made sure of the same thing. No point in death if you can't have a little fun beforehand."

"Why don't you hate it? Penn and Voss seem to hate how I've killed Fae."

Elspeth waved her hands. "I know your story, Scarlet. I can feel it around you. While I cannot see into your mind, I can *sense* it. The troubled past, the longing, the loss, the sheer volume of responsibility you have on your shoulders. You lost more than your world, you lost yourself. Some of us can relate to that for different reasons, and I understand why your history would have driven you to where you are now, Fae Slayer."

With a new level of understanding and closeness, Elspeth and I hiked back up the hill. I enjoyed her beauty and how she looked at things from all perspectives. Heck, I even liked how she viewed me as a whole person past the murderous surface.

It made me wonder about the truth behind Marcy's words.

Was there anything for me beyond the slaying? Could I have a normal future with no more blisters to heal?

As the sun descended our camp into darkness and firelight, time seemed to slip away. Penn set up Faerie lights around the perimeter, and Voss stood at attention as the other two settled into their bedrolls. Penn and Elspeth had whipped together a quick stew, but even with a full stomach and warm blanket, it took a long time for my eyelids to feel heavy. It took longer still for my brain to stop circling through the endless history of blood to toss me into oblivion.

❧ ✂ ❧

I woke up in the middle of the night to pitch darkness. The first thing I thought was how empty and alone the surrounding wilds felt. The second thing I thought about was how quiet it was. Too quiet. The blackness stretched so wide and deserted, not even a star peeked out of the sky.

"Penn? Elspeth?" I reached for my sparrowbone dagger, only to find my sheath empty. They had left me in the middle of nowhere with no supplies. Even the whinnies of the horses were gone. "Voss?" I hissed into the dark as a growl sounded next to me. I swallowed, scrambling backward only to feel a warm hand clamp over my mouth.

I bit down on the hand and sucked in a breath as I realized who it was. "Voss?" I muttered against his skin.

"Shut up," he whispered, bringing my body closer to his. He slipped noiselessly into the darkness, hauling me along with him. He was so strong my feet didn't touch the ground. It was as if I were a doll in his arms. I had enough wits about me to know now was not the time to argue with him. That growl had sounded like a deep rumble of an animal, and it had been close. Too close.

Grasses brushed against my ankles, and I cursed myself for taking off my boots. Everything had felt swollen after the day of riding, and Voss had assured me he had the watch covered. Yeah, right. This would be the last time I trusted a Fae with anything. Now my boots were out there in the dark.

And what of the horses? I had grown fond of my dappled mare and hoped she was okay.

The snuffling creature moved in the dark, its noise reaching my ears. It pawed at the ground, and as my eyes adjusted to the inky black night, I saw the outline of a giant bearlike creature. A fire pauldrin. According to the people who had seen one, they could breathe fire if frightened, and were frightened by just about everything. Herbivores with the most dangerous defense mechanism known to man. The man who told the tale had burns all the way up his arms, so I believed him.

It approached us, and I pressed myself against Voss. There was nothing he could do if it got spooked, but I prayed to whatever Fae god Elspeth believed in that Voss had us under a glamor. I had no idea if glamor even worked on lower Faerie creatures, but I was about to find out.

"Don't move," he whispered, his breath licking my ear.

My body was stiff against him, but he certainly didn't need to tell me twice. I knew my life was in danger the moment I woke up, but I had not imagined it being such a gentle giant.

The beast pawed the ground with long, dark claws, which caught on roots. It brought the food up to its snout. After a few moments of chewing like a cow with cud, it moved onto the next patch of earth.

A branch snapped in the other direction, and the creature leaped straight into the air, a good three feet above the ground for something as large as a bear. When it came down, its open mouth shot fire across the clearing, lighting up the prairie grass in front of it. Its sloth-like face and dark eyes widened at the sudden vision of flames, and it took off running.

Voss breathed, chest relaxing behind me.

"Why did you leave me sleeping near it?"

"It wouldn't attack you if you were sleeping. But you *woke up*."

The flames sputtered out as quickly as they had come and with the cover of darkness, Voss's arms around me tightened.

"I think you can let go of me now."

Voss complied, and I landed on a sharp rock. I swallowed a curse. "Where are Elspeth and Penn?"

With a wave of his hand, Voss summoned a small light between us. His eyes bored into mine. "Still sleeping."

"They slept through that?"

"It's still the first watch. Of course they slept through that."

"Doesn't seem very safe." I turned and headed back toward the camp, favoring my left foot over my right.

"What happened?" Voss came around to my side. His nose wrinkled, and a frown marred his lips. "Where are your boots?"

"I took them off because *someone* told me it was safe for the night." I scowled. "I'll be fine. It's just a small knick from a rock."

94

Voss stiffened, summoning numerous blazing lights around the camp with barely a wave of his finger. "Penn, Elspeth, wake up. We're leaving now."

"What's wrong?" Penn bolted up straight.

Elspeth wiped at her eyes, blinking several times, but the weariness did not leave her.

Voss inspected my foot like he wanted to set it on fire. I blinked a few times and asked, "Yeah, what's wrong?"

"Your blood." Voss dropped my foot, crossed the camp, pulled up my bedroll, and stuffed it into the same pack as his. It was seconds for him to react, but I still stood there like an idiot not understanding. He whistled long and low, and suddenly the horses came running toward us. Their hooves drove into the surrounding landscape from all different directions. "That's how I found you, and that's how Morna and Cumina will find you too if we stay any longer."

"What?!"

"She's bleeding?" Penn yelled.

Voss wasted no time explaining further, but forced me to sit down, showing them both the growing red patch on my sock. He took both of my socks off and set them on fire with a flick of his wrists.

"You didn't need to burn both of them. I don't have many of those."

"Elspeth."

She came to my side and pressed her fingertips to the sole of my foot. Her hand glowed, but as she pulled her hand back, she frowned. "Not even healing. She really is cursed."

"Shit. Shit!" Penn raced around the camp, gathering the rest of the supplies and tossing them onto the horses.

"I don't understand."

Voss grabbed my chin, tenderly running his finger over the small cut the Fae's fingernail gave me before he died under my knife. "Blood has a scent. Yours is very distinct, likely due to your immunity to our magic. When he cut you, a bit of your blood stayed on his finger. It was enough to track. It wasn't by chance that I found your friends or you. I followed you, your scent."

"And Morna and Cumina can do the same now." My face fell, because of course. Of course, there had to be a downside to this curse. I had never realized my blood could be tracked, at least not to this extent. "Will they be able to find me?"

"I'm going to do my best to leave a glamor behind and destroy all traces of it, but so long as you're actively bleeding, they can pick up our trail easily."

"This is going to make my period interesting."

Elspeth turned red. "I didn't think about that. Fae don't... We choose when to have young, but you..."

"Bleed once a month." I stared at Voss. "So once a month, I am going to be open target practice for all assassins?"

"Never mind once a month!" Penn yelled as he hitched up the last horse. "We have to worry about it *now*." He tossed a white cloth to Voss, who quickly wrapped the bottom of my foot in layers of it.

"You aren't wearing the boots unless you want me to burn those too. I'll carry you to your horse."

I narrowed my eyes.

"Do you want to be stubborn, or do you want to survive?"

Shaking my head, I gestured for him to get it over with. He was gentler this time getting me into the saddle. He hung my boots from one of the saddlebags, and the four of us were off into the night, with Faerie lights illuminating the road in the dark. It didn't take long for my adrenaline to fade and for exhaustion to kick in. I started dozing right in the saddle. Voss had to slow to steady me on top of my horse.

"How long does it take a human to heal?" His voice drifted into my lolling dreams.

"I don't know. I'm not human," Elspeth sniffed.

Likely longer than they wanted. Morna and Cumina would find our trail, but once I healed, would they be able to find us after that?

Nine

By the time we arrived at our next destination, I was half-asleep in the saddle, having snoozed on and off fitfully during our ride. It took a few moments for my brain to catch up to where we were. They had corralled our horses outside of a run-down farmhouse. Somehow, it remained standing in the middle of the wilds. The words scrawled across the top read *Keepers Inn*, whatever that meant. Voss held out his arms for me, and I gladly fell into them. I was exhausted, and I couldn't imagine how tired he must be since he was the only one of us who hadn't slept yet.

Gently, he unwrapped my foot, set the bandage on fire, and checked the cut. "It's clotted."

"Probably another day until there's a scab over it. Less time if I can clean it."

He sniffed. "I can still smell it, but it's fainter. I think we can get a few hours of sleep here. Besides, they are a day's ride behind us."

"You could smell it from that far out?"

"Assassins are able to blood hunt. It's why we're chosen by the king."

"The bright side is my friends are safe." I sighed and nuzzled into Voss's arms. Being this close to him felt natural, like breathing. I had done this with numerous Fae in the past, and maybe that's why it felt so easy and familiar. Or maybe this was the complete lack of sleep talking.

"Oh?"

"They decided not to leave the city. If Morna and Cumina are coming here, my friends will be safe from now on."

Voss gave a solemn nod. "Penn, take care of the horses. Elspeth, get us some rooms inside please? I am going to take Scarlet over to the water pump."

"Most places have plumbing."

"And I don't want to bring the smell inside with us if I can avoid it." Voss frowned. "I know you have no way of understanding how our senses work, but—"

"You're like sharks."

The intense sigh that came from Voss actually made me giggle. "No, no. Please, by all means. Take everything magical about the Fae and boil it down to 'you're like sharks.' Sharks aren't even mammals! I should drop your ass here and leave you for the vultures."

"But then I wouldn't be able to kill your king."

"I am beginning to wonder if it's worth it."

Voss found the spigot and gently set me down after scouring the ground for any sign of sharp objects. I moved the pump up and down until a steady stream of frigid water came out of the end and shoved my foot underneath it. I bit back a yelp as the ice numbed my entire foot. It took only a few moments to wash off the underside of my foot. Voss used a Faerie light to inspect the area again. It danced a blue glow across his face.

"The smell is less strong. Thank the Mother. I need sleep."

"Glad my healing pleases you."

"I would have preferred you not cut yourself in the first place. I have to warn you, we traveled all night going west."

"But that's away from Treborne's—"

"Scenic route now, I'm afraid. Morna and Cumina are good, but the change of directions will get them off our trail for a bit. We'll double back before veering off in two different directions tomorrow. It will take them longer to find us that way, and we'll be back on track tomorrow night." Voss frowned. "Or much later tonight, I suppose."

"What happens to you if they find us together? I saw the panic in your eyes."

His eyes flashed dark. "Nothing good. I'd rather not think about it. I'd be lucky for exile back to Faerie."

"Is it really that bad?"

"You know how your priests talk about hell?"

"Yeah?"

"That's what we turned it into."

"All because of the king?"

"He'll do the same here if we don't stop him. And then where will we be? We made your leaders and scientists off themselves." Voss shook his head. "It was a shame he ordered the culling of your people that way. They could have helped us more than the king realizes. And yet…"

"There was nothing you could do to stop him."

"Only you, I'm afraid."

Voss dipped his arm under my knees and behind my back, lifting me off the ground once again. "Do not get spoiled by this, little fox. I promise I will not be your chariot forever."

100

"Oh, and here I was getting comfortable being manhandled by a Fae assassin."

"You've been manhandled before and liked it."

"Are you shaming me?"

"Not at all. Everyone is entitled to enjoy sex. Even if it comes with a heavy dose of violence and death." Voss stopped walking when we were halfway to the building. "Is that why you want to kill Lord Treborne? Not because he's a vile creature, but because you want to get off one more time before you see the king?"

I rolled my eyes. "I don't need to kill people to get off. My hand is perfectly capable of—"

"But it's better when there's danger involved, isn't it?" Voss's irises swirled as he stared at me. His lips were so close, his breath warm, and his skin hot against me. I squirmed in his arms, wanting to be much farther apart to have this conversation. "There's nothing to be scared of. It's why I've never slept with a human. Too fragile, too easy. Where's the challenge?"

"I'm not." I crossed my arms, elbow digging into his leather chest plate.

"Because you can say no, of course. But you *are* fragile. Your foot is proof of that."

"I don't split open at the seams because of sex. That was a hard rock, not…" I rolled my eyes at the grin spreading up Voss's face. "I hate you."

"No, you don't." He carried me up the front steps of the farmhouse and headed into the lobby. Elspeth and Penn discussed the room arrangements with the man behind the desk.

"Is there a problem?" he asked, setting me down on the dusty wooden floor.

"There are only two rooms. I'll stay with… Lola so you can get some sleep, Voss."

The old nickname. I glanced at the keeper. The gentlemen wore a pleasant smile, but it didn't quite meet the edges of his eyes. Elspeth didn't feel like we could trust him. The man looked human, which meant any Fae who came along could influence him, including the two assassins likely chasing us. Penn's eyes were glowing a brighter blue when I gazed at him, and I wondered if he was already casting some kind of glamor on the man.

"No," Voss said, wrapping his arm around me. "If you watch her, then you won't be able to sleep, and we'll have to ride hard by noon. I want everyone to sleep well. We'll take a room together."

"Excuse me?"

"We're not sleeping together, just next to each other." Voss pulled me close, whispering in my ear. "Besides, would it be so horrible?"

"If there's no stabbing at the end, then yes. Yes, it would be."

Penn barked out a laugh, and the glow from his eyes faded for a moment. "Shoot." He blinked, and it was back again. The man glanced around, seeming to wake up from a daydream before slipping back into the stupor.

"Go before you distract him more." Elspeth held out the key.

"For the record, I hate this idea," Penn said, as Elspeth dropped the key into Voss's awaiting palm.

"Heard, acknowledged, and ignored."

"You're an ass."

Voss tossed him a fake kiss, grabbed my hand, and forced me up the stairs behind him. We found room number seven at the end of the hallway, and he turned the key in the lock. The door swung inward, revealing a sparsely decorated bedroom with one king-sized bed in the middle.

"Fantastic," I said. "I hope Penn and Elspeth love snuggling."

"They've slept in worse accommodations." Voss locked the

door behind us, slowly taking off his armor. "May I request you leave your weapons on the dresser?"

I glared at him.

"The last thing we need is for you to wake up in the middle of the night because of a nightmare and stab me in the chest. Again."

"It barely looks like I hit you at all."

"Because Elspeth is a remarkable healer." He eyed the top of the dresser pointedly.

"I can't remember the last time I dreamed, but fine. I will do everything against my better judgment to make you sleep a little safer, Assassin."

"I appreciate that, Slayer."

I arched an eyebrow. He had me there. Quickly, I stripped my weapons from my body, hoping the one in my boot still was intact, and took off the extra layers. I stood in front of him with just a bra and panties, and Voss assessed me for a moment.

"Most humans are more... modest."

Shrugging, I said, "I assume this is nothing new to you. Other than the body belonging to a human instead of a Fae."

"Nothing new, no." Voss took off his layers of armor, but it took him a long time.

I climbed into bed and pulled a pillow over to the far side of the mattress, not wanting to get anywhere close to him in the middle of the night. By the time I settled, he was pulling off his shirt. I glimpsed the scar rippled across the skin of his shoulder, looking pure white against his sun-kissed skin. It had healed, but I had left a mark.

While I loved looking at him, I hated him for it. He was perfection, with canyons carving a deep v leading straight to his pants, and his abs were practically a washboard. He had wider shoulders than most Fae and was broader overall. His pointed ears stuck out from under his sunlit hair, and I shook my head before pressing my eyes shut.

"It's rude to stare."

"My eyes are closed."

"You were staring."

"You have no proof."

The mattress sank as he climbed onto the other side of the bed. "If I had magic, I could get you to confess to all of your sins. Including the one of lust you just committed."

"Sinning is a very human concept." My words were steady, but I flinched as his body drew closer to mine.

"What are you doing?"

"Oh, you didn't think you were going to stay on this side of the mattress without me, did you? How else am I supposed to sleep?"

"On your own side of the bed." I turned to face him.

He was right there. His face inches from mine. His dark eyes churned with liquid amber that reminded me of the sky in the early moments of dawn. "If I'm all the way over there, you could escape in the middle of the night. You could grab your weapons and flay me open."

"That would serve no point now. I need you to bring me to the king, just like you need me to kill the king. Trust goes both ways."

"And do you?" He reached up and ran his finger gently along the scab left by the other Fae.

"Do I what?" My breath caught in my chest.

"Trust me?"

"No." Yes. I wasn't sure. I didn't want to trust him, but everything we had already been through showed me that maybe he was worth his word.

"Then why should I trust you?"

"One of us has to start first."

"And why not you, little fox?"

"Because I need... I have to... I don't know." My words left because his hands had traveled down my chin to my neck, toying with the strap of my bra. I had never had a Fae toy with me this way, tease me like I was worth the attention. It had always been about sex. Sex and only sex. Never anything more.

I wanted to hurt him, because whatever this was welling up inside me, I hated it.

"Turn around."

"No."

He growled, eyes sparking. "Turn around."

"See, even you can't stand it when I say no." My brows lowered in a challenge.

Voss grabbed my shoulders and flipped me away from him, dragging my body against his in one smooth motion. He fit perfectly against my backside, his hard length pressing against my ass.

"You said you'd never sleep with me."

"I know what I said."

"And?"

"Biology is not... I will not force myself upon you, Scarlet."

The part of me that had been ready for a fight relaxed. "So we're just sleeping?"

"We're just sleeping, and I don't trust you not to run away. That's all this is."

"And if I say no again, or I don't want to?"

His grip tightened against me. His breath caressed the edge of my ear as he said, "Go to sleep, Scarlet. We have a long day ahead of us."

I swallowed, reached over, and turned off the bedside light, plunging us into the haze of the early morning dawn. Voss's grip only seemed to get stronger in the moments of quiet between us. "I'm not going to run away," I whispered. "There's too much at stake now."

"You have no idea," he muttered as his nose shifted into my short cropped hair.

My eyelids were heavy. I couldn't believe I was allowing myself to fall asleep next to a Fae—my enemy and possibly my savior, an assassin for the king himself, Voss. Life was cruel, and perhaps this was the biggest joke of all—I *liked* how his body felt against mine. It unfurled something inside me, and I craved more than just violence for the first time in my life. I craved... this. Whatever this was.

Ten

Waking up several hours later, I was still delirious from the day's ride and the night's events. It took me several moments to realize someone was playing with the ends of my hair, and several more moments to realize I was draped across Voss's body.

I leaped off him, taking half of the covers with me in the process. For the first time in my life, I felt exposed in my underwear. I blinked and pulled the blanket around myself.

"Take as much as you want. I love being cold." Voss rolled his eyes.

"Why didn't you wake me up? Don't we need to go?"

Voss glanced at the clock on the wall. "We have some time. I asked Elspeth to get us a meal before we head out. She should be back momentarily."

"I'm sorry, Elspeth saw me like that? Across you?"

"You're... blushing?" His head tilted to the side. "That's a new look."

I grabbed the dagger off the dresser. "Give me one reason I shouldn't—"

The door opened, and Elsbeth took in the scene with the tray in her hands. Her eyes narrowed and shifted between me and Voss. "Do I want to know?"

"Scarlet blushed."

"The Fae Slayer blushed?"

"I will kill both of you."

"While blushing," Voss added.

"While blushing *and* in my underwear." I decided to own it.

"Go ahead then, be in your underwear." He gestured to the blankets wrapped tightly around my body. Scrambling off the bed so fast had taken away all of his coverage, and his chiseled chest was exposed. His nipples were hard, like another part of him, and he had no shame in hiding any of it. His pants were tight, and I saw *everything*.

"No."

He growled.

"I'm going to put this here and just…" Elspeth slid the tray onto the dresser and exited the room. I wanted to scream at her not to go, not to leave me here with him, because I may end up stabbing him after all.

"I meant it that time."

"I know." His eyes churned.

"And yet it still affects you, doesn't it?"

"Obviously."

"Why is that?"

"Because we're not used to it. It's different. Fae are… we're free flowing with our sex. We don't deny it from each other if we're in the mood, because why bother? There's no point in shaming natural desires. And humans, well, you know what happens to some of those who sleep with Fae. No human can say no. So when you say no, it's simply a reaction on an instinctual level. We want to prove you wrong, use our power to prove you wrong, but we can't use our power, so it's... It's basically being the biggest tease on the planet."

"Wow. Okay. I mean... Wow." I took a breath, not sure what to do with this new information. Refusing to look at him, I categorized the tray, which held some eggs, toast, a sort of fried meat, two oranges, and a pile of potatoes.

"It's your own version of magic. And you shouldn't be ashamed of it. I certainly wouldn't be if I were you."

I put the dagger down and snatched up a piece of toast. I shoved one end into my mouth before awkwardly grabbing the tray and putting it onto the bed in between Voss and I. "I didn't know it was such a... how do I say this?"

"Like touching a Fae's erogenous zone?"

"Yeah, that. Wait. You know about erogenous zones?"

He arched an eyebrow. "Doesn't every living thing on the planet?"

"None of the Fae I've been with ever took off my shirt, which is why hiding the dagger was so easy." I frowned. "Except the last one. But I assumed..." I gestured vaguely, letting the silence indicate my train of thought.

"You've been with the wrong Fae." Voss peeled open an orange with quick movements of his fingernails. "But you already know that. It's how you chose your marks. They didn't care about people, so they didn't care about you. They cared about one thing and one thing only, conquering whoever had the audacity to tell them no."

"But biologically speaking, you're... not all that different."

A sliver of orange paused on the way to his mouth.

ARIEL RAE

"I mean, if *no* causes the same reaction in you—I'm not saying you'll act on it—you're biologically like them."

"Biologically speaking, sure, I am like my brethren. We can, and should, control it. Just like humans should."

"But if I were to say repeatedly I'm never sleeping with you."

"It would become increasingly difficult to ignore."

"Hmm."

"I don't like where your brain is going, little fox."

"Just storing the information in case I need it."

"And why would you need to convince me to sleep with you? What would you possibly gain, I wonder?"

Other than possibly the best sex of my life? My body had thrummed under his touch last night, and I hated to admit how much I wanted to be that close to him again. But if I used his weakness against him, was I any different from the Fae themselves?

No. I wouldn't force Voss into anything, just like he wouldn't force me into anything.

"Maybe to make you ignore the knife in my hand so I can end you with it. Someday." I buttered the toast without looking up at him.

"It might work if you needed it to. Though, I pray to the Mother, little fox, I will never do anything to make you so angry with me." Voss swallowed an orange slice. It was so disgustingly erotic it made me want to slice open the scar on his chest.

There was something really messed up about me.

"Toast?" I offered him the butter knife handle first.

"Why is it I don't trust you with pointy objects, either?"

"It's not that pointy, but I was thinking about how satisfying it would be to stab you."

A quirk of a smile ghosted on the corner of his lips. "That makes sense." Voss took the knife from my hands, his fingers

110

grazing mine, but it was enough to send my body into a frenzy.

"I'm going to take a quick shower." I walked out of the room and slammed the bathroom door between us. Blinking hard, I tried to calm my body. In my entire life, I had never felt like this about any Fae, or any person. Not even Marcy.

Under the warmth of the shower, I tried to wash away the feeling, tried to rid my body of any leftover need. Every time I touched myself, I imagined the heat of him pressing against me. The solidness of his chest. The way his lips curled up in his obnoxious smile when he thought I was being obtuse.

I hated it.

I would stab him.

Someday.

Maybe after I killed the king.

☙ ✄ ❧

It took three hours to double back before we split off into two groups. Voss took my latest bandage with him and Elspeth, whereas Penn and I headed in the other direction. As much as it pained Voss to let me out of his sight, he acknowledged Penn was the better illusion creator. Thus, he should keep us out of harm's way if we passed by Morna and Cumina. Penn was more than pleased by the compliment, and Elspeth scowled at the insult that she had to be babysat as much as Penn did.

Out of the group, Voss and I were the fighters. While I had yet to see Elspeth fight, I had a feeling she was halfway decent in combat, likely better than Penn. If I wanted to escape, it would be now.

Except I trusted Voss would bring me to the king's court. The much guarded location was worth gold in my eyes.

Before we parted ways, Voss said, "Don't make me regret this."

He scowled as he veered his horse in the opposite direction from the two of us. Penn swallowed hard as we watched them go for a few moments before turning down the other path.

"He seems to trust you more," Penn said after a few minutes of riding.

"How so?"

"You're with me. And let's be honest, my knee still throbs from where you kicked it."

"It's not like I broke anything."

"Only because I'm Fae. If I had been human? Hobbled."

"Big baby."

"You kick hard. It's not being a baby, it's me being honest."

I shrugged.

"We're going to have to work on your mannerisms before we get to Lord Treborne's place."

"What's that supposed to mean?"

"He'll never believe your Voss's escort with the way you move, and if you plan to get close to Treborne during a party, you'll have to get in first. And right now? They wouldn't let you in the court, much less into his estate."

"There's nothing wrong with me."

"You move like someone with sights set to kill."

"Well, yes, because I *do*."

Penn snorted. "I'll have Elspeth work with you when we are back with them."

"You each have your specialties, right?" I said to fill in the silence between us. "She heals, right? Not much combative specialty in that."

"Don't say that to her face. But yes, she heals. Everyone except you, it would seem."

"Another downside to this curse."

"With as many Fae as you have killed, that's the last descriptor of your anti-magic I'd thought I'd hear from your mouth."

"You think I want this?" I gestured to myself, though I wasn't sure what my motion was accomplishing. "If I hadn't opened the door, my family would still be alive."

"And if you hadn't opened it, it would have called to someone else until another person found it. Your family probably would have died in a similar fashion due to proximity. You surely don't blame yourself for their deaths?"

Not the death of my parents, no, but the noise that escaped my lips got my brother killed. He sacrificed himself so I could live, and that was why I had to kill the king. My brother's death had to mean something. The terror in his eyes before he calmly pushed open the pantry door and stepped out into the light of the Fae had to mean something.

The emptiness I felt after had to mean something.

"No, it's your fault."

Penn gazed at me, eyes welling with hurt.

"The grand your, not... *you* your."

"Eloquently put. Definitely will fool Treborne."

"Why do I need to fool him, anyway? I can walk in there, tell him I won't sleep with him, and he'll be putty in my hands."

With a laugh, Penn pulled his horse in front of mine, stopping both of us abruptly. "Do you not realize the entire kingdom is looking for you now? Everyone knows your story. You seduce Fae with a single word and send them to their graves. You've become a siren for our kind, which would be a spot on comparison if sirens weren't horrific beasts. Everyone knows to avoid the word."

"But can they ignore the call once it's out there? Would you be able to?" I did not want to verbally touch Penn's erogenous zones. Now that I knew what I did, I was going to be more careful using my words around potential allies.

He scratched the side of his horse's neck, pondering this thought. "No, likely not. I would try, but… Elspeth maybe, if you wanted to test it on anyone else."

I narrowed my eyes.

"Oh, I've seen the way you test it on Voss. You're becoming his vile temptress." Penn moved the reins, guiding the horse to lead the way farther down the path. My mare fell into step behind his.

"I am doing no such thing."

I absolutely was.

And I liked it.

And I still wanted to stab him, because the blood blossoming on his leathers that first night had not been nearly enough for me.

"He's stronger than most Fae, but it's still a marvel."

"I will not garner respect for someone for doing the absolute bare minimum."

Penn snorted. "I agree with you; there is something biologically malfunctioning in Fae, but I also think that's because of our being cut off from your world for so long. We used to travel back and forth. We hosted humans for the duration of their mortal lives and treated them like royalty."

"Then what happened? Because that's not what you do now."

"The gene pool got smaller and smaller. Fae started experimenting with other species. Some of us aren't pure blooded anymore, for better or worse. I think there's succubus mixed in with some lines, and those end up being the worst of the worst."

"But why did you get cut off?"

Penn sighed. "It's a long story, but has to do with the king. He wanted power and control. And magic, the kind he used to bind the Fae to him, always has a dark side."

We were quiet for a minute as I digested this. There was so

much about Fae history I didn't understand. Riding in silence with Penn was easy. As much as I wanted to lash out at Voss, I had no animosity toward this male. He was easy to talk to, with kind eyes and a sorrowful expression.

"So, Elspeth is the healer, you're the best at mirages, and Voss is a blood hunter."

"Yes."

"What else can you do?"

"A lot of things. Water work and lights for me mostly. Elspeth is good with earth elements, and Voss has us beat in all categories. I think he could learn to heal if he'd be willing to tap into that side of himself."

"What side is that?"

Penn glanced at me, lips flattening. Shaking his head, he said, "Maybe we should ride for a bit instead of… this."

"You can't leave the conversation like that."

"I can, and I will. You and Voss can hash it out. I'm not getting involved in any of that."

He kicked his heels into his horse, and mine took off after him. I wasn't used to riding at such a fast pace, and my body felt like I was lurching on top of a rocking ship instead of having any of the eloquence I managed at a slower pace. Still, the wind raced through my hair, and for a moment, I was just a girl on a horse chasing after a friend in the wilds.

Within a few minutes, Penn slowed his mount to a stop, his eyes swirling brightly.

"What is it?"

"I have to concentrate for a few minutes. Please don't speak."

I opened my mouth, but when I looked at how his jaw worked, I shut up. Rummaging through my saddlebag, I grabbed out the dried fruits and nuts and popped several into my mouth. My eyes drifted to the horizon, watching the wind blow through the tall grasses as Penn's brows slipped farther over his eyes.

The beat of horses' hooves met my ears before my eyes caught sight of the two on the path. My heart kicked up in my chest, because this was it—the moment we had been worried would catch up to us. I shoved the food back into the bag, getting ready to launch my horse into action in case this went south.

Two figures drew closer and closer as they pushed their horses faster than I could ever manage. Froth had formed on both of the poor creatures' mouths, and the two women riders looked like harbingers. Their skin gleamed dark under the sun, with sweat pooling around their hair and necks. As one of the large geldings reared up, both of them pulled to a sudden halt. They were within five feet of us.

"They were here," Cumina gazed around us.

"Obviously, Cumina." Morna sniffed the air, scowling. "It's fainter than before."

"They do heal, you know?" Cumina's voice sounded like an operatic singer got shoved into a blender. It was haunting and beautiful, something so chilling it buried deep into my bones and told me to run into the forest.

"Obviously, Cumina." Morna's voice, however, was more like popping corn. It had crescendos and pings throughout each word, adding a strange, lilting accent to her voice.

"I think we need to go back to the main road. They spent the night somewhere, and if we can find out where, we can get more information."

"It feels like a waste. We're missing something." Morna's eyes flared, staring at us, but no... *through* me. Her eyes stared straight at mine, swirling pools of churning molten gold. She blinked, and the magic faded out around me. Ruffling her black hair, she shook her head. "Nothing."

"Like I said—"

"Obviously, Cumina!" Morna dug her heels into the horse and headed back down the road, chasing after the ghost of us.

Cumina sighed and rolled her eyes. "When I find this bitch." Her black mohawk swept in coils across her dark scalp. They were equally stunning and deadly, as most Fae were. Whenever I killed a Fae, I imagined it was a vicious assassin like these two, but now inklings of regret formed inside me. I might have been killing Fae that were like Penn.

Kicking the side of her horse, Cumina continued after Morna.

With still swirling irises, Penn nodded in the opposite direction. He put his finger to his lips, and we took off down the path. Once we were out of sight, Penn's eyes dropped back into their normal color.

"We still need to keep up the pace. They were racing those horses to their deaths."

"Which is good news for us," I called out to him.

"Explain?"

"Those horses will probably collapse at the inn, and that keeper didn't have any. They will be on foot after that." Poor creatures. No living thing should be treated that way, and if Morna and Cumina weren't looking for my head on a platter, I would attempt to fetch theirs.

"Regardless, I'll feel better when we're back in Voss's company. That was too close."

I swallowed, knowing exactly what he meant. We had gotten lucky, and luck wasn't something I wanted to count on twice. By the time we circled to the meeting point, our horses were ragged. Penn led both to a stream as I waited on the empty roadside for any sign of Voss and Elspeth.

Cursing, I thought about how everything could have gone better. First, if I had known my blood was a homing beacon for all nearby assassins, I would have been more careful with my footing last night. That lack of knowledge I could blame on Voss and his inability to give me the information I needed to be successful. Keeping me in the dark wouldn't make either of us survive. Second, if I hadn't insisted that we kill Treborne together, we would have never been in the clearing to begin with. Maybe it was a waste of time to head to Treborne's, but if I wanted my friends to be safe, I needed to lead the assassins somewhere else before going to the king.

At least I knew Morna and Cumina were hot on my trail, which likely meant no one else was poking around Raskos's territory for me. If the other assassins caught wind of my movement, the compound would stay safe. But I still hoped the three of them moved cities, just in case. I tried to shake off the thoughts of my companions, because the sooner I forgot about those I left behind, the better it would be for everyone.

With a sigh, I sat down on the dusty road and stared up at the sky, waiting for something to happen, any signal to say that this was the right path. The late afternoon sun slowly sunk toward the horizon, but nothing happened. No divine intervention, if there was such a thing, and no magic moment to convince me one way or another.

I had never questioned myself so much in my life, and I hated it. The second-guessing made me feel weak, and this would be the last dearth of certainty. I would allow myself this moment, and after, I needed to move on. Treborne needed to die to show that I was gone from Raskos's territory. Once that happened, we could kill the king.

And then…

What happened after that?

At the sound of two more horses, I stood up and dusted off my jeans. Voss pulled on the reins of his ride when he saw me standing alone, dismounting and staring into the distance, searching the horizon for Penn. By the way his brow pulled taut, it was as if he worried I had stuffed Penn into the sun itself.

"He's down the bluff, tending to the horses."

Voss let out an audible sigh. "Elspeth?"

"On it." She led both mounts in the same direction, leaving me with Voss once more.

His dark liquid eyes bored into mine. "How long have you been waiting?"

"About forty minutes. We ran into them on the road."

Voss cursed. "I was worried they wouldn't be fooled. We need to head out as soon as the horses get a drink."

I shook my head. "Their horses were about to collapse. They will either be stuck at the inn to let the horses recuperate, or they might have to walk. I think we have time."

A dark laugh escaped his lips. "Morna can anchor animals to her willpower. She'll run those two until they collapse, which if they are the geldings I saw back in Raskos's land, they likely have another day in them. They will catch up with us at Treborne's. We have to accept that."

"What makes you so calm about this prospect?"

"You won't be bleeding then. I can barely smell it on you now. They'll lose the trail. Remember, they still think you're a useless girl who was drunk on Faerie wine."

"How great for me."

"And how great for the ruse to get into Treborne's party."

"How are you so certain he'll throw one?"

"Elspeth sent a message."

I narrowed my eyes. "And how did she do that?"

"We have our ways." Voss stepped closer to me. "Are you okay?"

Huffing out a breath, I crossed my arms in front of my chest. "Am I okay? I don't know, Voss. Why don't you tell me what other secrets you've been keeping from me? Fae are a mystery, and the more I know about you, the more likely I will be to survive long enough to kill your stupid king."

"I thought you were a kill first, ask questions later kind of girl."

"I was."

"And?"

I set my jaw, lifting my nose. We stared at each other for a few unrelenting beats.

Voss sucked in a breath through his teeth. "Tell you what. For every night you don't kill me, I'll let you ask three questions."

"I'm not planning to kill you." *Yet.*

"Then you'll get a lot of questions." Voss's lips curled into that overconfident smirk. "Just be sure you ask the right ones."

"What is—"

Penn and Elspeth climbed up the bluff, leading the horses in their wake. The two that Penn and I rode looked exhausted.

"Can we afford to walk for a bit? Give them both a break?" Penn asked, eyes glittering with hope for the beasts.

Voss shook his head. "We can double up on ours for thirty minutes, give yours some time to relax. Then we have to get back at it. Morna won't slow down, and neither should we."

Nodding, Penn brushed the wet side of Switch. I was starting to love this mare. "I tossed some water to cool both of them off. If we keep a brisk but steady pace, I think they'll be okay. We weren't riding near as hard as those two, and they had a few moments of rest."

"We should make it to the court in the morning if we ride through the night," Elspeth added. "It'd be a lot on them, but once they are stabled, Treborne will spoil them simply because they are my horses. You, however—" Elspeth looked me over. "—need some work."

"Penn," I growled.

He shrugged. "We need to make this believable."

"Make what believable?" Voss quirked an eyebrow.

"Treborne won't believe just any human caught your eye. You've been actively avoiding them since the door opened thirteen years ago. No way will he think she changed you."

"Hey!"

Penn ignored me. "Elspeth will work her magic over the next day and teach her some poise."

Voss rolled his eyes. "Treborne knows I would never go for someone with *poise*."

"But you also wouldn't go for someone threatening to stab you at every turn," Penn said with certainty.

Voss's eyes flashed to mine, and I felt a spark inside me. Yes, he absolutely would. I knew because I felt it myself last night and this morning. There was something between us.

Besides, I *really* wanted to stab him. Not kill him. I wanted to stab him just for fun. If there was such a thing. And judging by the dark, lingering look Voss gave me, there *was* such a thing.

"Maybe a little less murderous would be good," Voss decided after a lengthy assessment.

"I hate all of you," I said.

"Come on, little fox. You'll ride with me for thirty."

"What if I've decided I want to ride with Penn?"

Penn's eyes widened, and he visibly moved closer to Elspeth, as if she could save him from my games.

121

"Then ride with Penn." Voss shrugged, climbing on top of his steed.

I turned around, but Penn and Elspeth were already sitting on top of one mount, neither of them wanting to get into the middle of this. It was clear from their heavy breaths that they had scrambled away from me in an instant.

At least I was still terrifying, even if it was the ire of Voss they feared more.

The edge of Voss's lips quirked up, and he knew he had me. Bastard. When he offered his hand, I took it, but dug my nails into his skin. He ignored the discomfort, lifting me up like I weighed nothing, and settled me behind him. The edge of the saddle dug into me in the least pleasant way I could think possible. "You have to hold on to me."

"And if I don't?"

He clicked the reins forward, and I almost toppled off the horse before I latched onto the back of his armor. I wrapped my arms around him, pulling myself closer to get off the edge of the saddle. With every movement of the horse, my body got closer to his and the heat of him flooded into me.

"If you want to stab me, now is probably an excellent time to do it. I'd be helpless," he said.

"Yeah, right."

"Truly."

I pulled the knife from my thigh sheath and ran it over the bloodied part of his armor. "I have a feeling you could disarm me easily right now, mostly because you could make the horse gallop and leave me behind in the dust."

"You want to try it?"

There was a challenge in his voice, and I ached to meet it. To watch Voss bleed under my hands, to feel him against me, to… I pressed my eyes shut and tried to cut off the heat spreading throughout my body.

"Is this your weakness, little fox? What makes you collapse to your knees and beg for more? What makes you want me even when you despise me?"

My fingers trembled against the knife. "Stop."

A growl escaped him, so deep I felt it in my arms and chest. "I think we need a new word other than stop."

"A safe word?"

"Yes, one that tells me when you want me to stop, and when you are playing with me but don't really want me to stop. Because I have a feeling things will not go the way you envision them at Treborne's."

"And what am I envisioning?"

"Quenching your desires."

"And why won't that happen?"

"Because we're killing him together, and I don't want to fuck Treborne."

I pressed my eyes shut and slipped the knife back against my thigh. "Switch."

"Switch, like my mare Switch? All the words on the planet, and—"

"And what? There's nothing sexual about your horse. It's the perfect name to take us out of the moment. And does it get you sexually charged when I say it? Switch?" I whispered the last word along his ear.

"It's like an annoying wind in my ear, so no. It does not."

"Good. It's settled then. We can both use it if things go too far."

"I pray it never gets to that point."

Me too, I wanted to add, but refused to admit it.

In another few miles, we changed horses again and rode on, a faster trot this time to gain as much space as we could on Morna and Cumina's failing steeds.

When the night fell, Elspeth and I took up a position at the rear of our party, surrounded by Faerie lights. She tried to teach me about Fae manners and how humans were expected to act around royalty like Lord Treborne. She caught me not paying attention numerous times, chastising me for my insolence, which made Voss cackle from the front of the line.

"I fail to see the point of this."

Elspeth huffed. "When we get to the King's Court, you'll need this more than ever to get an audience with the king. If you aren't subservient, he'll never allow you to get anywhere near him."

I sighed. "Fine. Can we take it back from the top?"

Penn chuckled. "She's hopeless."

Elspeth let out a long breath. "Okay, when we enter the court—"

I did my best to pay attention to rules of the courts and humans being present inside. It was a lot of *yes, sir and ma'am* and *how can I help you*? I hated the mask I was going to wear, but if learning how to appear meek would help me kill the king, then maybe I had to put some faith in Elspeth's words.

By the time the sun had risen, I was slightly less abrasive. Elspeth and Penn said it might be enough to trick Lord Treborne. After all, Voss wouldn't choose someone timid, but the more we rode together, I was less sure he would choose anyone shy at all. I think he craved violence as much as I did.

I wanted to rip him open and figure out what made him tick.

Eleven

As soon as we got to the court's stables, Penn set about taking care of the horses. He doted on the mounts, which made me like him more. I wished I didn't. This journey would have been easier if the Fae had been the monsters I had believed them to be. But they had history. They were full entities with lives beyond this moment. It made the world more gray, and I hated that.

It would have been so easy to kill them before now, but with our time and traveling together, I no longer wanted to slit their throats. Though, I would still happily stab Voss and paint his chest with his blood. I suspected that was because of how warm I felt inside whenever he was around.

In the simplest form, it was obnoxious.

"I need to freshen up, and I think we need to get this one something better for tonight. Elspeth hooked her arm through my elbow, forcing me to take a few steps with her. She grinned at me with pale lips and a mischievous look on her face. "We'll see you

125

boys later." Her fingers wiggled as she waved them goodbye.

"Do you think it is wise to separate?" Penn asked.

"I don't smell her. We'll be fine." Voss tossed my boots at me. They landed perfectly at my feet. "Though running around barefoot with your sensitive skin might not be the best way to stay incognito. Will you book us a room at the Barrest Inn for the night? Might be best for her to wash up before the party."

Elspeth nodded, tossing both of the males a kiss. After throwing on my boots, we turned into the city, and I was stunned by how much was left standing. There were streets lined with houses bearing weathered patterns straight down the street, and it seemed to stretch for blocks. They all led toward an old capitol building that looked converted—likely for Treborne's newly formed palace.

Shock formed around my stomach, because a lot of courts were in shambles held together by a prayer. Most cities had been destroyed. But this place held the original buildings humans had created as the town center, before the Fae took it away.

"I thought Treborne was one of the worst. How is… everything still standing?"

Lord Raskos's city looked like a bombed-out shell compared to the brownstones and rows of small shops in this place. And Raskos didn't have half of the reputation that Treborne did for treating humans poorly.

"Treborne wanted his city to become a destination for tourists. He reconstructed everything from the ground up, but it's a farce. Behind the facade, people go missing all the time. I know you won't be deceived by it, but he keeps it sparkling on the surface to cover up the rotten core."

"So, it's like eating an apple with a worm on the inside."

"He's worse than a worm."

"And you're using yourself to get us into his party this evening?"

Elspeth pulled me close, a glint in her eye. "There would be no party without me."

"Why do you have so much sway over him?"

"We dated decades ago." Elspeth waved her other hand. "When I walked away from his kingdom, it was like your power of saying no to a Fae. He's wanted me ever since, more now that I haven't killed a human. I think I ruined him by saying I could do better."

"Huh."

"I might have been a different person then, but Voss made me come to my senses. We had known each other for a long time before Treborne swooped in, anyway." I was about to ask her how Treborne caught her eye in the first place, but my thought was interrupted. "Oh!" Elspeth pulled me toward a window of a small shop that housed dresses and gowns. "Look!"

"I'm not the kind of—"

"Do you want to murder Treborne or not?" she whispered into my ear, and it was liquid moonlight rolling over my skin. I may be immune to magic, but Fae's voices held power. "Come on." She tugged me inside without waiting for my answer.

Elspeth wasted no time once we walked into the store. Every flutter of fabric and swipe of a zipper made me more nauseous when I looked at myself in the mirror. When I was little, I refused to wear dresses to family events, always stuffing a pair of my brother's pants into my dress so I could change when we got to whatever holiday we were headed to. My family realized it was a lost cause and let me wear whatever I wanted. Frilly dresses and the other items Elspeth dressed me up in now made killing Treborne seem like an impossibility.

"Spin," she ordered.

I crossed my arms in front of my chest and stayed still.

"You are the worst." Instead of waiting for me to spin, she walked around me, assessing. This dress was gray and silver, which matched the lightness of my eyes. I had to admit it looked good, but it also belonged on a different version of me, someone who never had to hide in a pantry closet. "I love it," she said finally. "But you hate it."

I took a step forward, judging how far I could stride with such a narrow waist. "This color is great, but do we have anything that screams more... Voss would choose me?" I doubted this dress was it. It was the kind hundreds of women would wear to grab the attention of a Fae. I doubted he'd find someone who blended into the crowd stunning enough to claim.

Elsbeth pursed her lips, looking at the material while thinking it over. She waved her hand around the dress.

"Hey!" the shopkeeper yelled. "I spend a lot of time on those, and your magic—"

"I'll pay you two hundred extra coins if you let me do what I want to this piece." Elspeth yelled over her shoulder. "It is remarkable work, but she's right. It's not her. Don't you agree?"

The man behind the counter let out a sigh. "Two hundred plus the cost of the original dress. And if she doesn't like it, you return it to the original condition before you leave."

Elspeth's eyes flared bright green for a moment. "Deal."

I gasped. "He just—"

"Yup, and I intend to keep my word. Now, stop fidgeting."

The shopkeeper went back to the receipts in front of him, unaware of my absolute horror. I had never seen anyone willingly enter a deal with a Fae, and he had sold his... Well, what exactly had he sold for the coins? A dress. He had sold a dress, in whatever form Elspeth wanted to buy it. I supposed it was a rather mundane deal, even if it was a deal with a Fae.

"I couldn't imagine doing that," I breathed as she waved her arm over me again. The dress flashed into a mini poodle skirt with a flowing blouse. "I will vomit on this. Is that what you want?"

"Stop being a child." She waved her hand again, and I had to suck in a breath to make the new version of the material fit. "No." That word repeated out of her lips as she tried look after look after look. Finally, she spun me around to face the mirrors.

I swallowed. The silver material drifted down my sides in a jumpsuit with wide legs, resembling a dress without being one. It arched against my middle, pulling tight around my breasts and over my shoulders in one piece. No sleeves, and nothing except the width of the pants to worry about in battle.

"The best part?" Elspeth showed me a hidden zipper lining the waist of the jumpsuit, all the way around. Once unzipped, the pieces would fall apart. "No pesky Fae ripping through your clothes tonight. Unless, you know, you want them to." She tossed a bag of coins on the desk for the shopkeeper. "She'll take it, and I'm taking this." Her fingers snatched an emerald piece as it was off the rack. "I love this color, and I can simply make it divine on my skin. Thanks much. Deal completed." Her eyes swirled, sealing the magic for a second time.

The man waved us off with a grunt, not bothering to count the coins before sweeping them into a drawer.

After changing back into my riding gear, Elspeth brought me through the bustling streets to the Barrest Inn. We checked in, brought the clothes upstairs, and looped back to the stables. However, only Penn was there by the time we arrived. He had a few strands of hay in his hair, and most of the horses were taking long drinks from the water trough, save for Switch. The mare was leaning into Penn, stepping from hoof to hoof.

"How did it go?" Penn asked as he ran a brush through Switch's long mane.

"Perfect," Elspeth said at the same moment I said, "Horribly."

Penn laughed. "Voss said he'd find us later at the inn. Had some business to attend to in the city before the Lord meets his..." His voice trailed off, no further explanation needed. Once we killed the Lord, this place would turn into chaos. I wondered how many people would perish in the temporary upheaval, or if another Lord would simply take Treborne's place.

I would ask about the courts next time I was with Voss. I hadn't killed him last night, so he owed me three answers. And I intended to get to know my enemy, because after the king died, there would still be more work to do.

I yawned as my stomach let out a hollow growl.

Elspeth nodded to the horses. "I'll take over here for a bit. You should stay with her at Barrest, in case. She'll need rest for tonight."

"How are you all still so... perky?"

"Magic can let us continue, though it's not always pleasant." Penn's eyes were swirling lightly, with the barest hint of magic around him. "Come on. You need to sleep."

By the time Penn and I made it back to the Barrest, I was trudging up the stairs. Penn promised to bring me a bowl of soup and bread, but before he could make it back to the rooms, I had fallen asleep.

∽ ✂ ‣

I awoke to the latch on the door closing. The dagger was out of my hand before I could think better of it. Voss cursed, barely avoiding the end of the blade as it hurled past him and slammed into the wall. It thudded to the ground and left both of us in a stunned moment of silence.

"I told you not to sleep with those."

"You shouldn't sneak up on me."

"I wasn't sneaking." His chest rose, eyes swirling to a liquid fire.

Sitting up, I assessed where the dagger had pinged off the door versus where Voss stood. I was an inch off, and he had been an inch too fast. Two inches. I was getting sloppy. "The next leg of the journey, we're doing target practice along the way. That should have been your heart."

Voss frowned. "And how happy would you have been if that were my heart? If I was bleeding out under your feet?" His eyes blazed as he looked me over. I felt his magic around me, swirling throughout the room.

Stretching my arms over my head, I licked my upper lip. "To be honest? I'd rather toy with you first. A dagger straight to the heart is anticlimactic, so I'd be disappointed."

"Good to know." He shifted the tray in front of him, and it was only with the movement that my eyes landed on the sight. My mouth gaped open, watering at the smell of fresh bread and steaming bowl of soup.

"This is mine," he growled.

"Really? You brought a plate in here for yourself instead of eating it downstairs in the tavern?" I tilted my head to the side in disbelief.

"It was going to be yours, but I've decided it's my second dinner now since you've attempted to kill me. Again."

"It's a habit at this point." I shrugged.

The liquid amber darkened in his eyes. "I figured you'd need to eat something. We have about an hour before the party. Lord Treborne is expecting all of us, including you."

"Including me, as in Scarlet?"

He passed the tray to me, the frown still not leaving his face. "No, not Scarlet."

I took the tray onto my lap, crossing my legs underneath it. The steam wafted up, hitting me in the face. I swallowed back my saliva. "What did you do?"

"It's what Elspeth did, and I'm still angry with her about it. Please don't stab my healer."

"What did she do?" My brows flattened over my eyes, knowing I would hate whatever answer came next. I tore off a hunk of bread and dunked it into the soup, shoving the sopping mess into my mouth, choosing to destroy the meal instead of the Fae.

"She elaborated. Instead of calling you my escort, she said I had taken an interesting human lover named Lola."

My lip twitched. "Interesting human lover."

"You are a human."

"Helpful, Voss. Truly." I sighed, taking a large gulp from the bowl of soup. It was some meat and vegetable stew, and the broth was delicate despite the gamy taste. "Why couldn't I have been just your escort?"

"How is that better?"

I wouldn't have to act like I was into Voss. I wouldn't have to look at him like I was looking at him now, with desire and anger and contempt and lust. The world wouldn't see what I had turned into in the last few days on the road. I hated Fae, and yet...

"What do I have to do?" I asked.

"You've already asked over three questions."

"Voss, these aren't questions about your life or your past or the Fae in general; these are about the plan. I need to know the plan if we're going to—"

"Relax, little fox."

"You're teasing again."

His grin made me want to carve his face open to permanently widen his smile and lick the blood from his chin. "The way you're looking at me right now? That's a good start. You're into me, but you're also your own person. Treborne wouldn't expect me to fall for anyone else."

"So basically, me." I wanted to scream at the part of me that was excited by the prospect.

"That's why the plan should work, despite my disdain for it."

"And how do we get Treborne alone?"

"You suggested it earlier. We do what you do best. You seduce the Fae. You suggested to me that you wanted me to share you as a *gift*."

"What?!" I balked.

"I would never offer to share with Treborne. *Ever*." Voss sneered at the thought. His eyes narrowed and mouth parted in a disgusted snarl. "But if my *lover* were to want something so horrible, I may entertain the idea out of pure curiosity. Plus, from our show at Raskos's club, it makes sense we would be lovers now." The Fae shook his head slightly. "Besides, it's only a matter of time before the other assassins catch up to us. If we put on a good show, like we're on a diplomatic journey for the king, maybe we can keep the others away from you. It certainly would make our journey to the king's court easier."

"Which is where again?"

"Nice try." Voss folded his arms over his chest.

"And if I bleed again?"

"Let's hope you don't."

"It feels like we're leaving a lot of things up to chance."

"Not everything. Treborne will believe us, and he will say yes. We'll easily get him alone."

"Why?"

"Because he's wanted everything I've had in the past. If I have you, he'll want you."

"Is that why he wants Elspeth?"

Voss coughed. "No, he wants her for his own ego. I've never been with Elspeth."

"What else of yours has he wanted, then?"

"Is that one of your questions? Because we're getting into non-mission territory."

"I hate you."

"I can't explain the entire history of my people to you. It'd take... years. Longer than we possibly have."

"Here are my three then: Why aren't you able to heal others? What does Treborne want that you have? And why have you never slept with a human?" My impulsiveness made me waste that last one, but my curiosity got the better of me.

Letting out a breath, he sat at the end of the bed, watching me eat for a few moments. "You have to be tapped into a softer side of yourself to heal. Most Fae aren't. Elspeth has the right temperament for it, so I let her focus on it, so I can focus on other things. I might be able to learn it, but that would take effort. It would force me to become something I am currently not. I am the king's assassin for a reason." His dark gaze settled on me, causing goosebumps to rise along my skin. "Treborne wants my title. And I've never found a human worthy of sleeping with. As I said before, humans tend to be fragile things."

"He wants your title of assassin?"

"You're out of questions, little fox."

"It seems like a stupid title to go after, especially if the king doesn't pay you anything for your services. Though I suppose people like Treborne are after power more than anything else, right? Otherwise, you wouldn't let me kill him."

"I'm not *letting* you kill him." Voss's eyes flashed, and a smirk curled on his lips. "We're killing him together, as it is a mutually beneficial sacrifice for the greater good. It will be my pleasure to watch the lifeblood flood out of him."

Voss watched me as I spooned more broth into my mouth, and this felt comfortable. It would be easy to fool everyone tonight, because he was a very attractive Fae. His golden hair flowed around his ears and had the perfect part, looking shiny and clean despite our travels. There was something so beautiful about him. Even though I thought a few more scars would make him more impressive.

When I shoved the last bite of bread into my mouth, Voss stood up and tossed the silver material at me.

"Let me see this dress."

"It's... not a dress." I had to catch it so it didn't fall into the bowl. "And I'm not changing in front of you."

"You didn't seem to care two nights ago."

"That was different."

"Why?" Voss took a few steps closer to me. The air in the room grew thin. "What do you think is going to happen when you tell Treborne you want to sleep with him? What do you think we're going to have to do together?" His fingers reached the collar of my shirt and fiddled with the seam. He was close enough I could taste the searing sun on my skin.

Voss scooped up my dagger and dropped the sparrowbone into a sheath at his hip. "I'm going to show you. Remember the word."

I swallowed, not trusting myself to speak.

Voss climbed behind me on the bed. "You okay, little fox?"

"Just get it over with."

He chuckled, running his hands over my shoulders, along my arms, down to my thighs. His fingers reached the inside of my thighs and pulled me open, as if presenting me to someone else who wasn't yet in the room. "I'm going to show him every part of you. You're going to tell him no." His voice was lava coiling around my ear, painful and stunning.

My back arched as I leaned my head against Voss's shoulder.

"You're going to tell me you regret asking, that you don't want him, you only want me." His words licked my ear, full of sin dipping straight into my core. He hooked one of his legs around mine, pinning me open for the rest of the world to see. I was fully clothed, but there was something so intimate about this, so close, so dangerously delicious.

"I'm going to give him permission to take you, to teach you a lesson."

"And then he's going to fuck me, and while he's fucking me—"

"You take the dagger from my side, and you slam it into his throat." Voss's hands slipped back over my thighs, up my hips, and stomach, and then they were gone. He lifted himself off the bed, putting space between us like none of this bothered him. My body missed the heat of his, and it made me violent on the inside. "And if you change your mind, you know the word to get out."

I rolled my eyes. "This is my job, Voss. I know how to handle myself against one male Fae. It's not a big deal."

"You won't be in a room with *one* male Fae, because I'm going to be there holding you back. We need that part to look real, and if you want me to stop at any point, I need to know you have a way out."

I swallowed. A way out.

If I wanted it.

But what if I didn't? What if I never wanted to climb out of the dark sex that I craved? What if I wanted to sleep with Fae for the rest of my life? What if I wanted to taste blood in the air while I came?

"I know the word."

"Say it."

"Switch."

Voss nodded, though his expression looked pained. "It still doesn't create any cravings. We might have to change it if..." He licked his lips, almost looking forlorn. "Well, we probably won't be in a situation like this in the future. Now, change."

I rolled my eyes and stripped down to my bra and panties. He watched me while I did it, his eyes roaming over my body. He was going to present me to the Lord tonight, so I needed to get used to his fiery attention before then. I showed Voss the zipper as I put the outfit together.

"Elspeth." He cursed.

"What?"

"You're like staring at the moon."

"To your sun, right?"

Voss pinched the bridge of his nose. "We will not go unnoticed this evening. I hope you are ready to enter the realm of royalty, Scarlet, because humans don't make it out unscathed."

"I hear I have some excellent protectors on my side."

His irises turned to fire. "In that outfit, you're going to need an entire fucking army."

Twelve

When we entered what used to be the capitol building, I had to swallow back my shock. If Raskos's land was the apocalypse personified, Treborne's court was a lavish British kingdom. The decor screamed of someone dripping with unlimited wealth. Every piece of furniture was polished with a bright sheen over rich dark woods. The marble floors were immaculate, with intricate inlay designs on top. Gorgeous artistic carvings snaked up the walls, flowing into the ceiling. This place felt brand new, like Treborne had ordered it to be created and modified for him.

The remodel must have cost a fortune, or required a lot of mindless drones doing his bidding. Since Treborne was one of the worst, according to Voss, the rumors of him disposing this original human workforce felt true. The world had collapsed around this place, but Treborne used people to mold it back into something ornate. Custom paintings hung on the walls, most portraying the same man depicted in many battles and with different human women.

"Let me guess—" I leaned close to Voss. "—those are all portraits of Treborne on the walls."

"Are you beginning to understand why I don't like him?"

Gold sconces with bright electric bulbs lined the hallways and huge crystal chandeliers swayed overhead. Music drifting in from the other room. Hopeful men and women stuffed the entrance, clambering for a chance to be let up the circular staircase to the second level of the manor. I hung on Voss's arm as he led the way up the steps. Elspeth had outfitted me with an elegant pair of ankle boots that could be used for kicking a kneecap in or for dancing.

Elspeth stayed close to Penn's side, and her sunken shoulders told me she was anxious about tonight. I wouldn't want to see any of my ex-partners either. Mostly because they were all dead, burned, or buried. It was easier not to have exes. Maybe I should suggest the same thing to her.

"We're going to have to make a few rounds," Voss said, pulling me closer to him. His outfit was simple, a button-down shirt similar to his riding gear but now with a black pair of breeches. Other Fae had put in much more effort than Voss, but somehow he looked wealthier than everyone else. He certainly stood taller than all of them. "I have some missives from the king that need distribution, which is our excuse for being in town this evening."

For a moment, I had forgotten he was the king's assassin. It was so easy with Voss to ignore his background, because he never acted like he wanted to be working for the king. His mention of missives held a hint of annoyance in his voice. However, that wasn't the only reason I could ignore his past. With his arm wrapped around me and his warmth flooding into me, it was easy to pretend we were something else. And with Treborne on my mind and how we would trick him into getting close, it felt like Voss was on my side.

"Whatever you're thinking about, keep doing it. Red looks good on you."

I scowled.

Voss brushed his nose and lips against my hair. He didn't kiss me, but lingered. I leaned into him, putting on a good show for anyone who was watching. The moment felt personal, but when our feet crossed the threshold into the ballroom, he was focused again. He nodded at Penn and Elspeth. The plan was for them to figure out where Treborne was in the throng of people while Voss languidly walked with me, making it seem like we had no agenda.

They pulled away from us, and I got my first real glance at the ballroom. Every part of the white room was lit by Faerie lights stuffed inside crystal candle shades. Shadows danced listlessly, twisting around the vacuous space. A live band played in one corner, a mixture of human and Fae instruments which created haunting, lurching melodies. Hundreds of Fae lingered around tables, eyes bright and swirling as human servants traveled in between them with plates of hor d'oeuvres. Some Fae had humans tucked under their arms in various degrees of undress. Others had put their human pets in the most eloquent of dress with diamond studded leashes around their necks.

The humans looked proud to be where they were, but I couldn't shake the feeling of entrapment by being here.

As we approached the first group and the Faes' eyes landed on Voss, most of their conversation and stilted laughter came to an abrupt halt. The first table he approached held three higher Fae, all with swirling bright yellow eyes and two human women in accompaniment.

"I didn't believe the rumors," the taller one in the middle said. Their eyes slid over me, stealing long glances at my body and my outfit. In a bored tone, he said, "But here you are."

Voss pulled me closer, his own eyes brightening. "She's proved to be a good time, much like most of you tried to convince me a decade ago."

My fingernails dug into his hip. We had discussed this. He had to treat me like an accessory, but it was one thing to talk about it and another to experience it. I hated feeling like I was a prop, an object, especially while I was the wolf in sheep's clothing. I was the one who would end the lot of them. Voss's fingers ran in slow circles around my shoulder, perhaps to calm the rage inside me or to show off his possession.

"She's unique, that's certain," the shortest one on the right said, eyes shimmering to orange for a moment. "Maybe I can copy the jumpsuit look for Zoe here." The Fae's eyes darted to the woman next to her in wonder. "I'm not sure the color would suit her, unfortunately."

"Whatever you wish," Zoe said.

"Of course, darling." The female stroked Zoe's face.

My nails dug harder, and Voss flattened his palm against my shoulder in either warning or annoyance.

"So what brings you to lowly Treborne's palace? Shouldn't you be—"

"Words from the king." Voss cleared his throat. His voice dropped lower. "The three of you are late on your payments, and it has not gone unnoticed."

The one who had been quiet dropped open his jaw. "I personally sent everything two weeks ago via scytheseer. You're telling me it never made it?"

"That won't do."

"We'll have to send another."

"That was three months of payment!"

The tallest one waved her hand. "Easy enough to get. We'll

make the blacksmith add in some additional jewels next time, as an apology for the effort his highness had to put in to send you here."

Voss nodded. "See that you do."

"Does this one have a name?"

I opened my mouth to spit the word *no* out at her, but Voss pressed a finger to my lips in what would seem like a commanding gesture. I would bite his finger again and taste his blood on my lips. If there was one thing I was not, it was a toy.

"She does, but I prefer to call her little fox."

I scowled.

"She seems to hate that." The Fae laughed. "Maybe we need a pet name for Zoe. What do you think?"

"Anything you wish."

My nails threatened to pierce his skin.

Voss leaned over, eyes flaring bright. "Stop doing that unless you want me to take you somewhere private right now. *Without* Treborne." His eyes drifted back to their normal black as he faced the other three Fae again. He had glamored them, I realized. "Ladies, gentleman, I will see you in a fortnight."

The night carried on, with us drifting from table to table. I wished I could be glamored so I didn't have to witness the hazy eyes and glazed over looks from the other humans underneath the Fae's spells. Would killing Treborne do anything to free these people? Would his death fix anything? I knew killing him would send another message to the king—I wasn't done yet. Maybe the fear would help, and maybe it would spark hope in the people who needed a way out.

Judging by how many humans wanted to break into the ranks of the Fae, I doubted nothing short of a revolution would make us be on equal ground. Someday, maybe once Quinn had figured out how to get the human networks back up and running in full, we could overthrow the Fae hierarchy. Maybe.

Until then, I remained latched to Voss's side as he made deal after deal with the other Fae on behalf of the king. I wondered what kind of king would also use his unpaid assassin for missives, but I wasn't surprised that a monster would use a monster as a glorified messenger boy. Voss commanded respect among them, which made my skin crawl at being associated with him. I became his pet, his prop and nothing more, and I couldn't help how my nails bit into his shirt from time to time. It took at least an hour for Elspeth to find us in the crowd.

"He's ready to hear your proposal."

Voss nodded, and I swore his arm tightened around me before leading me out of the ballroom and through a golden door at the top of what appeared to be a dais. I hated this Lord. The opulence and oppression were so much worse than Raskos. At least with Raskos, humans knew they were getting thrown into a narrow strip of protection against the wilds. At least he didn't cover up the fact that his city was dangerous, that *he* was dangerous. Treborne covered everything up with beauty.

And if Voss didn't like him and would kill him with me, that said something about this male.

My skin crawled as we slipped through the doorway, and it fastened shut behind us. I knew what I had to do. I had to act like this would be fun, like I wanted to have a threesome with Voss and this other Fae. While I might not have been a great actress, I was great at focusing on the end result.

Blood and death.

And *that* made me smile like a giddy kid off to trick or treat on Halloween.

"That's a gorgeous smile, little fox. Though I am terrified to ask what you're thinking about."

I licked the side of his neck. "Nothing good."

The door on the opposite end of the room opened and who I could only presume was Lord Treborne breezed in. His feet barely touched the ground. He was a tall, lanky male with a pointed nose, thick edges to his chin, and eyes that were a bit too narrow set. I had to hold back laughter, because Penn was right to laugh about Voss wanting to share with Treborne. While he was still beautiful, he did not have the ethereal beauty most Fae held, making him the least attractive Fae I had seen.

And I had seen plenty Fae.

"Voss, how nice of you to stop into my city unannounced." Lord Treborne scowled, purple lips parting slightly. The color of his skin was almost olive, a sickly green tinge to the hue. "Elspeth told me you had official business to discuss?"

"Well, not me exactly."

"Oh?" Treborne lifted an eyebrow, his eyes snapping straight to me.

I tried to put on a sweet smile.

"You see, this little one here has never met a Lord with such an elaborate court."

Treborne laughed, and it filled the room with a sense of ice cracking apart.

"And she asked if we could perhaps go to a Fae party. I told her you were the one who threw the best. When we arrived this evening, she was so taken by your decor she demanded to meet you, so I sent Elspeth to smooth the waters."

"The human who captured your heart. It's such a quaint story being told around my court." Treborne smirked. "But isn't that all it is?"

"No, Lord." I stepped away from Voss. I imagined how good the red tint would look seeping out from Treborne's throat.

144

Hopefully it was enough to give me the look of a girl in love as I looked into Voss's eyes. "There's something different about this Fae."

"And there's something different about this human. It was her suggestion to come to you, Treborne. She felt it was unfair not to give something back to the Lord keeping such good care of this city." Voss ran his fingers over the small of my back as his face expressed sole possession.

Another dark laugh from the male. "I don't think I've ever heard such complimentary words coming from your mouth, Voss, but I'll bite. What do you want?"

"I want him to share me with you." I swallowed, trying my best to make a blush cross my cheeks. The power of knowing what I was about to do rose inside me, making my heart flutter faster in my chest. "Demanded it, really."

"Demanded it. A human demanding of you?" Treborne fixed his gaze back on Voss. There were notes of distrust coming from him.

"She's very hard to manipulate."

This had been part of it too. Not giving away I was Scarlet, but announcing that I would be more of a challenge than most humans. No matter what, the prospect of a strong-willed human intrigued most Fae.

"Of course, but they all fall eventually. Turn around," Treborne said, his eyes flaring.

I didn't move.

He growled.

"Turn around." The purple hue in his irises grew with violence. I made my face into a blank mask and stumbled through an awkward turn, like I was fighting it but was unable to resist. "Interesting."

Voss pulled me back into him, righting me so I could face the conversation again. "It could be a fun way to bring the Lords and Ladies closer together, if we shared one thing in common."

"You've never shared anything in your life, and I am supposed to believe she is a peace offering?"

"Please, my Lord. It was my idea. I'd appreciate it very much. It's a way to unite the courts." I took another tentative step forward. "I can even pretend your magic always works on me, if it would make it better for you."

Treborne took a step toward me, and I flinched just enough. "You most certainly will not *pretend*. That is such a human notion and disgusting. Turn around." He demanded, his eyes flaring.

I shrank back into Voss, masking my giddiness with fear now. "Maybe this wasn't such a good idea."

Treborne chuckled. "If you aren't able to control her, what good are you?"

Voss wrapped his arms around me, possessive and strong. "I can make her do whatever I want." His eyes flared. "Take off your pants."

Slowly, as if I were captured beneath his will but still hesitant, I undid the entire zipper from the lower half of the jumpsuit. The material fell to my ankles, pooling there.

Voss's hand cupped my cheek and forced me to look at him. His eyes swirled as he used glamor on Treborne. "You know the word. At any point in time."

I nodded.

We turned back to Treborne, who watched me with hungry eyes. "So you listen to him, but not to me?" The snarl in his voice was coated with anguish.

We had him.

"Voss, I don't want to—"

"Nonsense. You asked for this earlier. It would be rude to take back the option from the Lord now."

"Spread your legs," Treborne demanded, his eyes growing hot with magic. I ignored him, only listening to Voss's signals now per our plan.

"You heard the Lord." Voss pulled me against him, my back arching as he lifted me up by my thighs. He held me like I weighed nothing.

I sucked in a sharp breath. I had envisioned us on a couch, in a chair, or against a desk. We practiced last night on the bed. This felt more personal somehow, standing in the middle of the room with him holding me up with a firm grip on my thighs. Voss's hands shifted to the inside of my legs, pulling me open for the Lord to inspect. I was wet, because all I was thinking about was my knife plunging into the male's neck. As I squirmed in Voss's arms, a rumble sounded from his throat. It cascaded like fire across my skin, so different from the way Treborne sounded.

"She can deny sex," the male sounded displeased. Good.

"She can deny a lot of things," Voss said. "It's what makes her interesting."

Treborne closed the gap between us. Playing into the part, I pushed him away with my left hand, but he shoved my wrist against my chest, pinning me against Voss. My right hand remained free, gripping tightly onto Voss's thigh, right above the dagger. "You won't deny me. Not if he demands it." His eyes swirled as he undid his breeches.

"I will deny you," I spat.

Voss's grip dug into my thighs, tightening so much I might bruise. His hands shook against me.

Treborne was free of his pants in a matter of seconds, playing with the end of his cock with his other hand. A sneer crossed his face. "We need to teach this one some manners." A glistening bead formed at the end of his erection.

"Switch."

I blinked. I was exposed to Treborne. Completely at the Fae's mercy, like Voss and I had planned. We needed to get close enough to kill him. Treborne was inching closer to me, getting so close and ready to penetrate, and I would take it.

But Voss's voice. "Switch, *please*, Scarlet. End it now."

His magic was hot against me, using glamor to cover up his voice from the Lord. I hesitated, not knowing if Treborne was near enough for a clean shot at his throat. If I missed, the Lord could scream and bring the entire castle party in here with us. I let Treborne get closer until he was primed to pierce straight into me. Voss's fingernails threatened to puncture my skin.

"Switch."

Remembering what he said about my blood, I wrapped my hand around the sparrowbone dagger and thrust it into Treborne's neck. It wasn't a clean shot. The male stumbled away from me, breeches catching around his knees as he fell backward onto the desk.

Treborne let out a howl. I jumped out of Voss's arms and scrambled forward, twisting the dagger and slicing it through muscle into his throat. His moans faded into gurgling blood and I stood there, staring at the waste of it all.

I whirled around, ready to scream at Voss for ruining the plan, but when I faced him my voice cut short. He was right in front of me, breathing hard, his eyes churning with violent sun storms. "I couldn't let him fuck you. I—" Voss grabbed my chin in his hands, delicate and possessive at the same time. "Say the word, and I won't do it."

My throat dried.

"Tell me not to."

"No," the word barely escaped my mouth in a whisper before his lips crushed against mine. The power of his magic swirled around us. I could taste it, taste him. He was liquid fire and lava, a scalding hot cup of cocoa against the roof of my mouth.

The dagger clattered against the floor as he backed me against the desk. Treborne's body twitched next to us, and heat curled inside me. Voss's hand wrestled through my hair, pulling it taut as he dragged me further into him. My lips threatened to burst against the violence of his mouth. I scraped my fingernails along his hips, finding the hem of his shirt. It went up and over and onto the floor, next to my kicked off pants and the pooling red blood.

"Fuck," he muttered against my mouth. "This is a bad idea."

"It's a terrible idea."

He growled against me, tongue tracing along my jaw up to my ear, then down to the sensitive part of my neck. His teeth sank into my skin in a bruising bite. If my blood wasn't on the tip of all assassins' noses, he'd have ripped my skin open. A part of me wanted him to.

"We should stop."

"You say the word, and we will." His other hand climbed up my side, brushing against the swell of my breast. "Say the word, and this ceases."

"No." I arched against his hand as this thumb traced over the hardened nub. I sucked in a breath, greedily wanting to feel it all.

The hand in my hair drifted lower, brushing over my shoulders and spine, sending tingles to every part of me. My arms trembled as I sank my fingernails into the skin on his shoulders. I shouldn't have dropped the dagger. I wanted to make him bleed.

But also, I wanted him.

"You can't say it, can you? Because you want this too much."

He cupped my ass, bringing my core against his hard length. The fabric rubbed into the sensitive part of me, and I hissed, feeling feral. "Admit it."

"No." I ran my hands over his shoulder and his chest as he pushed me back onto the desk. I scratched the corner of the scar I gave him and smirked as a bright red bead of blood seeped out of it.

"You're going to pay for that."

"Make me."

He shoved my chest down so hard and fast I slammed against the desk, next to Treborne's deadened eyes. "You enjoy looking at him, don't you? Seeing what you've done?"

I sank my fingernails into his wrist, and he hissed as he kept his hand on top of my sternum, nestled perfectly between my breasts.

Voss thrust against me, and I gasped as his heat pressed against my nerves through his pants. Dropping to his knees, he moved his hands to my thighs, spreading me wide before him. "It would have been unfair of me to share something so beautiful with a man so vile." He kissed my thigh, and his warm breath made my knees quake. His eyes looked up at mine, and I stared at him, amazed this was possible. I was breathing heavy, hot, and slick with desire for him, and no knife or dagger in sight.

"Please," I breathed.

"You want this?"

I wiggled under his touch.

"Stay still."

"No."

"Then you'll get nothing." His warm breath was over the sensitive parts of me, lips hovering mere inches away. A whimper escaped my lips as he brought his mouth down on top of me, engulfing me and burning me from the inside out. His wicked tongue split me open, easing into me and greedily rubbing against every piece of my skin. Slowly, sinfully.

I curled my fingernails into the wood on the desk as my thighs trembled against him, threatening to close. He pushed them wider and growled, low and long. It vibrated all the way into my core, and I gasped on nothing. I was on fire.

When he pulled away, a soft smile played on his lips. "You can be taught after all, little fox."

"Fuck you."

"Is that what you want?"

"No." *Yes.*

"No?"

"No," I heaved in a breath. "Not in a million years. Not if we were the last two living creatures on the planet."

"How about the last two living creatures in this room?"

I glanced again to the bloodied remains of the Lord, and damn it if I didn't feel myself shudder against Voss's hands as he toyed with me. The teasing was too much. His thumb against my clit was more than I could handle, but not enough. I wanted more, needed more.

"I need you," I admitted.

"And what if I don't want to give you what you want?" He kissed my thighs, my hips, my stomach, working his lips up toward the soft skin of my breast. His tongue ran over my nipple, and his teeth bore down on me. I arched my back into him, and his arm slipped underneath me, pinning me to his tongue as he pressed against me once again. The sensation like fire across my nerves, just like his voice and his eyes. Everything about Voss ignited something inside me, and I was terrified and whole at the same time.

"It seems you want to give me what I want," I gasped as his

teeth pinched my stiff peak.

He was about to say something more when the door opened.

Penn and Elspeth poked their heads in.

"Out!" Voss bellowed.

"We, uh, kind of need to go before anyone realizes the Lord is… dead." Penn swallowed.

"OUT!"

"Five minutes," Elspeth pressed.

They slipped the door shut.

"How is it that you smell wetter?" Voss's finger trailed down my side, circling around my hip, and heading straight to my core. "Is it because you enjoy being watched?" One of his fingers met my middle, and he chuckled. "You're full of surprises."

"I will stab you again."

"I don't doubt that. But not right now."

"No."

"You like that word a lot, don't you?"

"So do you."

"Do you want me to take you now, or wait until we have more time?"

"I never want you to have me."

"That's not the word."

I stared at him, glaring in a vicious challenge. My hands reached for his breeches and undid them in swift movements. I gazed at him, amazed at his size. Most Fae were larger than humans, and Voss wasn't much larger than the others. However, the desire I felt toward him made his erection feel enormous. Maybe because this was a monumental decision, to have sex with someone because I wanted to instead of wanting to get close enough to kill them.

Voss ran a hand over my head, soothing back my hair and gripping the top of my head. "Next time, I will take my time, giving you everything that you deserve."

"Presumptuous to assume there will be a next time."

"I'm fairly confident."

The tip of him pressed against my entrance. My legs wrapped around his hips as naturally as if we had done this a million times. With his hand firm on my head, he pressed into me, inch by agonizing inch. My body burst into flames as he sank deeper. He stretched me, consuming me from the inside out. When other people talked about sex with Fae, this is what I imagined. The fire, the passion, the ignition from somewhere inside me threatened to tear me apart. He sank all the way in with one long and slow thrust, and I screamed.

"Say the word."

"Stop checking in with me."

"Never."

"That's—" I couldn't counter, because he had slid out completely and thrust back inside so hard and fast, I stopped being able to breathe. My hands ran up his sides, feeling the smooth muscles of him as he worked his body over mine. I wanted to be closer still. I wanted to feel him in every part of my core and soul. I hadn't felt his other hand skating around my hips until he pressed his thumb on my clit.

My whole body clenched, and he had to push harder to stay inside me. I wasn't ready for this to be over yet. It usually took more time. I had to seek my pleasure from my partner, but Voss's lips found my neck as I scraped my hands all the way down his front. He growled at me, and it undid every part of my soul. My body tensed around him, exploding and cresting in a giant wave, and he kept moving, keeping the steady rhythm even as I could barely handle the rapid fire. His thrusts had discovered a part of me that made my thighs shake around him, and he didn't let up.

As the pressure inside me grew, I realized I could tell him to stop, but I wanted this feeling. This vulnerability of being touched in a part of my core that had long been ignored. I shook and screamed with every thrust, coming apart at the seams as he gripped onto the back of my head and dragged my face into his shoulder. I bit him hard and felt his own muscles clench as the rush of him pumped inside me.

Everything inside me let go, and I stopped being able to breathe as the pleasure rolled through me in shock waves. I was undone for the first time in my life.

Voss let me down gently, like he was afraid I had broken. And the way my thighs trembled, I wasn't sure he was wrong. His eyes searched mine, swirling liquid fires. "You okay?"

"For fuck's sake, Voss."

He grinned. "I'll take that as a yes."

"No, I am not okay." I scrambled out from under him. "We had a plan." I hopped off the desk and scooped up my two fallen garments. "And this could have gone very, very wrong."

"But I think it went the exact opposite." The boyish grin was back, and I wanted to slice him. "In fact, I would say this was a resounding success. We have a dead Lord and a fully satisfied Fae Slayer who didn't have to kill her partner to orgasm."

Scowling, I picked up the dagger and brought it to the scar on his chest. A single bead of blood still hovered there as he watched me. Instead of pushing the blade into him, which I so desperately wanted to do, I lowered the dagger and licked the blood off his chest.

Voss grabbed my chin, fingers burrowing into my skin. "You realize what that does with a blood hunter, right?"

I stared at him, because I didn't care. His blood was like candied ginger on my tongue.

Leaning in close, he whispered, "I'll be able to find you no matter where you are. Any place in the world until my blood leaves your system."

My face fell, confidence forgotten as I stood there naked and dripping in front of him, with him inside me in more ways than one.

"Don't look so terrified, little fox. A blood bond isn't something to be scared of. Besides, it's only as strong as the amount of blood you drink. If I had yours in my system, it would be an entirely different level of the bond, which we cannot risk right now. Though I hear it makes sex more intense." He pulled up his pants and grabbed his shirt. One sleeve had a splatter of blood across it. My shirt had fared worse, being right next to the artery when I split it open.

"The sex wasn't *that* good." Turning away from Voss, I wiped my blade against Treborne's pants, stealing the sheath off the floor where it had fallen. I secured it around my waist. I felt better with my weapon at my side.

Voss pressed against me, his hands going straight to my middle. He toyed with me, my body slick with him. "Your body says otherwise."

I trembled under his touch. "I will kill you."

"Maybe someday, but not right now. Put on your pants, unless you want Penn to see you naked again."

Rolling my eyes, I pulled on the jumpsuit, barely finishing with the zipper when the door opened again. Penn's eyes were roiling currents of the ocean.

"How bad is it?" Voss asked.

"It would have been better had you two not been screaming your heads off. Truly, Voss, can you be any less messy?" Elspeth breezed into the room. "He's really dead." Her eyes went soft around the edges.

"She trusts us now, right?" Penn asked, voice straining from the amount of magic he was using to keep us hidden.

My arms crossed over my chest. "I trust for you to kill Lords with me."

"She trusts us," Voss said adamantly.

"I can't keep this up forever. I'm making people think Morna and Cumina are in here with Lord Treborne, as it might buy us some time if they need to stay for questioning. You know they won't be held up forever, but it will help us get to the throne without much delay."

"Good work, Penn."

"I'd feel better about it if I wasn't using all of this energy while you got to have fun."

"You want me to fuck you too, Penn?" I asked, keeping my voice light and sweet.

Voss's voice dipped low, "Not happening."

"Can you please not make Voss kill me while I'm trying to save all of our asses?"

Elspeth poked the corpse a few times and then spat on him. "Good riddance. Let's go." Her eyes swept over both of us, her gaze lingering on my face. With only a moment of hesitation, she reached into the desk and grabbed out some items and tossed them into her bag before breezing out of the room.

Wiping the sweat from his upper lip, Penn urged, "Can we hurry?"

"Can you walk?"

"Stabbing is too good for you. Dismemberment maybe." I walked past him, hurrying out the door after Elspeth, letting Voss's chuckle chase after me.

Thirteen

We hurried through the long passages, but with Penn's magic trained on everyone's perception, they paid us no mind. It wasn't until we were out of the mansion's walls and into the meticulously groomed courtyard when we heard a scream from inside. An alarm sounded, and another person yelled, "The Fae Slayer is here! Lock the doors!"

"I can't keep this up for much longer," Penn said, eyes flaring. "It'd be easier if I switched to covering us instead of everyone else, but it won't work on her."

"Do it," Voss said. "I'll try to redirect them from just her." His eyes flared to life as relief flooded across Penn's features.

The iron gates inched down the walls, attempting to shut off our retreat. Voss focused on the man in charge of the gate, and the bars stopped moving long enough for us to slip outside.

"There!" a gruff voice yelled. "Open the gate! She's escaping!"

Voss swore, but kept his focus on the guard in charge of the gate, who kept inching the thing closed behind us.

"You're rusty, Voss," Penn snapped.

"Not the time." Voss's eyes glowed with an electric fire.

Once we reached the stairs, Elspeth tossed her magic onto our outfits, changing us into black attire. It would allow us to slip unnoticed into the night, and my ankle boots transformed into combat boots again. I breathed a sigh of relief at having my feet back in running gear.

What I wouldn't give for that kind of magic. It would have made camouflage so much easier.

Guards scrambled behind us, Fae and humans alike. But with both Voss and Penn working together, their eyes glazed over whenever they grew too close. We rushed toward the stables. There, Penn and Elspeth finished prepping the horses, and off we rode, the four of us disappearing into the darkness and leaving the city behind us. No one told me which direction we were going, but I figured we were proceeding as planned. Our next destination would be to kill the king.

There was an hour of silence into the ride. Penn finally broke down and said, "Are we going to talk about what happened back there?" Penn's skin glowed under the cool blue hue of the Faerie lights. Elspeth and Voss had lit them once we were far enough away from the court.

"No," Voss and I said at the same time. I glared at him for a minute. There was nothing to talk about as far as I was concerned. Sex went with violence. I had killed a Fae, and thus my body reacted in kind. Sleeping with Voss didn't change anything between us.

"I think it'd be better if we talked about it."

"Of course you would think that, Penn," Elspeth said, rolling her eyes.

Voss lifted an eyebrow.

"What is that supposed to mean?"

"You want to talk everything out. It's tiresome," Elspeth sighed. "Sometimes angry sex is just angry sex."

"Talking is better than sitting in awkward silence forever. Isn't it?"

"No," again Voss and I said together.

"Mother, they are like the same person." Penn tossed up his hands, which made his horse shake its neck in annoyance. "Sorry, girl, but it's true!"

"I am not the same as him," I spat.

"If you compare me to a human one more time—"

"Fine, fine. If you can admit to me there is nothing going on between the two of you, I'll shut up."

"There's nothing going on between us," I said firmly.

Voss nodded, but his eyes lingered on me and a feeling pulsed straight down into my core.

"Okay, if that's the case, then I will sleep next to you tonight, Scarlet. It can get cold on the—"

In a matter of moments, Voss charged his horse alongside Penn's, snaked his arm across the gap between them, and snatched the collar of Penn's shirt in his hand. He yanked them nose to nose. "You touch her and you die."

I swallowed.

"Holy. Shit." Penn reared back, bringing us to a halt. The horses pawed at the ground. None of them enjoyed being on the road at night, but they seemed more spooked when we weren't moving. "What happened in there, Voss? Because I wasn't being serious. I only wanted—"

"According to Scarlet, nothing happened." Voss tossed a glance over my shoulder. And wait, what was I seeing? Obviously there was possessiveness there, and maybe it was because I drank some of his blood, or maybe it was because we slept together. I heard male Fae could become territorial, but this seemed like something more. There was… anguish in his gaze?

"We had sex," I decided to say. "As I think both of you know because you almost interrupted it."

"We did interrupt," Elspeth corrected.

"It was… great sex," I added.

"Great sex." Voss's voice was flat. His fingers unfurled from Penn's collar. Voss kicked his heels into his horse and started us forward once again. Penn swung back to ride beside me, and Elspeth's mount trotted next to Voss.

"What did I do?"

"Other than calling the sex *just* great?"

"Not *just* great. It *was* great. That's a compliment." I shrugged. "What more am I supposed to say? Grovel at his feet? Declare him the master and commander of the universe?"

"Maybe I didn't make this clear in our previous conversation. When I said Voss never slept with any human, I meant it. For him to sleep with you… that's a big deal."

"It doesn't have to be!" I fought down the loudness of my voice. "It doesn't have to be messy and complicated. It simply was, and it was a good time."

Penn laughed, his voice sounding so sad. "What makes you think Voss is anything but messy and complicated?"

"Because he seems in control all the time with a giant stick up his ass?"

"He teamed up with *the* Fae Slayer to kill the king, but deviated from the plan to appease you. Then, he helped you kill another Fae in order to prove himself, all the while having no chance of a magical deal that will force you to uphold your end of the bargain. And after that, he slept with you. Does that sounds simple to you?"

I swallowed. "You make it sound like I am the monster."

Penn shot me a look. "I'm not the one Fae whisper stories about in the pub at night. You are."

Running my hand through my short hair, I tell him, "I didn't ask for this. I didn't want this."

"What do you want then, Scarlet? To kill the king? Or do you want something more?"

My eyes fixed on Voss's back. His shoulders were hunched, and I couldn't make out what Elspeth was saying to him. "I only ever wanted to kill the king. To avenge my family. To make it right."

"Okay, then don't sleep with Voss again."

"Who said I was going to?"

Penn shrugged. "He's not the kind of male that does anything casually. It's always intense, and unless you are ready for that, I suggest you don't give him any mixed signals."

Clenching my jaw, I bit back my feelings. I never told Voss I wanted more than sex. I never set up that expectation. And besides, Penn hadn't spoken with Voss privately, so what did he know about it, anyway? It was likely that Voss's ego was hurt because I didn't call our sex earth shattering. I failed to praise the ground he walked on after he gave me... the best orgasm of my life.

Maybe "great" hadn't been the right word for what happened between us.

⊱ ✄ ⊰

Several hours later, we found an old barn off the road. Voss veered off the path first, jumped from his horse, and pulled back the warped wooden door to the ancient looking building. The fields were dark, even under the half-moon, and this place looked long abandoned. Elspeth cast some lights inside the barn, and Penn led

161

the animals into the stables. Switch followed him as soon as I jumped off. I gazed out into the open fields, which hummed with the incessant sounds of the wilds.

Hopefully, no one would follow us from the mansion. Lord Treborne had plenty of guards, but with him dead, there was no one left to employ those people. I hoped none of them would follow us and focus instead on getting into the good graces of the next Lord or Lady to rise to power.

I had stayed hidden for so long because Fae relied too heavily on their magic. Humans had forensics and science to navigate the world, but the Fae relied on spells and casts which would never point to me. As I now knew, I could be traced by my blood, but I wasn't going to bleed for a while yet.

If the handsome Fae hadn't cut my skin back at Raskos's court, I wouldn't be in any of this mess, but I'd also be farther from the king than ever.

"You coming inside?" Voss asked. His voice was low and brisk; it felt like embers brushing against my skin. He leaned against the doorway, coolly watching me with his dark eyes.

"Eventually."

"It's not safe. We've been lucky to not come across any hoswisps on this journey." Voss pushed off the frame and approached me. A crisp wind rolled over my skin, sending a chill along my spine. "You were right. It doesn't have to be complicated."

I breathed out, watching a cloud drift across the sky. The edges were brilliant white against the dark night. "The thing I ask myself is this: would I have been ready for you had I not just killed someone?" I turned toward him. "Violence turns me on. Treborne's death turned me on. And I know that's all kinds of fucked up, but what if I can never have it any other way?"

What if Marcy was right, and I was going to be like this for the rest of my life, even after the king was dead, even after the revolution was on the way?

"There's nothing wrong with knowing what turns you on."

"And if that's it? If I have to kill someone to get off?"

Voss shrugged. "How is that different from some of the Fae?"

"I'm supposed to be different from the Fae. That's the whole point of killing—" I shook my head, frustrated. "I might never end up being normal, Voss."

"And that scares you?"

Turning back to the sky, I stared at the lone cloud. "What scares me more is ending up alone because I've killed everyone I've become sexually intimate with." I huffed out a breath. "I wanted to make you bleed."

"You did make me bleed."

"More than that."

"And now?"

"I'd still happily carve a smile onto your face to replace the cocky one you are wearing right now."

His smile stayed as he ran his tongue over his teeth. "And you think you might kill me because you liked fucking me."

"Yes."

"Thank the Mother."

"What?" I started.

"Here I was thinking we'd never sleep together again. But if you're worried you might kill me, I might have a chance to bury myself back inside you."

My mouth dropped open.

"And that, little fox, would be worth risking death over." Voss winked before turning back into the barn.

Their goddess needed to help me, because I could see myself

falling in love with Voss while standing over his grave. And he apparently had no sense of self-preservation. Messy and complicated was right.

As I ducked inside the barn, Elspeth helped me pull the door shut. Penn and Voss prepared a meager meal out of our rations of stale bread and large chunks of hard cheese. When we were done, Penn passed everyone an apple, which was our dessert for the evening. I sliced off a few pieces and fed them to Switch. She happily nibbled on them.

"You're spoiling her," Penn said, but his voice held so much affection I didn't believe him. He would do the same thing.

I ran my hands along her neck instead of acknowledging him.

"It's going to be a cold night, but we can't risk any fires. Once we're settled in the loft, the lights will go out too." Voss looked around the barn, assessing any weak points. "I don't think the hoswisps can get inside, so this is likely the safest place to crash until the morning. I am concerned about Morna and Cumina, but I suspect they are answering questions in Treborne's palace. Seeing as how Penn set up the idea that they were the ones committing the treasonous act, I think we'll have some time as they chase their own tails. We'll take off toward the king's court in the morning."

"Which is where exactly?"

Voss slid me a look. "You'll see."

"Still don't trust me, Voss?"

"Seeing as how you told me you might kill me, no, not really."

Penn choked on his apple.

"I wish there were some walls between us tonight," Elspeth sighed.

"Why? Nothing's going to happen," I stated.

"Yeah, nothing's going to happen." Voss's voice, however, dipped into a purr. His eyes flickered with the fire we didn't have, and I felt it caress along my skin. I could only imagine what he was trying to do to me.

"Very convincing, both of you. But if you can't keep your hands off each other next to a dead body, I doubt you'll keep your hands off each other in a hayloft," Elspeth said.

"I hear dead bodies are very sexy."

"That is *not* what I said." I glared at Voss.

Penn coughed.

"Live bodies *marked* for death are very sexy," I clarified.

"Tell that to Treborne's corpse. Or are you going to admit that it was me you were attracted to?"

"Please, continue to ignore the fact that there are other people stuck in this horse barn with you. I appreciate it." Elspeth rolled her eyes, clambering up and dusting off her pants. "I'm going to get ready for bed the best I can in this place. If you need me, I'll be attempting to keep my dinner down." Hay fell off her boots as she ascended the ladder.

"I should do the same," I said, deciding now was as good of a time as any to get away from Voss and Penn, especially as Voss's eyes continued to roam over me. I scurried up the ladder and chose a bedroll in the corner.

As I nestled under the blanket, Elspeth's voice reached me. "For what it's worth, I would have happily fucked someone next to Treborne's corpse, just to rub it in his cold, dead face."

It felt strange, having another group know my secret. Before now, I had relied on Quinn, Anya, and Marcy, but they had been a safe haven to go back to in between missions. None of them had joined me in the fray. They couldn't. There was too much risk, too much liability. It felt weird to be on this journey with other people, to have a mark and destination that we were traveling to together.

"Thanks, Elspeth," I said.

She grunted in return.

I covered my face with the flannel blanket, shut my eyes. It grew warm under the covers from my breath, and it wasn't long before I fell into a deep sleep.

Fourteen

The back door rattled in the frame as the pounding started up again. It had died down for a few seconds, and I hoped beyond hope that the beautiful strangers outside with fierce, murderous eyes had left.

"Pantry," my dad hissed, herding both my brother and me into the small space. "Don't make a sound. Don't move. Don't do anything." He slammed the door shut. The slatted door might have prevented them from seeing us, but it did nothing to shield our vision.

The front door blasted open as if by some explosive magic. Shards of wood spewed everywhere. Three gorgeous Fae stepped into the room. One of them was broad-shouldered with eyes and hair black as coal, another had dark skin and ocean pools of lightness in his eyes, and the third was a woman with long flowing blond hair and alabaster skin.

"So cute. Are you trying to hide from your new masters?" the broad-shouldered one asked, stepping front and center into the room, throwing out his hands wide. "We own this land now. There is no running from us. You will do as we say."

"Of course. Whatever you need." Mom's voice shook in her throat, tears *springing to her eyes.*

"Get on your knees." She hesitated, and the Fae forced her down so hard one of her knees split open, blood oozing against the kitchen tile floor. Red on white.

Dad watched. His eyes turned hollow as the three of them took my mother in every way possible. She never said no. She couldn't. No one could deny the Fae. The screaming only started after they tore her open.

My brother pressed close to me, his hand clamped over my mouth. Warmth pooled on the floor underneath us as fear struck hard into my heart.

And then they began on Dad.

A whimper escaped my lips.

Their vicious smiles turned toward the pantry door. "Come out, come out, wherever you are. We won't bite."

My brother let go of my mouth, rose to his feet.

I wanted to scream, tell him not to go. It could be different this time. I could save him. We could—

"Stop!" I screamed.

"Hey." Voss's voice pooled around me. "Hey." He pulled me into his arms before I could say one word otherwise. My limbs shook. My body wanted to shut down. It had been so long since I had been back there, a scared, helpless kid trapped in a closet. "Where were you?"

I breathed out, parsing through the nightmare. While dreaming was a rarity, whenever I had the nightmare, it changed. It was never quiet the real memory, and it was never the same horrific thing twice. The dream threatened to become reality.

I bunched his shirt in my clenched fist, pressing myself against him. "Back when the portal opened. When they—"

Voss ran his fingers through my hair, soothing it back behind my ears. "You don't need to say anything else."

"When I find the Fae who did it…" I shook my head, because I was going to tear them limb from limb. I was going to make them watch as I forced them to do all the things they made my family do, made my thirteen-year-old brother do. My stomach soured as I swallowed back bile. "I'm the reason my brother's dead."

"What makes you say that?"

"We were hiding in the closet, and I made a noise. My dad told us to stay silent, but I—"

"You were a child."

"If I hadn't—"

"It was those Fae who did it. Not you, little fox. You can't blame yourself for the villains in your life."

"I opened the portal." My eyes stung, and I swallowed heavily. "I made a noise. How is it anyone else's fault? I brought you here. I brought *them* here."

Voss's lips parted as he let out a long breath. "Come here." He tucked me against him, and he moved us easily toward the edge of the hayloft, where a loft-length window used to be. Over the years, the glass had fallen out, leaving a hole staring out into the long empty fields. The darkness around us felt enormous.

As Voss settled down with me, he pointed to the shadows on the horizon. "You are not to blame for this world, either. This was inevitable. Someone else would have opened the Fae door, and who knows, if that had happened, maybe it wouldn't have been someone as clever as you, little fox. Maybe they would have been discovered, and the human who could have been our salvation would have been lost forever. You survived. Most wouldn't have."

I wasn't so sure.

"Besides, the Fae likely would have commanded for anyone else to come out of hiding. Parents are known for hiding their young. The reason you survived is because of your gift."

I let out a long breath. "Ours was one of the first homes ravaged. My brother might have been fine, because they might not have known we were there."

"Only to die later." Voss leaned back, taking me with him. I sat against his chest, and his hand made idle circles along my arm, drifting toward my wrist and back down. "You can argue it however you want, but you will never know how the past would have changed. So you can blame yourself, or you can keep going to avenge them."

"I will always keep going."

"Good."

"I haven't had nightmares in a long time," I admitted. "Maybe it was the horrible sex last night."

Voss chuckled. "Do you want to ask your questions?"

I plucked at a loose string on his pants. "What will happen to Lord Treborne's court?"

"Unless he named a direct heir, someone close to him in power will take over as the Lord or Lady of the court. He had no offspring, so it's likely going to travel to someone at random. We can hope it is not a Fae as depraved as he was, but there's no way of knowing who will usurp the power. That's the thing about power. It's wanted by the greedy."

"And the heirs for the king? Are they going to be as greedy as the king himself?"

"The power usually shifts to the closest heir, and the closest ones should not be the ones who are greedy for power. They will probably get the power and ascend to the throne. The Fae cannot be without a king, so the king's power shifts quickly from one to the next."

"And if that Fae is worse than the king?"

Voss's fingers stilled on my arm. "I doubt very much that he would be worse than the current king, but I promise you, if he is, I will slaughter him myself."

"Careful, Voss, it sounds like you're making a deal with me. What do I have to give you in return?"

"I'm sure I can think of something." His fingers trailed up to my shoulder, across my collarbone, down my sternum and rested in between my breasts. "But maybe not when my two best friends are sleeping next to us."

"How is it they sleep so well?"

"You are out of questions." His lips brushed against my temple.

"I hate you."

"I glamored them not to hear us."

"So we could do anything we wanted?"

"Just about." He caught the glint in my eye. "We're not killing Penn."

"Just a small wound."

"Like the one you gave me?"

"You want me to cut you instead?"

He grabbed me tightly, bringing me between his legs. We sat like that, with me tucked into him, staring out at the endless night field for several minutes. On the breeze, I heard a rumbling, bleating purr.

My back straightened, and Voss held onto my hips.

"They can't hurt us here. Stay quiet." His voice was stern, but strong.

The haunting melody joined with the sound of their shuffling hooves a few moments later. Hoswisps by the hundreds roamed over the fields, darting in and out of the tall grasses. Their eyes glowed in the night, like hundreds of blinking orange fireflies, making the wilds sparkle. Their feet were hoofed with rat-like claws at the end, and they had large pointed maws like a parrot, body delicate as a newborn lamb. The most terrifying thing was their tails, which had a stinger with venom deadlier than a widow's bite. They traveled in large packs, but mostly kept to wild fields, as the Fae's magic and guards kept them out of most cities.

"You can keep them away if we need, right?"

"This many? I'd be lucky to, but they have no interest in hunting us unless we're easy prey. And we are not prey."

Their cries were like mourning whales, flowing in a tidal wave across the sea of grass. I shuttered against Voss.

"Do you not trust me?"

"If I were to push you into the lot of them, how long would you survive?"

"How long would we survive, you mean?"

I narrowed my eyes and turned to look at him. "You'd take me down with you?"

"If you pushed me, yes. Fair's fair."

"What's the worst thing you've ever done?"

Voss's eyes flashed. "You are out of questions, little fox. That one will have to wait until tomorrow."

"What if I tell you mine?"

"You can't make a deal."

"A story for a story."

His thumb circled around my belly button. Even through the fabric of my shirt, I could feel the heat of him. "If I like the story, I will share mine. Otherwise, tomorrow."

"This. This is the worst thing I have ever done."

He stilled against me, his breath warm against my neck. "Define *this*, please."

I pressed my eyes shut, because if I could see him, I was going to lose my nerve. "Liking how you make me feel. Liking this."

His fingers curled against me, pressing into my stomach. "And how is this the worst thing you have ever done, Fae Slayer?"

"I promised I would never trust a pretty face. It was one of my rules."

"You're saying you trust me?"

"I trust you with me. And that's a start."

"Huh."

"What?"

"You trust me with you, but what do you not trust me with?"

"Killing the king. There's still a lot you could be keeping from me. It seems too easy for you to show up on one of my hunts and whisk me away with the promise of doing the one thing I've been aching to do for the last thirteen years."

"I will help you kill this king."

"And the next one, if he's as bad or worse?"

"Yes." Voss turned me around so I was face to face with him. "Why is it easier for you to trust me with your body than with your plan, little fox? Do you think so little of yourself?"

"No, just—you seemed honest. During sex, it felt like you wanted me. Not because I was saying no, and not because I could give you something no one else could, but because you wanted me. Me as myself." I shrugged.

"I will try to not betray your trust."

"I believe you. Mostly because the consequence is another stab wound on your body, and I intend to make that one the much more permanent kind."

His chest rumbled with another laugh. "What are your other rules?"

"Never negotiate."

"As you know, you can't make deals with Fae."

"I didn't know that when I made my rules. The last is to never admit I opened the door."

"And yet…" Voss gestured to himself.

"You already knew."

"Still, it sounds like you are trusting a pretty face." He fluttered his eyelashes. "And you think I'm pretty."

"You're an ass." I turned back to the hoswisps. Voss placed his chin on my shoulder, and his hands found their way back to my hips. "You know, there's something beautiful about these creatures."

"Of course you would think that."

"Why?"

"They are deadly. You like dying things."

"I like things marked for death."

Voss suddenly stiffened. "You are not sleeping with the king to kill him."

"Well, if I—"

He growled. "No. We will get you close to him without the need for that ruse."

"Possessive much?" I glanced over at Penn. "And if Penn tries to make a pass at me?"

His teeth found a soft spot on my neck, and he bit down hard. I yelped. "Yes," he admitted, kissing the tender spot. "He touches you, he dies. Just like Treborne."

"Treborne never actually touched me."

"Close enough."

I laughed. "I'll keep that in mind if I ever need to turn you against your allies."

"I don't like this. Thinking of you with anyone else."

"Too bad."

"What can I do to convince you otherwise?"

"Tell me what you'd do to me if they weren't sleeping next to us." I dropped my voice lower because I couldn't help myself. I wanted to know all the terrible things he would do if we were alone up here.

Voss's chuckle caressed my neck. "Well, first, I'd reach under your shirt." One of his fingers played with the hem of my shirt, and he grazed my skin. "And as soon as I knew you weren't expecting it, I'd trail along your side, up toward your breasts." His hand followed his narration. "And as I pinched your nipple, I'd drag you closer against me with my other arm."

The second he pulled me into him, I felt his length against my ass. My back arched into him as my nipple hardened from his touch.

"And then I'd have to explore to see if you were ready for me, by teasing you at the hem of your jeans. I'd unbutton them slowly, like I had all the time in the world, fiddling with your zipper as I worked my thumb against your nipple in slow strokes. And when you arched against me again—yeah, like that—I'd feel underneath your panties and trail down to the most sensitive parts of you. I'd find you slick with yearning, because you can't resist me, even if you wanted to."

"I can resist you." My voice was breathless.

A low moan escaped him as I squirmed against him. His fingers danced expertly along my entrance, easing me apart.

"And when you tried to close your legs because you simply couldn't stand being teased anymore, I'd hook my legs around you and force you open. I'd tear off your clothes and watch as the wetness of you pooled between your legs. Only when I was certain you were good and ready, would I lower you on top of me, inch by inch. I'd take my time piercing you, thrusting inside you, making sure you felt every moment that I claimed you as mine."

"I'll never be yours."

His fingers stilled, no longer toying with any part of me. "Are you sure?"

"Absolutely."

"How about now?" One finger slid inside me, and I gasped in response, but shook my head against his shoulder. He trailed his other hand to my opposite breast and twisted on my peak so hard I cried out. The pain and pleasure cut straight into my core. He reached the part of me he had yesterday, stroking my nerves with his finger, long and hard. The feeling threatened to split me open at my seams, but still he curled his finger against me, stroking it with a constant assaulting rhythm. I bucked against him.

"Not. Now." I gasped each word, barely able to speak.

He grabbed me and dragged me farther into him. "I'm not going to fuck you tonight." Voss's lips nipped at my ear. "Because that would be rude to our friends."

"Your friends," I corrected.

Another finger joined the first one, and he pushed both of them inside me as he moved his thumb along my clit. I couldn't help it; I whimpered. I was being undone from the inside out. He released my breast only to move to my mouth, forcing my jaw shut with his hand.

"I'm going to make you scream."

I shook my head.

"I'll keep going until you do." His voice turned dark and husky. "But I do recognize you couldn't say our word even if you wanted to, so bite my hand as hard as you can if you want me to stop."

I wanted to bite his hand to make him keep going. My back arched again, and his hand tightened around my mouth. I was pushed back against his chest, feeling the warmth of him pressed against every part of me as the lower half of my body writhed with pleasure.

"It's going to be a delicate balance, little fox, because if the hoswisps hear you, we might be done for."

The glowing orbs of them were still floating around the field, but farther away. I tried to hold on to my pleasure, keep it in, because I didn't want him to know how good it felt. And if I did scream, Voss would know he had complete control over me.

He did.

I was putty in his hands.

And he knew it with each thrust of my hips against his hand, trying to seek pleasure in the same way he delivered it to me. I shook against him as an explosion reared up inside me. With the heat of him pressed against me, it was easy to imagine him inside me again. His nails dug into my cheek as he held me, and with several more strokes, I screamed against his hand, rocketing back and forth as my entire body came undone around him.

Everything inside me let go.

After the shock waves had left me, Voss released his grasp on me. He slipped out of my pants and brought his fingers to his mouth. "I like the taste of you." He licked me off him, his eyes swirling again.

"If you tell me I taste like some kind of food—"

"No, not anything so mundane. You taste of loneliness and death. You taste of endless night and darkness. You taste of jealousy and rage. You taste perfect and divine."

I stared at him. His description reminded me of how I thought of the Fae, the way their voices sounded, and the way their skin tasted. They were a myriad of things, never one item. "How are any of those things remotely a turn on?"

"How does thinking about death make you wetter? I felt it when I told you the hoswisps might find us if you screamed too loud. You seeped over my fingers."

I cupped the side of his face, bringing his lips to mine. I bit down on his lower lip, hard. Blood burned into my mouth. "You taste like fire and the sun."

His hand clawed into fists, one tangled in my hair and the other on my shirt. "You torment me. A blood bond isn't something to be done lightly, and this is the second time you have... You're strengthening it."

I licked the outside of his lips, pulling back with a small smile on my face. "Then enlighten me. How does it work?"

Voss breathed out heavily. "The hoswisps are leaving, and I think it's time we both went back to sleep."

I narrowed my eyes. "What does it mean, Voss?"

"For a mortal who wants nothing to do with Fae, you ask a lot of questions about us."

"Maybe because it will help me kill the king."

He picked me up in one smooth motion and brought me back to my bedroll, laying us both down on top of it. "Tomorrow, we'll talk about a plan, how we'll get you close enough to kill the king. Then tomorrow night, I'll explain what the bond is. I can't right now. There's... too much."

"Too much what?"

As his arms wrapped around me, he dragged me close. "This."

I felt him, and my body reacted instantly. *More.* I wanted more. He wanted more. I swallowed. We were going down a dangerous path together, but the scariest thing about Voss? I felt ready to step into whatever fire he brought my way.

"Tomorrow, little fox. I'll make sure we stay in a town with a bed, and I'll tell you everything you need to know about blood bonding. Including what promises you've already accidentally made."

I shrugged. "I can always kill you to get out of it."

He chuckled. "I'm looking forward to the day you try."

Fifteen

The next morning, we rode hard and fast. Voss was determined to get out of the hoswisps' territory before we became their next meal. There was no safe place to set up camp in these parts of the wilds. With every hour we rode, we were reaching the end of the state. I hadn't been lying to Raskos when I told him I'd never left the state; that much had been true.

For some stupid reason, I hadn't thought the king would go this far from the portal, but as we arrived in a borderland court, I was second guessing my knowledge. There was an old port city, which had been largely abandoned by humans after the Fae took over, mostly due to a band of fire pauldrins that burned the entire thing to the ground. Thinking it over, maybe that city was where the king had gone. In Faerie, they didn't have technology like we had, which meant their trade routes were likely based on waterways.

I could still be wrong, because we could be headed in this direction now only for Voss to lead us somewhere else later. The assassin seemed dead set on keeping our destination secret from me. I understood why. If I had no need for him, what was to keep me sticking around?

Other than the way he made my body feel.

A large stone wall seemed to crop out of nothing, surrounding the border of the court. Fae guards stood on either end of the entrance, but barely glanced at us as we crossed the line into the town. We drove the horses to a stable next to an inn near the outskirts. This place was between Raskos's bombed out remains and Treborne's overly lavish lifestyle. There were large farmhouses and some old brownstones which had been converted into a town center. The humans and Fae here seemed to be actually... getting along.

"What is this place?" I asked as I swung my leg to one side of Switch and jumped down from her back. I gave her a few long pats on her silken neck before turning to the three of them.

Penn gestured around us, eyes sparkling. "Welcome to Lord Alpin's territory."

I balked. "I heard—"

"You heard wrong," Voss grunted as he led his horse toward the stables. "Not everything you find on those human networks is true. While some Fae Lords and Ladies are much like Treborne, there are several like Alpin who try to rule fair for both human and Fae. He recognizes one cannot live without the other. There must be harmony between us."

"One good Fae doesn't undo everything committed by the others." I crossed my arms.

"Oh, get over yourself," Elspeth said. "No one said that. But Alpin is one of the nice guys, and this will be a great place to get a good night's sleep." She let out a long yawn.

"You slept pretty well last night," I said.

"Sure, I did. Keep telling yourself I have no idea what happened between you two." Elspeth led her horse toward the stable.

Penn stared after the other two as they disappeared into the darkness of the stable. He glanced at me. "Do I want to know?" His jaw dropped open. "You are *blushing*."

"I will cut you."

"Voss would be very upset if you did."

I narrowed my eyes. "I don't care what he thinks right now. He's not here, and my dagger is."

Penn ran his hand through his hair. "Why don't I take Switch off your hands?"

I handed him the reins, but trailed after the horses anyway. It was clear the three of them had been here before, and I needed to get my bearings. Besides, every time I turned my back, I felt like someone was watching me. No one in this town knew me, and I was well out of the territory I had traveled while performing my assassinations, but I still felt eyes focus on me.

Most people did not venture out to the borderlands, because crossing state lines posed a huge risk. No one made the return journey, and it was rumored that hoswisps ran in thicker swarms over here, more deadly and focused than in the areas closer to the portal.

Judging by how many we saw from the barn loft last night, I didn't doubt the numbers. But in this court, there seemed to be plenty of Fae guards around the perimeter, while the humans set to do the work on the interior of the gates. On the surface level, it seemed to be a good system. However, looking only skin deep was what got humans in trouble in the first place. Fae might be glamorous on the surface, but dark and vile things lurked underneath their skin and inside their blackened hearts.

"We made it a bit early. Want to check out the market?" Voss asked as he stepped out of the stables, sizing me up as my eyes continued to dart around the town.

"If it will pass the time."

He eyed me, and I wondered what he was thinking. Why was it easier to talk to him while staring into the face of danger? Without my life in mortal peril, it felt... difficult. This was difficult. Was that normal? Was anything about me normal anymore? I wished I could ask Anya. She'd know, and she wouldn't judge me for it.

Voss nodded toward a longer stretch of road. "Let's go then. Elspeth and Penn will deal with the horses."

"Why are you always making them handle the animals?"

Penn laughed from inside the stables. "Yeah, Voss, tell her why."

Voss frowned. "Because it's their job. Just like mine was hunting you."

"And how's that going for you?"

"I found you. So, quite well." His boot landed on the edge of a rock, and the stone skittered down the road. "However, I'm not planning to do what the king wants with you, as you already know."

"I wondered about that, actually," I said as he gestured down a worn asphalt walkway. I turned with him as we entered an alley between worn brownstone buildings. Only a couple of people milled about on the street, but otherwise, we were alone. "How do I know this isn't some elaborate ploy to get me to the king so he can do what he pleases with me?"

As casually as breathing, Voss slipped his arm over my shoulder and pulled me in close. "I suppose you don't."

"Great way to convince me to trust you."

"I can give you several more orgasms on the way to the king's estate, if that would help calm your troubled mind."

"Maybe I'll start by cutting you with a toothpick. See how

stabby I can get with that." I smiled sweetly at him.

He sighed and ran his fingers over my shoulder. "The king wants you dead. And if the other assassins catch up to us, you'll see why I'm to be trusted over them. They will torture you and drag you kicking and screaming back to the king's court. Likely for a brutal execution in front of the king directly."

"I would never scream."

"I seem to recall last night differently than you, then." Voss led us down another corner onto a narrow path. The end of the road was covered in shadows despite the afternoon sun. Just as I wondered where he was taking me, the passage opened up to a courtyard full of market stalls. Goods, produce, and wares were strewn throughout the colorful pop-up tents.

Voss took his hand back and walked a few steps ahead of me, gesturing widely to the market. My jaw was open, and damn him, he looked smug again. "This is how Alpin's people make their money. He has the best market on the border, so people travel here, despite the threat of the hoswisps, to shop."

I stepped next to him, staring at the bustling market. It was incredible to see artisans, blacksmiths, companion animals, and people and Fae from every walk of life here in one place. Most of the towns I had been in were like Raskos's, sad ghosts of what life used to be like. Nothing like this. Alpin had figured out what made people want to congregate and capitalized on that, making a safe haven for both Fae and humans.

"Why bother, though? Since Alpin could make these people give him what he wants for free?"

"Why bother with anything?"

"I don't get it. Power generally corrupts, and most Fae are corrupt, but here—"

"Here, Alpin created a town where Fae could remember why

they shouldn't destroy the new world. Faerie had been beautiful once, and Alpin saw the potential for beauty here too, so long as we didn't ruin this world like we had our own. Come, I have some coin, and you need new clothes."

I looked at the black outfit I wore and wrinkled my nose at the smell of hay wafting off me. "I smell like we spent the night in a hayloft."

Voss chuckled. "We can get some soaps, too. The inn we're staying at has hot baths. I wouldn't mind joining you for one."

"You wish." A warm bath sounded perfect.

"If you don't say it, I'll never stop." His voice was next to my ear and velvety soft against my skin. "But I don't think you want me to stop, do you? Would you let me take you right now? Right here in the middle of everyone?"

I whirled and pushed him hard in the chest. He barely moved an inch, the cocky smile back on his face. "Someday, your blood will flood into my mouth, and it will be the sweetest thing I have ever tasted."

"Don't tempt me." His grin was incorrigible.

With a sigh, I headed into the crowd, letting my eyes linger on the trinkets, baked goods, produce, and decorations available for purchase. I hadn't seen anything like this since I was a kid, with my hands pressed into my parents' as we strolled through shop after shop. It had been around the holidays, and we were bundled up in winter gear, my breath coming out in puffs. They were attempting to find my brother a video game, which was sold out in most stores. As a reward for my good behavior, they had given me a hot cup of cocoa with thick whipped cream with pieces of candy cane crushed on top.

I could barely remember what a candy cane tasted like.

But here in this town, the whimsical magic of the sanctified world felt preserved. It was as if the hoswisps hadn't ravaged the landscape, as if the Fae hadn't leveled our homes, as if fire pauldrins hadn't incinerated the trees.

"Here," Voss said, guiding me to a stall with riding gear, pants, and shirts. "What do you need?"

Shopping was never my thing. When I was with my parents as a kid, I only put up with it for the reward at the end. It was no different now. I grabbed several practical items in my size and gave Voss a shrug.

"That's all you want?"

"It's three outfits. Do I need more than that?"

His eyes roamed over my body, as if assessing whether giving me that information would clue me to our destination. "I suppose you could clean them if needed."

"Or Elspeth can."

"You would ask Elspeth to clean your clothes for you?"

"Magically, of course." I waved my hand over myself.

Voss grunted. "There's a difference between being clean and being *glamored* clean. You'd have to clean them yourself, but three should be plenty, you're right." He paid for the pile, and we were handed the lot in a weaved basket. The shopkeeper thanked him for his continued patronage.

"Come here often?" I joked.

"The borderlands are nice, despite the hoswisps. Alpin did something with this town I thought would be impossible under the current king's rule. I admire him for that."

As we strolled back the way we had come, I paused at a table sporting silver wires intricately wrapped around stones attached to delicate woven threads. Breathing out, my fingers hovered over a pure red stone, sensing something from it.

"Does it speak to you?" the woman behind the counter asked.

"Not many people can find the beauty inside a red jasper."

"It's pretty," I admitted, not quite understanding what I was feeling. The stone itself seemed to hum energy into the air. "Though I am not sure how practical it is to have something so heavy on a delicate band."

"Ah, I can assure you, it handles most everyday wear and tear. These threads were reinforced with Fae magic and should last a lifetime."

"The Fae work with you to make these?"

"I should hope so. He's my husband." The woman smiled as she twisted a wristband on her right hand, fiddling with an inlaid stone there.

I gaped at her.

"A bit unconventional, I know. I get that look a lot from people who come from out of town, but we've made it work. Do you want to talk price?"

Biting my lip, I knew I couldn't afford it. I didn't have anything myself, and there was no way I would ask Voss for money. The stone was a beautiful dark red, a scarlet color that matched the name I'd given myself once I became the Fae Slayer. It reminded me why I started this journey to begin with, why I had to continue it no matter what the cost, and why sacrifices had to be made along the way.

"Not today, I'm afraid. I don't have the money." As I moved to go, I nearly smashed into Voss. He had continued on without me, and I was startled to see him once again so near.

"But I do." Voss nodded to the stone. "How much?"

"Two hundred."

He narrowed his eyes. "One fifty."

"One seventy, and that's final."

Voss eyed me.

"I don't need it."

"One fifty and remove the band. I'll make my own."

Her eyes widened as she looked at both of us. She shrugged. "Fine, the bands take a lot out of my husband, anyway. It's not his typical magic." With deft fingers, the woman unthreaded the band and handed over the stone set in the silver wire. Voss passed her the coins, and he inspected the red jasper.

"Come." He led me away from the stalls to the darkness of the alley. With delicate fingers, he grasped my hand and placed the stone in the middle of my wrist. His brow creased with concentration as the silver around the stone expanded, multiplied out of nothing, spinning around my wrist until it connected on the other side. When he finished, he breathed out. "It's stunning on you."

I had seen magic destroy and manipulate people. I had never seen magic do... this. Tearing my gaze away from the stone, I looked at him. Voss watched me with a hungry gaze.

"The silver band will hold better than the ones her partner made. The magic on the threads was weak, only made to last a human's lifetime."

"I hate to break it to you, Voss, but I am human."

He stared at me and blinked once. "Of course you are."

"Is this a sudden realization you are coming to?"

"No, just—" He tucked a stray piece of hair behind my ear, and I shuddered at the lightness of his touch. It was more intense than the possessive way he typically held me. "There are a lot of things I wish to explain to you, but we're running out of time at the market. It closes a few hours before sundown to give the travelers a warning to pack up and get home before the night settles."

"Are there other beasts outside of these walls? Other than the hoswisps?"

"There are always other beasts."

Voss led us back toward the inn, but stopped briefly at a bakery which someone had built into the first floor of a brownstone on our way. He bought some fresh bread and a few pastries for us. I was shocked to see him eat something covered in powdered sugar. It was completely out of place. This wicked man who had been nothing but teasing and conniving and vicious ate a danish covered in powdered sugar like it was the most normal thing in the world.

My brain couldn't handle it.

As I licked my fingers clean, we reached the main road toward the inn where we were to spend the night. The setting sun glinted off my new bracelet, and a few times I caught Voss staring at it as we walked.

"What?" I said as I sucked the last of the sugar from underneath my fingernail.

"It looks like it has been there all along, like it belongs on you." A heartless chuckle escaped his mouth. "It figures scarlet would look perfect."

"The beautiful color of blood and death." I grinned.

"Always so morbid, little fox." He hooked a finger around the bracelet. "But this is hardly a morbid gift."

"I'll keep that in mind next time I use this arm to draw my knife across someone's throat."

"It will match perfectly," Voss said with little hesitation.

We arrived shortly before sundown. The light cast long shadows across the roads and in the distance, the low moaning of hoswisps could be heard. They stirred after a day of sleeping. The gates to the town closed, with more guards roaming the top of the wall.

As we entered the inn, I took in the converted farmhouse. The bottom floor was open, with giant wooden plank floors. A few small dining tables in the entry and what might have once been an office space spanned the space before the open kitchen. One Fae and several humans worked over pans and pots steaming with various items for the patrons already seated.

"Come, we get the same accommodations here every visit." Voss tugged on my hand, and we went upstairs, the steps creaking louder than the bustle of the inn below. On the first floor landing, we went to the end of the L-shaped hallway and he knocked on the door on the right.

Penn opened up the space. "Dinner in an hour. Elspeth and I are going to wash up." He dropped a key into Voss's outstretched hand. His eyes glanced between both of us. "Have fun."

I opened my mouth to protest, but Penn had already latched the door behind him. Voss used the key on the door across the hall, and we headed up a second flight of stairs.

Sixteen

Standing at the entrance of the third-floor suite, I was speechless. Voss set my new clothes on a bench at the foot of a king-sized bed with four ornate and expertly carved posts. He set about shucking off his own boots, but I was in temporary awe.

The suite spanned the length of the house, with a half bathroom tucked off to the side and a huge claw-foot tub was across from the bed. An inlay of marble surrounded the tub, which could likely hold three people. The bed had several plush pillows, and my body suddenly ached with the idea of sleeping on a soft mattress and comforter. The walls were painted wood, creating a beach-like feel to the room, despite being miles from any capes or coastal regions. It was a gorgeous space, a perfect oasis from the exterior world.

One could come here to forget everything had turned sour outside. Complacency like this was dangerous.

"You going to stand there and continue staring, or are you

going to enjoy the accommodations?" Voss had already put his boots off to the side, rummaging through the packs Penn and Elspeth had likely left for him. He pulled out clean clothes, and with swift movements, began filling the tub.

"The tub is… in the bedroom."

"Observant."

"You said it had hot *baths*, plural."

"The hotel has hot baths, plural, but this room only has the one."

"And you intend to use it?" I put my hands on my hips, eying him.

"Don't you?" He unwrapped the soap and passed the bar underneath the water a few times, allowing some suds to form inside the water. "You can opt to smell like a hayloft, if that is what you desire, but I will bathe."

"You planned for this."

"I plan a lot of things." Voss shrugged. "Can you blame me for wanting to see you naked again? Stripped bare before me?" His voice dropped lower and when he looked at me, his eyes smoldered, his magic flaring. I wasn't sure what he was trying to do, but I stared at him, dumbfounded. I couldn't bring myself to move in either direction. I was captivated by him and equally terrified of what this would mean.

While I wanted to make him bleed, I also wanted *him*. Fear of what that meant for my future as the Fae Slayer wrapped around my heart. Maybe this entire trip was a ploy to convince me that Fae were not terrible. Maybe this was the secret mission of the assassin: if he convinced me Fae were good, then he could convince me to spare the king's life. Maybe that was his end game, to use me for the king's own ambitions.

The thing was, Lord Treborne didn't fit into that theory. Voss told me Alpin was off limits, and from being inside Alpin's court, I had a better understanding of why.

The king was known for his brutality. That's why we were in this mess. As much as I wanted to mistrust Voss, something told me he was telling the truth. He wanted to overthrow the king so a less corrupt ruler would take over.

"What else have you planned, Voss?" My voice came out as a squeak, and I wanted to lash myself for showing weakness in front of him.

"You want details like in the loft, or would you like me to show you?"

"I'm not talking about the bath."

"But I am." His eyes flared again, and the suds in the tub multiplied. His hands went to the hem of his shirt. He lifted it up and over his head, and I was stunned into silence. I still hadn't moved a muscle farther into the room. His body was perfection, chiseled in a way that made me feel like I could sharpen my dagger on his muscles. "Care to join me?" He reached out, hand hovering steps away from me.

Screw it. I wanted a hot bath, and if it had to be with Voss, then fine. I could bathe with him. I had slept next to him in a loft, I had fucked him, and he had presented my naked body to a Fae Lord. Joining him in some water would be easy.

I tossed off my boots, stripped out of my clothes in smooth movements, and grasped his hand in mine. He paused, frowning at the mess I had left in my wake on the floor. "What? Not clean enough for you? Didn't seem to bother you when we were surrounded by blood."

"That was different. I have no love for Treborne's court."

Forcing a pout, I stepped up to him, closing the gap between us. "I'm a messy person, Voss."

"I'm aware, little fox." He looked at our hands wrapped together, eyes flicking to the bracelet again. "I'm keenly aware."

"So, what are you going to do about it?"

"What do you want me to do?" He ran his tongue over his teeth as he eyed me.

I shrugged, using his hand as leverage to get up and over the edge of the claw-foot tub. He relinquished his hold on me, and I slipped underneath the suds. Warm water caressed my aching thighs, making my muscles relish the respite.

Voss removed his pants and climbed into the opposite side of the tub, watching me as I reached for the soap. He snatched it first, working a lather around his palms. "You want this?"

I scowled at him. "That's the entire point of getting into a bath, is it not? *Bathing?*" Crossing my arms over my chest, I leaned into the bubbles he had magically produced and gazed at him.

He ran the soap over his pectoral muscles, up around his arms and shoulders, making every part of him slick. I imagined it being blood; us being surrounded by it, drenched in it instead of water. I swallowed hard.

"What are you thinking about over there?"

"Nothing."

"I can practically hear your lust through your heartbeats."

My scowl deepened.

"Tell me, how dead am I in this scenario?"

"You're very much alive, much to my dismay."

"How injured am I?"

"You aren't."

"How injured is someone else?"

"Gravely."

"Come here."

"No."

"Come here," he demanded, his nose wrinkling with annoyance.

"No."

His teeth bared, eyes turning back into liquid lava. His blond hair was still dry, hanging around his ears and framing his angled jawline. "If you continue not to listen to me, I will punish you."

"I find that hard to believe." I flicked a few bubbles toward him. "You wouldn't."

"Say the word, and I won't."

I bit my lower lip. "No."

One moment, I was on my side of the tub, staring at him. The next, he latched his hands around my ankles, dragging me so quickly toward him that my head sank underneath the water. As I sputtered for air, he placed his hands on my hips, pulling me hard against him. My legs were on either side of him, and if this position didn't make me feel helpless in the best way possible, I didn't know what would. His length pressed against me.

"Your fantasies are incredible." His words purred against my skin. Liquid ignition ran throughout my body. "And I think maybe someday we should explore them a bit more."

"Like when?"

"Maybe after killing the king. Maybe before."

I squirmed in his hands, and he gripped me firmer against him. A whimper escaped my mouth.

"Have any other Fae heard that sound?"

My head shook without my permission.

"Good." Voss's hands left my hips and found the bar of soap again. "As much as I would love to explore exactly what you want me to do in that sadistic little head of yours, I do recall there is a point to *bathing*, as you said." Once the soap had created a lather in his hands, he brought the bar down across my exposed chest.

I shuddered.

"How many Fae have touched you this way?"

"None." I gasped as his hand curved underneath my breast, heading back over the top of my chest, trailing bubbles behind. He made slow, languid circles around my skin until the bar reached my peak. He dropped the soap, and it slipped right next to his length against my core. His thumb rolled over my nipple, making me suck in a gasping breath. He grasped my skin, pulling lightly, and a cry rolled off my tongue as my hips bucked against him. Voss's other hand settled on my waist and forced me to still against him. I whimpered again as he rolled my sensitive skin in between his thumb and pointer finger.

"If the other Fae had made you feel like this, would there be a trail of bodies in your wake?"

"I may still kill you." The words came out on the end of an exhale. I tried to move, but his fingers dug into my skin, forcing my hips to stay secured against him, feeling the heat of him wedged between us was unbearable.

"I doubt that." Voss cupped warm water in his palm and brought it over my soapy skin. It dripped along my breasts. "Who else would allow you to constantly threaten them?"

"Probably many people, as long as I said the magic word."

His hold tightened around my hip as he brought more water over my breast. Each droplet felt electric. "Wrong answer."

"You know I'm right. All it takes is one word, and you're like putty in my hands."

"Then do it. Make me putty."

"Never."

Voss reached between us, fingers trailing along my stomach as he searched for the missing bar of soap. "See, here's the weird thing about you telling me *no* so much." His erection was solid against me as he brought the soap back up, starting slowly around

195

my other breast. "I know I can have you, and I know you're mine, whether you realize it or not."

"I'm not anyone's."

He used the corner of the soap to tease my nipple into a turgid peak. I arched against him. "That's where you are wrong, little fox. But keep telling yourself you have the power here. Keep trying to admit you dislike this feeling."

"And what feeling is that?"

"Being completely out of control." His fingernail grazed the edge of my skin, and I bucked against him. His other hand kept me flush with him, and he pressed right against my clit, making my nerves ignite. "As much as you want to condemn or hate me, you enjoy being helpless under me. For once in your life, you've met someone who does something different to you, and that terrifies you, enrages you, but also arouses you." As the suds dripped off my skin, he kissed the side of my neck. "You want me to own you." His teeth grazed my skin.

"Fuck you, Voss." I pushed on his chest, but his hands were too fast, already locked onto both of my hips. "I don't want to be owned by anyone."

"Then say it." He pulled away from my neck, looking at me with his liquid fire eyes. "Say the word, and I will stop."

I pulsed against him with need, and his eyes widened.

"You can't deny me anymore, can you?"

I didn't want to, but I hardly got to say words, because he moved against me. The length of him ran along my entrance and made my thighs quiver. "I could," I muttered, my voice sounding weak even to my own ears.

"Say it. Prove you can, little fox." One of his hands trailed toward my center, slipping down my stomach. "Prove you can say no." His thumb pressed against me, coercing a moan from my mouth despite my attempts to hold it back. As I rose against him, searching for more, a growl emanated from his chest. "It doesn't matter that you can't say no, because I want you like this."

"Like what?"

His other hand came up my side, trailing along my shoulder, then my neck. He grasped my chin and forced me to look at him. "Equally consenting partners. Even if you are imagining someone dead in this room with us right now."

I bit down on his thumb maliciously hard, because it was the only thing I could think to do. Voss was hitting the truth, and it frustrated me, creating a hateful well of emotion inside me. I *liked* him. I liked sex with him. And I didn't need to imagine a dead body to fuck him. We were consenting partners.

And that meant I had lost a part of myself along this journey, lost it to him. Why did that make me feel strong and incredibly weak at the same time? Why did it make me feel confident and utterly helpless?

As my teeth ground into his skin, blood warmed my mouth. He still tasted like candied ginger, and it made me wonder what other parts of him would taste like when he felt like fire.

He growled and lifted me up so the tip of him hovered underneath my entrance. "You're stunning."

I ran my tongue along his thumb. He traced a line back down my body, leaving a trail of blood in his wake, my skin marked by him. I wanted to tell him I didn't belong to him, but watching his blood mix with the water between my breasts as he worked his way much lower along my body, I knew it wasn't true. Voss had slipped underneath my walls, somehow pierced straight into my heart, and that terrified me more than anything else in the entire world.

And he was right. I liked being terrified.

He moved my hips back and forth against him, stroking the tip of his erection against my clit. When he aligned with my entrance, he toyed with bringing me down on him. I felt each pulse of pressure as he teased me. It was too much, and I was already gasping for breath.

"I want to hear you say it," he said, bringing my hips back down to nestle against him. The feel of him right there, right near where I desperately wanted him to penetrate. I needed him inside me. His tongue ran along the skin of my neck, up toward my jaw, then over my chin and finally onto my lips. His kisses drank me in hungrily as his tongue swirled into my mouth. I wanted more as I moaned, leaning into him. His touch set my body on fire.

Voss pulled back, eyes swirling. "Admit you want this. Want me."

I ground my teeth together, staring at him. His fingers caressed my stomach, hovering there, waiting. "What happens if I don't?"

"Then you get nothing."

The words echoed into my very soul. I doubted my ability to walk away from this, from his touch, but also from him. There was something about Voss which was deliciously protective, bordering on obsession, and the way he looked at me like I already belonged to him was hot.

His thumb traveled lower, teasing the skin below my belly button, but not venturing far enough down. I arched my back, aching to feel him inside me. "What will it be, little fox?" His hands stilled. He stilled. The fire was inside me, all-consuming, driving my brain and my mind to the brink. I needed him.

"I need you."

"Need?" Voss's smile made me want to cut him. "Not just want, but need?"

I moved my body so his thumb slipped lower, hitting the exact right spot. I sucked in a breath, feeling a slight relief at the tension.

My hands gripped his shoulders as I rolled over his hand. "Want and need," I admitted, voice coming out more solid despite how desperate I felt.

He applied pressure with his thumb, making lazy circles around my nerves, creating another fire inside me that threatened to be let out. "You are mine, little fox. Say it."

I moaned as his thumb picked up the pace. My thighs shook. Everything inside me wanted to let go, release.

His tongue trailed down my neck, over my chest, to the sensitive peak. He drew my nipple into his mouth and pressed his teeth into my skin. "If you want my cock inside you, say it." His tongue wickedly danced on my nerves, making my body shudder. His thumb trailed down farther, toying with my entrance, playing with me. "I can feel how much you want it, how much you need it. Your body is quivering. You're mine."

I shook my head, but I wasn't able to process words. Everything was red hot and liquid fire, just like his smoldering eyes as he looked up at me. I wasn't going to last much longer, and I wasn't sure I could bite back the words from him.

"Need more convincing?"

He moved me then, positioned me so that once again the tip of his arousal pressed against me. My body begged him to be inside me, and I tried to move my hips down, but Voss wouldn't allow it. "You're mine," he said again with finality.

There would be no arguing.

"I am yours." The words felt thick on my tongue, like I was half in a dream and half in the real world.

He didn't wait any longer. With one quick thrust, the entire length of him was inside me, stretching and filling me. The hollow emptiness I felt moments before was gone, the ache relieved. I yelled out as my thighs settled flush against him, no more space between us. My breath came in waves as I adjusted to having him inside me, and he waited until my sex pulsed against him, begging for more.

"I like the way you feel." He lifted me up, pulling out of me and pushing back in. My legs wrapped around his waist, and it became a steady rhythm. Voss rolled his hips with expertise, hitting all the right spots in my core. I was filled again and again. His teeth trailed long marks down my neck, and my hands wrapped around him. The feeling of his skin against me, smooth and hard, made us connected. I was vulnerable, and he was fire, and I liked the way we moved together.

He lifted me up out of the water, and my legs naturally latched around his thighs. A low growl rumbled in his chest as he brought us both soaking wet over to the bed and laid me down underneath him. He never took himself out of me, still having us locked together. I liked that. I liked him being inside me.

He smoothed my wet hair back away from my face. "I could fuck you all day."

"Is that a challenge?"

The corner of his lips quirked up in a smirk. "Maybe for the future." He pulled back, almost entirely out of me, and another soft sound escaped my lips that sounded too much like begging. He rolled his hips, moving the tip of his erection around my entrance.

"Please." I needed him.

His eyes widened as he bit his lower lip. With another thrust, he plunged back inside me. His rhythm became long, hard, and fast, stretching me tightly around him as I came close to the edge. My fingernails found the skin on his shoulders, and I pulled him down into me. Our mouths connected, and a hunger drove me to stick my tongue into his mouth, tasting everything that burned inside him. I wanted all of him. I wanted him to be inside me, own me, complete me. I wanted to feel him filling me.

This was so different from our time in Treborne's court. I had needed him for an entirely different reason, but now, I needed Voss as himself. My body shook as he let out a low moan, pumping in and out of me with a fast fury. His muscles tightened, and I felt his release inside me, my own one chasing right after his. Every part of me tensed and tightened around him, bucking in rhythm as I took my pleasure for all it was worth. Stars filled my eyes as I finally felt relaxed for the first time since entering the room with him.

Voss held himself up with trembling arms, watching me as I came back down to reality. Propping himself on one elbow, he took my right hand and kissed the skin right next to the bracelet he made for me. The intimacy, the heat of his lips on me while he was still inside me, made heat rise to my cheeks.

"Another Fae Slayer blush?" Voss's fingers wandered back up my arms, and his thumb ambled along my cheek. "You're remarkable."

"Sometimes I think I hate you."

"It doesn't matter, though. You already admitted you're mine."

"Why do I feel as though you're going to make me regret saying that?"

He shook his head, a smirk playing on his lips. "I will never make you regret it, at least sexually."

I tried to cross my arms over my chest, shield myself from him, but he captured one of my hands in his, interlocking our fingers together.

"You are beautiful, you know?"

"Yeah, I know."

He huffed a laugh and drew one of my fingers into his mouth, slowly tracing my skin with his tongue. "Dinner's soon. Are you hungry?"

As if on cue, my stomach let out a low growl.

Voss's laugh was like a tickle of flames dancing along my skin. He pulled out of me slowly, and my body ached from the loss of him. "Let's get you cleaned up and head downstairs."

I nodded, though I was unsure how to move. Everything in me was languid and relaxed, and never once in my life had I felt so... fulfilled.

Seventeen

By the time we reached the first floor of the inn, Penn and Elspeth had chosen a table in what used to be the office of the farmhouse. The table had a wide berth of space between it and the other patrons. Elspeth looked me over as we approached, and her brows knitted together. My hair was still damp, and I was wearing the new riding clothes Voss had purchased for me this afternoon. His hand hovered on my lower back as we wound through the dining room.

"We ordered for the table," Penn said as Voss pulled out a chair for me.

The two already sitting exchanged a glance.

"I'm not helpless."

"Never said you were." Voss's smile said more than I wanted it to. While he said he enjoyed being on equal footing to me, it was obvious he wanted to be more than that.

Elspeth narrowed her gaze on me, looking up and down and scrutinizing me. "What's that on your wrist?" Her voice went up an octave as she looked toward Voss. She was silent for a moment, before adding, "Spending our money on frivolous things?"

Penn frowned, his eyes also darting to the bracelet. His hands wrapped around a tankard of ale and brought it up to his lips, nearly choking at how quickly he sucked down the beer.

"I told him I didn't need it."

"I bet," she said, scowling.

"It looks good on her, does it not?" Voss captured my wrist in his hands, the grin spreading wider up his face as the other two frowned. "Perfect color."

"I hope you know what you've gotten yourself into," Elspeth said to me with pointed words.

"Fantastic sex?"

Penn choked on the ale. "He doesn't need more of an ego."

Elspeth's brows remained furrowed. "It's a *very* charming bracelet, Voss. I didn't think you were interested in getting anyone jewelry. Last time I recall, you called such a thing... What were your words?"

"Covering up your mediocrity by announcing yourself to the world."

"Yup, that's the one. Thanks, Penn."

"Anytime."

"It's just a bracelet," I said, fiddling with the material on my wrist.

Voss ran his thumb over the stone. "Sometimes a male has to eat their words when something feels perfect. And it looks incredible on her." He tossed me a grin. "What do you want to drink?"

I shrugged. "Wine? The human kind."

"Obviously. I wouldn't dream of giving you any more Faerie wine."

"She did seem more into you when she was on it," Elspeth said.

"She's into me plenty now."

I narrowed my gaze at Voss and yanked my wrist away from him. "I still have the capability of gutting you."

"Sure, she's into you *plenty*." Elspeth laughed.

"I do like her, though." Penn nodded at the bracelet. "She's good for you, I guess."

"I'll get us some drinks." Voss winked at me and stood.

"And another round for us. You two took your sweet ass time." Elspeth shook her empty tankard at him. As soon as Voss neared the kitchen staff, her eyes shot back to me. "What is your angle with all of this? Are you seducing him so you can kill him someday?"

"The thought has crossed my mind," I answered honestly, but then glanced over at him as he leaned against the counter. His black eyes flashed up to meet mine. They crinkled around the edges when he met my gaze, and my stone cold heart warmed. "But not anymore."

"And when the king is dead? What then?"

"I don't know. That feels like a lifetime away." In truth, I wasn't sure I could continue this relationship with Voss once the king was dead. There was so much to do in the human world, so many people I needed to connect with to start the revolution and fight back in this unending war against the Fae. I couldn't continue sleeping with the enemy while that was happening.

But the thought of leaving him behind made something go sour in my stomach.

I turned back to Elspeth. "Maybe I've gotten too soft, but I kind of like him."

Penn snorted. "She kind of enjoys getting her brains fucked out of her skull."

"I can cut you too, you know? Or break your kneecap, for real this time."

"Empty threats. If you weren't cozying up to Voss, I'd be shaking in my boots." Penn sipped at his ale delicately. His light eyes swirled with mischief.

"How am I supposed to kill the king if I am losing my edge?"

"Oh, trust me. Your edge is fine. That proves it." Elspeth pointed to the bracelet. "You and Voss are going to make a good team, but we have to talk about how to infiltrate the court."

"I've already thought of that." Voss sat down and placed a glass of wine in front of me along with a bottle. He floated two tankards to his friends, and he swirled some kind of mixed cocktail in front of him. "I am the king's assassin, after all, so what better way than to walk right in?"

"Walk right in? With her?" Penn laughed. "Now I know you've lost your mind."

"As a captive, of course." Ice clinked against his glass as he took a hefty gulp.

My jaw dropped open. "As a captive." My throat felt like it was going to close. There were so many ways for that plan to go wrong, namely if I was placing my trust in Voss and he turned against me. "I hate it."

"It's a simple plan," Elspeth said, "with a major issue. The king ordered her dead, not delivered to his doorstep. He'd think something was up if we showed up with her alive."

"And I'd very much like to be alive, with free use of my hands."

"If there's another way, please tell me." Voss gestured to the three of us. His thumb circled around the top of his glass. Confidence oozed off of him, and I wanted to slam him against the wall.

And then do other things to him that were far less violent than

I was used to.

"We could disguise her as someone else," Penn said.

"You know glamor doesn't work on the king," Elspeth spat.

"Well, it would work long enough to get her inside without alerting the guards to her presence. She can act as our prisoner after that, if we get caught."

"It'd be safer if we don't deceive the court with anything other than the obvious." Voss glanced at me. "This, of course, has to be okay with you."

I took two gulps of wine before casting a solemn glance around the table. "I'll agree to it only if we do not find another way."

"There might be one." Elspeth looked between the two of us. "But I'm not sure your little fox is going to like it. Though, I suppose she might not have much choice in the matter?" She raised her eyebrow at Voss in what appeared to be a challenge.

Voss growled at her.

"A wedding," Elspeth said right as a server brought the meal for the table. "If the king thinks she's agreed to work with you, then she might get to live without being a captive."

Voss's eyes land on mine.

"Absolutely not," I said.

Elspeth's eyebrows rose for a moment, as she slid a glance at Voss. It was only a second before her eyes settled back on me. "You already look the part, especially with how you continue to stare at him like you want to come apart at the seams while he has his way with you."

"I do not."

"You do," Voss said, a smirk spreading up his cheek.

"It's not unheard of for humans to be so infatuated by Fae that they would literally die for them. What makes you any different?"

"I am different. Magic doesn't work on me."

"I hate to break it to you, but love *is* a kind of magic," Elspeth said.

I sucked in a breath so fast it sounded like a hiss. "I am not in love with him."

"But you love having sex with him. It's practically the same thing." Elspeth shrugged, stabbing at a large hunk of meat with her fork.

"It's a start," Voss muttered, somewhat deflated. I arched a brow in his direction. He shrugged. "Well, we have two options, both of which you hate. We can find alternatives. I personally love the idea of tying you up."

"I'm sure you do." I tore off a piece of bread and dipped it into the sauce covering the meat. The smells were incredible. The inn's kitchen had both Fae and humans working alongside each other, and if the resulting food was this good… It was easy to imagine this future, envision what Voss thought the world should be.

"Tomorrow morning, we need to take off at sunrise if we have any hope of getting to—"

Voss coughed. "We're still not telling her."

"Oh, so you're fine dressing her up in jewels, but not telling her our destination?" Elspeth gestured at my wrist again. She was making me feel self-conscious about this stupid bracelet. I never wore jewelry before in my life, and it wasn't like I could take the thing off now that Voss had permanently attached the bangle to my wrist.

"Precisely. From what I understand about Scarlet, and she can correct me if I'm wrong, if she had no use for us, there is no telling what she would do at that point. Possibly run back to her human crew and try to infiltrate the king's court without us." He looked levelly at me. "Tell me I'm wrong."

"You're not *not* wrong." The piece of meat melted apart in my mouth, deliciously tender and rendered pure.

"Well, fine. We still need to leave early to avoid an onslaught from the hoswisps. Less than one hour after daybreak, and we should be on the road. Heard?" Penn stared at us in turn.

"Fine by me," Elspeth said.

"I'm not worried about you." Penn gazed at Voss. "Can you keep it in your pants long enough for us to get on the road?"

Voss slipped me a glance. "Can we?"

"I hate you."

He winked, and I flipped him off. "We will be on the road one hour after daybreak, else we are stuck here for another day, giving the assassins more time to play catch up." Voss licked a bit of sauce from the corner of his mouth. "If I feel the need to get rid of any more aggression, I'll be sure to do it tonight."

My steak knife made a satisfying thwack as it sunk through his hand and pinned him to the table.

Everyone stared at me.

Voss scowled, ripping the knife from his hand. The injury instantly stitched back together, because it wasn't sparrowbone and would do no real damage to him. A single bead of blood dripped onto the table off the end of the steel.

I grinned. "My aggression is taken care of."

"I don't know whether I should kiss you or punish you."

Leaning close to his ear, I said, "Why not both?"

Voss cupped my jaw in between his fingers, bringing his lips to mine with brief ferocity. It felt more like he was claiming me in front of the other two, and everything inside me tensed. "Please don't stab my hand again. I like this hand. It's useful."

"Oh please, a steel knife won't do anything to you."

"Other than hurt his precious feelings," Elspeth laughed.

"Am I the only one who is incredibly freaked out by the way

they interact?" Penn asked incredulously. "It's not entirely safe pairing him with her, is it?"

Elspeth shrugged. "Would you rather keep watch over her, Penn?"

Voss growled.

The other male instantly shook his head. "Not anymore. Voss will kill me."

"Indeed." The fire in his eyes died down as he stabbed his fork through a roasted carrot and tore it in half with his teeth.

"Do all male Fae get this way after sex?"

Elspeth looked at me. "No. Not all Fae, but I suppose you wouldn't know that, since you never gave them the chance to react."

"I rarely them a chance to come either."

Voss choked on his vegetables. "Fuck."

"You know, I admire you for being a selfish lover. Not enough females chase their own pleasure. Good for you." Elspeth nodded at me.

"Seriously?! We're just... leaving that as is? She could still murder Voss in his sleep, and then where would we be?"

"Yes, little fox, where would we be?" Voss leaned his chin on his hand and gave me a long, level look.

"Likely I would be running from the two assassins. And I wouldn't know where to go next, since you haven't told me. And then Cumina and Morna would find me in about two weeks when I have my period. That sequence of events sounds... unbelievably frustrating." I frowned, thinking the progression of events over and wishing I had a better plan in place than depending entirely on these Fae. I had come to like Voss, but I still wasn't sure I could trust him.

"And the alternative is staying with me, getting fucked as much as you want, and traveling in style straight to the king's court. Which do you think sounds better?" Voss arched an eyebrow at me, and I wanted to tear it straight out of his skin. There was something about the way he looked at me that ignited me all the way to my core.

"In either scenario, I imagine myself killing the king so I could live with both outcomes."

Penn snorted. "Of course you would choose a girl who wouldn't fall head over heels for you. But I'm with Voss on this. You would prefer the latter option, no matter what you say." His eyes swirled with turquoise whirlpools, and I realized he must have been glamoring our conversation, otherwise we would not have been able to discuss everything so freely.

"The latter option does have better food."

Elspeth's gaze did not waver from me. "I know you don't care to hear this, Scarlet, but I honestly think you two are good together. You balance each other out, and I hope you remember that after the king is dead."

"I'll try to keep it in mind."

The slightest hint of a downturn appeared on Voss's lips as he looked over at me. He inhaled a long breath. "See that you do, because everything between us has been entirely and completely real."

"I still don't like this," Penn said with finality.

"Since when did I listen to what you wanted, Penn?"

"Never. But that doesn't mean I'll stop trying." He shrugged, biting off a large hunk of cheese and staring at me.

"For what it's worth, I do not intend to kill Voss. Yet."

Penn swallowed hard. "It's the *yet* that is terrifying."

Our table fell into easy conversation after that. We talked about the journey ahead, which would continue to be a flat and long ride with stretches of plains between here and there. I suspected we were headed into the port city, but I didn't want to suggest it and scare poor Penn even more, though I did like messing with Voss's friend. I ate and drank my fill, and then some, feeling a little light-headed from the glasses of wine. At some point, Voss had switched his glass for a stemmed glass and joined me in finishing the bottle. Once everything was gone, the four of us retired. I was a little unsteady on my feet, and Voss laid a hand on the small of my back, leading me up the staircases to our accommodations for the evening.

I shed my boots and clothes quickly, jumping into bed with nothing but a shirt on. As I stretched underneath the covers, I watched Voss. He was so neat and pristine, the way he did things. My pants, socks, and jacket were in a haphazard pile next to my boots. He folded his clothes neatly in a pile, placing them at the bench at the foot of the bed, with his boots lined up beneath. His dark eyes glowed for a second as he forced all of my things into a neat stack next to his.

I arched an eyebrow. "Nice trick."

"Which I wouldn't have to do if you weren't the messiest person I've ever met in my entire life."

"Voss, we fucked on a desk above a puddle of blood. Whatever gave you the impression I was an orderly person?"

"I'm fine with sex being messy, but these are clothes. There's a difference."

I snorted.

"I'm serious." The bed sank under his weight. He had taken everything off except his loose fitted shirt and pants. "Also, I sleep nude when I have the privacy."

"Of course you do." I didn't look away.

His irises swirled as he slowly unbuttoned his shirt and removed his pants. He was glorious. Everything about Voss screamed with crackling energy and fire. The angles of his abdomen heading toward his cock, the planes of his taut muscles, and his slightly broad shoulders. He lifted the covers and slipped under them with me, his heat hitting me first.

"We're sleeping tonight," he said as he watched me.

"Sure."

"I mean it."

"Sure. I mean it too."

Voss kept his gaze on me.

I moved my body close to his, drawn by the warmth of him and the surge of attraction I felt inside me. We didn't sleep for several more hours, and he made good on his promise to make me scream his name.

Eighteen

Hazy, diffused light of dawn covered the room when I awoke in the morning. My body was wrapped around Voss, legs draped over him with his thigh pressed against the most sensitive part of me. Slowly, I removed myself from him, feeling sore as I shifted. We had overdone it last night, but I couldn't seem to help myself when I was around him. What made it worse was how much I enjoyed the taste of his blood. None of the scratches I gave him left any marks, but the beads of blood had left a delicious aftertaste on my tongue. Staring at him now was as perfect as watching a morning sunrise.

As if sensing my gaze, Voss opened a single eye and met mine. The corner of his lips curled up in a lazy smile. "Good morning."

"You never told me what blood bonding does."

He went rigid. "Little late for that now."

"Is it?"

Voss blinked, rubbing his eyes. He propped himself up on the headboard and stared at me. "You drank my blood, and if I take any from you, we'll be bonded for quite some time."

"And what does that do?"

"Can I get a 'good morning' first?"

"Good morning. What does that do?"

He frowned and let out a breath. "For starters, it would make tracking you easier. Right now, I get a vague idea of where you are, but if I drank from you, it would be like a compass pointing toward you. I'd be able to find you anywhere, regardless of whether or not you were bleeding."

"That doesn't sound... horrible."

"And since you've had my blood, we'd start to sense each other. Feelings, emotions. They'd start to... mix. It can be quite frustrating if you don't like the person you are bonded to. There's more too, like lives being intertwined, but... it's hard to explain to someone who doesn't have magic."

"Is any of it permanent?"

Voss shook his head. "Lasts some time, depending on your system. A month usually. A lot of bonded mates share blood frequently to continue the bond."

"Would it work on me? Since I'm immune to magic, how do you know it would?"

"You're immune to manipulation, a blood bond is different."

"Would it help us kill the king?"

"It wouldn't hurt." Voss reached over and ran his thumb over the bracelet he gave me. "You shouldn't make the decision lightly, little fox. It's a commitment to me. It's a way to say you trust someone holy and purely with all aspects of your soul, because you begin to feed off each other mentally and emotionally. You should never accept blood from a Fae you don't trust."

"But you let me drink yours."

"The bond isn't complete unless I partake in yours, and

honestly, I enjoy thinking about how many pieces of myself are inside of you. I'm selfish like that."

I snorted. "Spoken like a true Fae."

A loud knock slammed on the door, and I jumped.

"Voss? Come quick. I can't find Penn." Elspeth's voice called up the stairs.

Voss glanced at me for a second before we were out of bed and throwing on our clothes. I was grateful he had spent the time to organize our outfits last night, because within moments we were scrambling down the stairs and opening the door for Elspeth with our packs in hand.

Her eyes were wide and red-rimmed, hair an unkempt mess and a flush across her cheeks. "Is Penn with you?"

"No. What happened?"

Elspeth's breathing was ragged. "I left him at the stables this morning. He wanted to get the horses ready early, so we'd be able to leave as soon as you were awake. I came back here to put together some food for us before the kitchen staff woke up. When I finished—" She shook her head. "He said he'd find you once he was done, but when I got back to the stables to pack up our food, the horses weren't ready and he was gone. I hoped he had come back to find you, but Switch had mud caked on her hooves, which was so unlike him." She took a staggering step back and glanced toward her door. "I asked a few people who were out, and no one remembers seeing him leave the barn."

Voss hissed.

Elspeth's eyes grew watery. "Are they here?"

"I'm hoping Penn saw them and went into hiding." The frown on Voss's face didn't convince anyone with his failed attempt at a lie. "I'll head to the barn and check it out. Do you still have his vial?"

Elspeth reached into her pocket and pulled out a small glass vial with blood red liquid inside.

"Good, I might need it."

She nodded with a sniff, brushing her hair behind her ears.

As Voss rushed toward the exit of the farmhouse, I asked, "What is that?"

"Penn's blood," Elspeth said as we followed behind Voss. His demeanor had changed, shifting to all business and no nonsense now that one of his own was missing.

"You think it's the assassins?" I asked her.

"Of course I do."

"And Voss will be able to track Penn with that?"

Elspeth nodded. "If we gave Voss our blood all the time, he'd be able to find us at any point, but we don't want to risk accidentally bonding. It's... uncomfortable."

"He told me about it."

"Really? How did that come up?" She slid me a glance.

"I've kind of... licked his blood. Multiple times."

She stared at me with a dead expression in her eyes. "You know what, I'll unpack that entire sentence once we find Penn." Elspeth's eyes dropped to the bracelet around my wrist. "And that."

"It's pretty, but I told him he didn't have to."

"And you think a Fae will listen to you when you tell them no?"

"Good point."

When we arrived at the stables, Voss gestured for us to stay back. My fingers instinctively wrapped around my sparrowbone dagger. If the assassins were here, I could help Voss. They wouldn't be able to use their abilities on me, but Elspeth grasped my shoulder and shook her head. "They aren't here. Give him a minute to do his thing."

I swallowed, waiting on shifting feet.

A few moments later, Voss exited the shadows of the stables. His brow creased and anger pulsed off his veins. "They were here."

"You're sure?"

"The assassins?" I asked at the same time.

"I'm not sure why they would bother taking Penn, especially since an ambush on the road would have served them better at this point."

"Because Penn is the weakest of us, and they know it." Elspeth stamped her foot. "I shouldn't have left him behind."

"It's not your fault. If I hadn't been—" Voss's gaze swept over me. The word *distracted* went unsaid. He didn't have to say it. Guilt floated off him in thick waves. "It doesn't matter. Give me the blood."

Elspeth handed over the vial. Voss uncorked it and took the entire contents down in one swallow. A small amount of red lingered on his lips.

"Stay with her at the inn." Voss's eyes ignited with a deep, pooling amber.

"I'm not staying behind," I said. "I can help. They can't use me against you, and I can fight."

"Not against two assassins." The fire in his eyes landed on me. "Elspeth, make sure she stays at the inn."

"You know as well as I do I cannot make her stay, Voss. So let's be smart. Why don't we use her to our advantage? What if she acts like a prisoner?" Elspeth pulled on my arm.

"What?" His eyes flared bright. While he seemed to like this idea with the king, his eyes narrowed with disgust at the idea of using me as assassin bait.

"If she's our prisoner that we're taking back to the king, why would Morna and Cumina need her? Especially if the king's orders have changed?"

There was something about the way her voice dropped at the mention of the king's orders. I narrowed my eyes at them. It was the first sensation I had since starting this journey that I wasn't getting the entire picture.

"They would never believe the king would want the Fae Slayer alive."

"A public execution might make them believe. I have rope in my saddlebag." Elspeth gave me a sympathetic look. "It won't be pleasant, but it's better than losing Penn, right?"

"I can't fight with my hands tied behind my back."

"Then we tie them in front on a leash. But you have to look like you lost." Elspeth frowned at me. "No, more pissed off and morose. Pretend Voss did something incredibly stupid, like... let you sleep with Treborne."

Voss growled.

I looked at him, annoyed. "That *had* been the plan."

"Yes, that's perfect!" Elspeth rushed into the stables and came out with a thick rope. I offered my wrists with a heavy sigh. With quick efficiency, she had my wrists bound in front of me within moments. "Let's go rescue Penn!"

Voss watched with hungry eyes.

"Don't get any stupid ideas, Voss," I snarled.

A smirk appeared on his lips as he took the lead of the rope. I glowered at him, feeling more like a pet than ever before, but Voss barely registered my expression. He pressed his eyes shut and after a few moments of concentrating, he took off toward the outskirts of town, outside of the wall that kept the wilds at bay. His nostrils flared as he took a sharp left onto a smaller offshoot, a worn dirt path that led along a dried creek bed.

"This feels far, Voss."

"Have I ever steered you wrong, Elspeth?" His eyes swirled liquidized amber as he glanced back at us.

She shook her head in response.

It felt like hours, but the sun had only risen slightly higher from the horizon. We rounded another dried out bend in the creek. A disheveled cabin stood in a cropping of gnarled trees. The roof was missing numerous shingles that had been blown off, and a gaping hole appeared blasted out from the top, likely where the chimney had collapsed.

Morna waited with her arms crossed, leaning against the thick wooden door that hung lopsidedly on the hinges. "The boy's inside. What's left of him, anyway." She had a dagger in her hands, and she ran a calloused finger over the sharpened part of the blade. Her eyes flashed bright gold, opposite of her sister's silver ones.

"I swear to—"

"Relax, I only meant mentally." Morna tossed Voss a sickening smile. "Cumina trapped him in his own worst nightmare. He'll be fine physically, but—" She shrugged, pointing to her temple with her knife. "You have something that I want." Her eyes landed on me, looking feral and predatory.

"You mean this?" He tugged on the rope, forcing me to take a staggering step forward. "I believe I've already gotten it. You were too little, too late. As usual, Morna."

She sniffed. "I'm not interested in this conversation. Cumina has the girl dead to rights with her bow. You hand her over or she dies, and then Penn dies."

"It's of no consequence to me."

My frown darkened.

Voss straightened. "But it might matter to the king who called for her public execution."

Morna's eyebrow arched before she let out a haunting laugh, all rough pops in the air. "You want me to believe you're still working for him? You think I'm stupid enough to fall for the oldest trick in the book? No, *assassin*. I won't play this game with you, because I have a plan to get both me and my sister back in the king's good graces." Her eyes roamed over the three of us. "Because as I expected, you had no idea the king *has* changed his plans. He called for an execution, publicly. And while I would love to kill her right now, if I do, it puts all of us in danger."

"The easiest thing to do is to walk away, Morna. Let me take her in and release Penn immediately."

"You see, I'd love to consider your terrible offer, but the king has also called for the execution of anyone who has been aiding her." Morna toyed with the dagger, twisting the tip against her finger. It didn't so much as make a mark against her skin. "I do like you, and I would rather not have to kill you to bring the human back, but considering she looks well taken care of, I'd say you had other plans for her."

"She's a means to an end," Voss said, keeping his voice stiff. He pulled on the rope again, and I forced myself to stumble forward. "*I* need to bring her in, not you. It needs to happen this way, otherwise there will be consequences."

"For you, maybe. But I am not one of your lackeys who will follow you to the ends of the earth."

"Screw—"

Voss held up his hand, stopping Elspeth's insult.

"And besides, since this is the only way I have to get back on the king's good side and not turn you into the dear old man, I have a backup plan if you don't comply." Morna took a step away from the door, twisted the knob, and forced the heavy wood inward.

On the other side of the door in the ransacked, rotted out cabin interior, two people were bound to equally rotten chairs. Their eyes were glassy and blank stares went into oblivion. One was Penn, but the other—

"No." I stepped forward, fear snaking through me and making me forget my place.

With a snarl, Voss shoved me back.

"This is an easy trade. We get the girl, or we kill both of them." Morna shrugged, a cruel smile spreading across her face. "I'll give you two minutes to decide. And don't worry, Cumina can kill them by simply erasing their minds if you do anything stupid. I'll give you some privacy." She disappeared as if she were mist.

"Who is the girl?" Elspeth asked.

"Marcy," I whispered. My voice was dry ice in my throat.

Voss's eyes spun as he turned toward the two of us. "We're glamored. I'm making it seem like Elspeth is arguing with me right now. We need a plan and fast."

"I go with them," I said. There was no time to come up with something better.

"That's not a plan, but a surrender."

"If we blood bond right now, you could find me with it, right?"

Elspeth sucked in a breath.

Voss grimaced. "You still don't understand how serious a blood bond is. Being separated from you afterward will be like madness."

"Do you see another way? You tracked Penn with his blood, so you can track me, too. I trust you, Voss." I could barely believe the words escaping my lips, but I did trust him. And if this was the only way to ensure the other two were safe, I'd have to do it.

"It's a lot to ask of two people not in love." His irises swirled as he watched me.

"She's right, though." Elspeth's voice was soft and gentle. "While I agree, it's a lot to ask, perhaps too much, you would find her. We could ambush them in a day or two, or wait until they get to the king's court and find the right moment to free her. With you and Penn working together, you could hide us from the entire court, let alone sneak up on the assassins."

Voss swallowed. "And you'd allow this, knowing it's going to join us together emotionally? Knowing there's more I didn't explain to you? A blood bond with a blood hunter is not without difficulties."

"If it will save Penn and Marcy, yes. I'd—" I swallowed. "I loved her once. Maybe I always will in my own way, and she doesn't deserve to die like this. I couldn't live with myself if I let her die."

Pinching the bridge of his nose, Voss turned to Elspeth. "I don't like this idea. What if I can't sense her as well because of her magic nullification?"

"You've said it before, Voss. A blood bond is bigger than magic. And there's only one way to find out, and we're almost out of time."

"Kiss me, little fox. It might be the last time for a while. And put your tongue into it."

"At a time like this? Really?"

He clasped the back of my head and drew him into me. His tongue parted my lips as he thrust inside me. I met him in kind, pushing my tongue in between his teeth. He bit down, hard. Blood filled my mouth, and he swallowed against my lips. A growl rose inside him as he sucked on my swollen tongue, but I dug my nails into my ropes, wishing I could drag him into me.

Voss pulled back, leaving me breathless. "It is done." His irises swirled. "And it worked. Don't talk while you're still bleeding, little fox, or they'll know we did something. Elspeth, start yelling at me about how I am too headstrong for my own good."

"Gladly," Elspeth said.

The swirling in Voss's eyes disappeared as quickly as it had come. As soon as it did, I was hit with an essence of him. *Fear, worry, and a melancholy about what will happen next.* It was strange, like having a shadow inside my head. None of it made sense, but it was there, lingering in my peripheral vision. It felt more intense than having him inside me, than feeling him take me sexually.

And now I understood why he didn't want this for us without there being something more. I could feel him, sense him. Having him inside my mind was invasive and personal.

As Morna reappeared, I forced myself to straighten, putting on a blank face as Elspeth breathed in sharply.

Elspeth acted like she hadn't skipped a beat. "And your nature is going to get us all killed someday. So I say we hand over the girl. It's an easy trade for Penn's life, or does he mean nothing to you anymore?!"

The female Fae cocked an eyebrow at us, but there was nothing in her body language to indicate that our ruse hadn't worked. At least, I prayed this had been a ruse *with* Voss and not a ruse against me. I failed to see the point in creating such an elaborate plan in the first place, because Voss had me dead to rights that first night.

"So, what will it be?" Morna said, yawning. Her dark skin shone in the sun, lighter freckles dancing across her nose.

"I'll make a deal."

Morna's brows came down over his eyes, and a smirk ticked up her lips. "What are your terms?"

"You hand over Penn and Marcy physically, emotionally, and mentally well—"

Morna scowled at that last part.

"—and I will give you her." The mental shadow of Voss danced around my head, jumping from emotion to emotion with such rapid fire, it made me dizzy.

Morna's eyes lit up. "And you promise not to retrieve Scarlet before the execution or do anything to interfere with the execution of Scarlet the Fae Slayer."

Voss glanced at me, and my spine went rigid. We hadn't talked about him making a deal with her, and this one felt fairly solid. If he made it, I would be doomed to arrive at the execution. His tongue ran over his teeth inside his mouth, and he swallowed. "Deal."

My jaw slackened, but Elspeth was fast on her feet, snapping my mouth shut before I could get out a word. She gave me a wide-eyed expression, and I knew she hadn't been expecting Voss to take the deal either. If he didn't retrieve me or interfere with the execution, I was as good as dead. *What was he thinking?*

Except I felt his thoughts. He was whirling thunder and constant movement. There would be a way out of this, at least, he believed there would be.

I wanted to ask Voss, wanted to know what was coming next, but Elspeth's quick hand had been right. If I spoke now, the blood on my tongue would make Morna suspicious. The Fae had given me a pleading look, and I had to believe there was something in the deal I wasn't seeing. I had to trust Voss, despite his whirling emotions of worry and fear.

I felt woozy.

Morna's eyes went from shining gold back to a dull brown with the deal officially sealed. "Excellent. Cumina, come out and rescue these pawns from their pits of despair. I am going to find us two more steeds."

Cumina scuttled down from the nearby tree she was hiding in. Her skin glowed deeply under the late morning sun. "Did you know this one's biggest fear is snakes? We don't even have those in Faerie. He's pathetic, and if I were you, I would have kept the girl instead of getting him back." She waved her hand in front of Penn's eyes, and he lurched forward out of the chair, as if waking from a long dream.

His eyes didn't look pained or full of horror, so I had to wonder if they had been telling the truth. Had they really been trapped, or was it a show to manipulate us into doing what they wanted? If so, we had played right into their hands.

"And this one is curious." She ran a long fingernail along Marcy's skin and licked her lips. "Her biggest fear is about to come true in real life right now. So while I will relinquish my hold on her, I am not responsible for the outcry that happens next." With another wave of her hand, Marcy was free, and her frantic eyes met mine as if we were magnets.

"No!" She stood up from the chair and ran to me, hitting me hard in the chest. "Scarlet, I'm sorry. I was a fool. I thought I could help you, but..." She glanced around at the sheer amount of Fae around us. "What are they going to do to you?"

"A public execution," Voss said, back straight and voice hollow. His thoughts were a dark collision in my mind. "It's only a few days' ride to the king's court. We'll see you there, *Scarlet*."

I swallowed, trying to make sense of what was happening. Had he sold me out intentionally?

Names. Deals. Names. Names. Names. His thoughts whirled, and I tried to push them out of my head. They were impressions at best, and threatened to take over my mind.

"Come, Marcy, we'll get you home." Elspeth put a hand on her shoulder.

"No!" Marcy screamed, shoving them off. She wrenched out a sparrowbone dagger. "I might not be able to hurt any of you, but... I will try."

Cumina snorted. "Such charming words from a little human."

Penn blinked a few times. "What did you do, Voss?"

"What I had to. That's what I'll always do. Follow the king and do what I need to. Let's go. And bring the human girl. I have no use for her, but we might as well get her back to safety."

"Look at you going soft," Cumina taunted, toying with the string on her bow. "Never thought I'd see the day where the wicked—"

Voss was in front of her before I could blink. "I might have promised to give you the girl, but nowhere did I promise not to kill you. Watch your words, Cumina."

She narrowed her eyes at him. "Whatever. My sister and I have everything now. I don't need anything more from you." Slinking around him, she gathered the tether to my wrists. "Remove the leech from her side."

"Scarlet, I'm sorry. Say something."

I shook my head, instead kissing her cheek as gently as I could. Tears sprang to Marcy's eyes.

"Let go, Marcy," Elspeth cooed. Her eyes swirled to life, a rich golden green. Marcy relaxed under her words, and Elspeth extracted Marcy from me.

I lurched forward as Cumina pulled on the leash again. The four others turned away, leaving me with the wicked, gloating smile from Cumina. I watched them retreat, wishing I could tell Marcy it'd be okay. I'd find a way out of this.

Voss tossed a final look over his shoulders, eyes swirling. And he winked.

I scowled at him, wondering if he was coming back, but no. They kept walking, Elspeth putting a firm hand on Marcy's back to get her to move away from us.

I breathed out of my nose, trying to piece together what had happened and what Voss's meaning was. He could follow me now, but if he couldn't interfere, then… What did he have planned?

An apology rose in the darkest corner of my mind, a shadow of the male who left me behind.

I hoped he knew a loophole I was not yet seeing. My life was in the hands of a Fae I barely trusted. The pain in my tongue disappeared as I realized how incredibly useless I was now.

Nineteen

Less than an hour later, Morna had procured two stallions. "The guy tried to sell me another one, but I told him we planned to make that one walk." She took a step toward me, her black skin glistening under the late afternoon sun. The horses snuffled behind her. "You can walk, right?"

I shrugged.

"Talking doesn't seem to be her strong suit," Cumina answered. "I haven't been this bored since we tracked down Lord Mistish. Do you ever wonder what happened to that partner of his?"

"No, I'm not a psychopath."

"I hardly think wondering makes me... You know what? I am not prepared for this. Not in front of her. It's creeping me out. Look at the way she just... stares."

"I liked it better when she looked shocked after he sold her to us so easily." Morna leaned forward, coiling a lock of my black hair around her finger. "I have heard many interesting stories about you, but I never thought your hair would be so dark."

"Almost like mine."

"This is like the night. And her eyes…" Morna frowned. "I wonder about you too, about how you seduce the Fae into doing what you want simply by saying words they wish to hear. So tell me, seductress, what do I want to hear more than anything?"

I kept my mouth shut.

"Isn't that how you got him to work with you? Distracted him like the Fae siren you are?" Morna sighed and pulled away from me. "It's no matter. We rescued him from her, and the king should be pleased. I did, however, expect her to have more teeth. So many dead at the hands of this." The gesture at me was shaped with apathy.

As much as I wanted to hurt them right now, my position was precarious. If I opened my mouth, fresh blood would be on my tongue. If Voss got caught with his plan this early on, maybe they would try harder to hide me from him. So instead, I held onto hope that Voss was coming back, but if an opportunity to escape presented itself, I would take it. If Voss didn't rescue me, I would find a way out of this.

Though, with my hands tied and my only weapon a sparrowbone knife in my boot, I had never felt more alone. Save for the night I woke up with the fire pauldrin nearby, but that was only for a second because Voss hadn't left then.

He was gone now. They all were.

The rope dug into my wrists as Cumina hitched me to the saddle of her horse. "I hope you enjoy running, Fae Slayer, because we're going hard."

Morna rolled her eyes. "We can't kill her before the king gets a hold of her. We're going steady, but step lively, because we're not stopping if you stumble, and that'd be a hell of a way to go."

If I bled, it'd be easier for other assassins to find me, easier for

Voss to find me. Maybe that was a better solution, to cause more chaos in the ranks of assassins. Voss had promised the assassins he wouldn't rescue me, but someone else still could. Elspeth or Penn had not made a promise. Maybe that would be the angle.

I wondered if there was another assassin out there who didn't want me dead. It was probably a one in a million chance I would stumble upon someone like Voss again.

Most Fae didn't want to go against the king, but Voss… Voss seemed like he would go against the king simply because he wanted better for the Fae and humans. He knew Alpin's court could exist elsewhere in the world. Now that he was gone, I ached to know more about him. Putting my faith in someone I barely knew anything about felt horrific.

If I didn't find a way out myself and Voss rescued me, then I'd be forced to trust him. I already believed he would take me to the king. I wanted to trust him, truly I did, but breaking a lifelong promise to myself was hard. If Voss came for me, then there would be no more excuses left. There would be no more reason to second guess his motives.

Please, Voss. I told him in my head. *Please find me.*

The dark corner of my mind seemed to stir around me, engulfing my thoughts with his own. *Patience, little fox.*

I wanted to kick him, and I swore I could hear his laughter in between my ears.

Cumina mounted her horse and started us off down the path. I trailed behind, clambering over broken pieces of rubble as the horse's hooves expertly navigated through the debris. The sun was high in the sky without enough time to ride to the king's court, and here Cumina was leading us away from the safety of the town and into the wilds.

I knew little about these assassins, but they seemed willing to do anything for the king, even if it was at their expense. Maybe I could exploit that down the road, or maybe they were so eager to please the king that no plan of mine could deter them. I hoped it was the former, because my life was in their hands.

ﻬ ✂ ﻬ

We continued on for several hours after sunset, neither of the assassins using Faerie lights. I honestly wasn't sure why. It made traveling on horseback with Voss, Elspeth, and Penn feel like a dream in comparison. My feet throbbed for a respite, and I finally got one after the sky descended into near inky blackness. I had tripped over so many rocks and stones from my inability to see, and that was what made them finally pause with a heavy sigh.

Once Morna and Cumina swung off their horses, Morna barked orders at me. Over the next hour, enshrouded in darkness, I prepared the soggy camp for the night and attempted to start a fire. I had never started a fire out of nothing, and dewy moisture coated everything, my boots included. The chill in the air ran under my skin, seeping its way toward my bones. My teeth clacked together, and I was more than miserable, still bound by my wrists. Everything in me hurt, but I couldn't fight back against them without using my words.

I cursed inside my head, because while Voss's plan might save me in the long run, he had ruined the one advantage I had over the Fae: my voice.

"Maybe you'd move faster if we threatened your little friend again." Morna growled from the corner of the camp. I could barely see their outlines; let alone what I was doing with my hands.

I swallowed back every challenge I wanted to say.

Morna and Cumina didn't scare me, but I knew with only the sparrowbone knife and my hands tied, I was no match for the two of them. They were assassins, but I had a secret weapon I could use once my tongue had healed a bit. I could make them both whimper at my words with a few licks of my voice.

My tongue still felt numb, and I knew they'd be able to smell the wound if I spoke too soon. I didn't understand much about the blood bond connection Voss and I had, but I felt the rumblings of his presence, the way it was steady and sure. I couldn't ruin the potential for a surprise attack.

Literally biting my tongue had never been so hard.

Cumina groaned. "Didn't they teach you humans how to do anything?" With a few waves of her hands in the dark, the tent I had been attempting to set up went upright. Then a fire burst to life out of the soggy wood and cast a glow around us. The warmth flooded against my skin, and I breathed a sigh of relief.

"We should have made her suffer longer." The scowl on Morna's face deepened. I was beginning to think she always looked that way.

"I was tiring of watching the sheer helplessness of it. Besides, we need the fire to keep the hoswisps away. I haven't heard them yet, but you know as well as I do they are out there."

"Whatever. At least now we can eat something." Morna let out a bored yawn, and I realized she did this a lot, like everything in her life was a chore and she wanted no part of it. Yet, here she was acting on behalf of a king for free or, I supposed, for the glory of bringing me in.

I wondered what would happen when they presented me to the king. What was in it for them? There had to be more than the promise of notoriety. The Fae wanted more from their lives, but in this world, they could have whatever they wanted. By all accounts, every single Fae, no matter how weak, was notorious. Humans would do anything the Fae asked of them.

Why bother with the king when they could live like royalty themselves?

From the little I knew of Fae politics, which admittedly wasn't much, there would be no ascension for them. They were assassins, and they would stay assassins unless they carved out their own courts. They wouldn't become Lords or Ladies by delivering me onto him. So what was in it for them, other than a weak male's praise? Because at the end of the day, the king *was* weak. He demanded everyone to do his bidding, but never stepped foot outside of his court.

If he wanted me dead, he should have the balls to do it himself in a fight to the death. Face the Fae Slayer one on one and see if he caves to my charms like all the rest. Of course, he would, because they all did. Once my tongue healed enough for me to have my way with these two, I would. Morna and Cumina were dead Fae walking, and it was only a matter of time.

With deftness, Morna threw a bunch of dried vegetables and meat into a pot. She poured water from a skin over the mess and placed the heavy steel near the fire. They both waited, watching it in an eerie silence.

None of the bleating purrs of the hoswisps met my ears, so I hoped my bones wouldn't be stripped clean tonight.

I awkwardly sat down near the edge of the fire and wondered what had changed. Voss had seemed genuinely surprised when these two mentioned the public execution from the king. Between the time that he had been assigned to track me down and these other two had found me at Raskos's, something had shifted.

Question was: how did they know these updates when Voss didn't? What leg up did they have on Voss that I wasn't understanding?

It took another thirty minutes for the stew to heat, and fifteen minutes after that for the two of them to gobble down most of the food, minus the remains at the bottom. Cumina offered the dregs to me, but I shook my head, refusing to open my mouth despite my stomach grumbling.

"Suit yourself, stupid human." She ate the rest of it in a few more bites.

"Not like she'll starve along the way." They shot idle banter back and forth, mostly at my expense.

As I stared into the flames, I started plotting. Tonight, I would attempt to free my hands. Tonight, I would get my knife out of my boot and saw my way to freedom. Then, I'd bring the sparrowbone down onto one of their throats. Morna first, I decided. Once one of them was dead, I'd deal with the other one and ride off on horseback quick enough. I might risk bringing the wilds down on me, but if I rode the horse fast enough, maybe I could make it out of here alive.

I had things I needed to do, like kill the king and tell Marcy this wasn't her fault. It was inevitable either way. The Fae would have traded my life for Penn's in an instant. I saw it in the way Elspeth and Voss stood, a moment of vulnerability from both of them. They depended on each other, needed each other. As much as Voss said he needed me, the bond to his friends was more like family. Elspeth and Penn might have been working under Voss, but he cared about them just the same.

I missed my group, having people who would lay their lives down for me. I felt homesick for the first time.

Inhaling slowly, I also realized I needed to know why Marcy had deviated from the plan. What had possessed her to stray from the path and put herself in danger? We had discussed this. My life was important, but not nearly as much as Quinn's connections. Once I killed the king, it was up to the revolutionaries to take over.

That had always been the plan. I was the assassin, the martyr, the fuse, but I was never supposed to be the leader for the rest of our lives.

I was invaluable only until the king met his demise.

"Come on, Fae Slayer." Morna stood up, dusted off her pants, and snatched the end of my tether. She didn't give me time to scramble upward, so I was half-dragged over to a nearby tree. With quick movements, she tied me against the trunk. I barely had a few feet to move, and it would be harder to get out of this, but not impossible.

"Go to sleep, Fae Slayer. We have a long day ahead of us." Morna's eyes flared with color, and I knew she tried to use magic on me. Her face pinched in a scowl as the magic left her eyes. Morna glared at me, shrugging it off like it didn't bother her. "I could always hit you across your head instead. Cumina, take first watch. I'll take over in a few hours."

As the two assassins bickered over their own tiredness and settled down on bedrolls, I tried to twist into a more comfortable position. Pressing my eyes shut, I evened out my breathing to appear like I was asleep. I listened to their conversation with fervor, hoping to glean information. It took about thirty minutes for them to discuss my sluggish pace.

"With her dragging us like that, it will take ten hours to get to court."

And finally, it gave me an idea of where we were. Ten hours after sunrise, I would either figure out how to kill the king or be trapped in a dungeon. The port city I was thinking of was closer than a ten hour on foot journey, so the king's court had to be somewhere beyond the port city. If I escaped these two, I would go to the port and figure out the rest from there. At least now I had a destination in mind.

My feet throbbed with the idea of walking for ten hours tomorrow, but being this close also ignited me. If I could get away, maybe I could kill the king by myself. Maybe I wouldn't need Voss, but why did that idea leave an empty feeling in my stomach?

I swallowed my emotions. If I followed the road past the port city, I could hope that the next court I came across was the king's court—if no one in the port city gave me any ideas on where to go next.

I fought off the weight of sleep, and eventually, Cumina's eyes drifted shut. Morna was still asleep herself, with her sister not having woken her for her watch. The fire had burned down next to nothing, and if the hoswisps came toward us, these two would be the least of my problems. I had to get out now.

Pulling on the tether, I flexed away from the tree as far as possible, which ended up only being a foot or so. Folding my legs toward my hands took effort. Inch by agonizing inch, I pulled the knife out of my boot. By the time I was done, I was sweating, but at least I had my sparrowbone. I twisted it around and ran the blade back and forth against the knot between my wrists.

In the dark of night, I had no way of knowing how much time had passed, save for my tracking the dim waning moon. It might have been hours, but I was sore and ached all over. Sleep threatened to overtake me until a growl sounded in the dark.

Cursing, I shoved the knife back into my boot and tried to pretend I had been asleep while Morna bolted upright.

"Cumina," she hissed. The other Fae slept like a rock. "Good help is so hard to find these days." I could practically hear her eyes roll as a bunch of Faerie lights appeared throughout the clearing and a fire burst to life in the middle of our camp.

The growling grew closer.

Morna cursed and grabbed a spear from the ground. "Cumina!

Up!" Smoke curled from the cuff of the sleeping Fae's pants.

"What?!" Cumina yelped as she jumped up from the ground. The Fae whirled around, barely able to snatch her bow from the ground in her panicked state.

I swore in my head. Personally, I would never let my guard down like this. It had been too easy for something to sneak up on us—on them—and I was certain if the other assassins were around, I would have been as good as dead. I had to find a way out of their clutches and fast, because staying with these two was a surefire way to get me killed before we reached the king's court.

Whatever the beast was, the ground shook underneath the thunderous paws, and even with the Faerie lights, the animal was enshrouded in darkness.

"It's a freaking caltula," Morna hissed.

Cumina cursed as she shot a few arrows into the dark. The arrows ignited the moment they left her bow, creating steaks of light in the night. Nothing moved. Not a single thing shown out of the endless blackness. It was like the creature had disappeared.

I tried to think about what the caltulas were, but nothing came to mind. Hoswisps were the biggest problem, next to the fire pauldrins. Other wild creatures lived out here, but usually stayed clear of humans and Fae alike. I had never heard of a caltula, but from the way both of their voices dipped, I didn't imagine anything good.

Twisting my boots up again, my fingers shook with an ache to be set free. I debated telling the two of them I could help, but worried about my tongue. It felt a little better, but I had no idea how good their senses were. If Voss could track me from a small cut on my face, there was no telling what these two could do. Still, being tied here made me feel like a target. If this creature turned on me, how long would I have to get away?

"Do you hear it?"

"Shut up," Morna hissed. Her ears pricked, trying to listen to the sounds in the dark. I was right there with her, straining to hear any movement.

Something slammed against the ground, creating a shock wave that rolled through the dirt like an earthquake. My ears rang as Cumina staggered on her feet, taking aim and shooting again into the dark. This time, the fire arrow slid by a beast as black as night. It was nothing but shadow, but as big as a house. It seemed to be a ghost, barely coming into focus before the fire arrow sputtered out.

The Faerie lights flickered out one after another.

"Morna!"

"On it." She threw out more lights, but as soon as she cast them, they winked out of existence, plunging us into nothing. In the moment of light, I saw a velvety purple around the creature's black gaping maw.

Screw this. If I got caught with the sparrowbone knife, it was better than being reduced to nothing by the rumbling beast in front of us. I pulled out the weapon and kept sawing at the bindings.

Cumina shot off several more arrows, and the fire flickered out on those as quickly as it had come. She cursed and threw one of her daggers into the dark. A bucking roar slammed over us, making the earth tremble in its wake. "Got something on it."

"Not enough." Morna gripped her spear tighter, casting out more lights. Sweat broke across her brow.

I continued to attack the rope.

The beast took another step or two forward, and with each footfall, the earth threatened to split open and swallow us whole. The enormous size made me shiver against the tether. Stupid Fae tying me up like I was nothing. I could be an asset right now. We could be running. But no, I was tied to a stupid tree. A few threads on the ropes were frayed through, but I still had so much more to go and I was about to curse the heavens. Wretched Fae and their strong ropes.

The dark part inside my head grew with an ebbing sense of violence, and I felt like Voss was here with me.

"I have about twenty more arrows and a handful of throwing knives. After that, it's hand to hand combat."

"With a caltula," Morna huffed. "Not a bad way to spend the night."

As another thread popped apart under the pressure of the knife, relief spread through me. At least I would be free to fight this beast soon. Instead of fighting against it, I turned toward the darkness in my mind, the presence of Voss. *What is a caltula?* There was no immediate response, so I tried a different tactic, thinking the same word over and over again.

Until I got a sickening wave of panic, *Run, little fox.* I almost vomited from the sincere terror that lanced through my brain. It was from him, and if Voss was worried about a caltula, I needed to get out of here and fast. Morna and Cumina were not as competent as I wished.

Another few threads came loose.

Cumina shot off more arrows. One sizzled as it struck absolute darkness. The roar that came next was deafening, and the creature wasted no more time. All of the Fae lights blinked out again, and my vision was slammed into absolute black. I forced my rapid heart to focus on the knife, the movement, even without seeing.

Morna wailed, and I couldn't tell if it was a battle cry or her getting injured. Cumina's arrows shot through the night, giving glimpses of the scene in front. Morna rushed to one side. The beast prowled toward Cumina. Morna jumped onto its shoulder, if the shifting inky black could be considered a shoulder. Cumina tumbled to one side as a giant paw came down. And another round of black nothing took away my vision.

"Cumina!" Morna yelled.

The sound of my beating heart threatening to overpower everything else. I needed to break free, get out of these bindings, and find safety, but where? I didn't hear the horses anymore and wondered if they had taken off in the middle of the night without us.

"Die, you bastard." Morna grunted, and the sound of air escaping her lungs after a thud on the ground was the most eerie sound. It sounded like the beast had killed her.

I swallowed. Once it was done with them, what would happen to me?

After more precious moments, the knots on my wrist loosened, and I yanked back. The ropes tore at my skin, and I could feel the moment my blood hit the air, mostly because the beast with all its focus, turned toward me. I was in the dark, but I felt the giant eyes land on me. It was night. It was blackness. It was an abyss, nothingness, and it would have been so easy to step forward and let it consume me.

Something in the air shifted. Inside my head, I swore I heard something ancient, something wicked and ethereal, something unearthly. *The moon.*

Morna let out a gut-wrenching howl. A wet squelching sounded as something connected in the dark, followed by heavy feet. The ground shuttered, rumbled, and shook. I backed up, trying to get my footing, but was knocked back when the beast fell onto the ground, shaking the earth around me with a sickening wave.

Lights flew up everywhere after that, blinding and brilliant around the clearing. My bloodied ropes were near the tree. Cumina laid with a cut across her chest but she was still breathing, and

Morna… Morna was covered in a thick viscous blackened liquid, her eyes on fire and breathing hard. Her golden eyes caught sight of me.

"If you run right now, so help the Mother, I will not wait for the king to get his hands on you." She turned to her sister, ignoring me, thinking her threat had been enough.

I glanced around the clearing, figuring now was possibly the only time for leverage. I hoped my tongue was healed enough, because I needed it for this next trick.

Twenty

I took a few steps toward the sisters. "It's cowardly of the king to make you risk your lives while he sits high in his court without ever getting his hands dirty."

Morna ran her fingers along her sister's open chest. Cumina's eyes fluttered, but she didn't stir. "What would you know about it, human?" Morna's voice turned to ice.

"I know you're at the mercy of a dictatorship. I know you have little to no control over how your lives turn out or what you become. Why work for a king like that, anyway?" I took another step forward, holding out my hands as Morna tossed me a look of bitter contempt.

"You talk like you know us, but you know nothing." Her gaze turned back to Cumina, whose chest was rising and falling shallowly. "And what would we do instead? Work for one of the narcissistic princes? There are shades of darkness in every world, and the Fae have their own. There were worse rulers before this king, and there will be worse rulers after."

"Why a king, though? Why not a queen?"

Morna snorted. "I would love to see that, but that's not the way we work."

"And why not?"

"The power of the Fae has always been with the king. What the king decides is what happens to our society. A female ruler would not hold as much power or influence, for only the king can change the world." Morna's eyes whirled, and her hand brightened as she placed it on top of Cumina's shredded skin. "Some Fae have theories about you, Fae Slayer. It is believed that the king will break you, as he holds more power than all of us. He can manipulate Fae and humans alike. He controls us, not the other way around. If we want any semblance of freedom in our world, I have to voluntarily do what he asks. The ones who don't, well, they are the ones with little tomorrows."

"Doesn't sound like freedom to me."

"That's because you've never known true captivity."

This conversation was not going well. "If no one else has magical influence over me, why would he?"

"Because he's more powerful than all of us. By the time he's done with you, you'll be begging to drag your own dagger across your throat."

Cumina coughed and sat up, almost knocking her face into her sister's forehead. "Fuck. That hurt."

"We'll test the theory at court tomorrow." Morna flashed me a grin. "Your chance to run is over."

"Let's be honest, Morna, there was never a chance to run." I shrugged. "But think about it. This might be your only chance to overthrow the king. Wouldn't it be better not to work for him? Maybe take a chance on someone else?"

"You can't make any deals with me, Fae Slayer. I am not stupid, so don't bother trying."

"Suit yourself, but I think there might be more than one way to get into the king's good graces."

"Oh, yeah? What would that be?" Cumina wheezed out a breath, glaring at me. "I liked it better when she was mute."

"I could make him a deal."

"You can't make deals, as I've already said." Morna sat back with a sigh, staring up at me with squinted eyes. Her head cocked to the side.

"You want to tell the king about my influence over Voss, right?"

Her eyes narrowed farther.

I didn't give her a chance to respond, plowing ahead. "Well, give me a chance. Let me show the king how I do it. What do you have to lose?"

Cumina sneered. "Your influence won't work on him. Now shut up and go to sleep."

"Or make yourself useful and find some herbs to help with this."

"Make me," I said, giving Morna a challenge.

Her eyes widened. "Oh, so that's how it is?" The irises glowed with electricity. "You wrap them around your finger with simple words?" The sneer on the corner of her lips widened, but she made no move to approach me, not like other Fae did.

"You won't get very far with her." Cumina moaned as she rubbed at the newly formed skin on her chest. She glanced around the clearing toward the large shadow. "I thought those had gone extinct."

"Same."

"What do you mean, it won't work on Morna?" I asked.

"Morna is… oh, what do you call it here?" Cumina frowned for a moment. "She doesn't have sex."

"But I *am* still annoyed that she won't listen to me." The other Fae scowled, eyes swirling with bright golden fire. "Sit."

I shrugged.

"*Sit.*"

"It won't work."

Morna growled. "I could force you through other means."

I rolled my eyes and sat down. "Happy?"

"No, not in the slightest." She let out a long breath that sounded similar to a sigh of relief, though.

"What about you?" I looked at Cumina.

"My sister would kill you, while I would be helpless. If you want to make it to the king alive, I suggest you don't try anything with me."

"So you're open to my idea?"

"I never said that."

Morna folded her arms across her chest, eyes roaming over me. They landed on the bracelet on my wrist. Her lips drew taut. "We may have a problem." She sent a glance to Cumina.

"Other than the constant ache in my chest?"

"You'll heal fine, but what does that look like to you?" Morna gestured to my wrist.

"Rope burns? Does it hurt?" She dipped her voice with mock concern.

"No, the other thing."

Cumina ceased rubbing her chest and let out a sigh. She waved her hand, making one of the Faerie lights drift toward me. The glow poured over my body. Her whirling silver irises narrowed as she stared at the bracelet. I rotated my wrist over, feeling a little self-conscious under their gazes. I may be free, but I was no fool. These two took down a beast together, and even if I could manipulate them slightly, I would be no match for two Fae.

"A stone," Cumina said slowly.

Morna frowned and stared at her sister for a moment.

"Oh," the word escaped Cumina's lips on a breath.

"Yeah, *oh*."

"But he was being manipulated by her, wasn't he?"

"Was he?" Morna sniffed. "What do we honestly know about him? I'm thinking this information might be more interesting to the king than the Fae Slayer herself." Without warning, Morna lunged forward and grabbed my wrist. "What is this?"

I shook my head, trying to wrench away from her, but her fingernails dug in, tearing into my skin. Fresh blood bubbled up from the wounds.

Morna cursed. "Stupid girl. What is on your wrist?"

Flashing the sparrowbone knife, I said, "You should remove yourself."

She shoved my arm away, and I quickly tore off a piece of my shirt and wrapped it around the wounds. I didn't know how many other assassins were out there or how many Fae were chasing me, nor did I care to find out. If one of them stole me away from Morna and Cumina, would Voss still be able to find me? Would they be worse than traveling with these two? And how bloodthirsty would they get, knowing the prize at the end was the king's gratitude?

"It's a stupid bracelet."

Morna sneered. Her hands grasped my cheeks in both of her hands, forcing me to look at her. "I know it's a bracelet, but how did you get it?"

Deny. His voice welled up inside my head, and I mentally screamed at him for leaving me to die against the shadow creature. Voss chuckled darkly.

"It's an old thing." I shrugged.

She turned to her sister, scrambling away from me as if I were on fire. "It looks like a wedding cuff to me."

I snorted. "I would never—"

"And I think she's bound." Morna frowned.

"What does *never* mean to you?" I accused.

Morna let out a breath and cursed again. "He's likely on his way here as we speak. I don't want to kill her, Cumina, but I think the king would understand, given the circumstances."

"You think he's working to overthrow the king?"

"He'd be a fool to put a cuff on a woman if he wasn't planning to keep her."

"But you made a deal with him."

"And he's cleverly found ways out of them before. That male is a genius at loopholes, which is why I don't want—" Morna shook her head, glaring at me like this was my fault.

Wedding cuff? I screamed at the shadow of him in my head, but I didn't receive any reply. *Oh, now you go quiet.*

"No one is keeping me," I growled. "Except myself."

"It hardly matters what you want, human. This is bigger than you," Morna snapped. "I need a reason not to strike her down where she sits."

"You're looking for a way into the king's good graces, right?" I suggested, keeping my voice level, though my panic spiked. "Bring me to him and tell him what you've learned." At least then I could get close enough to him to kill him myself.

"You're not denying that it's a wedding cuff?" Morna gaped at me.

"It's not. If it is, I will kill Voss myself."

"I think that's the most true statement we've heard out of her," Cumina grunted. She shook her head, massaging her temples like she could parse through all the new information. "It's a wedding band, but the question is, why?"

"It's *not* a wedding band."

Voss's presence stayed eerily quiet inside my head.

I screamed at his shadow. *If this is a wedding band, you will die.*

Make me bleed. A command, loud and clear, came through. I almost growled out loud.

"How much do you know about Fae culture, girl?"

"None, most likely. She kills first and never asks questions. Did I get that right?" Cumina rolled her eyes.

I spat at her, but it landed short.

She laughed, high-pitched and chilling. "Well, that answers that question."

"If he catches up with us, I will expect you to put up a fight against him, because you, Fae Slayer, have married one of the Fae." Morna's laughter turned dark.

"There was no ceremony, nothing. We're not married," I insisted, but Voss's thought rolled around in my head. *Make me bleed.* I gladly would at this point.

"The band is the wedding."

"It's just a stone from the market." I shook my head, more adamant now, because it was not true. However, I remembered the look on Penn's and Elspeth's faces when they saw the bracelet, their questions. It clicked into place.

"And where did the metal come from? The jeweler?"

"From…" I couldn't bring myself to say it, because my mouth had dried out.

"Him?" Morna's eyes filled with delight. "So tell me, Fae Slayer, did you blood bond before or after the wedding?"

"I'm not—"

"Pretty words from a mouth that can't be trusted."

That was it. I wasn't going to listen to this anymore. *Screw your plan*, I shouted at Voss's shadow in my mind. I scrambled forward, lashing out at Morna with my knife. I caught the edge of her jaw before she fell back. She used the momentum of her fall to kick my hand. My fist threatened to lose the knife, but I clamped my fingers down harder. I snarled, taking a few steps back, shaking off the ache.

"Really?" Cumina sounded disappointed. "You could have walked with us the rest of the way untethered. No chance of that anymore."

"If you're going to hand me over to the king anyway, there wasn't another way this would go."

Morna pulled out a saber and opened her arms wide as an invitation.

"Not going to fall for it."

Her irises swirled to life. "Bring it, Fae Slayer. Show me everything you're made of."

I shook my head, taking a step back. "No, there's no point."

Morna roared and charged toward me, because at the end of the day, she still was Fae. And no Fae could resist being defied. As she ran, I brought my center of gravity low enough to get a good shot in. She swung, the blade whipping out, and I ducked low as the silver whizzed over my head. Thrusting my hand forward, I slammed the knife into her stomach. I tried to twist it, but was wrenched off by the other assassin. Cumina wrapped her hands under my arms and behind my head, pinning me to her. I flailed the knife as much as I could.

Blood bubbled from Morna's lips. "You're going to regret that." She spat, clutching at her stomach. The red seeped slowly, already closing underneath her fingers as her magic swirled to life. "Fucking sparrowbone."

"Let. Me. Go." I slashed down with the knife, but barely grazed Cumina's hair from this position. My shoulders were practically wrenching out of their sockets. There was only one way out from the awkward hold she had me in.

Down we go.

I kicked off the ground, forcing both Cumina and I backward. I turned the knife away from us, not wanting to stab myself during the fall. We hit the ground, and the wind rushed out of my lungs. Using the momentum, I rolled off and away from both of the Fae. I clutched the knife out in front of me.

"You don't have to die for him. Because let's get one thing straight, the king will die. I will kill him, and you don't have to go down with that ship."

Morna brought up her saber again, readying for another challenge. The blood had clotted on her stomach, and I wished I had that kind of trick up my sleeve. Cumina joined her, but she had the bow in her hands, arrow not yet notched. There was no way out of this for me, unless I got through them.

I wasn't afraid of a fight.

"Cumina, I'll never sleep with you."

Morna growled. "Stop your games."

"We need to cut her tongue out," her sister gasped.

I grinned at them. "I'll say no until the end of my days. Tell you to please not stick your fingers deep inside me—"

Morna charged again, but her sister stayed put. Good. The saber slashed out, and I used my knife to edge the sword in the other direction, mere inches from my face. I snarled and kneed the Fae in the crotch. She whipped her elbow back, and it smashed into my nose. Blood splurged out, covering the front of my clothes. Her nostrils flared as she whipped her hand back, readying to swing out again. I was too dizzy to react as the steel flashed down.

But everything stopped. It took a moment for my spinning brain to catch up. Morna had stopped mid-swing, but not by her own choice. Cumina had stepped in, holding her sister's hands from delivering the killing blow.

"Tie her up," Cumina demanded. "And I will have my way with her."

I smirked.

"Oh, Morna. She's useless against me. It's cute, isn't it?" I blinked with innocent eyes at the other Fae.

"We kill her now," Morna growled. "She'll continue to manipulate us until—"

"Then we gag her."

"I'm so scared," I mocked.

Morna's fingers shook on her blade.

I took a few steps back, the two of them still locked in indecision. "I'm not sure how I'll ever get over this fear in my heart with two big bad Fae after me."

"I want her dead."

"And I want her bound."

"Unfortunately for you, neither is going to happen." Out of the darkness came Voss's voice, not in my head, but from the night. "Which is a shame, really, because I agree she looks good wearing a rope."

Morna shook her head, her magic draining from her eyes as she snarled. "You said you wouldn't interfere."

"Ah, yes, I wouldn't interfere with you bringing Scarlet the Fae Slayer to the king." Voss stepped into the light, his liquid fire eyes swirling. "But that's not your name, is it?" He flicked his attention to me. *Maxine.* His voice was like lava inside my head, rushing around my brain, claiming some wild part of me.

"It isn't my name. Not officially," I admitted.

252

Morna cursed, but gestured to my wrist. "Care to tell her what you did?"

He glanced down at my wrist. "I gave her a pretty piece of jewelry that she liked from the market. I think it looks clever on her."

"It's a wedding band," Morna snarled. "And she's not pleased with it, are you, Fae Slayer?"

"Is it a wedding band?" I demanded.

"You can make me bleed later."

"Fuck you, Voss."

"I look forward to it." He swept his eyes back to the two assassins. "As you can see, I am coming back to claim what is mine. And you have no right to her any longer. I was going to wait until you got to the king, as I figured it would be easier to get into the castle that way, but unfortunately, you tried to kill her. Quite a few times."

"She's not manipulating you, is she?" Cumina glared at Voss, stepping in front of her sister like a shield. Her glare could cut diamonds. "You're going against the king."

"Did you expect anything less of me? You know the type of male he is, and it's time for a new era. We are, after all, in a new world. New leadership will be good for the Fae."

"You're an arrogant—"

"Watch what you say, Morna. You tried to kill my wife."

I flung the knife at him. His hand snatched it out of midair, and Voss cut me a look. I gave him one right back, because *fuck you.* The feeling rippled through my mind, straight into the part of him that was inside me.

Later, he purred.

Later, he was going to be flayed open like venison.

"And you two are fine with this?" Morna called out to the dark.

"Of course." Elspeth lit a Faerie light. Penn right beside her. "The kingdom needs to change. The king is going to destroy this world just like he did Faerie. You know it just as well as we do, Morna."

Cumina cackled, which quickly turned into hysterical hiccups. "You'll have to kill us, because we'll tell the king everything if you let us go."

"Shut up," Morna hissed.

"I could do you one better." Voss stepped up to Cumina. They gazed at each other for a long moment. He bent down and whispered something in her ear.

She stilled. "Why didn't you say that earlier? You're truly an idiot."

He shrugged. "You didn't give me a choice. Besides, I heard there might have been a wild caltula left roaming around here, and I thought it'd be great if you two could finish it off. Can't really have darkness itself taking over towns in the aftermath of changing kings, can we?"

"You're an asshole."

Morna watched the exchange with a stiff back. "You have twenty-four hours. And if things are not better by then, you know what we're going to do. That's the longest we'll give you for our silence. Any longer, we'd be risking our heads."

Voss nodded, turned toward me, and offered me the handle of the tiny blade.

I crossed the remaining space between us and snatched the knife back. He captured my wrist in his hand, pulling me into him. His body pressed against mine.

"Try stabbing me again, and we'll see what happens to you after that."

"Take the band off."

"Like I said, it looks clever on you."

"You disgust me," Morna said.

"How is that any different from normal days, Morna?" Voss tossed her a smirk while placing his hand on the small of my back, guiding me away from the two assassins.

"What did you say to her?" I asked once we were a few yards away.

"What she needed to hear to walk away. Our horses are close. We're going to ride hard, because I'm not sure I can deliver that promise in twenty-four hours."

"But you didn't make a deal."

"Yes, but not keeping your promises as a Fae is bad manners, and I already backed them into a corner once with you. I'm not going to make my enemies hate me more. Plus, this is beneficial for everyone, including the humans, if we succeed."

I cut him a glare. "We have a lot to talk about."

He chuckled as Elspeth and Penn lit our way with floating lights. "And they have many feelings to add to this, too."

"For the record, I hate the idea," Penn said.

"And I think it's simultaneously charming and sheer stupidity," Elspeth added.

"I want it off."

Voss shook his head. "Not happening." We reached the horses, and I noted there were only three. "We had to give Switch to Marcy, as she needed a ride away from town to get back to safety. I traded for a saddle big enough for the two of us."

A part of me wanted to thank him for making sure she remained safe, but the other part of me was still furious that he *married* me without my knowledge. "Ride with Elspeth then. I want nothing to do with you."

He made a humming sound inside his throat, and I swear it

sounded pained. Still, they ignored my protests, with Elspeth and Penn climbing their mounts and leaving me with Voss. He offered his hand. "Unless you want to wait for the other assassins to smell you. I didn't get much of a fight tonight, so it could be fun."

I sighed. "We're going to have to burn this shirt, aren't we?"

"Yup. I have your clothes, but we're going to ride until dawn, about another hour, then find a stream for you to bathe in once the air warms."

I huffed, taking his hand and letting him lift me onto the saddle. Voss swung up and over easily in front of me, taking the reins in his hands and clicking the horse forward.

"Penn, I need you masking our scents as we make the rest of the crossing."

"On it."

"Elspeth, lights please."

"Of course."

"And you," he whispered back to me. I leaned against his shoulder, feeling exhausted with the rhythmic strides of the horse. *Sleep.* The voice came from deep inside my head, and as much as I was angry, as much as I wanted to fight him, as much as I wanted to scream at him for everything he had put me through, I did exactly what he asked.

Twenty-One

"Wake up, little fox."

Voss's words licked at my skin. My eyes fluttered open to blinding sunlight. We were outside of a forested area, and the two other Fae were already dismounting their horses. I blinked several times to make the watery film over my eyes disappear.

I yawned. "Can I go back to sleep?" I mumbled half of my words into his back.

"Maybe once we get you cleaned up. The other assassins won't be so easy going if they catch up to us." Voss pressed his back against me until I begrudgingly stirred from the saddle. He helped me down, and I stretched my arms over my head. A few of the bones in my spine popped, and I let out a loud groan. He smirked as he slid from the mount. "Not comfy enough for you?"

Another yawn escaped my lips. "Riding on horseback against your bony shoulder was perfectly comfortable. I have no idea what you're talking about."

"Ouch."

Elspeth laughed. "You sure know how to pick them, Voss. She's right, though. You are bony."

He cut her a glare, his eyes swirling. She swatted at something that didn't exist for a minute, cursing as Voss's magic faded away. "Serves you right."

"You should get her cleaned. We'll get the horses rested up."

Voss nodded to a small trail between the trees heading into the woods. I walked after him as my muscles screamed in protest. Everything hurt. It could have been from fighting with the other Fae last night, riding asleep upright on a horse, or having to contort my body in order to cut my way free. Probably a mixture of all the above. I was happy to be liberated from the other assassins, but I would have to confront Voss about everything I had learned.

Specifically, about the bangle dangling heavily around my wrist.

The woods parted with a deep, slow running creek trailing in between the trees. It was about four feet wide and three feet to the bottom. It was crystal clear, showing all the way to the bottom brown sand. I started removing my clothes, but caught Voss's eyes on me.

"What?" I said.

"You're going to be shy now?" He held out his hand.

I tossed my bloody shirt at him, and it went up into flames instantly. I was still in my undergarments, which also had blood on them. He flicked his hands to those too.

"You don't own me, you know?"

He arched an eyebrow.

"But that's what this is, isn't it?" I gestured to the bracelet.

"The rest of your clothes, little fox."

I sighed and finished stripping, shoving them at him. His eyes swirled as flames burst through the materials. The heat rose against my skin for a moment.

"I have soap in the pack, along with your new clothes." He shrugged off the pack as I hugged myself, feeling every part of me hardening from the cold. Chuckling, he wasted no time producing the soap and stepping out of his clothes.

"What are you doing?"

"Going in with you. It's been a day, and I'd prefer to smell nicer."

I glared at him as his shirt went up and over his shoulders, fluttering to the forest floor. His shoulders rolled back as he stretched.

"Get in," he told me.

"I'm not for you to command."

"Aren't you?" His eyes flickered to the bracelet.

"If I get in, will you tell me what this is really about?" I accepted it was a wedding band. Morna and Cumina had no reason to lie about that, but I needed to know why. It didn't seem necessary with the blood bond between us. Though, at the time Voss gave me the band, he had no idea I was going to accept a blood bond.

"Yes."

Dipping my toes into the water, I hissed and pulled back. "It's freezing."

Voss's pants were off, and I forced myself not to look at him, instead staring at the water I was going to have to wash in. It was frigid, and I wouldn't be staying in long. As I took another step toward the water, steeling myself for the chill to hit me, Voss scooped me up and jumped.

I screamed as we both plunged into the water, his arms firmly lodged around me. The cold seeped everywhere, between my thighs, under my arms, around my breasts. It made every part of me cry out, but just as quickly as there was a numbing chill, I was warmer.

As Voss set me down, I stared at him. The chilly air swept over my body, but the surrounding water was warm now. His irises glowed from magic.

"Neat trick."

"I'm full of them."

As he said that, a snake of warm water swirled around the inside of my thighs, tracing lines up and down my skin. My body clenched as Voss smirked.

"But that will have to wait. Turn around."

I crossed my arms over my chest.

"Turn around," he demanded, his eyes swirling.

There was a small part of me that told me to listen to him, begged me to give into him, but the stubborn word came out of my mouth. "No."

"Fine." He made a thick lather of the soap in his hands and pressed his hands over my breasts. "I can start on this side, if you prefer."

The suds turned pink as he worked them over my skin, beginning to remove the mess of my blood. His thumbs rolled over my nipples, which were already hard from the chilly air. I sucked in a breath.

"Your body amazes me. So responsive to such simple touches." His fingers trailed a line under each of my breasts. "Rinse off."

I shoved him, trying to grab the soap out of his hands, but I was slick with suds, and instead of accomplishing much of anything, I made us crash into the water. Before I breached the surface, his lips were on mine, crushing against me and pulling me into him. I couldn't breathe, but I also didn't care. Something about Voss's fire was all-consuming, and I wanted to burn.

He pulled me out of the water, and a gasp sputtered on my lips.

"You're even more beautiful when you're furious with me." His hands grabbed my ass and brought me against him. He was hard, pushing against my core.

"Is it a wedding band?" I demanded.

Voss swallowed and at least had the foresight to look sheepish, before he admitted, "Yes."

"Why?!" I forced my wrist in front of him. "Take it off."

"Fae bands are for life, I'm afraid."

"Why?" I asked again through gritted teeth. My anger at him only fueled the fire in my stomach. I could make him bleed. I could use this against him. I could destroy him, and the thought of it made me wet, wanting him inside me all the more.

"There are many reasons, none of which will be adequate for what you wish to know."

"Try me."

Voss reached below us, scooping up the soap that had fallen. He kept me cradled against him as he made another lather. He brought it down over my shoulders, under my arms, washing me like I was something precious and worth the time.

"Make me understand," I said, my voice lighter and more pleading, because no Fae had ever looked at me like this or had treated me this way. It terrified me, because I wanted more. I wanted this forever. I wanted what the band meant, but it was too soon to have these powerful emotions.

It was too soon to have a dark part of him inside me like a shadow.

"Do you want me to show you instead?"

"What does that mean?"

"If we strengthen our blood bond, you'll be able to see more of it, see more parts of me. Instead of an impression, I could show you the reason I felt like it was important to link myself to you."

"You want to drink my blood."

His eyes lit up, and he solemnly nodded. "It tasted like moonlight under an autumn sky."

"Hm." I stared at him, but also at the piece of him inside my mind. *Why should I trust you?* I asked him through my thoughts.

His hands stopped their slow descent down my back. A frown pursed his lips. "Because what I've done has only been to make you stronger."

"So you heard me those other times?"

"Impressions, mostly. But I could hear you a lot clearer if we strengthen the bond."

"Tell me why first, and then you can show me."

He sucked in a breath. "Unmarried humans can be controlled by any Fae. Once you are married to a Fae, only that Fae can control you."

"That makes no sense. I can't be controlled by any Fae."

"There are rumors about the king."

"Morna and Cumina told me."

He stiffened against me for a moment, but continued. His hands roamed over my skin with the bar of soap, washing away the blood from the night before. "If the king controls you, you can't kill him. This was a precaution to make sure the king can't control you. Even he cannot break through a married Fae bond."

"So you made me your wife because of a rumor?"

"I have reason to believe it's true."

"So this is to kill the king? If it can't be broken, then... what happens after?"

A frown creased Voss's lips, and I swore I saw a flash of regret or sorrow. "I hope after everything is settled, you will like the idea of being my wife. But I won't force you into playing the part. Once the king is dead, I'll set you free."

"But you said this was unbreakable."

"It is, but you can still live your life, and I can live mine. You won't be able to be controlled by Fae or marry another Fae."

"I wouldn't marry any Fae."

He looked at me.

"Fuck you, Voss."

His hands stilled. "Maybe once we're finished talking, little fox." With quick motions, he made another lather and rubbed it along my neck, up my jaw, around my cheeks. "Close your eyes."

I did as he said, mostly because I wanted to revel in the feel of his caresses along my skin. My anger hadn't abated, but sex and violence always went hand in hand for me. As much as I wanted to flay him alive, I also wanted him inside me. Once he was done scrubbing my face, he asked me to hold my breath and dipped me under the water once again. When I came up, I smelled clean and felt better.

"Being your wife doesn't make me yours," I said, but my voice was quiet with little enthusiasm behind my words.

"I understand."

"But you claimed me. In front of the other two assassins, you essentially marked me as yours. Won't they use that against you with the king?"

"Not if I get them what they want. And I have a feeling if we kill the king fast enough, we'll be able to get them everything they need and more."

"So the court isn't very far, is it?"

Voss swallowed. The location of the king's court was the last thing he had kept from me, not wanting me to scamper away to kill the king on my own. At this point, I wouldn't give up his help. He had kept true to his word and protected me, even working around a Fae deal to do so. We had continued to travel the way Morna and

Cumina were taking me, so I trusted him in a way.

As much as a Fae Slayer could trust a Fae Assassin.

"Bond with me again?" His irises swirled in liquid lava.

A tingling sensation ran up my spine, and it felt like I was going to fall off the edge of the universe. The next words out of my mouth would change my future forever. But I found myself wanting to taste his blood on my tongue, wanting to feel him deep inside me in more ways than one.

"Okay."

He smirked.

"Don't do that."

"What?"

"Act like you've won something."

"Oh, but I have." The soap trailed along my skin again as he reached down between my legs. "You are a prize."

"I am not an object."

He moved the soap against my nerves, and I bucked against him. "You're right. You're better than a prize. You're a dream."

"Cheesy."

Voss tilted his head and pressed his lips against mine. It was a slow kiss, sensual and full of promise all the while he worked the bar around me. Then the soap was gone, and it was his fingers, toying and playing with me. I arched against him. He cupped me, pulling me toward him. I wrapped my legs around his hips, but left enough space for his hands to keep working.

"Greedy little fox."

"Mmm," I muttered into his mouth.

He brought my lower lip between his teeth and bit down hard. I gasped as he pulled blood straight from my lip into his mouth. I dug my fingernails into his shoulder, wanting to taste him just the same, but I was trapped in this position, with his fingers splaying me apart and testing my entrance. Voss drank deep, and I shuddered when his presence became bigger and larger inside me. I felt his pleasure, felt how his fingers ached to be inside me, felt how much he ached for me.

He pulled back, eying me. "Your turn. And don't hold back. I know you still hate me."

"You can feel that through the bond?"

"Vague impressions," he reiterated. "But I want to feel more. Like this." He pulsed his cock, and I felt it. In my mind, I felt the muscle contract. I felt like I was him and me at the same time.

"Fuck," I said.

"And I want to feel what this is like." He pushed a finger inside me, and I gasped. "What does it feel like to have me invading you?"

"It feels—" I didn't get a chance to finish, because he ran over the spot that made me lose all of my senses.

"Show me." He arched his neck, presenting his skin to me. "And don't hold back. Give me all the anger you have."

My mouth watered at the thought of his blood, the taste of him. Never did I imagine myself drinking Fae blood, but on some biological level, I craved it now, craved *him*. Voss was right. I was still angry. Angry enough to press my lips against the pulse in his neck. Angry enough to sink my teeth into his skin. My agitation fueled the fire to rip his skin apart, and soon, his blood burst into my mouth. Fiery ginger hit my senses, and I swallowed deeply, pushing myself against him so flush he could barely move his fingers inside me.

His frustration at being held back was clear in my mind, which made me grind against him. His cock ached, hardening to the point of it being painful as I drew long gulps from his neck.

"Enough."

But I wanted more.

With his free hand, Voss tore me off of him. "You're dangerous."

"Of course I am." I grinned, and I could see myself the way he saw me. Blood coating my teeth, standing out against my pale skin and black hair. I looked like the moonlight—a blood moon—to his sun.

"I like how this feels." Voss got enough space to pump his fingers again. "This spot right here? That's the—" He groaned as I bucked against him. The sensation of my wetness coating his fingers, the tightness encompassing him, and feeling it from his perspective and mine was almost too much. "I see why you like it so much."

I wanted to explore this. The sensation of being him, feeling me through him. I ran my fingers down his chest over the sensitive tip of his erection. As I wrapped my hand around him, my body clenched, and I felt the pull of me against his fingers at the same time. It was exquisite. With every movement of my thumb along his erection, he ached to be inside me, to stretch me, to split me open until I begged for release. As much as I felt powerless against Voss, he felt the same way with me.

As he pumped his fingers, I applied pressure with my hand, slowly moving up and down. The swell of him in my hands, the feel of him consuming me, the pleasure he got from watching me squirm.

I like you like this.

Like what?

Helpless. Mine.

Fuck you, Voss.

He chuckled as he withdrew his fingers, and we moved as one. I guided him against me, and he worked himself inside, filling me.

Feeling his pleasure was like lightning. The tightness of me around him, the force in which he had to push to get me to open wider, the warmth pressing against him, around him.

One of his hands roamed to the back of my neck, while the other one slid under my ass. He pushed me farther down onto him. I bit back a cry as I grabbed onto his shoulders for stability. His forehead rested against mine, and we gasped the same air.

I felt the slickness of my walls around him. I felt the push and pull of him inside me. I felt his emotions crest into a solitary thing. He chased his own pleasure with each thrust inside me, with each pulse of him and me. I gasped as he moved his hand from the back of my neck to the front. His eyes swirled as he stared at me.

Fuck, he is gorgeous. And as I had the thought, his stupid smirk appeared on his face, and I scowled until he pierced me so deeply that my thoughts disappeared from my head.

You are too.

He flexed inside me. So many sensations flooded my system, and I rocked harder and faster until everything inside me welled. As every part of my body tensed, I felt it through Voss. The friction, the wetness, the intense pulse that ached through him. He thrust in me as deep as he could go, claiming me and marking me as he came. I felt his release along with my own. It was an eruption, a surge of every emotion inside me as stars burst through my head.

I wanted to scream, but it came out more as a whimper while my body shuddered.

Voss was delighted. I could feel his smug pleasure surrounding me, but he was also… happy?

"Yes, little fox. Happy." He pressed his lips against my cheek. "Let's clean you up." As he pulled out of me, I watched as the water around us filled with the essence of him.

"Fuck, Voss. How did we get here?"

"Easy. You find me attractive."

I glared at him.

He pointed to his head. "Don't deny it. I know you now. And we have a common goal." Voss found the soap again and passed it to me. We finished bathing quickly and more efficiently than the first time, as the sun was rising higher in the sky. Our clock was ticking. There was an urgency to his movements, and I could feel the thoughts in his head, the promises he was worried he couldn't keep. A lot of it was fuzzy, not exactly him, but an impression of him.

"Can you hear all of my thoughts now?"

"Not all. But a lot. Like how your thighs are quivering and you want to taste more of my blood, which really, little fox, didn't you drink enough?" Where I bit him had already healed to the late stages of a bruise, the cuts completely healed.

"No." The inside of my lip was faring much worse than him, but I knew why he chose there. As swollen as it was, it'd be harder for the assassins to track us with an injury inside my body.

Voss stepped out of the water and grabbed a towel from the pack to dry off. Without his presence and magic warming the water, it cooled fast. I clambered out after him, grabbing another towel. The cold air nipped at my skin as I dried off.

One of Voss's thoughts ran through my head, wicked and wanting.

"What was that?"

"Just wishing I could use magic on you, because there are a lot of things I could make even better if I were able to use it."

I ground my teeth together. *Better than that?*

"Yes, better than that. And if you're still worried about having me inside your head, you'll get used to it over time."

"Have you blood bonded with anyone else?"

"Yes, but as I said, it wears off. It's not a permanent bond, not like the bracelet. So if you hate having me in your head, we won't have to do it again." A wave of disappointment hit me, like Voss was already expecting me to say no.

"I didn't hate being bound to you with the sex."

His lips quirked. "So you admit to enjoying it?"

"Not hating something and enjoying it are very different."

"You say one thing, but your mind tells me another." His voice drifted over my skin, and I forced myself to get dressed quickly, else I was liable to jump him again right there. We had a king to kill. "Trust me, little fox, when everything is over, I plan to do that and more."

Twenty-Two

As we arrived back at the temporary camp, Penn eyed us. "What took you both so long?" His eyes swept to Voss's, and he scowled. "Don't answer that. We were supposed to be fast, per your promise with Morna and Cumina. You're letting yourself get distracted." He let out a breath and gestured to the horses. "They are ready to move, but you both need to eat something."

"I saved some bread and cheese for you. The bread is stale, and we dipped it in tea to make it better, but I drank it all." Elspeth pulled herself up onto her horse. "It's the first thing in your saddlebag. You can eat while we walk. We also need to come up with a plan, as it won't take us much more time to get to court."

"Thanks, Elspeth." Voss sounded sincere. "You okay to ride?"

"You're not that big."

He frowned. *Liar. I can feel how sore you are right now.*

"I think I liked it before you were inside my head."

"You exchanged more blood?" Penn gaped at us, shaking his

head before he mounted his mare. "Reckless."

Voss offered me a hand up, and I gratefully took it, swinging my leg over. This time, he rode behind me, giving me the reins. I glanced at him, questioning this turn of events. He struck me as someone who was always in control, and this was giving up a bit of it.

Not giving it up. I'm right here if needed.

"Stop that."

His tongue ran over my ear. "You like it. And besides, I'm hungry." Voss fished around in the saddlebag and produced a hunk of bread and cheese. "We'll trade off in an hour or so, once I've had a chance to feed you."

"You are not feeding me. I'm not a child."

"Never said you were. That'd be weird anyway, considering how old I am."

I stilled. "How old... are you?"

Elspeth snorted. "Now you ask?"

I groaned.

"We're all very old," Penn said. "But compared to Voss, I'm a baby."

"Only by twenty-three years, Penn."

I groaned. "Wait, were any of the Fae I fucked young?"

"Hmm..." Voss rested his head on my shoulder. The stubble on his chin dug into my shirt, prickling my skin through the material. "I think one might have been under one hundred."

"Remind me again why I shouldn't kill you?"

"Because." Voss didn't say any more, but put a small piece of cheese in front of my mouth.

I bit it and him.

He yanked his hand back. "Fuck."

"It tastes better with your blood on it." As I said the words, I

271

could feel him growing hard against me. His erection was uncomfortable in the current position. "Serves you right."

"I could make you uncomfortable too."

"Oh?"

His fingers toyed with the hem of my pants, dipping underneath them. "I could make you drenched before we get to the court."

Penn coughed. "Can we not? For like... five more hours?"

"Jealous, Penn?"

He cursed from his position in front of us.

"I hate to break up the little party you are having, but we need to talk about what's going to happen once we get to court." Elspeth slipped into her no-nonsense voice, tossing both of us a stern look.

"None of this is my fault."

She narrowed her gaze at me. "Do we want to do the captive route or the marriage route?"

"Marriage," I growled. "It makes the most amount of sense, seeing as how it's the truth."

"But can you pull it off?"

"Pull off a marriage that is essentially real? I don't see why not."

"The king has to believe you like each other, and while I'm convinced you to love *fucking* each other, your actions don't speak of a newly wedded couple." Elspeth shrugged. "It has to be believable for us to get close to the king, and I'm not sure both of you are prepared for that."

"I acted in front of Fae for a long time before you found me. Voss?"

He put a piece of bread in front of my face. "Eat."

"Stop it," but he took the opportunity of me speaking to pop it into my mouth. Heavens above, it *was* stale. Elspeth hadn't been kidding. It took a while for my saliva to make it somewhat malleable to eat, and in that time, Voss carried on the conversation without me.

"We can look in love. This one only needs to think about all the blood that will cover her hands after she slits the king's throat, and she'll look content and satiated."

Elspeth huffed. "Is she going to be able to listen to everything you say once we're inside those walls?""

I stiffened. And Voss already sensed my question as I continued chewing, so he clarified, "If we're married, you would be bound to whatever I said. So if I suggested something, even in the slightest, it would be expected for you to act accordingly."

"Of course there had to be a catch," I said, mouth still half-full. I swallowed hard.

"That's the part she can't pull off," Penn challenged with a laugh.

"I'm very good at following directions, if they are ones I *want* to follow." I maturely stuck my tongue out at him as Voss fed me another piece of cheese.

"I like your name. Have I told you that?" His words licked my ear. "Maxine."

A shiver tore up my spine. I hadn't heard that name since I was a kid. "Max," I said absently. I had never gone by my full name, not with my family, not with my friends, and not with anyone alive now. He had been the first to speak those syllables to me in thirteen years.

"Max."

My muscles clenched, actually clenched, as the word caressed my skin.

"I've heard hearing your name from a Fae's lips is erotic, but this… it's like touching all of your erogenous zones at once. Isn't it, Max?"

I shivered against him as he chuckled. "I could elbow you in the stomach, kick you off this horse, and speed away without you."

"But then, who would feed you cheese and bread?" He tempted me with another slice. I tried to bite his fingers again, but he was too quick this time. "And wouldn't get mad when you tried to take off a digit along with the food?"

"You're a lovesick fool." Elspeth shook her head. "Sometimes, I wonder why I am dedicating my life to you."

"Because I have fantastic ideas."

Penn snorted. "Like forcibly marrying a woman who wants all Fae dead?"

"Like I said, *fantastic*." Voss nuzzled his lips against my neck, pressing the lightest of fluttering kisses against my skin.

"Besides, this is a means to an end. Right?" I asked.

He hummed into my ear.

"We're not really married. I mean, we are, but it doesn't mean anything."

"You keep telling yourself that," Elspeth muttered.

I ignored her, not wanting to think about this any longer. Voss was having fun with me, like any Fae would. We were desperately attracted to each other, but this was part of a plan, a ploy to kill the king. It didn't mean anything. Sure, the sex was great, but that didn't mean we were going to spend the rest of our lives together. Someday, I would be dead and Voss would move onto someone else, someone better suited to be his actual wife, someone he loved.

But why did the idea of him being with someone else make me feel viciously hollow?

Because you're a jealous little fox.

Get out of my head.

He presented another piece of cheese. *You need your strength. I can feel how hungry you are. Please don't bite me this time.*

But you taste so good.

"Mother, I can practically hear your thoughts." Elspeth faked a retching noise. "Riding with you two is like being around horny teenage Fae." She kicked her horse's sides and rode a few more paces ahead, next to Penn. The surrounding forest had grown dense, and I wondered how much longer it would be before we got to where we were headed.

I took the cheese and tore my teeth through a few more pieces of bread until Voss was satisfied. It was weird to have him know me this way, know what I was feeling, not just emotionally but physically. And likewise, there was a piece of him I could prod. I suspected he got more out of our link than I did, but maybe that was due to him being Fae and my being human, or my immunity to magic. I could sense him, but it was still a vague impression, unless he was intentionally opening to me.

You can block your thoughts from me.

"Would have been nice to know before now." I frowned. "How?"

"You have to work at it." He rested his hands on my hips, making slow, lazy strokes along my skin. "If you don't want me getting a direct look inside your head, focus on blocking the part of me inside you out. Otherwise, I hear pretty much everything."

"Everything?" I blanched.

"Everything."

"And how is this not a method of controlling me? You could tell if I was going to turn against you."

"But you aren't."

"That's not the point. My privacy is gone."

"It's true, you have no more secrets from me. But isn't it better that you can be yourself? Your absolute worst and vile self, because I still very much want to feel myself split you open."

The feeling of his arousal rose in the dark part of my mind, the shadow of him in the corner of my brain. "Stop it."

"Make me. Convince me you don't want me, Max."

Hearing my name on his lips made every part of my body clench, making my nipples hard in an instant and running shivers down my spine. I almost yanked on the reins from the suddenness of it. "This is why I never told anyone my real name."

"I promise not to abuse it. Too much." Voss ran his fingers along my arms, settling on my hands that were white-knuckling the reins. "Calm down, little fox. We still have a few hours to go, and I can't have you this tense when we get to the castle. Maybe we should practice between now and then."

"Practice what, exactly?"

"You need to do what I say when I say it."

I narrowed my eyes, twisting around to get a good look at him. His eyes sparkled with delight. "I hate you."

"But you don't."

I shot a few thoughts at him, dark ones where his body lay in a twisted bloody heap underneath my naked writhing form.

His eyes widened. "What does it say about me that I find it incredibly sexy when you think like that?"

"That you're fucked up."

"And what does it say about you that you're completely wet right now?"

I cursed inside my head, and his chest rumbled against me as he chuckled.

He pulled me close, making our bodies completely flush. "We'll start practicing with something small. Drop the reins from your right hand."

Fuck you, Voss. I didn't want to do it. Everything inside me screamed not to listen to the Fae, not to obey him. I didn't have to do it, but he was right, if he suggested something while we were in the castle before I got close enough to the king, I would have to listen to him in order to sell us as a couple. We had to make this marriage band a reality and hide my identity as the Fae Slayer.

Hide it until it was too late for the king to do anything. Hide it until my sparrowbone ran right across his throat.

I dropped the reins from my right hand.

"Good, now pick them up again."

I rolled my eyes.

"It's good practice to start small."

Picking them up again, he kissed the side of my neck. "Now take your right hand and pinch your left nipple." As I stiffened, he tightened his grip on my hips. "Hesitation like that will get you killed."

Sighing, I did as I was told, taking my left nipple in between my thumb and forefinger, twisting slightly.

Voss tensed against me, and I could feel his thoughts whirling inside me, seductive ones. He was insatiable.

"You don't know the half of it." He reached over me and took the reins in his hands. "With your left hand, reach down your pants and touch yourself."

"Voss," I said, feeling numb. I had never done this in front of someone, and frankly, it was embarrassing.

"You think the Fae court is going to expect anything less from me? They know how ruthless I can be as an assassin, and they'd expect my wife to accept whatever I throw at her. We could always go back to tying you up. I won't say it doesn't make me hot thinking about—"

I shut him up by reaching down my pants and pressing against my clit, shoving the feeling of it straight toward him. He shuddered against me, and I knew he was experiencing it through our link.

Interesting that this could be considered a weakness.

"Which is why you don't bond with people—" Voss sucked in a breath as I slipped a finger in between my folds, toying with my entrance. I had to lean against him to get a better angle. "—that you don't want to experience everything with, and I mean everything."

"Is this enough for you?"

"Now stop."

I hesitated.

"I said stop, little fox."

Scowling, I withdrew my hand from myself.

"Take back the reins. And stay absolutely still." His right hand reached down into my pants, teasing my skin. His fingers trailed along my thighs, but not touching the one place I wanted him to. "Don't. Move." He reiterated as his other hand reached for his own arousal. I felt it as he stroked himself, both inside my mind and against my back. The feeling he gave himself while toying with me was enough to make me want to buck against him, make his hand find the spot I needed him to touch. He moved languidly, rolling his thumb over his head and squeezing himself lightly, sending the feeling of it through my mind and making me wish he were inside me instead of in his own hand.

"Do you think you can listen to me?"

"Yes," I panted, trying not to move.

"Tell me what you want."

"Release."

"And what happens if I don't grant it to you?" His voice was sultry and low, breath caressing my skin. "What happens if I focus on my pleasure?" He sent a jolt of feeling toward me again as he swiped his thumb over his cock, playing with the beads forming there.

"That is your decision to make," I wheezed, barely able to think.

His pointer finger grazed against my core, and I struggled not to move. A whimper escaped my mouth.

Helpless and mine.

Fuck you, Voss.

He chuckled, pushing his other fingers against me in slow deliberate circles, increasing the pressure until my nerves buzzed against his hand. His other hand continued to stroke his own pleasure. "If I tell you not to, would you be able to hold it back?"

I whimpered mentally, hating how he brought this carnal desire out of me.

"Could you, or are you incapable?"

"I'm capable."

"Prove it." Voss continued his assault on my senses, making me feel his even strokes on his cock. I felt it swell in his hand. I sensed the pressure against and around him, the desire he had to penetrate me, invade me. It grew inside my mind, building up as he continued the circles against me, making me come alive underneath his touch. "Hold off."

I could feel Voss prodding inside my head, entwining his thoughts with my desires until all I could think about was how he was driving me to the brink only to deny me my release because of this stupid game. His chest rumbled as he laughed. I could tell how much he liked it, toying with me, being able to use me simply because he suggested it. I could deny him, but I wouldn't. We both knew that now.

His thoughts flooded into me, with how excruciatingly hot he found it that I could say no, I could stop him, but I was choosing to be helpless against him. I was giving myself over to him. And it made him more amused to find how angry it made me.

"How are you feeling?"

The inside of me was threatening to explode. I could see stars at the edge of my vision as every muscle in my body coiled tight.

"Good, then?" His strokes became more even and sure against himself, pulling at his skin and moving his hips to get a better angle. I thought of him claiming me in more ways than one. I wanted him to release on my back as he rubbed me and demanded that I hold off. I was dripping.

"Fuck," he whispered with the same breathlessness I felt. He was near the brink too. "Do what you need to do, little fox, but do it silently. Hold back your screams, scream at me inside your head, but don't let anyone else know what you're feeling right now. Take from me what you need."

With his permission, I rode his fingers, trying to keep my hold on the reins steady and even. I wanted to break the sound barrier with the tension built inside me, but I internalized it, let it race inside me like a red hot lightning rod. The orgasm shot through me, rolling over my body as his fingers pulsed against my nerves. My shoulders arched back against him as I felt the heat of his cum against the lower part of my back. Mentally, he was grabbing onto me. I screamed through the blood bond, letting everything out even as no sound escaped except for a few heavier breaths.

Shaking, Voss relinquished his mental hold on my mind, and the forest in front of us became sharper. I was able to focus again. We were hundreds of yards behind the other two now, and the canopy above us opened up.

Voss laughed against me. "I think it's time we gave the mare a break and walked for a bit. Plus, I have to get you cleaned up."

I groaned. "How many shirts am I going to ruin being with you?"

"I paid for them. I reserve the right to destroy them however I see fit." The smugness of his grin hit me without seeing it. As I pulled our mare to a stop, Voss hopped off and handed me a new shirt from the saddlebag.

"I feel like I should say thank you, but then it feels like I am forgiving you for the mess you created."

"In good news, I think you're ready for the king."

I glared at him. "Like I said, I am good at following directions when they are ones I want to follow."

The cocky smirk was back. "And you wanted to follow those." It wasn't a question.

"I wanted to make sure I was ready for the king's court." I stripped off the shirt and tossed it at him. He caught it before the mess hit him in the chest. He wasted no time by setting the whole thing on fire. "Seems so wasteful," I said, pulling the second one over my head. "Maybe we wash them in the future?"

Voss's eyes settled from their liquid amber back to black. "As I said, I can destroy them however I want."

"I'll listen to you, but can you try to go easy on me? This is our only chance, Voss, and one wrong move could have me sent to the dungeons or killed."

He frowned. "We both want the same thing. I won't demand anything I don't think you can handle. And besides, you have a safe word."

"Which would seem so natural to come up in conversation." I rolled my eyes.

Offering me his hand, I took it and we walked along the path for a bit, letting the mare take a long needed break. A few miles later and the forest disappeared, becoming a large endless rolling plain, what used to be farmland but was now a heaping waste of wilds. It took us hours of walking and riding, trading between the two so the mare didn't get exhausted, but as the sun set, the plains stopped abruptly at giant stone walls that came out from nowhere. It took us longer still to actually end up in front of the colossal structure.

This place was about two hours north of the port city in the middle of nowhere, and not an area that would have come onto my radar. With as many Fae as I had fucked and killed, none of them admitted to the location of the king. But seeing it now in person, it was unbelievable we would ever miss it. This place was enormous.

Penn and Elspeth had dismounted, waiting for us to catch up to them.

"Welcome to the King's Court," Voss announced.

Twenty-Three

The guards stepped out of the turret posts on either side of the enormous gates. One was Fae and the other was human. The human looked ready to collapse, with dark bags under his eyes and a hollow look to his cheekbones.

"Ah, welcome back," the Fae guard said, saluting Voss with a flourish. "I take it the travels went well?"

"Not as fruitful as we would have hoped."

The male Fae eyed me, looking me up and down while assessing. "What brings you back here, then? You promised—"

Voss waved his hand, effectively silencing the male with nothing more than a look. "I found something more delightful than the wretched Fae Slayer. This woman captured my heart." He grabbed onto my hand and pulled me toward him as if I were a prize. I tried to keep my smile sweet and light, but felt like the show wasn't good enough.

Think of something bloody instead. Voss kissed my knuckles. *That's better.*

Elspeth rolled her eyes. "And yes, he's been this obnoxious about it the entire journey, demanding for us to return to his majesty's court in order to make everything official." Her hands went onto her hips. "It's been most aggravating, but if we could get the ceremony along, then we could restart our search in earnest for the slayer."

"You? Settling down with a human?" The male snorted. "Never thought I would see the day that—"

"You think too much, then. Open the gate." Voss's words dipped into cold calculation.

The male eyed him, swallowing before opening up the space. "Of course. My apologies. You are right. There should be no delay in celebrating such a momentous occasion. The king will be pleased, I am sure. She is a fine specimen."

I gritted my teeth as Voss slid an arm around me.

"I tell her that every day."

I will kill you.

I would love to watch myself bleed underneath you.

The tension I was holding leaked out of me, already excited by his proposal. Voss chuckled, and I forced myself to give him a big grin—one a girl in love might do.

"I was so lucky to have found him. Right place, right time, I guess." My voice trickled into vapidness, becoming light-hearted and airy. It was sickly sweet and so unlike me, it made everything inside me cringe with instant regret.

The guard, however, seemed satiated.

"I can send word to the—"

"No need," Elspeth stepped forward. "I will make the preparations, as I know what will make him happy. We shall celebrate this evening, after we have cleaned ourselves from the journey." Her nose tilted up, like in challenge for the other male to contradict her.

"Of course. I will get the gate." He turned to the human guard, eyes swirling. "Lift it."

The other guard nodded, gaze vacant and empty. The puffiness around his eyes grew more prominent with each passing second. Reaching for an older style pulley chain system, he heaved his weight onto the mechanism. It groaned underneath him, but barely moved a few inches. Slowly, the gate crawled upward, while the Fae guard watched, not lifting a finger to help the man with the heavy barred gate.

I sneered, but Voss's arm tightened around me.

This is how it is here for now. Watch your emotions.

This isn't fair.

You're right, it's not. But if this man can hold on for a little longer, we can get him the rest he deserves.

I wasn't sure he would survive much longer, judging based on his sluggish movements. Tapping my foot, I tried to get an air of impatience. "Surely you can make this go faster."

The male Fae stiffened. "Well, of course." He waved his hand, casting a spell over the door, which seemed to make it lighter. The human's burden was lifted, and the gate opened at a rapid fire pace.

"Thank you, as we have a ceremony to prepare for." A giggle escaped my lips. "Oh, this is going to be so wonderful." I danced a few paces in front of our group as the gates lifted enough to allow us to pass. "I have heard so many wonderful things about this court, and to think, I get to see it with my husband at my side!" I breathed in deeply and did a twirl, spreading my arms out wide.

I turned back to find them gaping at me, including the human guard who had now secured the gate latch and was no longer under control of the other Fae.

You terrify me, little fox.

Grinning wildly at Voss, he closed the gap between us and scooped me up. "If I recall, there's a tradition that humans have about carrying you across the threshold."

"Oh, that old thing." I slapped him on his shoulder playfully.

"Yes, that old thing. But you know what?"

"What?"

"This is better for you." With an adjustment, Voss tossed me over his shoulder, my ass hanging in the air. *Not so smug now, are you?*

I slapped his ass. "Always."

The guard eyed the show, but Penn and Elspeth led our horses inside as we trailed through the city.

As I looked around from my rather uncomfortable perch over Voss's shoulder, I vaguely remembered this place. My parents had brought me to the zoo and the aquarium here. There were still remnants of the bustling metropolis it used to be, but a lot of it was like all the other cities and towns. It was a hollowed version of what it once was, with less vibrancy, life, and more crumbling facades.

A few winding blocks away from the guard station, and Voss dropped me down. His body lingered next to mine as he stared at me, shaking his head with a bit of wonderment.

"What?"

"Using status and power to your advantage while still somehow remaining innocent in all of it. I like the way you think." He tucked my hair behind my ear, his fingers lingering on my cheek.

"Do you think all the people are like that here?" Unlike Alpin's haven, these streets were relatively quiet. Several Fae milled around, talking to each other in muted voices, but no one looked happy. A few nodded at Voss as we passed, but the movement seemed respectful rather than out of fear. Maybe I was right to trust him after all.

So you do trust me.

Get out of my head, Voss.

He chuckled, smirking. He linked his arm with mine and leaned close to my ear, like someone in love would do. "Most humans are worked until they drop dead. So yes, all people are like that. This is what we're here to fix. Think of the end goal, little fox, and don't let the current status distract you."

I could stay here for weeks on end, systematically killing every Fae who treated the humans poorly, but Voss was right. The end goal was in sight. We had walked into the court of the king, something I wouldn't have been able to do so easily on my own, but having the king's assassin on my side had its perks.

More than just a few.

A flash of him pushing inside me made my body shudder, and I growled at him. "If you don't stop doing that, I will use my dagger on your pride and joy."

"Again, I'd love to see you try."

As we rounded a corner, another wall cropped out of nothing, blocking the higher part of the town from the lower part. Another set of guards stood between us and the king's buildings. The most powerful Fae in the world had built a wall around the largest and most luxurious high rises in the city, which could have easily housed hundreds of people. Instead, most of the city was in tenements and smaller dwellings outside of the high rises. Despite the streets being relatively empty, I could feel the underlying thrum of people. I questioned whether they were staying inside because they wanted to or because the king made them feel so unsafe that they needed to hide.

This was no way to live, not when the king had access to so much.

These guards were not chatty, but they were both Fae. They

nodded at Voss and lifted the gate using pure magic, their eyes whirling to an almond hue as the thick iron rose from the ground. Once it was well above our heads, we walked straight inside. There was a private set of stables to the left, which Penn veered off to immediately with the horses.

Elspeth grabbed onto the upper part of my arm, practically yanking me away from Voss. "We need to get ready, and I know if I leave you with him, you two are going to miss your own dinner because of... him being him."

Voss gave her a mock wounded look. "You act like I have no self-control."

"I act like you fuck her whenever you get the chance to because you like it *and* because you have no self-control when it comes to her. Besides, I have a much nicer tub than you."

"There is nothing wrong with my tub." Voss looked offended this time.

"Nothing wrong, yes, but yours lacks jets." She turned to me. "I promise you, it's worth it."

I glanced between the two of them, knowing full well that I needed to look the part this evening for an introduction to the king. If Voss and I messed around, we could ruin our opportunity. "The less I'm around you right now, the less likely I am to mess up when you give me an order. I think it's probably better for me to go with Elspeth, since she won't be able to control me anyway, right?"

Voss let out a breath, his head hanging slightly. "It's a fair point. Very well. I will come to fetch you right before dinner. Elspeth—"

"I know. You don't have to say anything."

"And if anything goes wrong—" His eyes landed on me. "—you can reach out here." Voss placed his lips right in the middle of my forehead, giving my skin the lightest kiss possible. It was so intimate; I wanted to strip him naked, shove my knife into his kidneys, and fuck him right then and there. "And I adore your twisted little mind."

I tossed him a grin before skipping after Elspeth.

As we walked toward the high rise on the right, Elspeth pointed out some places to me. This building used to house a commercial space on the bottom, so there was a commissary kitchen which had been converted to feed the king, along with a tailor, a butcher, a library, and a vault of wine. Of course there would be luxuries tucked away for the king while the rest of the world went to complete hell. He was here while humans had to fight for their lives, either against Fae who would use them until they dropped dead and inside the vicious lands of the wilds. It was disgusting.

"And this is our building's entrance. The king lives in the other one."

I glanced across the street. "In the entire building?"

"Well, there's a ballroom on the second floor, a gorgeous mezzanine, and plenty of other spaces inside to keep him busy, but yes, he's the only one who resides in the building. If he were to marry, then he would house her there as well, but it has been a long time since the king has had a wife."

"What happened to her?"

Elspeth glanced around as we swept through the lobby of her building. She pressed a code on the exterior of the elevator and called it down. This place also had a steady thrum of electricity. In a lot of towns, they ran on fumes and broken grids that pulsed with frequent blackouts. Here, there was a steady rhythm and hum of moving parts.

"Let's get to my place." She pressed the button for the second to the top floor.

I understood her unspoken meaning; it wasn't safe to speak

openly here. Instead, I asked, "Let me guess, Voss lives in the penthouse?"

"Does it bother you?"

"That you get to live in this, while the rest of us are struggling to survive? No, it's fine." I crossed my arms and leaned against the cool steel as we rose slowly.

"This wasn't a life we would have chosen for ourselves, you know? Well, maybe you don't, because you still think of us as..." She let the last word go unsaid.

"I don't, not anymore," I admitted. Somewhere midst the traveling, I had seen their struggles. I still hated that so many Fae lived in opulence while the rest of the human race fought over scraps, but we were here to change that.

When the elevator opened to her floor, there were two doors. She took me to the left one, and I had to assume Penn had the other one. Figured. The king's assassin and his two assistants would get the best accommodations in the city, even if it seemed like they weren't here half the time.

"If it makes you feel better, I keep a maid employed, and I pay her very well and offer her protection for everything she does. She's human and not compelled." Elspeth shrugged off her jacket and hung it over the coat rack as we walked inside.

It was odd to walk into this apartment, because it was sleek and modern, looking so very human, like something out of an old magazine. It was barely lived in, with not an ounce of dust or anything out of place.

"When we first came over, I was ecstatic to get a second chance. New horizons and adventures, being able to live without suffering. Earth was it, our time to integrate with the human race and become something more, learn from our mistakes, and not drive the planet into the ground like we did Faerie." Elspeth stepped out of her boots. I stayed in the entryway, watching her. She put her boots underneath the coat rack. When she looked back at me, she smoothed her auburn waves.

She continued, "As you likely remember, the fights started up shortly after we arrived. Battles between the human army and the Fae who felt they were above listening to anything the humans had to say. Slowly, the politicians were killed, anyone in a position of power slain so the king wouldn't have to deal with competition trying to sway people. He wanted to rule by fear, because he thought it would be easier, and in some ways, it was." Elspeth gestured half-heartedly to her apartment. "We got all of this, along with a world we could take from and do whatever we wanted with."

"But then the wild creatures came over," I said. "And it got worse."

She pressed her lips into a thin line. "We could have used those munitions we made everyone destroy. Instead, we repeated our mistakes, forcing everyone back into the practical dark ages so we could be the ones in charge. I admit, Scarlet, it wasn't right. None of it was, but I can't go back and fix it. Also, there was no fighting the king. We were looking for you. Ever since we learned you could stand against the king and possibly kill him, we searched for you, hoping we'd be the ones to find you before the others."

"Pretty convenient how he sent you after me then, isn't it?"

Elspeth shook her head. "Voss asked for the job. We were already hoping to find you in secret, but when the king ordered it, it was the perfect opportunity. Once we found you, we could finally cut him down. Believe what you want about our race, because I know power can corrupt and some Fae are greedy once in power, but try to remember that some of us aren't your enemies. Some of us wanted a new beginning. Some of us were sick of watching the land turn gray and the sky turn dark with ash. We have a chance here, and I want that more than you know."

She let out a long breath, weariness creeping around her eyes as exhaustion weighed on her shoulders. "I'll get the bath drawn for you. The water takes a while to warm up, but it's heaven. Take off your boots and gear, and I'll get everything settled."

"Am I going to get stuffed into another gown tonight?" I asked as I slipped off one boot. It thudded to the ground.

"You are announcing a marriage in front of the king, a king who still believes in gender roles. What do you think?" Elspeth disappeared into a room off to the left, and I continued to undress, laying everything out at the ready.

I couldn't bring myself to remove my sparrowbone dagger. It felt too good having it back, like a part of me had been missing for the night I spent without it. Running my fingers along the blade, I realized I should sharpen it soon, perhaps tonight if I had a chance. I wasn't sure when it would be a good time to swipe it across the king's throat, but I couldn't risk the cut being shallow. I couldn't risk his healing.

With as much security as the king had, it proved he was paranoid. There would be no second chances. I had to get this right.

"Whenever you are ready." Elspeth poked her head out, eying me. I still had on my trousers and shirt, rumpled from a day of riding pressed against Voss. She shook her head and gave me a sad smile. "I hope to see a day where you can put your guard down."

I tapped my fingers against the grip on the dagger, dragging my lower lip between my teeth. It was still sore from Voss, which made me think of his shadow in the corner of my mind. He seemed to sense whenever my thoughts landed on him, because his essence took pleasure in my internal wanderings.

You wet yet?

Touching my dagger, so not yet.

And thinking of me?

Stabbing you, yes.

So then you are soaked. He chuckled through our bond.

I shook my head and focused back on Elspeth. "I hope for that too." The words, however, were more to convince myself that such a world was possible.

Twenty-Four

When Elspeth said her bath was worth it, she hadn't been lying. Even I could admit how much of a necessary relief it was to ease the tension in my body. I let the jets and added salts melt away the last bit of self-doubt and fear I had over the evening. The warm water washed away my exhaustion, the ache in my spine from sleeping upright, and allowed me to focus. I went through fighting stances, meditating on how it would feel to swipe my dagger across the Fae's throat. I imagined a world where humans no longer had to bow down to a corrupt Fae king.

It was a beautiful dream, and with it being so close at hand, the thought made me excited. The end was within sight, but if anything went wrong tonight, I could lose everything. In the worst case scenario, Quinn would still work with his network to find other weaknesses, other ways for the humans to start the revolution. I knew our group would continue on without me; they would be okay.

But if I could remove the head of the snake tonight, it would be a morale boost. It would be easier for the humans to gather if we didn't have a king to fight against head on. And if the Fae became divided after the new ruler rose to power, even better. One of the princes would take over, but surely the kingdom would suffer some moments of disarray.

In those weeks of chaos, the revolution would start. Quinn would spread word, and the war would begin again. We would rise against the corrupt Fae and push them out.

I hoped that Fae like Elspeth, Penn, and Voss would be spared. Our side needed to be better than the Fae and realize not all of them needed to be overthrown. I sent a silent prayer out into the universe as I got out of the tub and dried off.

That's a lot of desires, little fox. Promise me you'll keep that fire.

Get out, Voss.

Make me.

I tried to slam down on my thoughts, but he only chuckled. Instead, I sent him the most gruesome thoughts I could think about and felt his mood sour. *You're welcome.*

Please stop thinking about dismembering Penn. I kind of like him.

Get out, and I'll stop.

He went quiet, thankfully.

Once I was dry, Elspeth helped me prepare for the rest of the evening, using some of her Fae magic to alter her gown to make a form-fitting dress for me. The outfit would have been better suited for a queen than me.

I gaped at myself in the mirror, tucking my hair behind my ears. The short, black bob cut such sharp angles along my face, but the rosy fabric was flowing and feminine. It was graceful, elegant, and expensive. Plucking at a piece of it, I cast Elspeth a glare. "This is too much. Don't you think this is overdoing it to announce a wedding between an assassin and his wife?"

"The king's favorite assassin, you forget." Elspeth twirled her hands, and I obeyed by doing a small spin for her. She frowned. "I think... this." She waved her hands over the piece, turning it bright scarlet red, just like the stone Voss had wrapped around my wrist.

I gawked at the dress. The tight bodice, the ample amount of cleavage, and the strapless dress was stunning even if it didn't suit me. But how could I possibly kill a male while wearing all of this?

"Oh, and one more thing!" Elspeth breezed out of the room and came back with a bejeweled sheath attached to a garter. "I don't think you should kill the king tonight, for the record. If you stay here a few more days, he'll put his guard down more and more, but I know you wouldn't want to go anywhere without it. While it'll be hard to reach—"

I hugged her.

Elspeth froze underneath my arms, and I could hardly believe myself either. "You're welcome?"

Laughing, I pulled away, taking the sheath gently in my hands. "It's perfect. Thank you." I ran my fingers along it before lifting my skirts and attaching it around my thigh. It fit my dagger perfectly, and I felt like I could breathe easier with it on. The dress was a princess cut away from my hips, which hid everything underneath it.

"If I get a chance, I am going to take it."

"I doubt that will be tonight. Do me a favor and try to enjoy the dinner. It's good food, decent entertainment, and try not to think about the corruption outside. Leave it be for one night so you can get the king to drop his guard. Then do it. Too soon, and I worry about what will happen."

"Too late, and I risk discovery because Voss demands too much."

"I'll make sure he watches himself."

"As if you could do that." Penn's voice came from the other room. Elspeth and I scowled at each other before walking into the living room. Voss was perched on the end of a couch while Penn lazed across one.

The Fae Assassin looked like his usual smug self. His eyes landed on me, hot and heavy.

"How long have you been in here?" I asked.

"Since the sheath, which I will enjoy taking off with my teeth later." His smile was wide enough to reflect the last rays of sun. He raked a hand through his hair, tousling the blond locks. His dark eyes consumed me.

He cleaned up well. Voss was spouting a slick pair of dark pants, a white button-down shirt, and a gray vest. His blond hair swept away from his face, featuring his arched cheekbones and striking eyes. Underneath the black irises, there was a hint of his whirling power, ready to turn to liquid lava at a moment's notice.

Watching him eye me sent a jolt of excitement straight through me. He looked hungry, and the self-consciousness I felt earlier in front of the mirror drifted away as if it were a dandelion seed caught in a breeze. I swallowed.

"Shall we, my queen?" Voss extended a hand to me. It was as if the air was sucked out of the room hearing another nickname on his lips, one that showed his utmost confidence in me. We would do this. We could turn the tides. We could change the future.

I placed my hand in his, and his fingers interlocked with mine. His skin was warm, and he smelled good enough to eat. My stomach, in flattering form, growled.

"It's a good thing we're going to get food, then. I wish you had said something."

"When should I have? When we were running for our lives?"

"I could have given you more cheese and bread."

"Stale bread, yay."

Voss pulled me into him, wrapping his arms around me with such care I wanted to wiggle out of his touch. I was beginning to like this with him. It felt comfortable and familiar, but that also wedged fear inside me.

This couldn't last forever, could it?

"I missed you," he whispered.

"You're insatiable."

"Yes, I've been told. Come. Let's go announce our delightful marriage to the king."

While I had been in the bath, Elspeth had met with a lot of Fae and humans. She vaguely ran down everything with me, and she promised me that the humans she had working for the event tonight were compensated. She promised to extend as many protections as she could to them. Regardless, she had organized everything in a blizzard, getting the event together within mere hours so Voss and I could be announced before the king.

"Is this how it always is in the king's court for a wedding?"

As we left the room, I realized Penn walked in front of us and Elspeth behind, like guards would. They had always been around Voss, so that wasn't new, but this felt more formal, more poised, likely because we were in the court. Here, they were acting differently than when we were away from prying eyes.

In the elevator, they stood in front of the doors on guard and stoic. It was unnerving seeing Penn this way. His creased brow of concern was gone and his expression was flat. Normally, I could expect a side eye of confusion or complaints from him, but his stature right now was pure seriousness.

"This is a special occasion. It has been a long time since anyone has announced a wedding inside the king's court, and never has a

Fae married a human in this court. So this is more about...
acceptance. We are asking for the king's blessing with our
marriage."

"And if he doesn't bless it? Do I get locked in a dungeon
forever?"

Voss frowned. "If he doesn't bless it, there's nothing he can do.
As I said, a marriage vow is forever. I will be bound to you for the
rest of my life."

"Or the rest of mine."

Voss swallowed. "I don't like that you are now pointing out the
flaws in this plan, little fox."

"I had a lot of time to think in the bath."

"The king won't risk pissing you off, Voss, and you know it. He
won't order her death unless he discovers the truth." Elspeth cast
me a glance. "So no pressure, but remember to follow everything
Voss says."

"And remind him not to be an absolute ass about it."

Voss's free hand cupped my jaw, pulling me into him for a
quick kiss. "You know the word. If you scream it at me in your
thoughts, and I'll stop. But remember, no shocked looks, no angry
expressions, you're a woman in love." His jaw worked as he looked
at my narrowed eyes and furrowed brows. "Yeah, that won't do."

He pushed a thought into my head of his scar opening
underneath my fingernails with his cock pushed deep inside me.

"Fuck." I practically stumbled back, but he tightened his grasp
to steady me. "Don't do that."

"I'll do what I want. Besides, it's show time." The grin Voss
gave me was horribly wicked, and I absolutely loved it.

The elevator pinged as the doors opened, and we headed across
the street to the other high rise. The building's entrance was lavish,
decked out with quartz tile, giant marble pillar facades, and a huge

ivory staircase leading to the second-floor ballroom. A plush red carpet ran along the length of the stairs, and I could see why the king had chosen this building over the other one. Both were expensive, but this was exquisite, with no cut corners to bring out the most ornate features. The sheer magnitude shocked me, and by the time we reached the staircase, Voss had to shut my mouth by tenderly pressing against my jaw.

"Careful, little fox. It almost appears like you enjoy our surroundings."

"More like I am crafting how to burn it all to the ground." My voice dipped into a hiss.

He squeezed my hand as we walked up the steps and entered the ballroom. On one side, there was a long banquet table, already loaded with the first course laid out underneath silver covers. Voss straightened his spine, marching us across the length of the room and presenting me in front of the king.

The king—the one I had tried so many times to get close to—was now within my reach, save for the insane amount of fabric between me and the dagger.

"May I announce my wife, Maxine."

I swallowed, not realizing my real name would be laid out before the king, but there it was. It was liquid gold racing across my skin as the syllables escaped Voss's lips. Obviously, he couldn't call me Scarlet, but I had assumed we would go back to Lola. Perhaps that would raise too many red flags, as that identity had also been compromised when I was fished out of Raskos's land.

The king looked me over and stated, "Maxine." The sound made me want to retch. People told me that their name on Fae's lips was like hypnosis, a sexually charged tension. When Voss said my name, it felt exactly like that, fiery touches trailing against my skin, inviting, soothing, and hot all at once. I wondered if it was because of who Voss was or because of the bracelet, or if maybe it was because I stupidly was starting to like him.

Or at least enjoyed having sex with him.

When the king said it, however, it held an air of disdain, a loathing so deep it felt like bugs crawling under my skin. His voice disgusted me.

But that was where the king's individuality stopped. If he were in a lineup of other Fae, there was nothing to make him stand out. There was nothing identifying about this man. Like the other Fae I had slain over the years, he held an air of mediocrity. He had high cheekbones, darker set eyes, and a straight nose, but those features could be said about plenty of Fae. He had lighter hair with gray that seemed to glow even underneath the dim atmospheric lights of the ballroom. The male had wider set shoulders and wore a suit, which looked immensely out of place on a supernatural being.

"She looks… normal. I expected more."

I gritted my teeth as Voss pulsed his fingers around my hand. The dark part of him inside my head was physically holding me back. His emotions wrapped around my anger, encapsulating me and reeling my rage back in so I wouldn't lash out at the king. There were tons of guards. Elspeth had been right; if I reacted now, there was a high likelihood I wouldn't make it out of this alive. As much as I trusted the revolution to continue without me, if I could avoid dying, I would.

"Since the moment I met her, she has intrigued me. The Fae at Raskos's court were naturally drawn to her. I wanted to know why. And when I tasted her, I knew. She's sweeter than most."

"And how would you know? You made it a habit not to taste." The king shifted his gaze to Voss. "Wasn't that your stance, boy? Don't mess with the humans?" The older male rolled his eyes. "Such childish behavior that I am thankful to see you straying from. Well, don't stand there. Sit. Let's celebrate this occasion, and maybe I'll figure out what *that* is doing in my court." His eyes flicked back to me.

I bit my tongue so hard I tasted copper inside my mouth.

"Of course." Voss pulled me to the other side of the table and sat in the other head chair, a position of honor. I had to wonder exactly how many people Voss had killed in order to get propped into such a position.

Someday, I would ask him.

I expected Voss to pull out a seat for me to sit in, but instead, he pulled me onto his lap like I was nothing more than a prop.

Don't bite me when I feed you this time, Voss scowled.

No promises.

The king's eyes lingered on us for a moment before he waved his hands. As soon as the king set in motion, a bunch more Fae filed in from the outskirts of the room. Elspeth and Penn stood off to the side, not joining us at the table, which made my stomach hollow out. Voss made slow circles on my lower back, and I could feel his calm through the bond. His resolve was set, and mine needed to be too.

But when the Fae sat down at the table with us, it was overwhelming. While Fae magic didn't work on me, these Fae exuded authority. The room crackled with magic, sweeping over my skin like tiny pinpricks. The sheer magnitude of their powers let me know the king was more formidable than he appeared to be, because nothing compared to the energy wafting off him.

The higher Faes' eyes ran the gamut of colors, several sets of pink and lavender, others more pale than a robin's egg. It was like being thrown into a den of vipers. I had been around a lot of Fae in my life, had watched their magic and blood drain out of them too, but being near this much power made me feel helpless.

Voss ran his tongue up the side of my ear, because I had frozen at his side. I shot him a smile, but in my head, I was screaming. I pressed my dress down, trying to shift to take out the wrinkles and look as elegant as I could while being nothing more than a toy.

Steady, little fox. He ran his fingers along my thigh, soothing my nerves. Annoyingly, I could feel how much he enjoyed this, disarming me in a way no one else had to date. I wanted to fight him over it. *Later. I promise.*

"So nice to have you join us for this momentous occasion. It's rare to find myself surprised, being as old as I am, but alas, this joining has me rather speechless." The king gazed at Voss from down the table, lifting a golden goblet in front of him. His nails were filed into perfect points.

The rest of the table copied his movements, including Voss. I did not have a goblet in front of me, so I sat there, staring at them while trying to look pleasant and poised, like I wanted to be nowhere else in the world.

The table raised their glasses as one and downed healthy gulps of Faerie wine. Voss licked his lips afterward. "What can I say? I do like creating entertainment for you. It was about time someone did something interesting."

"Yes, you do." The king's narrow gaze settled back on me. "How rude of me. Get the human regular wine from the cellar. And her own glass as well. The boy can't have all the fun this evening, after all. What an oversight on my part, because of course the pet would need their own plate."

"I am fine sharing with my partner, your majesty, but thank you for thinking of me." I plastered on the widest grin I could muster. It made my cheeks hurt.

The king snorted, an absurd noise to come from the one that had ruled over the earth with an iron fist. "At least she has manners. The same cannot be said for you. So, girl, where did he find you? The side of the road? He has a habit of finding strays."

I ignored the jab and lifted my chin. "At a nightclub, actually."

"A club. You?" The king's eyes shifted back onto Voss. His jaw worked as his gaze slid between both of us. I tried to ignore the warning bells going off in my head. The way he spoke felt too performed.

Steady, little fox.

"I had business to attend to in Raskos's land. The Fae Slayer—" A collective inhale rose around the table from the other Fae, but I noticed how intensely quiet they were. They watched the volley across the table as if the two males were the only ones in the room. Voss cleared his throat and began again. "There were rumors the Fae Slayer had taken up residence there, a lot of deaths, but I'm afraid she had moved on by the time I arrived. Instead, I met this lovely creature at the club as I was asking Lord Raskos for any updates."

I tried not to glare at him when he called me *creature*. The way they spoke about humans made my skin crawl.

Voss wrapped one of his arms fully around my waist, bringing me close to him as he plucked the goblet up with his free hand. He ran small circles around my stomach, apologizing internally to me. "She had quite a mouth on her before I charmed her."

Charmed me, ha. More like made me drink Faerie wine.

Charmed, definitely.

"Well, she seems amicable now. Tell me, what is your true nature?" His eyes swirled to life with magic, a dark liquid reddish brown. The power coiled around my skin, trying to get into my head. I could feel the essence around me, invasive and hot.

"I'm afraid she's under my protection now, but go on, Maxine, tell him. What is your true nature?" Voss's eyes lit up.

I stiffened, making my eyes go glassy like Voss's magic was working on me. His energy circled around me, but this felt like a warm welcome breeze compared to the king's crackling lightning. "I'm human, of course. And I get quite stubborn and aggressive…" I flashed Voss an award-winning smile. "In bed."

A few snickers rose from the other Fae.

I shook myself out of the pretend stupor and tried to blush. Voss pressed his fingers against my skin as he flashed me an appraising look. *Not bad, little fox.*

When an attendant came over with a bottle of wine exclusively for me, I was grateful for something else to do with my hands. I felt like the room was running out of air. The person poured a hefty amount of wine into a clean goblet for me, and I nodded in thanks, picking it up and taking a delicate sip.

"I like her," one male said from farther down the table.

A female sitting across from him nodded. "She is very decorative. She is a perfect opposite of you. Look at the shine of her hair. Maybe I should go short next time. Do you think I could pull it off?"

Banter rose around the table with talks of clothing, festivities, and other superfluous things. I forced myself to down a glass of wine, because without it, I'd end up snarling at everyone due to their idiocy. Their lives were so… mundane, full of events with no real value while humans were out there dying from the hoswisps and starving from the lack of supply chain. The Fae effectively ended our society when they came over, and they had no remorse.

It won't always be like this, Voss whispered from the corner of my mind. He kept running his hand over my dress above my stomach, and it calmed me to have him pressed against me. *Remember, we have a lot of work to do once the king is out of the picture. These Fae? They will fall in line with the new ruler. Trust me. They are followers. We only need to get this right.*

While his words helped quell the fire underneath my skin, I still struggled to hold myself together, especially when a nearby couple started bickering over who had the most handsome human servants. All the while I sipped wine and forced myself to keep a neutral expression, because the king's eyes roamed the table, landing on me more often than not.

The first appetizer was announced with little fanfare. It was a green vegetable puree with a delicate oil based sauce. The plate was enormous for the tiny amount of food on top of it, and it almost made me laugh. I had remembered watching a movie like this when I was little—where the girl was thrust into royalty and her meals resembled this. I forced myself to eat the meager amount on my plate. The portion being so small indicated that there was much more to come, but it made my stomach rumble with hunger.

Did the Fae experience hunger like the humans do now?

In Faerie, yes. We've been privileged here. I won't deny that. Not all of us forget where we came from, what we came from. Not all of us are so eager to go back or to drive humans to do the same now.

Voss's dark eyes settled on me, an assessing look on his face. "How do you find the first course?"

"It's delicious, of course." The disdain spreading through me must have hit him through our bond, because he barely hid the flinch off his face.

Cautious, Maxine.

My name through our bond set a fire down to my nerves.

"While it is pleasant, I imagine after such a long journey, you are hungry." Voss kissed the side of my neck. "It's okay to admit it if you are."

"I'm famished," I conceded.

He nodded. "King Balgair, do you think we could speed onto

an entrée? I worry my wife is growing weary and must rest before whatever ceremony you have planned."

The king glanced between the two of us again. I squirmed under his gaze. "I'm afraid I won't speed up the process, even for you, boy. It is customary to have a seven course meal prior to the wedding events. Surely, even you have enough control over her to make it to the end of the meal."

I swallowed. "Whatever my husband wants."

"I didn't ask you to speak, girl." The king's cold eyes focused on Voss. "Control her or else receiving my blessing will be the least of your problems."

Voss's grip tightened on me. He swirled his wine and whispered in my ear, "Be a good girl and don't speak unless I tell you to." I didn't have to look at his irises to know they'd be blazing, because I could feel the air shift around him.

The hair on my neck rose, more so because of the scrutiny from across the table, and I forced myself to nod.

I'm sorry.

It's not your fault. From the lack of sustenance with so much wine, I was already feeling the effects by the time another attendant filled my glass again. *I can't drink anymore.*

Pretend to.

"Raskos's club." The moment the words left the king's mouth, the table plunged into silence. The hair on my neck rose.

The attendants dropped the second course on the table, pulling away the gleaming silver lids to display a bowl of red soup. It smelled like tomatoes. I couldn't remember the last time I had tomatoes.

"Never thought I'd catch you dead in a place like that, let alone taking a street urchin from one to bed."

"Like I said, I was following a lead."

"Raskos told me how many people died in his court. It's a wonder the Fae Slayer didn't try her hand on Raskos himself."

"I'm sure she would have, but Morna and Cumina were obviously extra guard detail."

"Yes, they never had a thing for subtlety. The problem was what to do with them once their mother died. They yearned for my approval, unlike some others, but I admit, they were not trained as you were."

Voss stiffened under me. "Their mother never saw the art in training them. It's a shame, really. I had hoped they would prove more useful on this side of the portal." Without looking at me, Voss raised the soup spoon in front of my face. I tried to be dainty while sipping from it, but hunger was getting the better of me.

What's going on between you and the king right now? I asked.

"Though, perhaps if their mother had trained them, maybe they would become like you." The king stared at the two of us. A utensil clattered to the table.

"What is that supposed to mean?" Voss asked, narrowing his gaze in a challenge.

A hush went over the room. The Fae collectively stopped breathing.

"Be honest, girl, what have you done to the male sitting behind you?" The king's eyes landed on me, roaring to life with magic again.

My spine straightened. "I am not sure what you mean, my King." I swallowed my resentment at those words escaping my lips. Never did I want to call this man *my king*.

"I do not believe this act." The king's lip curled as he tossed his gaze back to Voss. "Raskos told me about the woman you left with, and he had his suspicions about her. And now, you are entirely too complimentary, entirely too concerned with the well being of her. I know you. You're selfish and arrogant. Never would you ask to leave such an event like this for anyone but your own reasons. I am supposed to believe this ruse? Believe you care?" He gestured between the two of us. "She is not nearly gorgeous enough to have you be so stupid."

"What does he mean?" I turned to Voss, trying to keep a mask of innocence even as my stomach turned to ice.

Voss had frozen underneath me. I could feel the panic through our bond, but none of his thoughts were coming to me. I felt alone, despite sitting on top of him.

The king rose from his seat. "You see, it took me some time to realize it. Something happened at that club, did it not? The day you left Lord Raskos's court with this girl, this *Maxine* as you call her, the killings stopped." The king stood tall as he stalked toward us around the table. I was frozen to my spot, not knowing what Voss or I should do next. There was still the dagger. There was still the chance. "I was willing to play along, because perhaps I was wrong, because Raskos claimed her name was not Maxine, but Lola. This is where the story gets stranger still. You were seen leaving a party the night of Lord Treborne's unfortunate demise. More strangely, most Fae don't recall the events of that night. Most people don't remember seeing you, save for a single guard who swore he saw you fade into the night with her at your heels."

King Balgair lowered himself on top of us, leaning so close to me I could smell his breath. It was rotted and corrosive, just like him. "So tell me, girl, what have you done to the male you sit with? What vileness have you done to his mind to curl him around your finger? What magic powers do you wield over us? Are all the rumors about you true, I wonder?" He licked his lips.

There was too much fabric between me and my dagger, but my fingers itched to retrieve it anyway.

Forgive me. There's no time to explain this change of plans, little fox.

I started at Voss's sudden intrusion in my thoughts, but my eyes flew wide as he jumped out of his seat, taking me with him. He pushed me away from him as if I were on fire, and I stumbled a few feet as the chair crashed onto the ballroom floor, making a monstrous sound in the cavernous space.

"She does have powers," Voss said, scrambling for words and sounding unhinged, unlike his usual poised self. "She convinced me to—" He shook his head wildly, as if trying to push me out of his thoughts. "Seize her before she does it again!"

I barely had time to blink before several Fae had their arms locked around me. I fought and scratched, not quite understanding what was happening, but the look of betrayal I shot at Voss said enough. He threw me under the bus to save his own skin. The king assumed I had influence over Voss, and Voss played right into it.

Trust, he asked, eyes pleading.

Without being able to do anything else, but still wanting the satisfaction of doing something, I spat right in the king's face. "You're next."

As my spit dripped down his cheek, the king sneered, assessing me as one would a rat. "You won't be so confident tomorrow, when I watch you hang from the gallows."

Twenty-Five

It didn't take long for me to get carted away. I left to the sounds of Voss's made up story. He weaved a tale about the monster he met at the nightclub, a monster who could use Fae magic against them. He claimed I bent him to my every whim. I wondered how he made them believe it, but his eyes were swirling the entire time. The king was the only one questioning parts of his story, but the Fae still seemed content to blame the affair on me—the lowly human he could crush under his fingers.

This is the second time you've thrown me into the path of danger, Voss.

But the first time it was my idea. With that thought, the link between us broke off on his end as he went quiet inside my head.

As soon as I was shoved into the cell, I stumbled forward a few paces, whirling to fight the guards, but hesitated when I saw it was Penn and Elspeth.

"We know about the dagger," Penn said, keeping his voice calm and level.

"If you don't hand it over peacefully, we will take it by force,

311

and I would hate to destroy my creation." Elspeth swept her eyes over the dress.

Two of the guards hung back, arms crossed over their chests as they watched the exchange. Their irises were swirling oceans of blue. Penn's eyes blazed to life with bright turquoise pools.

"Don't hold it against him. We'll find a way out of this."

"Of course we will, just at the expense of my comfort. Again." I sneered, pulling up the edge of my skirts to reveal the garter underneath. I unsheathed the dagger and brought it out in front of me. "Give me one good reason I shouldn't cut my way out of this, especially if you are glamoring them?"

"Because you won't make it very far after that. Penn can't glamor the king. We'll come up with a plan to make sure you get out alive, and the king does not."

Shoving my dagger at her, I took a step back once the handle was in her hands. "Voss seemed pretty quick on his feet up there. Was this the back-up plan the entire time?"

Penn shifted his gaze to Elspeth, but the look he gave her was enough. "We didn't know if you could keep it together."

Elspeth let out a breath. "Honestly, I'm surprised Raskos reported back to the king. That weasel usually wants royalty out of his business, not in it. The king had made up his mind about you early on, but I think he was biding his time to see if Voss was involved." She gently tucked my dagger in her belt. I wished I still had it on me. The absence of it weighed heavily on me. Anything could happen between now and tomorrow, including Fae visitors. "I'm shocked you didn't break under the pressure. I felt all the magic swirling around you. It was incredible, because even married humans would have a hard time under that amount of pressure. Maybe not full influence, but faltering. You were flawless."

"Flawless enough to get shoved into a caged room underneath

the building," I grumbled.

She shrugged. "You're still alive."

"For now," I spat.

"And we'll make sure you stay that way. We got you this far, didn't we? Be ready tomorrow. And try to get some sleep tonight."

"On the cold stone floor with barely any food in me, sure."

Penn winced, taking a step back. "I can't hold it much longer."

"Until tomorrow." Elspeth spun and marched past the guards with Penn on her heels. They closed the iron gates with a heavy creak. The lock clicked into place, and the guards exited up the stairs as well. Soon after, the lights flicked out.

Great.

Perfect.

Rage boiled inside me as I sat against the wall, huffing with frustration. I threw every single insult I had at Voss, which only made him chuckle against our connection. Threatening him never worked, but it made me feel better. Meanwhile, in the dark, I tried to poke through to his side of things to see what Voss was experiencing with his freedom, but I couldn't. He had shut down almost everything between us. The power was entirely in his hands right now, which furthered my frustration.

Instead, I focused on blocking him out. I had nothing better to do, so I stared into the darker part of my mind, the part that housed him. I built a box around it, stuffing every part of him into it and isolating him in my head. As soon as I was done, the walls crumbled away instantly.

Try harder.

I hate you.

But I did. I kept building and rebuilding the box to pass the time, as there wasn't anything else to do other than shiver from the cold licking at my skin. What felt like hours later, but may have only been forty minutes, a sliver of the light sliced through the opening of the entrance, and the lights flooded on above me.

A female Fae walked down the stairs, keeping her nose held high as her heels clicked against the stone floor. She stopped outside of the bars of my confines and glared at me. "The Fae Slayer, *Scarlet.* You don't seem so tough now."

"Come inside and see how dangerous I can be." I picked myself up off the ground and faced her. She had pink lilac swirling eyes, watching me with scrutiny. The curves of her jaw and brows looked familiar, down to the upward bend of her ears. There was something about her.

"You killed my brother."

Ah, there it was. The last one before Treborne. They shared similar features, these two. I had been right to assume that Torin was a high Fae. If I had gotten information out of him, I might have gotten the location of this court.

Except no matter what the king's court believed, I had no magical powers over the Fae. I simply had a word, a word they hated hearing and wanted to prove wrong. Even if I had gotten Torin to talk, he might not have told me the truth.

"I've killed plenty of Fae," I admitted. "What makes you think your brother is special enough to remember?"

She snarled, wicked and feral. "He was a monster, but he was *my* monster. You had no right to take him from me."

"Why don't you teach me a lesson, then?" I leaned toward her. Without my sparrowbone to defend myself, it was stupid to goad a response, but frankly, I was bored, hungry, and angry, a combination that didn't allow my logical brain to step in. "Or are you as weak minded as he was?"

Growling, she stepped up to the bars. "Come here." Her magic flared to life around me, caressing my skin with demands. I shook them off like I had every other Fae's magic, letting it drift into nothingness around me.

"No, thank you."

"Come. Here."

"I don't want to." I shrugged and crossed my arms, arching an eyebrow at her. "What are you going to do about it?"

She marched over to the gate's lock and broke it underneath her palms, crushing it into nothing. I took a step back.

Well, damn, that was one way to do it.

The female threw open the door and prowled toward me. Usually, my mouth kept me out of trouble, but I had pressed the wrong buttons this time. At least if I got past her, I could run for it.

"I will make you pay. Blood for blood." The Fae leaped at me, but I ducked under her outstretched hands and attempted to dart around her. She screamed and wrenched on my stupid petticoats. I was about to tear this dress off with my own teeth if it meant getting out of this cage.

She yanked hard against the fabric, but the material didn't so much as lose a thread, and I stumbled backward into her. This Fae was no fighter. She lashed out with her hand and barely grazed my cheek, but it was enough. Her nails carved out a part of my skin, blood coming to the surface.

With a snarl, I punched her straight in the face, making red burst out of her nose. "Why does everyone keep making me bleed?!" I screamed, punching her again, this time in the jaw. My hand throbbed, because this was not the type of combat I was used to, and Fae bones were strong.

The Fae kicked out, which was so unexpected, I barely had time to lean backward. Her heel connected with my thigh, and a stabbing pain lanced up my leg. I gasped as she used her forward momentum to grab hold of my hair, yanking me upright with a tight grasp on my scalp.

I grabbed onto her wrist with both of my hands and dug my small nails into her skin.

"You disgust me," she said as some of my hair ripped out of my scalp.

It hurt. I clawed at her, but a whimper escaped my mouth as she yanked harder, tears making my eyes water. Switching tactics, I lashed out with one hand, catching the sore spot on her jaw, but the impact was more like a slap. The move must have annoyed her further, because her other hand latched around my throat.

Stupid. I had been so stupid to taunt her. If I had my dagger, she'd be dead, and I'd be standing over her bloodied corpse, but now... now I wheezed in a lackluster breath as she squeezed harder against my windpipe.

"Drop her." Voss's voice rang against the stones. Nothing happened for a moment, and my vision blackened. "Orders from King Balgair are a public execution, so everyone knows the Fae Slayer is dead. I said drop her now, Emille."

I fell to my knees as the Fae released me all at once. The bone jarring crack of my knees slamming against the floor made everything inside my body ache, but I could breathe. I had air.

"She deserves something more painful than the gallows, but at least I know she won't enjoy her night." Emille stomped out of the stone room, her footsteps reverberating off the walls as she went.

"Are you okay, little fox?" Voss's words wrapped around me, and they were the last things I heard before my vision went black.

❧ ✄ ❦

I awoke on the cold stone floor, my head cradled on Voss's lap. His eyes were dark pits of anger, watching the entrance to the dank cells with intensity. I groaned, feeling like my head was ready to implode.

"What the fuck," I said.

He soothed back my hair, tucking it behind my ears. I was afraid to move. "I will kill her."

"That's my job."

Voss let out a grunt. "She touched what was mine."

"Don't start with that macho possessive bullshit again." I tried to get up, but my head swam. "I've never been strangled."

His eyebrow cocked as his eyes settled on me.

"Outside of sexual encounters and when people were on their last breaths, which hardly counts."

"You scared me."

"I'm fine." This time, I found the strength to sit up, leaning away from him. My stomach swam with what meager food I ate earlier. I felt horrible. "How did you get down here, anyway? Aren't they worried you're going to release me?"

Voss nodded to the door. "I locked us in here with instructions for them to come check on me in two hours once I teach you a lesson."

"And what kind of a lesson is that?"

"I'll show you when the time comes." His eyes pulsed with a flash of lava for a moment before settling back into black. His shoulders deflated as he exhaled. "I have grown rather attached to you."

"I hear marriage does that."

"It's not out of obligation. I like your sharp edges and harshness. I like how you will fight any Fae you come across, even when the odds are stacked against you. I admire you. Fighting Emille was very brave."

"Stupid, more like," I grumbled, pulling my knees to my chest. "You sat at the head of the table tonight."

"Yes."

I narrowed my eyes. "Do all assassins get held in such high regard? Because Morna and Cumina—"

"I'd rather not talk about them right now, seeing as how I will be delayed on my promise."

"What was the promise, anyway?"

"Their freedom."

"Ah, if we had killed the king."

"Not *if*. We still will. It will be… delayed." Voss's eyes sharpened as a shadow passed the door, but no one made a move to come down. "Penn is blocking our voices for anyone going by."

"How can you be sure no one is doing the same thing to you?"

"I am more powerful than most."

"Let me guess. You're powerful because you are just that good."

"Remind me to make you say that when I'm deep inside you."

I glared at him, and his wretched smirk made its appearance. "How many people have you killed for him?" I asked.

"Too many humans. And too many Fae. The king wants what he wants, and he isn't afraid to sacrifice to get it, even if that means putting us in harm's way."

"The other assassins made it seem like there was nothing they could do to escape their situation. Is it similar for you?"

"Worse." Voss hung his head. "I owe my entire life to the king, and the sooner he is dead, the sooner I will also be free to do what I want. Trust me when I tell you, little fox, I don't make my decisions lightly. There are many reasons the king needs to die, more than you will know, but humans will benefit from it. That I can promise. He doesn't view you as anything more than servants, pests he needs to control, worse than the hoswisps."

"That female, Emille? She said I killed her brother."

"You killed a lot of relatives, I'm afraid. As have I."

"I never thought about it before. I mean, you have families and pasts and histories, but to me, in those moments, it was nothing but survival of the human race. I wasn't thinking about any of that, and now I feel…"

"Ah." Voss cupped my chin in his hands, staring at me for a few solid moments. "You cannot allow yourself to go down that route. What is done is done. There is no moving backward, only learning from your actions and changing the way you react in the future."

"You make it sound easy."

"It comes from many decades of practice."

"And your age again would be?"

"Not as old as you are thinking and not as young either."

I tried to reach into the shadow of him, the part of him that connected us, but hit an impervious wall. "You'll tell me one of these days."

"If you kill the king, once the dust settles, I'll tell you anything you want to know."

"And if I ask now?"

Another shadow went by the door. Voss cursed. "Let me tell you the plan first and see if we still have time after that. They've set up the gallows in the courtyard. The king will preside over it, but because he's conceited, he'll be on a dais not far away from the execution. If you are able to get free, you'll be able to sprint to him and kill him, hopefully without too many Fae realizing what has happened."

"Fae are much faster than people."

"Yes, but Penn and I can block most of the crowd from realizing what is going on, at least to buy you enough time."

"Okay, so how do I escape?"

Voss smirked. "I'm a genius, that's how."

"Stop looking so smug and tell—"

"We frayed the rope. Elspeth's idea, since she's so good with fabric. She made the rope age tremendously. It's not strong enough to lift a baby hoswisp, let alone you. The floor will fall out from underneath you, and you'll drop to the ground. Under the gallows, we'll hide your dagger. You'll see it. Grab it, sprint to the king, kill him, and we'll be free."

"And if the rope doesn't break?"

"I will ask Morna and Cumina to assist. Cumina is a great shot, and I will be in her debt if it comes to that. She'd appreciate me being indebted to her, but I don't think the plan will fail. If it does, then you have to hang on tight for a few agonizing moments before the arrow slices through the ropes."

"Gee, sounds fun."

"No worse than what Emille did to you. I really will kill her."

I stretched my legs out in front of me. "If this doesn't work, Voss..." I licked my lips, not knowing exactly where I wanted the thought to go. There were a lot of things I wanted to say to him. But overall, it had been very nice to get to know him, pleasant, and not at all what I expected.

He frowned, apparently getting my emotions through our bond. "It will work."

"How much time do you think we have?"

Voss glanced at the doorway, which had remained relatively quiet. "Not much, I bet. Someone will come to check up on me at some point, and then the show begins."

"So what does that punishment look like, exactly?"

He arched an eyebrow. "You want to know?"

"Why wait for an audience?" I cocked an eyebrow.

Without moving a muscle, Voss thrust the thoughts into my

head, images of him so deep inside my throat I had tears streaming down my face. My skin red and raw from being slapped. And how it felt for him to be penetrating me, forcing me open brutally and repeatedly.

"Of course, all of that is with the utmost respect," he added.

"Uh huh."

"If this is our last night together, little fox, and I hope it's not, then I want something no other Fae has ever had from you. Tell me, what haven't you done?" I didn't get a chance to say anything, because the two thoughts ran through my head and instantly the side of his lip twitched up. "So you agree? I punish you for real, so when we are discovered, it is believable? You know the safe word."

"Stop checking in with me and do your worst, Fae."

He closed the distance between us in a flash. His lips captured mine, moving against my mouth with a fury. I opened for his tongue, and he invaded me. Our kisses grew with passion and abandon. I didn't care who saw us, because I was desperate for him. Voss created a fire in me that only he could quench.

When he pulled away, he said, "I'm going to enjoy this. Probably a lot more than you."

"Don't assume anything, Voss."

"Get on your knees." He stood up, loosening his pants. The bulge of him was hard against the fabric, and I wasted no time scrambling to my knees.

With as many Fae as I had been with, male and female, I had never done anything with my mouth. I never had to. Fae usually fucked me within moments of hearing me say no. It was quick and pragmatic. Fae told me other demands, like turning around, shutting up, sitting down, begging. Never this.

This time, when Voss told me something, I listened. This male with golden hair, sun-kissed skin, and black eyes made me ache with need with four simple words.

He dropped his pants, springing his erection free. In this position, he seemed bigger, so close to my lips and face. The tip of him glistened. That cocky smile appeared on the side of his lips as his hands curled through my hair.

"I'm going to fuck your mouth now."

"Just—" I didn't get to finish, because he pushed forward in between my lips. He gave me a second to adjust, and I flicked my tongue along the tip of him, swirling it along his length.

"Fuck."

Do it, I told him. *If you want to own me so bad, do it.*

His fists tightened in my hair, forcing me to move at his pace and rhythm. He pushed himself inside me as far as he could go. I choked on him for a second before he pulled out, gliding along my tongue. He went slow for the first few pumps, and I could feel his hesitancy.

It won't look real. The taunt was meant as encouragement, but it worked.

Still trying to be in charge from such a helpless position. He pulled my hair taut and pumped faster inside my mouth, fucking me in earnest this time. I reached up and rolled his balls between my fingers. He groaned, but continued the quick pace, hitting so far back tears sprang into my eyes as I fought back a gag.

You know the safe word if you need it.

Fuck, Voss. Just fuck me. And show me.

You want to see?

Fuck, yes.

As soon as I asked, I saw this from his eyes and felt my mouth the way he felt it. His erection swelled every time he pressed into my lips and with each sweep of my tongue along him. As the tears welled into my eyes and a few trickled down my face, his own biology wanted to explode cum over my face and claim me entirely as his. He focused on my mouth, my lips around him, pressed with perfect pressure, and whenever he hit the back of me, he felt like he was claiming me, staking me as his own. And my eyes, the way my moonlit blue eyes gazed up at him with reverence.

The connection between us fizzled out as a Fae guard entered the room.

Annoyance grew. I was so wet from experiencing this from his perspective, and I wanted him to keep going, to feel more. I wanted to feel everything.

"That's where you went off to."

"Out," Voss said. "I'm busy."

"I can tell. The king wanted me to check on you. Said it had been a while. He was worried you would succumb again."

"As you can see, I haven't. And it's been a while for obvious reasons." Voss grunted, still steadily moving my head and mouth against him as the other male watched. "You can tell the king I am punishing her for what she did to me. I will have my way with her tonight. It's the least I can do to repay her."

"Shit, you're as fucked up as he is. She's fucking crying." The guard shook his head. "Sometimes, I'll never understand the way—"

"Careful what you say. If it is treasonous, we could have two bodies hanging from the gallows tomorrow."

I gagged on him as he hit a little too deep. Voss kept going, keeping up the facade, but I liked it. I liked how he had no regard for me at this moment, owning me like no other Fae had. I had no idea I would actually like being watched, but wasn't that part of the experience in the barn? The idea of getting caught?

The guard swallowed and ducked out of the room.

Voss withdrew from my mouth, pulling me up and into his

arms, pressing his lips against mine. The force of him was so powerful and quick that we stumbled back into the wall. My back slammed against it as he pressed both hands on either side of me. "Fuck," he breathed. "I'm sorry."

"I'm not."

After a few blinks, he wiped the tears away from my eyes with gentle fingers. The same fingers that had been threaded viciously through my hair. "I like this dress on you." He nuzzled into my neck, placing a kiss against my skin. "Now, lift it up."

I obeyed, staring at him. He had about a half a foot on me in height, and as I pulled the fabric up, he picked up my thighs, wrapping me around his hips. The tip of him rested against me.

"No panties?"

"No panties."

"Naughty Fae Slayer. I should teach you a lesson about being indecent. Because this—" Voss reached around my lower back, roamed over my ass, and hit my core. He ran his fingers over my wet entrance. "—is mine. And if other Fae knew you were wandering around like this—"

"I'd kill them if they got too handsy."

"You don't understand." His irises swirled as he maneuvered me so my back was flat against the wall, my legs wrapped around him. The layers of my red dress draped over us. With a firm grip on my ass, Voss thrust inside me in one solid motion, making me scream. "I would kill them. And I'd make you watch, so you'd be wet enough to take me afterward." Voss pulled out, then slammed back into me. He picked up the rhythm, pulling out slowly and shoving into me fast and hard.

"I—" I gasped out a breath as the length of him buried in me so intensely that my head struck the wall, making me see stars. "Don't—" One of his hands wandered up my ass, over my side, and up to my breast, where he squeezed my nipple hard. "Need—"

"Need what? My help?" Voss pushed all the way inside me with agonizing slowness. He stayed like that, challenging me.

I clenched my muscles around him in response.

"Fuck."

"I don't need you," I said.

His eyes swirled. "I think you do." His fingers trailed across my sternum to my other nipple. With a featherlight touch, he brushed his thumb over my hardened peak. "What will it take for you to admit it?" His thumb and pointer finger wrapped around the nub. "How hard do I have to punish you for you to admit you want this?" The pressure he applied shot through me, painful and intense and glorious. "You need me to bathe you in someone's blood and fuck you until you are boneless? Because I will." As if to prove his point, he pulsed his erection inside me, and my body jerked in response.

"Admit you like this."

"Fuck you, Voss."

He twisted my nipple hard enough that I cried out. My scream echoed off the walls. If anyone walked by, they would believe Voss was giving me what I deserved. This kind of torture was different, though, because it was pure pleasure and teasing. He had stopped moving inside me, and my hips tried to force a new rhythm. He growled, pressing me against the wall, and I lost my leverage. I was pinned and helpless between him and the cold stone.

"Admit it." His hand curved around my breast and trailed to my neck. Voss applied the lightest amount of pressure there. "You want me to fuck you. Use you. You want to feel helpless underneath me. You like it when I make you feel this way. You like it when I challenge you to be less than you are."

His presence roared inside my head, wrapping around my brain and searching through my thoughts. I tried to shut him out, but he was invading me in more ways than one. He rotated his hips against mine, moving his cock a few agonizing inches. It was not enough. I gasped out in need. I was useless against him.

There it is. How you really feel.

Fuck you, Voss.

Inside my head, he caressed my thoughts, whirling my sensations together. They unfurled in front of us. He was right, after all. I wanted to be used. I wanted him to take advantage of me. I wanted to be owned by him. And not so secretly anymore, I liked how he had made me his wife without giving me the choice. All along, I had been hoping for this, a Fae to challenge me, a Fae to stare into the darkest part of me and revel in it. The night we killed Treborne, Voss had seen the wickedness inside me, and he loved it.

With a growl, he pulled out of me and brought me to the floor. I landed hard on my ass, but he was lifting my hips up before I could protest and shoving back inside me.

"Fuck!" I screamed as he rocked into me hard, unrelenting.

Admit it. I want you to say it.

Voss was everywhere. Inside my mind, inside my pussy, his hands firmly wrapped around my hips, keeping me upright as he slammed into me again and again. I could barely breathe from the intensity of his pace.

You're mine, Max.

Using my fingernails, I scraped long lines down his arms until I felt the skin give and blood come out. The growl that escaped him was feral. He lowered my hips to the ground and pinned my arms to the ground. Bringing his head down to my breast, I gasped as his teeth sank into the tissue next to my nipple. My skin burst open, blood flooding into his mouth. He drank long and deep, and as he did, I felt his presence become clearer, thicker inside my head.

Voss made me feel how he felt. Each thrust of his dick inside me, the pull of me along the length of him, the tightness as I clenched around him. The rush of conquering me, inside and out. How he wanted to watch me beg, how he craved for my lips to be pressed against his cock. How he wanted to fill me until I came apart under his hands.

This was more blood than he drank last time. He was invading every part of me, ripping me apart piece by piece. And maybe that was his plan all along as my body bucked against his. I needed more. I wanted more. I needed him.

"I'm yours," I admitted on the end of a breath as he slammed into me.

Voss pulled away from my breast, a drop of my blood on his lips. "I want you to scream." He moved my arms so one hand pinned both wrists above my head, and the other trailed down to my clit. He rubbed his thumb against me, pressing down on my hips with the rest of his fingers as he pounded into me. Everything inside my body tightened. "So little to make the great Fae Slayer come undone."

I whimpered, trying to move my hips to get a better angle, so he would hit deeper and harder than he already was. He held me firm with his hands, pressing so hard on my nerves I had to succumb to him.

I was his. Completely. He was right. Voss had conquered me, but only because I wanted to be conquered by him. During our journey together, we had transitioned into something more than enemies. I no longer wanted to see him bleed. Except...

"If you want," he whispered in my ear, "I could still give you that fantasy, you dirty little fox."

My mind flashed with images of him, blood dripping down his

throat, over his stomach, flooding across my skin. It was like fire to me, igniting me from the inside out. Voss held me down, but fed me images of a knife in my hand, of me conquering him the way he conquered me. He made me feel his lust, his power over me, all of it pulsed inside me as he pushed and pushed. My body was on fire. I was endless need.

I screamed, gasping desperately for air, which didn't seem like enough. I fell apart underneath him and felt the moment he spilled into me. His thumb continued to roll over my clit until my shuddering body finally stilled.

"Just think. Once everything is sorted, I'll be doing that to you every night." He pulled out of me and tucked himself away into his pants. He helped me sit upright and stared into my eyes. "Will you be okay until tomorrow?" His eyes swirled again, letting me know our conversation was private. "I don't want to leave you like this."

"Leave me like what? In a dungeon, dripping with your cum?" I rolled my eyes. "I'll be fine. Tomorrow, I will kill the king, and I will watch that pretty neck of yours bleed underneath me."

"Remind me again why I like you?" He tucked my hair behind my ears. His fingers were so gentle compared to what we just did.

"Because I can tell you no."

"Mmm, no, that's not it. I think it's because you've told every other Fae no and have used your yeses as a weapon. But with me, you mean it when you say yes."

"You're full of yourself."

"And you're full of me." Voss kissed me. The quick caress was unexpected, sweet, and chaste. When he pulled away, that pesky smirk was back on his face. "Until tomorrow, Fae Slayer. Try not to dream of me."

Twenty-Six

Early the next morning, two guards entered the dungeon. They were wearing earplugs, and I had to laugh at the precautions. There was an entire court full of Fae ready to hang my ass, and these two were spouting earplugs like I was some siren. As far as I knew, sirens didn't exist. Though, Penn had mentioned they were real in Faerie.

I supposed to most Fae, I had become a legend, a mythical creature capable of dragging the Fae to their deaths. A seductress singing songs of promising sex before the Fae was flayed alive. The idea of the Fae fearing me, a mere human, made me smile.

I can feel your smugness from here.

Get out of my head, Voss.

Are you ready for this?

I promised to make you bleed after I killed the king, and I intend to keep that promise.

He chuckled through our connection.

I was in the same dress from yesterday, and annoyingly, my

thighs were still messy from Voss last night. If I failed today, I would die covered in a male Fae's cum. I wasn't entirely sure how I felt about that. If I succeeded, maybe I could watch Voss bleed again in real life. I promised myself to have fun with that male, once this was all over. After I got my revenge on the king, I would get revenge on the assassin by making him cry out the same way he made me. I wanted him to beg for it.

Unlikely, Max.

As I attempted to shut down the connection to him, my nerves thrummed. The guards cuffed me behind my back and escorted me up the stone steps. I left the heels to my ensemble behind in the dungeon, but neither guard seemed to notice or care. I decided to go barefoot, because running in heels was not for me. I debated how to deal with the handcuffs as they opened the door to the dungeon. I was fairly petite, and perhaps my shoulders could handle me maneuvering them from the back to the front if I had to, but that would take precious time.

I wouldn't have time once the rope cut.

As we ascended into the courtyard, a piece of metal touched my hand. I wrapped my fingers around it quickly, glancing over at the Fae who gave it to me. Penn, irises whirling a bright turquoise, nodded once before disappearing into the crowd. I clutched the metal with force, not willing to open my fingers for anyone. If he had given me a key, I needed to hold on to it for dear life.

The guards shoved me forward, and I stumbled below the dais. The gallows were on the right, next to the dais and the king, as Voss said they would be. It would be a clear shot to him once I got free. The rest of the crowd—the Fae who had been at dinner last night and a few new faces—stood around the courtyard, ready to see the sacrifice of the great Fae Slayer.

"Maxine Storm, the Fae Slayer who opened the Fae Door." The

king looked me over, eyes assessing. "How did my assassin treat you last night?"

I knew what he was looking for, but I wouldn't give him the pleasure. "Like the perfect gentleman." I lifted my nose up as Voss laughed inside my head.

King Balgair's eyes flared, and I could feel his magic press along my skin. "Don't lie to us, girl. We heard you scream."

They had, of course, but I glared at the king instead of speaking.

"It's no matter. You are a pest. A nuisance. There was going to be a day where it came down to you or me, and it was always going to be me. You are a weak, pathetic human. What did you think you would accomplish?"

I shrugged. "Killing you, of course."

He snorted, as if this were the most preposterous idea. His arrogance would get him killed soon. "And how is that working out for you?"

"We'll see."

"You are locked up and about to be hung from the gallows, girl. Your time is up." He snarled, turning back to the crowd. His graying hair hung around his head, and I wondered how old this Fae was if he was actually showing signs of aging. Most Fae looked young, stunning, and beautiful, but rarely had I seen them older. He still looked attractive for his age, but I wondered how much longer he would have left without my interfering. Years? Decades? Millenniums?

"For the deaths of the following Fae…" The king listed a bunch of names. Honestly, it was boring after the first five. I wondered how long my list was and was surprised when he kept going. So many, and somehow still not enough to get me to him until Voss came along.

You've been busy, little fox.

I didn't show any sign of hearing Voss inside my head, but he was there, in the darkest part of me. *You knew I had history.*

And that's all it is. History. From now on, it's only me.

I agreed with him there. Once the king was dead, I would have no reason to sleep with random Fae to locate the king's court. Of course, none of the Fae had given me the king's location, because they were loyal to a fault, but there would be no need to carry on after today.

Unless, however, the prince who ascended to power was equally bad.

"For these crimes, you have been sentenced to death."

I thought he was going to go on forever.

Jealous?

A bit, yes. I may have to do the other thing no Fae has done to you to make up for it.

I hated how my body pulsed underneath the dress at the thought.

"And now you will hang from our gallows. Guards!" The king swept his hand back, again not willing to be involved as they carted me to the wooden structure. I tripped on the last stair, and they pulled me upright. I felt Voss growl inside my head, and my eyes swept over the crowd, finally meeting his black gaze.

Licking my lips, I stepped forward toward the ropes, much to the surprise of the guards behind me who stiffened. One approached me, glancing me over with narrowed eyes. He slipped the hangman's noose over my neck, tightening it. He opened up the space between us and nodded to the other guard, who lifted the rope up with a pulley. It stretched against my skin, making it hard to breathe.

My heart raced, worried this might not work.

Calm, little fox. I won't let you die.

"Any last words?" The king asked, glaring at me.

Frowning, I thought for a moment, using the opportunity to adjust my grip on my key. "No." I winked at him.

King Balgair growled. "Hang her." His voice dropped low.

They flipped the switch, and the floor dropped out from under me. For a horrendous second, my weight caught on the noose, clutching my neck and threatening to tear my spinal cord. It lasted only a moment before I continued falling, dropping to the hard cobblestones below. I had been ready for this, my knees bent and braced for the impact. The shock still hit my legs and spine hard, but I bounced into it.

I whipped out the key, slammed it into the lock, and unhooked one of my wrists. It was only a matter of seconds to get free, but it was enough for the crowd to erupt with shocked expressions and loud protests. The dagger was right where Voss told me it would be, and I grabbed it, charging toward the dais.

Voices rose around me, but my eyes were dead set on the king. The king who stared at me in horror.

But he had enough time to collect himself, and as I swung forward with my hand, he danced up and behind the throne. I cut into the upholstery and growled at him. "Not so tough now that no one is protecting you, are you?" I leaped again, but he jumped backward, toward the stone wall that rose behind the dais.

"You have no idea who you are speaking to."

"Don't I? A coward."

"I am the *king*." He prowled toward me. My moment of surprise was gone.

"Then kill me, your Majesty." I spat the words as he charged. Swiping down, I missed him by a hair as he ducked around me. He grabbed the cord of rope around my neck and pulled. I was knocked off balance as he dragged me back to the dais.

While stumbling, I took another swipe at him, but his free hand wrapped around my wrist—he was *so* fast. His fingers clenched around my muscles, his sharp nails digging into my skin until I bled. Under the immense pressure on my wrist, my hand opened, and the dagger clattered to the ground. The king yanked on the handcuff still attached to my left wrist and latched the other side to the throne.

"Clearly, he did not teach you enough of a lesson." The snarling words were meant for me as the king's rotten breath curled around my face. "Maybe hanging was too easy for you. Maybe you deserve something much worse, worse than my assassin gave you last night." King Balgair spat in my face, grabbed my neck, and forced me over the throne, my ass in the air. Using the noose, he lifted my face for the crowd to see. "Look at the Fae Slayer, about to get fucked by the king of the Fae. Bear witness to how easily she will be defeated."

I swallowed my fear, choking on the helplessness running through me. I had been so close, and now... I might as well have been back in the pantry, watching the horrors unfold with my family while being unable to act. Pressing my eyes shut, I tried to make myself be anywhere but here, anywhere but trapped again.

As my skirts rose under his grubby hands, a growl sounded. It wasn't from me, but from the shadow in my mind, the part of me that belonged to Voss, and it grew louder.

"Get your fucking hands off her," he said from so close.

Everything stopped. The king's hands were just above my knees. The crowd stilled. A hush settled over the courtyard as everyone realized what was happening. I was no longer alone in my fight against the king. Not a single Fae moved to get involved. They stared at us, watching like we were actors on a stage. No one seemed willing to get their hands dirty if their magic couldn't do the work for them.

"What did you just say to me, boy?" The king whirled toward Voss, throwing out his fist. The king's knuckles slammed into Voss's jaw with a resounding crack.

Voss barely moved an inch backward, but his lip had split open, eyes narrowing into deadly points. "You heard me. You don't fucking touch her. She's mine."

With my free hand, I loosened the noose around my neck and slipped it off, then looked frantically around for the dagger.

"I touch who I want. I do what I want. I am the king, and you cannot control me, boy." Spittle flew out of Balgair's mouth. "You will die alongside her. So tell me, was her pussy worth it? This court bows to me. They will kill you on my word."

Voss gestured at the crowd. "I don't see anyone moving. Did you forget that you have to control them for them to listen to you?"

The king threw another punch at Voss's face, but he caught it mid-air. The two grappled.

And there. The dagger was a few feet away from the throne. I reached for it, but it was too far away. Twisting around, I stretched my legs toward the blade, desperate to hook my toes around it.

"You were always a sorry son of a bitch."

"You would know."

"I should have listened to my advisers. You were always too unhinged to make into an assassin."

"Too late for that now." Voss punched the male in the gut, shoving him backward toward me. I ducked in time for the king to stumble past the throne. Voss prowled forward. "You made me this way, and you'll die because of it."

"You can't kill me," the king taunted.

My body ached as I stretched for the dagger, and my big toe

wrapped around the blade. It cut into my skin, and I hissed, but forced myself to keep tugging it toward me. Fuck, it hurt. I adjusted my aim to get to the handle now that it was close enough, closing the gap between me and it inch by inch.

"Why do you think I rule over this?" King Balgair's eyes were liquid fire. "Because no one can challenge me. No one has the power to do so. When the Fae door opened, no Fae can die without the Slayer. And she's already shown she's not a fighter."

My hand wrapped around the pommel, and I shifted my grip on the hilt. Success. *Voss, I have it. Send him here.*

"She might not be, but she's smart. And you're forgetting one thing."

"And what's that?"

Voss leaped forward, grabbing the other male by the neck. He wrenched him around, using the momentum to swing the king toward me. The giant male tripped on his own two feet and fell, hand stretching in front of him as if that could save him—save him from me.

The dagger pointed at his throat. It sunk into his hand, through the skin and muscles, and out the other side, straight into his neck.

"I'm not working alone anymore," I snarled, twisting the blade.

Blood shot out from the wound, spreading around his hand and splattering my dress, soaking it through. Gurgling choked the king's throat, but the body weight was too much for me to handle, and I grunted under the effort of holding the male in place.

Voss tore him off me. The king shook, but the blood loss was too much too quickly. Slowly, the fire died in his eyes. Voss used a second key to open the cuffs and offered me his hand. I took his in mine, and he wiped a drop of blood off of my cheek. He lifted me to my feet, staring at me with awe.

Fucking stunning, little fox. Absolutely perfect.

The air around us was thick, charged with a shift that was hard to place. Disbelief, maybe? Shock? Penn and Elspeth stepped forward from the crowd and were the first two to bow down. They pressed their hands to their hearts, looking straight up at the dais, up at Voss and me.

"All hail to the new king. King Devoss Balgair."

Twenty-Seven

My mouth went dry. My mind turned to stone. I hadn't heard Penn right, had I? I stumbled backward, a few feet away from Voss as he looked over the crowd. A surge of power rushed around us, and I felt myself sway on my feet as something inside me hollowed out. My bones turned to liquid, and I felt woozy, like my legs could no longer hold me upright.

Pressing my eyes shut, I tried to rid myself of the seasickness. When I opened my eyes again, more Fae had begun to bow in the crowd, getting on their knees and copying what Elpseth and Penn had done. Voss's eyes were swirling liquid lava, a brighter shade than I had seen before as magic spun around him, inside him and out. It kissed my skin, making my thoughts flounder.

"De*voss* Balgair?" I swallowed as disbelief crept up my spine. I shook my head as Voss turned to look at me, that sickening smirk appeared again on his face, more sinister than it had been before. "You said—" Swallowing, I realized he had told me exactly what would happen.

BLOOD HUNTED

The closest prince would ascend to power.

He neglected to mention that he was an assassin *and* a prince.

"You lied to me."

"I *never* lied to you." The words were heavy.

I thought back to everything he told me, every mention of what the future would look like. Had he been telling the truth when he said he wanted something better for people and Fae? The Fae in the courtyard were in stunned silence, falling to their knees to usher him in as their new leader. Was it that easy to stage a coup and take over? Just one quick death?

"You see, Max." A shudder went through me as he spoke my name. "I needed you to kill the king because of the curse of the Fae door. Once it was open, the only person who could kill a Fae was you. We were invulnerable to everyone except you, including the Fae king. I needed you to kill my father—the male who was leading us toward a future of devastation and would happily usher in the apocalypse if it meant continuing his rule over the Fae. He was corrupt and greedy. I had planned to kill him myself before the portal was open, but he finished the curse, binding our two worlds together and making us immortal to all but one. You finished joining our worlds, and you became the only one who could kill him, the only one immune to our magic *because* of magic."

He stepped toward me, closing the gap between us. His gaze was piercing. I took a step back, trying to calm my speeding heart.

"But killing the king ended the curse. The Fae can die now, and any traitors to the new crown will be killed." His eyes glanced back at the crowd. "Anyone have any objections?" The silence was deafening.

I staggered another few steps back, toward the stairs of the dais.

"No, you don't. Not yet." He closed the gap between us again, grabbing onto the back of my neck. His eyes swirled, and

339

something inside me liquefied.

"What is that?" I asked, breathless, speechless, in complete disbelief. The dagger was still in my hand, but I couldn't bring myself to swipe out and kill him. As much as I wanted to drive it into his heart for his lies, deceit, and betrayal, it stayed useless in my grasp.

"It's my magic. And you can feel it now. You broke the curse, so now I can use it on you." He leaned close to my ear. "I'm the only one who can use it on you." When he pulled away, his face wore his signature smirk.

His magic coiled around my body, penetrating through my skin. I watched in horror as my wrist lifted without my permission. My body trembled as I traced the blade down Voss's chest, almost with a lover's touch.

"I trusted you." My voice barely broke above a whisper.

"It's as you said. You should never trust a pretty face." Voss placed a long, lingering kiss on my lips. I didn't return it. My body was frozen in place as a single tear escaped my eye and ran down my cheek. My hand with the knife tightened around the blade, but I still could not drive it forward into his chest.

Voss pulled back, catching my tear on his finger and bringing it up to his lips. He licked it off and gave me a wicked grin. "You should be thanking me. You're free. Run, little fox, run."

The words were a command, drilling straight through my body and forcing my legs to move. I turned away from the blood, away from the chaos, away from the kneeling Fae, away from the kingdom I felt like in some way was also mine, and ran out of the courtyard, through the streets, and beyond the gates of the court.

It wasn't until I passed through the gates that I could force my legs to stop. I bent over, heaving breaths out, my lungs starving for air. I looked back the way I had come. The gates slipped shut behind me, locking me on the other side away from the new Fae king.

I still had the dagger in my hand. My feet were cut to pieces after running through the court, and to make it worse, I was still in the filthy mess of a dress covered in blood. I had no idea where to go next, but I knew one thing and one thing alone.

Revenge.

I will fucking kill you, I thought at the dark shadow inside of my head. I was wet from the idea of plunging this dagger into his chest.

His laugh surrounded me, invaded me. *As I said, I'm looking forward to the day you try.*

Acknowledgments

Okay, let's be real for a second. You want to throw this book across the room, right? You want to hate me and lament the fact that you have to wait for book two to come out? Or perhaps you are more like me and binge read entire series. Regardless, I know you. Because I am you as a reader.

I want to throw books across the room all the time.

But think of the precious pages. Don't hurt the poor book. It didn't do anything to you. I did. I'm a hot mess, and you are welcome to join me in this chaotic journey that is... well, my author life.

Okay, now to the thank yous. Thank *you* for picking up this book and starting the journey. Thank you for trusting me. I hope you pick up book two, because I don't think you'll regret it.

I want to thank so many people in this writing journey. First, Amber. My gosh. What a joy it has been getting to know you and having you read my work. The amount of time you had me gushing over your commentary was so endlessly helpful in this battle against my own mental anguish. *Why do I do this to myself?*

Lindsey and Shaye at the Good Girls PR team for making me gush before Shaye even read the book. And Lindsey for being a particularly early champion. Honestly, the angry texts I got in the middle of the night: priceless.

My partner put up with nights of chaos prior to this book coming out. My eyes hurt, my back hurt, and my voice was gnarled and broken, and he still looked at me with a smile and made jokes. To which I told him: there are no time for jokes when I must correct all the grammar. Seriously, he's the best, never breaking despite my utterly intense existence.

To my parents, who I am demanding do not read the following chapters: 12, 14, 16, 21, parts of 22, and the last half of 25. Yes, I do recognize telling you after the fact really has no bearing on your reading experience. Uh, so I guess let me apologize. I am sorry that I cannot be more ridiculous and make jokes about this kind of thing in real life. It's awkward. We're all human beings, but talking about this kind of thing is just weird. You know what I'm saying? Sure. You get it.

Except you probably don't, and you're wondering, "Where is my child?" I am here. Trust me. Let's never talk about it ever again, okay? Unless you want to compliment me on my literary achievements and say how absolutely gorgeous the writing was. My point is: thanks for allowing me the space to become myself. Yeah, that's where I intended this rambling to go all along.

Insert sweat drop emoji.

Maybe I shouldn't write acknowledgments super late at night. Ah well, so it goes.

Subscribe to the publisher's newsletter on https://www.spacefoxbooks.com for regular updates or apply to become a Cadet Fox and join the street team!

Follow the publisher on Instagram, TikTok, or Facebook @spacefoxbooks

Thank you for reading.

About the Author

Ariel Rae also writes as R. A. Desilets. She was raised in a small New Hampshire town, but left it behind to attend Emerson College in Boston. After graduating with a degree in Writing, Literature, and Publishing, she moved to southern California.

Working as a barista, she somehow turned her life into a cliché and met her husband while serving him coffee. They fell in love, got married, adopted a bunch of cats, moved to the rainy side of Oregon, and eventually moved back to New England.

When she's not writing, she plays video games, drinks tea, reads way too much (though, she wonders if there is such a thing as too much reading), and snowboards.

Find her online at https://linktr.ee/radesilets

@radesilets

Other Work

Connect with R. A. Desilets
https://linktr.ee/radesilets

Free Short Stories with Newsletter Sign Up
https://subscribepage.com/radesilets

Made in the USA
Middletown, DE
23 September 2023

39122236R00210